Romantic Suspense

Danger. Passion. Drama.

Deadly Secrets
Cathy McDavid

Texas Revenge Target
Jill Elizabeth Nelson

MILLS & BOON

DEADLY SECRETS
© 2024 by Cathy McDavid Books, LLC
Philippine Copyright 2024
Australian Copyright 2024
New Zealand Copyright 2024

First Published 2024
First Australian Paperback Edition 2024
ISBN 978 1 038 92175 8

TEXAS REVENGE TARTGET
© 2024 by Jill Elizabeth Nelson
Philippine Copyright 2024
Australian Copyright 2024
New Zealand Copyright 2024

First Published 2024
First Australian Paperback Edition 2024
ISBN 978 1 038 92175 8

MIX
Paper | Supporting
responsible forestry
FSC® C001695

Published by
Harlequin Mills & Boon
An imprint of Harlequin Enterprises (Australia) Pty Limited
(ABN 47 001 180 918), a subsidiary of HarperCollins
Publishers Australia Pty Limited
(ABN 36 009 913 517)
Level 19, 201 Elizabeth Street
SYDNEY NSW 2000 AUSTRALIA

Cover art used by arrangement with Harlequin Books S.A.. All rights reserved.

Printed and bound in Australia by McPherson's Printing Group

Deadly Secrets

Cathy McDavid

MILLS & BOON

Cathy McDavid is truly blessed to have been penning Westerns and small-town stories for Harlequin since 2005. With over fifty titles in print and 1.6 million-plus books sold, Cathy is also a member of the prestigious Romance Writers of America's Honour Roll. This "almost" Arizona native and mother of grown twins is married to her own real-life sweetheart. After leaving the corporate world seven years ago, she now spends her days penning stories about good-looking cowboys riding the range, busting broncs and sweeping gals off their feet—oops, no. Make that, winning the hearts of feisty, independent women who give the cowboys a run for their money. It's a tough job, but she's willing to make the sacrifice.

Visit the Author Profile page
at millsandboon.com.au for more titles.

Ask, and it shall be given you; seek, and
ye shall find; knock, and it shall be opened unto you.
—*Matthew 7:7*

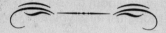

DEDICATION

To Pops, the best grandfather ever.
Could you have ever imagined when you rode the
rails from Montreal to Arizona as a young teenager
that your granddaughter would one day move to
Arizona and write about the same mountains you
travelled through? I miss you and love you still.

Chapter One

The old woman stood on her dusty concrete porch stoop and leveled an arthritic finger at Deputy Elena Tomes. Tucked in the crook of her other arm, a fat gray cat hissed and growled and dug its sharp claws into the woman's skin deep enough to draw blood. She didn't appear to notice.

"What are you going to do about it?" she demanded.

Elena silently prayed for patience. "As I explained to you when I first arrived, there's nothing I *can* do."

"That vicious dog next door keeps coming into my yard and scaring poor Peaches."

"You have to call Animal Control."

"I did. And they said because the dog wasn't on my property when they got here, all they could do was issue a verbal warning."

Elena glanced over at the neighbor's backyard

where the dog in question, a white ball of cork-screw curls hardly bigger than the cat, played chase with a pair of giggling girls. Vicious? Elena doubted it. More likely the dog was defending itself against Peaches's assault.

She noted the bent chain-link fence with its many holes separating the two properties. "Maybe if you repaired the fence, the dog wouldn't get into your yard."

"Me?" the woman gasped. "Their dog is the one trespassing. Fixing the fence is their responsibility."

"Have you told them that?"

She squared her shoulders, the bony knobs visible beneath her droopy cardigan. "I have. They refuse."

"Then maybe you should take them to court. Let a judge decide. But in any case, this isn't a matter for the sheriff's department. You can't keep calling with nuisance complaints."

"Nuisance?" Vivid red splotches bloomed on her wrinkled cheeks. "I'll have you know I won't be voting for you in the next election."

Elena swallowed a sigh. "I'm not an elected official, ma'am. You're thinking of the Cochise County sheriff. I'm just a regular employee."

Elena had been hired on four months ago at

the Ironwood Creek Sheriff's Substation. Her recruitment was part of the governor's new program to fill deputy vacancies with female and underrepresented candidates.

But Elena didn't explain any of that to the old woman. There was no point.

"What's the name of your supervisor?" the woman demanded. "I have half a mind to report you."

"Sergeant Deputy Jake Peterson. I can write that down for you if you want."

"Oh, trust me. I'll remember."

"If that's all, ma'am…" Elena tugged on the brim of her dark green ball cap. She didn't much like the regulation headwear, but it did protect her from the sun, relentless in this southeastern corner of Arizona even during winter.

Besides, the hat, combined with aviator sunglasses, made her look tougher and older. With her small stature and youthful features, few people took Elena seriously. That included her fellow deputies, much to her consternation.

She felt the old woman's stare burn into her as she walked to where her county-issued black-and-white SUV sat parked alongside the narrow street. Curtains parted and blinds separated as nosy people peered out their windows at the goings-on.

Elena paid them no heed and climbed into the driver's seat. There, she squeezed her eyes shut, already dreading the paperwork for this unnecessary call.

"Lord, I know You led me here for a reason, and I'm willing to wait until that reason reveals itself. But in the meantime, I could sure use a bit of encouragement."

After a moment, she sat up and radioed the station. Ironwood Creek was what her *Abuelo* Carlos called a service town, meaning it existed solely to support local industry—which in Ironwood Creek happened to be cattle and agriculture. Besides Jake and the deputy chief, Elena shared duties with two others. Not much ever happened of consequence, and protocol leaned toward lax. A hundred-and-eighty degrees from Elena's last position in Phoenix.

Sage Blackwell answered with her usual even tone. "How was the ever-congenial cat lady?"

"Let Jake know she may be calling him to report her dissatisfaction with me. Over."

"He'll love that." Sage had been the station secretary and deputy chief's assistant for the past three years. Nothing fazed her.

"Maybe you can run interference? Over."

"I'll try. Can't promise."

Elena nodded to herself. She liked Jake. He was the only member of the station's informal boys' club to treat Elena like an actual deputy and not Sage's underling, good only for brewing coffee, answering the phone and dealing with nuisance calls. Not that he'd taken Elena under his wing. He had a reputation to maintain with his buddies, after all. But at least he talked to her with respect and, when no one was listening, offered advice.

"Thanks. I'm going to patrol behind the abandoned pecan orchard. See you at the station in about an hour. Over and out."

"Be careful." Sage recited those two words every time and to everyone when she signed off. In that regard, Elena was an accepted member of the team.

Patrolling the abandoned orchard had been the first duty assigned to her when she arrived in Ironwood Creek. Grunt work for the untested rookie considered to be a liability in the field. Elena wasn't sent on calls to investigate stolen cattle or defuse a domestic situation. She didn't bust drug dealers or even break up bar fights.

Instead, she helped tourists move their disabled vehicles from blocking traffic, picked up homeless individuals in the park and drove them to the shelter, and responded to irate older women with fat cats who didn't get along with their neighbors. On occasion, and when no one else was available, she was called for backup. Like the time an enraged man had held his ex-girlfriend hostage in his parents' barn.

Incidents like that, however, were few and far between. Whether because she was new or a woman or both, Elena's fellow deputies and the chief didn't trust her. And neither had they given her the opportunity to prove herself. Yet.

The ancient pecan trees came into view, the late-afternoon sun glinting through their spindly barren branches. According to Sage, the orchard had been abandoned a decade ago and, to this day, the land remained tied up in a family trust, going unsold and untended. It had become a favorite party spot for errant teens. Not to mention a hideout for runaways and a magnet for stray dogs.

Elena's second pass revealed nothing more troublesome than a small herd of deer in search of grass, sparse in colder weather. At her appearance, they bounded away and vanished among the trees. She was just executing a U-turn when Sage's voice hailed her on the radio. Elena pressed the button on the transmitter.

"Deputy Tomes here." She always identified herself. Her protocol wasn't that lax. "What's up, Sage? Over."

"Chief needs you to head to Ridge Burnham's place. You know where that is?"

"I do. What's going on?"

"He called in. Found an old handgun buried under his well house."

All right. Not exactly a hostage situation, but more exciting than scaring away deer. Elena decided Oscar Wentworth, the other deputy on duty, must be busy. Otherwise, the chief would have sent him.

"I'll radio in when I arrive. Over and out."

"Be careful."

Elena knew Ridge Burnham, or more accurately, she was acquainted with him. He attended Hillside Church, the church home Elena had found since coming to Ironwood Creek. They'd met a few times through Jake, who also attended Hillside Church with his family. Jake was married to Ridge's older sister, Gracie. They had two adorable daughters, aged three and six.

That was another reason Elena thought Jake secretly helped her. Women like Elena were paving the way for little girls like his, showing them by example that they had no limits and could be whatever they wanted.

Five miles down the road, she turned into the Burnham place. A long dirt drive flanked by mesquite trees and the town's namesake iron-woods took her to the main house. She could imagine that a generation ago, the former cattle ranch had been a showplace. Now, it sat in dis-repair, a victim of weather, neglect and vandal-ism. Jake once mentioned that Ridge had retired from a successful rodeo career with the intent of restoring the family ranch his late father had driven into the ground. From what Elena could see, he had his work cut out for him.

As she drew nearer to the house, she slowed. Ridge appeared from the doorway of a shed and waved her over. She pulled up next to an ATV and parked. Adjusting her cap and aviator sunglasses, she got out and started toward him.

"Afternoon, Ridge."

"Thanks for coming so quickly."

He took off his leather work gloves and stuffed them in the pockets of his fleece-lined jacket. When they shook hands, her slim fingers dis-appeared inside his larger, stronger ones. The sensation wasn't entirely unpleasant, but Elena instantly dismissed it. If she was interested in dating, Ridge's handsome features would appeal to her. But her career came first, and that wouldn't change until she'd established herself.

"I'm told you found an old handgun," she said.

"Yeah." He led her to the back of the ATV. "The main pipe in my well house has a leak. I was digging under the side of the well house when my shovel hit something that shouldn't have been there." He reached into the ATV's small bed and lifted a burlap cloth. There lay a .40 caliber revolver coated in dirt. "I found this."

Elena leaned closer. A Smith & Wesson, she thought, though that would need to be confirmed. "You should have left it there and waited for the professionals. It might have accidentally discharged."

"The gun's not loaded."

"You checked?"

"I did."

Elena had learned since coming to Ironwood Creek that most of the ranchers in the area were knowledgeable about firearms. The difference between rural and urban living.

"You're fortunate," she said. "Had the gun been loaded, you might not be standing here."

"I guess God was watching out for me."

"He was," Elena agreed. "I'm assuming you don't recognize the gun, or you wouldn't have called."

"I've never seen it before."

"Okay. I can take it to the station for you."

"And then what?" Ridge wasn't wearing sunglasses, and his intense blue eyes bored into hers.

"The serial number will be traced. Hopefully, we'll find the owner of record. Learn if the gun was reported stolen or used in a crime."

"The serial number's been ground off."

"You checked that, too?"

Rather than answer, Ridge asked, "Am I required by law to turn the gun over to you?"

"Is there a reason you wouldn't? You did call."

"I think it might have something to do with my dad's homicide."

"Ah." Elena had heard about the late Pete Burnham's murder eighteen years ago. The case remained unsolved and ice-cold.

"I don't want the gun to get buried at the bottom of some box in the evidence room or sent off to a lab, never to return."

He sounded like he was speaking from experience.

"Why do you think the gun's connected to your dad's homicide?"

"Because of this." Ridge removed more of the burlap cloth to reveal a rusty metal strongbox. Beside it lay a pair of bolt cutters and a padlock, the shackle split in two pieces. "Take a look."

He lifted the strongbox lid. Inside were neat stacks of what appeared to be banded hundred-dollar bills, each securely wrapped in plastic.

Elena felt her jaw go slack. "Huh."

"I found the strongbox after I called the station," Ridge said.

"That's a lot of cash."

"My rough count, over forty thousand dollars."

And rather than keep the money for himself, he'd reported it to the authorities. *Interesting*, thought Elena.

"I'm convinced my dad was either killed for what's in this strongbox," Ridge said, "or he hid it because he knew someone was after him."

She retreated a step from the ATV, the gravity of his discovery sinking in. "I need to call for backup."

Ridge watched Elena as she rested an elbow on the hood of her SUV and talked into her radio. Deputy Tomes, he amended. She was here on business. He'd met her a few times at church and seen her once or twice around town. On those occasions, she'd been out of uniform. He'd had trouble imagining the petite, dark-haired beauty wielding a gun and taking down criminals. She'd seemed too delicate.

He didn't have that problem today. She exuded a confidence worthy of admiration.

Because she was new to town, she may not know all the details of his dad's homicide. That could come in handy for Ridge. Or work against him. It was too soon to tell and too early in their acquaintance.

If things were different, he'd remedy that and ask her out for coffee. But his focus was elsewhere. Specifically on rebuilding the ranch and restoring his family's good name. Both had been damaged by his late father, and solving his homicide could help significantly with the latter.

Besides, Elena gave off strong not-interested-in-dating vibes. Ridge didn't take the slight personally. She gave off the same vibes to every unattached man who attempted to flirt with her, leastwise according to his sister, Gracie. As the church's self-appointed matchmaker, she'd know and would have moved mountains to put an attractive, available single woman like Elena in Ridge's path. Since he'd retired from the professional rodeo circuit and returned home, she'd made it her personal mission to find his soulmate.

Ridge wanted that, too. Someday. Just not yet.

Elena finished her radio call and returned to where Ridge waited by the ATV.

"Chief Dempsey will be here shortly. He's stopping to pick up Jake first."

Ridge nodded. He'd rather the chief came alone. Not that he didn't get along with his brother-in-law—Jake was a good husband to Ridge's sister, Gracie and a loving father. He and Ridge were fans of the same sports teams and enjoyed nothing better than riding the mountain trails surrounding Ironwood Creek. But they didn't agree when it came to Ridge's late father. Jake thought Ridge should leave the past in the past and move on with his life. In Jake's opinion, Pete Burnham had been a drunk and a good-for-nothing and undeserving of the effort and emotion Ridge expended on him.

"Would you like a water?" he asked Elena.

"Thank you."

"Come on inside. We'll be able to see when the chief and Jake arrive through the kitchen window."

Elena followed him to the rectangular courtyard at the rear of the house. Three citrus trees—a lemon, an orange, and a grapefruit—stood guard. This time of year, like every February, they were still heavy with fruit.

Ridge opened the wooden gate and motioned for her to precede him. He did the same at the door leading to the kitchen. Warm air enveloped them, a welcome relief from the forty-degree temperature outside.

"Make yourself comfortable." He indicated the kitchen table and then continued toward an ice chest on the floor, where he removed two bottles of water. Returning to the table, he handed a bottle to Elena.

She perched on the edge of the seat, every muscle rigid. When she removed her sunglasses, her large brown eyes met his gaze before traveling the room and noting every detail.

"You're remodeling," she said matter-of-factly.

Ridge hung his cowboy hat and jacket on the back of his chair before sitting across from her. "One of my many projects."

"Must be hard to fix meals with no appliances and no cabinets."

"I eat a lot of fast food. There's also a microwave and toaster oven on the TV tray over there." He unscrewed his bottled water and took a long swig. "The new cabinets will be installed the first of the week. The appliances after that."

"Should look nice."

"I'm limiting the inside work to the kitchen and bathrooms. For now. Most of my repairs and restorations will be to the outbuildings and grounds, which, I'm sure you noticed on your way in, are in bad shape."

"Like the well house?"

"Like the well house."

Elena considered for a moment. "What makes you think your father is the one who buried the gun and the money? Could have been anyone."

"Well, it wasn't my mom. That's for sure."

"You asked her?"

"No need. She'd have dug up the money years ago if she knew about it and kept every dime."

Ridge's mother shared Jake's low opinion of her late husband and disagreed with Ridge's efforts to rebuild the ranch, constantly pestering him to sell. Ridge refused. Pete Burnham had inherited the ranch from Ridge's grandfather and passed it on to his children. For now, Gracie supported Ridge's plans to renovate. That could change. Their mom pestered Gracie, too.

"My sister and I were young when Dad died,"

he said. "Who else but him could have, or would have, buried the gun and strongbox?"

Elena sipped her water. "Let's assume for a minute it was your dad. How did he come into such a large sum of money? I heard he...didn't work much."

"That's true." Ridge tried to ignore the eighteen-year-old ache in his chest. "Worse than that, he drank away most of what little money he did earn. So, no, I have no idea how he acquired forty thousand dollars. Except my gut tells me he's the one who buried it there. If a cartel drug runner needed a place to hide money and a gun, they'd have buried it in the mountains, not beneath someone's well house where the owner might find it."

Elena sat up. "Drug runner?"

"Didn't anyone tell you when you took the job?"

"Tell me what?"

"Ironwood Creek has a pretty unsavory history."

"Really?"

"Look it up. We used to be a gateway town for bringing illegal drugs into the country. At night, you could see headlights winding through the outskirts of town. I used to watch them from my bedroom window traveling the far edges of our ranch. When I asked my mom about the headlights, she told me I was imagining things. My dad said to just ignore them and go to sleep."

"What was done to stop the drug runners?"

"Nothing. People bolted their doors and stayed inside."

Elena shook her head. "I had no idea."

"An altercation with a drug runner is the explanation we were given for my dad's homicide. He must have encountered one of them, who then pushed him off the ledge into the ravine. Evidence at the scene pointed to a possible struggle."

Elena studied Ridge thoughtfully. "But you don't believe that story."

"Not for a minute."

"Why?"

Her talents were being wasted as a deputy. She'd make a fine investigator. Not only because she asked questions, but because she listened and observed.

"Earlier on the day my dad was killed, I went out to the barn looking for him. When I got there, I heard him arguing with some guy. I was curious and a little scared. My dad seldom raised his voice. I ducked around the side of the barn and snuck in the back entrance. I hid behind the tractor and eavesdropped. They were too busy yelling to notice me."

"What were they arguing about?"

"Someone named the Hawk who was on the way. My dad apparently had an agreement with them."

"Them being the Hawk?" Elena asked.

"I'm not sure. Not much of what they said made sense."

"What else?"

"The guy kept saying my dad gave his word and going back on it would cost him and his family. That's when the two of them got into a scuffle. Next thing, the guy shoved my dad to the ground, told him that he was a dead man and stormed out. I ran to my dad and helped him up. He insisted he was okay, that it was nothing, and not to tell my mom."

"Did you describe this man to the authorities?"

Ridge snorted in disgust. "For all the good it did. Long hair. Scruffy beard. A brown T-shirt and jeans. I might have been describing any random fifty guys in Ironwood Creek. The detective said it didn't matter, anyway. I was young and, according to him, an unreliable witness."

"How old were you?"

"Twelve. Almost thirteen."

"Not that young," Elena commented.

She was the first person to agree with Ridge.

"My age was irrelevant," he said. "People were determined to discredit me."

"What people?"

"I don't know. Maybe those who stood to benefit the most from the mass amounts of illegal drugs being moved through the area. Millions of dollars' worth. Operations that size don't exist without help and without law enforcement and elected officials turning a blind eye. For a percentage, I'm sure. Isn't that how these things work?"

"That's a serious accusation. Do you have anything to back it up?"

"Only suspicions." He shrugged and took another swig of water. "Which, I've learned, will get you nowhere."

"You think your dad was involved with the cartel?"

"Involved or a witness." Ridge leaned forward. "My dad wasn't the only one killed. See for yourself. Find his case and read about it."

Elena also leaned forward. "Do you suspect the man your dad argued with killed him?"

"Yes."

"What evidence at the scene made the police rule your dad's death a homicide?"

"Footprints and broken branches, plus the location and position of my dad's body, all indicated he'd been pushed. Nothing to identify who did the pushing. No game or security cameras. No witness driving by."

"Unfortunately, that's not uncommon."

"But I found something in the barn that day," Ridge continued. "On the ground, in the dirt. A gold chain. It must have belonged to the guy and fell off when he and my dad scuffled. When I showed the chain to my dad, he ripped it out of my hands and shoved it in his pocket." Ridge swallowed what felt like a tangle of barbed wire. "Five hours later he was dead, and the gold chain wasn't in his pocket."

"You think he hid the chain or that whoever might have pushed him took it?"

"My guess is he hid it."

"Why?"

"Insurance. To use against the guy he argued with."

Elena released a long breath. "I wish I could say differently, Ridge, but that doesn't prove anything."

"If I can find the chain, it might. My dad

didn't leave after the scuffle, and no one else came over. It wasn't until later, near dusk, that he hiked into the hills. Since the chain wasn't on him, and he didn't give it to any of us, it must be somewhere on this ranch."

"What if he disposed of it?"

"I went through the trash. I wanted to show the police I wasn't inventing stories for attention."

Anger and frustration rose anew and clawed to the surface. He heard again the accusations made by thoughtless individuals that had shaped his future life, almost as much as losing his father at a young age had. Years of riding bulls and broncs hadn't driven away the pain. Neither had prayer, nor counseling from his Cowboy Church preacher. He hoped restoring the ranch would finally bring him peace.

Perhaps his brother-in-law was right and Ridge needed to let go of the past—but he wasn't ready. And finding the gun and money felt like a sign from above for him to continue seeking answers.

"Why did your dad hike up into the hills?" Elena asked. "Seems a strange thing to do so late in the day."

"Not that strange." One of the fond memories Ridge had of his dad returned. Too often, it felt like he was the only one who remembered the late Pete Burnham with affection. "He was an amateur prospector. We went out together a lot. Never found much to brag about, but we had fun. That's what counts."

"Was any prospecting equipment found at the scene of the homicide?" Elena asked.

"None."

"Okay. So, if he didn't go into the hills to prospect, then why?"

"To meet the Hawk?" Ridge suggested.

"Or to get away from him."

He sat up, suddenly energized. Why hadn't he considered that before? After the argument with the bearded guy, Ridge should have realized his dad had been running from danger.

The next instant, a different, more alarming scenario occurred to him.

"Dad could have been drawing his killer away from the ranch. To save me, my sister and my mom. The guy he'd been arguing with did threaten the family."

"That's possible," Elena agreed. "But unfortunately, you'll probably never know."

For the first time, emotion showed in her expression. Ridge saw compassion and empathy mixed with sorrow and felt a sudden bond with her. Perhaps, like him, she'd suffered loss and had failed to receive needed closure.

Before he could respond, they heard the rumble of an approaching vehicle. Ridge pushed back from the table and stood. Elena followed suit, and they both glanced out the kitchen window.

"The chief and Jake are here," he said, and reached for his cowboy hat and jacket.

She put on her sunglasses and followed him outside. Ridge readied himself for what would no doubt be yet another battle with law enforcement.

Chapter Two

Ridge watched Elena from the corner of his eye as they strode to where Chief Dempsey had parked his SUV next to hers. If this were a social call, Ridge supposed his brother-in-law would have clapped him on the back. Instead, Jake and the chief made straight for Elena, giving Ridge no more than a cursory nod and brusque "Hello."

"This way," she said and motioned for them to accompany her. "The gun and strongbox are in the back of the ATV."

The four of them formed a semicircle and stared wordlessly into the bed. Chief Dempsey removed a pair of disposal blue gloves from his pocket and slipped them on, tugging the ends for a tight fit. They were the kind of gloves Ridge had seen used by lab techs and nurses.

Only when the chief was satisfied did he lift the lid on the strongbox. "Would you look at that?"

Jake moved in closer and emitted a low whistle. "Hoo, doggie."

With his damp hair, he looked like he'd showered and dressed minutes before being fetched by the chief. Likely true as he'd pulled the graveyard shift this week. Ridge was certain the chief had brought Jake along only because he and Ridge were related by marriage, and Jake might "talk some sense" into Ridge.

A similar talk had happened once before when Ridge returned home six months ago and insisted he be given access to old mugshots—his goal being to see if he recognized the guy his dad had been arguing with in the barn. He'd been denied, and Jake was called in. Ridge had wanted Jake to go to bat for him. When he refused, the brothers-in-law hadn't watched football together for weeks. A birthday party for one of Ridge's nieces had provided the opportunity both were seeking to set aside their differences.

"Jake." The chief hitched his chin at his SUV. "Grab a couple evidence bags, will ya?"

"Yes, sir." He hurried off.

"What are you going to do?" Ridge asked the chief.

The silver-haired man paused to assess him. Despite his short, stocky frame, he exuded a sense of power and authority that garnered law-abiding citizens' respect and intimidated law-breakers.

"What would you like me to do?"

Ridge didn't miss a beat. "Reopen my dad's homicide."

"The case isn't closed."

"No one's investigated it for years."

"There's been no new leads."

"Until today."

The chief grunted, his gaze cutting from the strongbox to Ridge. "Nothing to indicate this gun and money are related to your dad's death."

"His murder."

"That hasn't been fully established. Could have been an accident or self-defense."

Ridge gritted his teeth. Condescending tones had that effect on him. "Then why didn't the person turn themself in?"

Jake had returned by then. "Come on, Ridge. Give it a rest, okay? We're not going to solve what happened to your dad today."

"We might. If the chief sends these items in for testing."

"What do you think they'll find?" the chief asked, opening the first evidence bag.

"Fingerprints or DNA. My dad's. His murderer's. Both."

"These items look to have been buried a long time ago. Evidence degrades." The chief placed the gun inside the bag and sealed it. "You said you found these by your well house pipe. There'll be water damage."

"Have the items tested, Chief."

"Be reasonable, Ridge," Jake cajoled. "We'd be wasting taxpayers' money."

Ridge refused to back down. Not this time. "Drug runners transported their product across our ranch. That's a fact. My dad, who may or may not have been on the take, was killed. That's also a fact. A gun and money were buried beneath my well house. You can't convince me the three aren't connected."

Only Elena looked as if she believed him. The chief and Jake exchanged here-we-go-again glances. Ridge tamped down his rising temper.

"My dad may not have been a model citizen or father of the year, but he never hurt anybody in his life and didn't have a mean bone in his body. He didn't deserve to be pushed off that ledge and left for the turkey vultures."

That was how the search party had found

Ridge's dad two days after he'd gone missing: vultures circling in the sky above the hills.

"No, you're right," the chief agreed, dialing his gruffness down a notch. "I understand your need for answers."

"Then you'll test the gun and the strongbox?"

He nodded and placed the strongbox into the second evidence bag. "I'll send them to the lab tomorrow."

Ridge took what felt like his first real breath since finding the gun. "Thank you."

"No promises on what they'll find. And the results could take some time."

"Any chance you can expedite the request?"

The chief furrowed his brow, his authoritative demeanor back in full force. "Don't push it."

"What about the money?" Jake asked. "What happens to it, assuming the tests come back inconclusive? Can Ridge make a claim?"

"You'll have to check into that, Ridge," the chief said. "There's a procedure. Paperwork to be filed."

Jake grinned. "Wait till Gracie hears."

Ridge's sister. Naturally, she'd be entitled to half of anything found on the ranch that they were allowed to keep, and Ridge would see that she got her fair share.

The chief carried the evidence bag containing the strongbox to his SUV. Jake trailed behind him with the bagged gun. They secured the items on the floor of the rear seat. When the chief shut the door and turned, Ridge was waiting for him.

"Mind if I call you in a couple of days?" he asked.

The chief frowned. "I'll call you."

"You need my number?"

"Jake has it."

Ridge's brother-in-law did clap him on the shoulder then in a show of forced camaraderie. "Relax, buddy. Don't get yourself tied in a knot."

He caught Elena's mildly exasperated glance—aimed at Jake. The earlier bond he'd felt with her grew. He really liked Ironwood Creek's newest deputy sheriff.

"Let's go, Jake," the chief said and ambled toward the driver's-side door as if in no hurry at all.

Regardless of what he said to the contrary, Ridge knew in that instant that the chief would put little weight on his discovery. What else was new?

"Deputy Tomes?" the chief called over his shoulder. "You coming?"

"Yes, sir. I mean, I'll be along shortly." She stood taller, an accomplishment considering the top of her head barely reached Ridge's chin. "I thought I might have Ridge show me the well house so I can take a few pictures. For my report."

"Look at you," Jake singsonged. "The rookie deputy covering all the bases."

Ridge sensed Elena stiffen.

"Don't be too long," the chief said.

"No, sir. I won't."

The chief and Jake climbed in and drove away, the vehicle's rear wheels sending twin plumes of red dust into the chilly afternoon air.

Ridge shoved his hands into his jacket pockets and stared after the SUV, his thoughts too tangled to sort. *Please, Lord, let this discovery help reveal the answers I seek.*

"Ridge?"

Rousing himself, he faced Elena. "Yeah. Sorry."

"Do you mind taking me to the well house? If you have somewhere else to be—"

"I don't mind. Anything to move the investigation along."

She smiled. Not much, just a slight lifting at the corners of her mouth. He imagined the reserved deputy's face alight with joy. That, he supposed, would be a sight to see, if an unlikely one. Which was a shame. She had nice eyes, and it was too bad she always hid them behind those sunglasses.

The two of them walked side by side through the barn, empty of livestock for almost two decades now. Birds flitted between the rafters, annoyed their tranquility had been disturbed. Once, the Burnhams had owned an old horse, a couple of nanny goats and a flock of chickens. Ridge's mom had sold eggs and goat's milk to bring in extra money. Ridge and his sister looked after the animals, as well as tended the vegetable garden behind the house.

During lean times, when Ridge's dad wasn't working or when he drank up his weekly wages, they'd survived on corn and squash and eggs and the kindness of friends. Ridge had learned at a young age how to pasteurize goat's milk, which they drank themselves when that was all they had. To this day, he hated it.

He and Elena passed by the ancient tractor Ridge had hidden behind on the day his dad argued with the bearded stranger. It hadn't run then and still didn't. One of these days, Ridge would haul it to the junkyard.

Reaching the back of the barn, he slid open a latch and threw wide the door, the hinges protesting from lack of use.

"Guess I need to grease those," he said.

Elena stepped outside. "How far is the well house?"

"At the top of that rise." He pointed to a small, square structure. "My granddad built the well on high ground. Gravity carries the water to the barn and house by an underground pipe."

"The well is wind powered." Elena nodded at the tall tower beside the well house with a spinning windmill on top. "Very eco-friendly."

"And less expensive than electricity."

They trudged up the rise. The wind increased the higher they went, stinging their faces and forcing them to hold their hats to their heads.

He took her around the backside of the well house to the hole he'd dug. Water dripped from where he'd taped the leak before going down to meet Elena. His shovel, pick and other equipment lay scattered on the ground where he'd left them, along with a toolbox.

Elena began snapping pictures with her phone from different angles.

"Don't take this question the wrong way," Ridge said, "but would you mind calling me tomorrow and letting me know the chief shipped off the gun and money for testing?"

She paused, her demeanor guarded. "If you're worried he won't—"

Ridge cut her short. "I am worried."

Her chin tilted up a notch. "I don't appreciate what you're implying. The chief is a public servant sworn to uphold the law."

"My dad's homicide was swept under the carpet, and the case has been left to rot for eighteen years."

"Ridge." She paused as if mentally counting to ten. "You were young when your dad died, right? And then you left town five years later, returning only occasionally. You may not have the clearest, most unbiased recollection of events."

"Are you done taking pictures?"

"Almost."

She snapped several close-ups of the hole.

Their return walk to the house was in uncomfortable silence. At her SUV, Elena opened the driver's-side door and sat, filling out paperwork.

"If I need additional information," she said, "I'll contact you."

"I'm sorry if I offended you, Elena."

"You didn't."

"Your boss, then."

She filled out a small white card. Emerging from the SUV, she handed him the card. "Here's the incident number, in case you need it."

He glanced down, noting she'd included her name and badge number as well. "Thanks."

And then she was gone. Ridge watched her taillights growing smaller and smaller and wanted to kick himself. He'd hoped to find an ally in Elena. Any possibility of that was now ruined, thanks to him and his inability to keep his opinions to himself.

She wasn't going to read up on Ironwood Creek's history or confirm the chief sent the gun and money to Tucson for testing. In fact, he'd be surprised if she ever talked to him again.

Elena sat at one of the two desks occupying the station's central room, her eyes glued to the computer screen as she clicked through pages. Jake had been at the other desk when she first returned from the Burnham ranch but was currently out on a call. A guest at the Creekside Inn had reported their car broken into and expensive photography equipment stolen.

Just as well he wasn't here. Elena was still a little annoyed with him. His remark about her being a rookie deputy had stung. Jake normally treated her with more respect than that. She wondered if he'd felt he had an image to uphold in front of the chief or Ridge. Maybe both. Frankly, she had little use for people who tried to make themselves appear superior by putting others down.

Shaking off the irritation, she continued reading and was soon engrossed. So much so, she didn't notice Sage Blackwater until the station secretary was standing behind her and peering over her shoulder.

"I thought you were off duty a half hour ago," she said.

"I was." It was too late for Elena to minimize the screen. "Just finishing some paperwork."

"That doesn't look like a report on the cat lady's complaint."

"It's not."

Sage leaned closer, her purse hanging from her shoulder and an empty reusable cup in her hand. When she arrived at the station tomorrow, the cup would be filled with a green power smoothie. "Isn't that the police report on Pete Burnham's death?"

Having been busted, Elena chose to come clean. "I thought I might read up on him. In case something comes of the discovery at the ranch today."

"Hmm."

"You know anything about what happened to him?"

Sage straightened and smoothed her long black ponytail with her free hand. "That was way before my time here."

"But you've lived in Ironwood Creek your whole life. There must have been talk."

"I was taking classes at Cochise College and working part-time when Pete died. I didn't pay much attention to local happenings. Too busy."

"A homicide is a big deal." Elena had the distinct impression Sage knew far more than she was willing to reveal.

"I can tell you this," the secretary admitted. "I remember my parents arguing. With each other and friends. Apparently, the whole town was divided. Half the people believed Pete was a drunk and a loser and had probably fallen to his death regardless of the evidence at the scene. His wife included."

"That must have been hard on Ridge and his sister."

"I don't know them well. I've met Gracie a few times through Jake, and Ridge because of his dealings with the station. But I can imagine being the subject of gossip for your entire life must be hard. I'm told Ridge idolized his dad." She sighed. "Children can be naive. They don't see their parents' faults."

Elena pictured Ridge as a twelve-year-old, losing the dad he loved. Hopefully, restoring his family's ranch would help him heal, whether his dad's homicide case remained stalled or was eventually solved.

"What about the town's other half?" she asked Sage.

"They were upset and afraid."

"Because a killer was on the loose?"

"No one was sure the deaths were accidental or intentional. And if intentional, then…"

"Deaths?" Elena's interest sparked. "As in plural?"

"There were other unsolved homicides over the years."

"Related to the drug trafficking?"

The typically unflappable station secretary reacted, her glance cutting to the door. "That was never proven one way or the other."

Ridge had been right. Ironwood Creek did have an ugly history. And a scary one.

"How many?" Elena asked.

"Two, other than Pete Burnham."

"When did they occur?"

Sage hedged. "The first one twenty-two, twenty-three years ago. Then Pete. The last one about eight years ago. It was just before Sheriff Cochrane was elected and implemented his crack-down-on-crime program."

The same sheriff whose participation with the governor's new hiring program was responsible for Elena landing the job at Ironwood Creek.

"Not that our problems were the county's worst ones," Sage hastily added. "Crime rates in Benson and Sierra Vista were soaring then, too."

"Tell me about the other murders," Elena said, circling back to their original topic. "Who were the victims, and what happened to them?"

"Sorry. Can't. I have to go." Sage retreated a step. "I'll be late picking up the kids from basketball practice. See you tomorrow."

"Have a good evening."

She all but fled, leaving Elena alone. The chief had already gone home for the day, and Jake hadn't returned from the inn. Elena used the opportunity to sidle over to Sage's desk and check out the shipping boxes the secretary had packed earlier. Per the printed labels, they were headed to the forensic crime laboratory in Tucson.

The chief had kept his promise to Ridge. Elena reconsidered calling him as he'd requested. After reading the report on his dad's homicide and talking to Sage, she found she'd softened toward him.

Not that Elena had much experience with homicides—all right, almost none. In Phoenix, where she was from, deputy sheriffs didn't investigate homicides. That job fell to local police. But even to her novice eye, this report lacked details. As if the investigating detective, a Frank Darnelly out of Bisbee, had exerted only the most minimal effort required.

Ridge's accounting of his dad's argument with the stranger in the barn wasn't even included. In the detective's defense, no proof existed the stranger had been involved in Pete Burnham's death. Nonetheless, the incident was noteworthy and should have been included in the witnesses' reports. It certainly established motive. Someone had been angry at Pete Burnham and threatened him and his family.

Printing out a copy of the police report, Elena folded the papers in half and carried them to the breakroom in the rear of the station. There, she keyed in the combination on her locker, retrieved her backpack and stuck the papers inside.

Taking a copy of the report wasn't illegal or even against policy. She could justify her actions as background research on the gun and money discovery. But she'd rather no one knew. She took plenty of grief from her fellow deputies as it was. They were bound to criticize her interest in the case and poke fun at her rather than commend her for being thorough.

Returning to the central room, she paused. She could lock up, arm the security system and leave. The place wouldn't be empty for long—Jake would be returning soon. He'd only come on duty early in order to accompany the chief to the Burnham ranch. Why, Elena couldn't be sure. Her first thought had been because the chief didn't trust her, but after seeing Jake and Ridge together, she wondered if there was another, entirely personal reason. More than Ridge's frustration with the lack of interest in reinvestigating his father's homicide.

Rather than head home, Elena returned to her desk and resumed her research, looking online for information about Pete Burnham. There wasn't much. A few brief newspaper articles revealing little more than she'd already learned and an obituary. Exhausting that avenue, she accessed the sheriff's department records archives available to her. There, she had a bit more success.

Pete Burnham had been arrested four times on petty charges. Public intoxication, disturbing the peace, trespassing and shoplifting. That last charge appeared to be more of a misunderstanding. He'd walked out of a convenience store with a bag of chips and a beer, claiming he thought he'd paid for them. Considering he went no further than the curb where he sat down to eat the chips and drink the beer, Elena tended to believe his claim.

He'd had enough money on him and offered to pay for the items, but the store owner insisted on pressing charges. They'd wanted to discourage Pete from ever darkening the market's door again. Apparently, he was a regular customer and a regular troublemaker. Loud. Pestering the other customers. Loitering. His mugshot showed a happy, disheveled drunk.

If Pete Burnham had any juvenile offenses, those records were sealed. Elena assumed there were none, since his offenses and apparent penchant for public drinking didn't appear to start until he was in his mid-twenties. If he drank before then, he'd managed to control himself and avoid trouble. What had changed for him? A quick side search revealed he'd gotten married about then, and Ridge's sister was born a few months later. A coincidence? Were the pressures of marriage and parenthood too much for him?

Elena did another search on crime in Ironwood Creek. Here, the results were mixed. There was a lot of it, no question. But again, sparse on details. Most of the articles and opinion pieces appeared in newspapers outside the immediate area. Sierra Vista. Tucson. Phoenix. Ironwood Creek had made the list of Arizona's top-five towns with the highest crime rates for a dozen straight years. And yet, from what Ridge had said, no one ever did anything about it until Sheriff Cochrane came along.

The sudden opening of the station door gave her a start.

"Hey. What are you doing here?"

This time, Elena acted fast and clicked out of the page she'd been viewing. "Hi, Jake. Just finishing up. About ready to hit the road."

By the time the sergeant deputy came around to her side of the desk, the computer screen was blank save for the sign-in screen. Elena released a quiet sigh of relief.

"Everything go okay at the inn?" she asked, grabbing her backpack and standing.

"What a mess. I mean, who leaves five-thousand-dollars' worth of photography equipment in their vehicle? He was practically begging to be robbed. Don't tourists realize burglars constantly case hotels looking for easy marks?"

"That's a shame."

"What's a shame is that he tried blaming the inn. Then went ballistic when the manager pointed out the small print on the agreement he signed stating the inn isn't responsible for items left in vehicles parked on the premises."

"Was there any security footage?"

"Didn't reveal much. The perps, two of them, were wearing hoodies and ski masks. They knew what they were doing. In and out of the car in less than five minutes."

"I hope his equipment was insured."

"He was on the phone with his insurance agent when I pulled out."

"That's good." Elena gave Jake a half smile. "See you tomorrow?"

"Yeah, but..." He grinned sheepishly. "If you

got a sec. I'm glad I caught you, actually. I sort of wanted to clear the air."

"Oh? About what?"

He removed his ball cap and tossed it onto the desk across from hers. "What I said earlier at Ridge's. About you being a rookie and covering all the bases."

She waited in silence for him to continue, not making it easy for him.

"You were doing a good job." He cleared his throat. "I was out of line."

"Did you tell that to the chief? Or Ridge?"

"What?" He chuckled, only to sober. "Seriously? Come on, Elena."

"Is that all? Because I'm getting hungry."

"Don't be mad."

"I think I have good reason. At Ridge's, you implied I'm inexperienced in front of our superior and the victim. But now, when no one's around to hear, you tell me I'm doing a good job. Which is it, Jake?"

He had the decency to blush. "You're the first female deputy any of us has had to work with. Ever. And you're just a kid, for crying out loud. You have to expect to take a little ribbing."

"How old were you when you started here?"

"Twenty-six. Fresh out of police academy."

"I'm twenty-eight."

"No fooling?" His dark brows shot up. "Cuz you look—"

She held out her hand in warning. "Don't say it."

"Okay, okay." He rocked back on his heels and patted his belly where it hung slightly over his belt. He wasn't out of shape, but Jake had the appearance of someone who never missed a meal. He liked to brag he knew his way around the backyard barbecue, and his smoked ribs were the best in town. "Just give us a little more time, okay? We're not a bad bunch."

"All right. Apology accepted."

"Good girl."

Elena stiffened. "Girl?"

"Oops. My bad. I've got daughters. It slipped out. Forgive me."

"Fine. On one condition." Elena went out on a limb. "You answer a couple questions for me."

"What kind of questions?"

"Tell me about the drug trafficking that used to go on here. You were a deputy then."

He frowned. "Why do you want to know that?"

"Because Pete Burnham's death may be related."

"You've been listening to Ridge."

"It makes sense."

"What, that a drug runner killed Pete? You'll get no disagreement from me. And I reckon one of them could've buried the gun and the money. It sure wasn't Pete. A drug runner is the only reasonable explanation. But if you're trying to tie Pete's homicide to the gun and money Ridge found..." Jake chuckled. "That's a stretch. A mighty big one."

"People have been killed for less than forty thousand dollars."

"Pete was killed because he saw something he shouldn't have seen or could identify someone who didn't want to be identified."

"Like the Hawk?"

"The what?"

"Never mind." Elena changed tactics. "It'll be interesting to see the test results on the gun and money."

Jake glanced over at Sage's desk and then snorted in disgust. "Nothing's gonna come of that. Those things have been in the ground too long."

"The chief must think it's worth checking into. He's sending them to Tucson."

"Don't be so sure. He's just going through

the motions. Easier that way. Ridge can make problems for him otherwise."

"He doesn't strike me as the type."

"Oh, he's the type. Likes to call the county sheriff's office and complain."

"He's searching for answers."

"Don't get swept up. I'm warning you, Elena."

"Warning me?"

"Yes, I am." Jake's features darkened. "I was here when the cartel reigned king. They wielded their power over the entire town, and everyone in it. No one was safe. If Pete Burnham was involved with them, and I'm not convinced he was, he died because he made the wrong person mad."

"What are you saying, Jake?"

"Ridge is going to find himself in the same position as his dad if he's not careful. And you, too, Elena, if you insist on getting involved."

"We have a duty to investigate Pete Burnham's death."

"The cartel has never showed mercy. And they don't forget. They may have gone underground, but they're not gone. That's why I want Ridge to quit stirring the pot. Not because he's wasting his time. Because I'd hate for my wife to lose her brother as well as her father."

Jake's comment stayed with Elena all that evening. But rather than scare her off, it convinced her she needed to speak to the chief at the first opportunity. He was the only one at the station who could, and possibly would, willingly answer her questions.

Chapter Three

Elena sat in the third pew from the back, her usual spot for Sunday morning worship service at Hillside Church. Funny how regulars had their favorite seats. Her family in Phoenix would arrive to their church with no less than six and sometimes as many as ten in their group. As a teen, she'd roll her eyes whenever her parents laid claim to "their row."

And now, here was Elena, just like them.

She smiled to herself. In only four months, she'd embraced life as a resident of Ironwood Creek—at least inasmuch as having her regular seat at church. All that remained was being accepted by her peers at work and making a few friends.

She'd been remiss with that last one, though who could blame her? Friendship required effort and time. She worked long, unmanageable hours. Hard to make plans with gal pals when her schedule changed one week to the next, and she might be called in on a moment's notice.

Not that she related well to other women when she did get together with them. They didn't like hearing about her job. Elena's sister called her a downer. A downer! She was in law enforcement. There was no cooler job on the planet.

Her sister also said Elena scared off potential friends. She intimidated them with her job and her no-nonsense attitude. Ridiculous. Elena wasn't no-nonsense. Levelheaded, yes. Pragmatic, perhaps. But those were good qualities.

Except, she apparently scared off men, too. If Elena believed her sister, they were attracted to her until they learned what she did for a living. She refused to accept that. If men were intimidated by her, it was because being married to someone in law enforcement wasn't easy for everyone. The job took a toll on relationships and families. As the daughter of a detective and granddaughter of a police sergeant, Elena could attest to that.

"Have a lovely day."

She blinked and discovered Mr. Harmon's smiling face at the end of her pew. "Same to you, sir."

She realized then that the sanctuary was nearly empty. Everyone had filed out at the end of the service—which was a good one. The minister's sermon had touched on the role of parents, and she found herself missing her own mom and dad. Her siblings, too. Her older sister and cousin were both expecting babies. Elena's mom had begun dropping hints to Elena about finding someone special and starting a family. She wasn't particularly keen on Elena following in her dad and grandfather's footsteps, citing the job's inherent danger.

At least Phoenix wasn't that far, a three-and-a-half-hour drive, so she visited monthly. Her family visited her, too. Elena's mom liked to fuss over Elena's small apartment and reorganize her cupboards. Her little brother and sister brought their swimsuits and workout clothes so they could use the apartment complex's trendy pool and gym. Her dad tuned up her car and engaged in cop talk. He was considering retiring in a year or two. Elena made enchiladas for everyone using her *abuela*'s recipe. The visits were always wonderful and filled her emotional well.

She made a mental note to call her mom when she got home.

Outside the sanctuary, several groups of people lingered in the foyer, chatting and laughing. Elena smiled and nodded, weaving her way toward the church's double glass doors.

"Elena. Hi," Olivia Gifford, the church bookkeeper, called. "Will you be joining us for coffee hour today?"

Beverages and sweets were served every Sunday after morning service in the fellowship hall. Elena usually ducked out, often because she had to work later that day or had worked all night and needed sleep. She started to tell Olivia no, only to remember her earlier thought about expanding her social circle.

"Sure. Sounds good."

"Great." Oliva brightened. "See you there."

Elena's flats echoed on the concrete walkway as she crossed from the sanctuary to the fellowship hall. She rarely wore dresses. Church was one of the few exceptions. Elena's mother had insisted, and the habit had stuck long past Elena moving out to attend college.

After graduating from the police academy, she'd considered joining the force like her dad and grandfather. A recruiter from the sheriff's department changed her mind. Amazing how a day, a plan, a life, could take a sudden and unexpected turn.

Kind of like spotting Ridge the moment she stepped into the fellowship hall. He sat at a table with his sister and Jake, and his nieces.

With his back to the door, he didn't see her, and she considered leaving. They hadn't spoken since their brief phone call when she'd told him the gun and strongbox had been shipped to the lab in Tucson. She'd intended that to be their last discussion. And while the idea of the gun and strongbox having something to do with Pete Burnham's death was intriguing, there was nothing concrete to connect it to Ironwood Creek's violent drug trafficking history.

And yet…

Her conversation yesterday with the chief had changed her opinion. As she'd listened to him, she found that some of Ridge's remarks that day at the ranch no longer seemed far-fetched. Elena wanted to tell Ridge about what she'd learned and help if she could. But not here and not now when he was surrounded by his family.

Granted, she should probably mind her own business. She wasn't a detective and felt unqualified to investigate an eighteen-year-old homicide. Moreover, the case didn't involve her, and she'd only get more flak from the chief and the other deputies. Not to mention Jake's concerns for her and Ridge's well-being if they kept poking into the drug cartel. But nothing about Pete Burnham's homicide added up, and Elena was having trouble ignoring the constant gnawing on her insides.

All at once, Ridge rose and headed toward the beverage table. He caught sight of her, and their gazes connected. Elena started forward. Neither of them looked away, not even when they were standing two feet apart.

"Morning, Ridge."

"Can I get you a coffee?" He held up an empty Styrofoam cup.

"Um…" Elena noticed people casting curious glances in their direction. Jake and Ridge's sister, Gracie, openly stared. "I was wondering if you had time to talk. About your dad's case."

"Now?"

"If you're free. I'm on duty later today."

"Absolutely." He indicated the room with a tilt of his head. "We can grab an empty table."

She shot a quick look at Jake and Gracie. "Have you had breakfast?"

"Just a stale donut before church. I was going to stop on the way home."

"More fast food?"

He smiled. "Guilty as charged."

"We could go to the Sunnyside Café." The nearby breakfast and lunch spot was a favorite of Elena's.

"Real food. How can I refuse?"

"Meet you there?"

"Let's go." He motioned toward the door.

"Do you need to talk to your family first?"

He chuckled. "I don't want to give my sister any ideas, particularly the wrong ones."

Elena thought they might be too late. From Gracie's hearts-in-her-eyes expression, she was entertaining all sorts of ideas.

Fifteen minutes later, Ridge met up with Elena at the café entrance. As expected for a Sunday morning, the place was packed, and they had to wait for a table.

"Apologies in advance if my sister corners you and gives you grief," he said.

"Grief? About what?"

They stood elbow to elbow with people on all sides and had to lean close in order to be heard above the din of clattering dishes and noisy conversations. Delicious aromas filled the air and caused Ridge's stomach to rumble.

"Gracie will jump to conclusions about us leaving church together."

"Oh." Elena gave Ridge a firm look. "But you'll set her straight."

"I'll do my best. My sister can be intentionally obtuse."

"How does she feel about your dad's homicide? Can I ask?"

Ridge took his time before answering. "She's older than me and saw more of Dad's drinking and the bad side of our parents' marriage. That's not to say she didn't love Dad and regret his death. She's just happier not dwelling on our miserable childhood and would rather I let the case lie."

"What did she say when she learned about the gun and the money?"

"She's mad I showed you the strongbox and wishes I'd split the money with her instead. Which I get. She's half owner of the ranch and feels I should have talked to her first. She and Jake have two daughters and can use twenty thousand dollars."

"You'll likely get the money back," Elena said.

"Hopefully. But you have to remember, she has Jake in her ear. And our mom. They all three want me to sell the ranch."

"I hope you turning in the gun and money doesn't drive a wedge between you and your family."

"It won't. At least I don't think it will," he said. "Even if Gracie and my mom don't always agree with me, they love me. And Jake loves Gracie. He'll go along with whatever she wants."

"I have to admit," Elena said, "I was surprised you turned the money in. You're renovating the ranch and could also use twenty thousand dollars."

He shrugged. "I did okay rodeoing."

"Five World titles, I heard."

"Something like that."

"Impressive. When did you retire?"

"About six months ago. Which is also when I began renovating the ranch. And pestering Chief Dempsey to reopen my dad's homicide."

Before he could say more, the hostess called out, "Table ready for the Burnham party."

Ridge touched Elena's shoulder and guided her past a family with teenagers. He meant nothing by the gesture. The space leading to the table for two tucked in a corner by the window was narrow. That was what he told himself, anyway.

A young man wearing a green apron appeared and held up a thermal carafe. "Coffee?"

"Please." Ridge pushed his mug forward, and the young man poured.

"Do you have any herbal tea?" Elena asked.

"Be right back."

"Tea?" Ridge asked after their server left. "I thought all cops drank coffee."

"I'm on duty this afternoon until midnight. I'll be drinking my daily quota of caffeine then."

Ridge winced. "Rough hours."

"Comes with the job." She set her menu down. "You were telling me about the ranch and your rodeo career."

He sat back, relaxing into the conversation. Normally, Ridge avoided talking about himself and his family, but opening up to Elena was easy. As he talked, the hum of twirling overhead fans and loud chatter faded into the background.

"Growing up the son of an alcoholic isn't easy. One day, Dad was great. Loving. Attentive. Teaching me how to rope or helping me build model cars. The next day, he'd be hungover and in bed until noon. Or he'd disappear for days. When he was killed, let's just say kids can be cruel. Whatever remarks their parents made about my dad at home, the kids used them to taunt me at school. My dad was a drunk. A loser. A lazy bum. I struggled and became what the school counselor called moody and withdrawn. I might have gotten into a fight or two." He tried to make light of his troubled youth.

Elena's expression softened. "I'm sorry, Ridge."

"Mom thrived on being angry. At Dad, at God, at life in general. No one was safe. She vented her wrath on anyone and everyone. Gracie left before the ink was dry on her high school diploma. She came back a few years later after bumping around the southwest and 'finding herself.'" He emphasized the last two words and then chuckled. "I shouldn't criticize. She had her ways of coping, and I had mine."

"Is that when she met Jake?" Elena asked. "After she returned?"

"Yep. He joined the sheriff's department while she was away. They met her third day home and fell head over heels in love. Married less than a year later."

"That's sweet."

Ridge nodded. "They balance each other."

"You say that like you're surprised."

"Our parents weren't exactly the best role models for a good marriage. I've often wondered, when the time came, if Gracie and I would have the tools we needed to make a long-term relationship successful. She clearly figured it out. I'm less sure about myself."

The reality was, Ridge had yet to be in a relationship that lasted more than a year. To be fair, much of that was because of his rodeo career. Constant travel took its toll on a couple. But he wondered if the real reason was that, unlike his sister, he hadn't figured out what tools he'd need.

"Awareness is half the battle," Elena said. "And the right person is the other half. That's what I learned from my parents."

He smiled. "Good philosophy."

"Did you also leave after high school?" she asked, changing the subject.

"My uncle introduced me to rodeoing when I was about fifteen. His way of trying to drag me out of my shell."

She smiled. "It seems to have succeeded. You don't strike me as moody and withdrawn."

"You haven't seen me on a bad day."

Their server chose that moment to reappear with a mug of hot water and a basket of various herbal teas. Ridge was thankful for the interruption. Otherwise, Elena might have noticed his utter captivation with her.

"You ready to order?" the young man asked. She nodded. "I'll have the avocado toast."

Ridge chose biscuits and gravy with two fried eggs on the side and a large orange juice.

Elena gawked at him. "I'm gaining two pounds just looking at all those carbs."

"Renovating the ranch is good for burning calories. So was rodeoing, not to mention good for someone with issues and needing an outlet to vent them." He sipped his coffee. "I did well and saved the bulk of my winnings. I always planned to renovate the ranch. It sat mostly empty for the last ten years, which makes my job harder. No one was there to keep the place up."

"You didn't come home?"

"Not often. Every few months for a few days to visit Gracie and Jake and the girls."

"What about your mom?" Elena asked. "Where's she now?"

"She moved to Sierra Vista once I began rodeoing professionally. Dad left the ranch to me and Gracie. Another reason for her to be angry at him. She refused to stay there after that."

"Ouch. She got nothing from his estate?"

"Life insurance. It was enough for her to make a fresh start in Bisbee where things turned out for the best. She has a good job and married a nice guy who treats her well. I keep hoping her happiness with him will rub off on her and that we might get along better."

"Is that possible?"

"Who knows? She thinks Gracie and I should sell the ranch. For the longest time I wasn't sure what I wanted to do with my life after quitting rodeo. Then something changed. Turning thirty maybe? I was always convinced nothing remained for me in Ironwood Creek. Until I finally realized I was running away from my past rather than facing it. Does that make sense?"

"It does. I've felt the same way myself at times. It's one of the reasons I decided to transfer to a new town."

They had something in common. He liked that.

"My plan is to buy Gracie out at some point, if she's agreeable," Ridge said. "She's not attached to the place like I am."

"You seem to enjoy fixing it up."

"Renovating the ranch is my dream. More than that, I'm convinced it's God's plan for me. Does that sound crazy?"

"Not at all. I believe law enforcement is God's plan for me."

Another thing in common. This was getting better and better.

"No more rodeoing, then?" she asked.

"Naw." Ridge shook his head. "I'm tired of life on the road and the aches and pains. I want to make a fresh start here. We still had a few head of cattle when I was little. My dad sold them off, along with most everything else. If something could be converted into drinking money, it was. Once I finish repairing the fences, think I'll invest in a new herd. Raise cattle like my grandfather."

"That's great, Ridge. Your plans, I mean. For the ranch and making your home in Ironwood Creek."

"What about you? Are you contemplating putting down roots in our little town?"

"I think so. Yeah." She glanced out the café's large picture window with its view of the street's quaint mixture of old and modern western ambience. "I like it here."

"Our first female deputy." Ridge didn't hide his admiration. "That has to come with some challenges. Ironwood Creek isn't as progressive as places like Phoenix and Tucson."

She laughed. "A few challenges, yes. Fortunately, I have some experience working with male law enforcement officers. My dad's a detective for the Phoenix Police Department. My grandfather's a retired sergeant with the Buckeye PD."

"Really? Third generation. I'm impressed, Deputy Tomes."

"I think my dad was counting on my brother carrying the torch. Instead, I am. My brother wants to be a graphic artist."

"Interesting." Ridge studied her. "So, why Ironwood Creek and not something closer to your family?"

"Several reasons. My dad and grandfather are well-known in Phoenix area law enforcement circles. I wanted to go someplace where they were less known and feel confident any promotions or special accommodations I received were because I'd earned them and not because of my last name."

"Makes sense."

"When the opening came up in Ironwood Creek, I liked the idea of a small town, and I thought my efforts might stand out more in a field of fewer deputies."

Their food arrived then, and they both dug in. After a few moments, Ridge got to the point. "So tell me, what did you want to talk about?"

"I researched the town's history like you suggested, and you were right. It's unsavory. And unsettling that it went on for years and years unchecked."

"There's a reason for that. Money. It buys silence and cooperation."

"True." She took another bite. "I also researched your dad. There wasn't much to find. Nothing you don't already know, I'm sure." She filled him in. Ridge ate in silence, listening. "I was going to forget the whole thing," she continued, "until Jake warned me to stay out of it."

Ridge's head shot up. "Warned you how?"

"He doesn't want you winding up in danger like your dad. And he said I would, too, if I wasn't careful."

"That sounds almost threatening."

"It wasn't. If he came across strong, it's because he cares."

Even so, Ridge worried for her safety. "The last thing I want is for anything to happen to you."

"Nothing will." She set down her knife and fork, seeming to struggle for words.

"What is it?"

Elena firmed her jaw. "I'd like to help you find out who killed your dad."

Ridge stared at her, taken aback. "I'm sure I must have heard wrong. I thought you said you wanted to help me."

Their server abruptly appeared. "Can I get you anything else?"

And then, Elena's phone rang, bringing their conversation to a grinding halt.

While Ridge ordered more coffee for him and tea for Elena, she talked to her mom. Her attempts to cut the conversation short and return the phone call later were thwarted. Her highly observant mom had instantly jumped to a wrong conclusion and insisted Elena reveal the name of her deep-voiced companion.

"You're on a date?"

"We're having lunch, Mom."

"Lunch or *lunch*?"

Elena bit her tongue rather than rise to the bait her mom dangled. "It's not like that. We're working on a case together."

"I want to hear everything. What case? Where did you meet him? Is he good-looking?"

She sighed. "I'll call you in an hour, Mom."

"You'd better, *mija*."

Thankfully pocketing her phone, she refocused on Ridge. Same as he was focusing on her.

She enjoyed the moment for a few heartbeats. No harm in that, was there? Her next thought was of her mom's unending questions.

"Sorry. My mom doesn't always take the hint."

"You two are close," Ridge said. "That's nice."

"It is. Most of the time. When she doesn't have her nose in my business."

"She cares, Elena." There was a trace of wistfulness in his voice. "You're blessed."

Though curious about his relationship with his mom, she sidestepped the personal and potentially sensitive subject. "I meant what I said about helping you, Ridge."

"I'm glad. Seriously. But I have to ask why."

"I talked to the chief the other day. Asked him what he knew of your dad's murder and the drug trafficking. It clearly struck a nerve. He shut me down and suggested I mind my own business."

"You don't appear to be doing that."

"My interest was piqued. I had to ask myself, what wasn't he telling me?"

Ridge considered briefly. "The chief has always seemed to me to be a decent man. He probably shut you down because he's worried about you, like Jake is, and believes the cartel is still around. Just lying low."

"That's not it." Elena dunked a tea bag in her fresh cup of hot water. "He's hiding something."

Ridge sat forward. "Like what?"

"I don't know. He's been at the station a long time. Oscar Wentworth, too. The chief was promoted from sergeant deputy when the former chief retired. There's a picture of him and the former chief hanging on the wall in the station."

"I remember my mom talking about Dempsey's promotion. There was apparently some bad blood between him and Wentworth at the time because they both wanted the job. And then between Wentworth and Jake when Jake was promoted to sergeant deputy."

"I can see that," Elena mused aloud, thinking of her coworker and his short fuse. "You don't suppose there's a connection between the chief's promotion and your dad's homicide?"

"What kind of connection?"

She sighed. "Forget it. I'm grasping at straws. The chief wasn't promoted until years after your dad's homicide." She sipped her tea, knowing she should ignore the direction her thoughts had taken, but not quite able to do that. "You said there were people who stood to benefit from the drug trafficking. What people were you referring to?"

"Higher-ups. Elected officials. The former chief. The mayor. Council members. Property owners who took kickbacks to look the other way, one of whom may or may not have been my dad."

"Him taking kickbacks would make sense, I hate to say. Money is all too often a motive for murder."

Ridge studied her. "You think Chief Dempsey is protecting certain people? Or himself?"

"No." Elena heard the lack of conviction in her voice. "But I keep asking myself why the drug trafficking went on for so long before anyone put a stop to it. And three homicides were swept under the carpet. All of them unsolved. Did you know that?"

"I did." Ridge sat back, a slight smile tugging at the corners of his mouth. "Seems like we have our work cut out for us, partner."

"I'm wondering how much help I can be with both Jake and the chief keeping a watch on me."

"They have a point, Elena. There could be risks. And you have no vested interest in my dad's case. Unless..." He paused.

"What?"

"Don't take this wrong, but are you trying to prove yourself to the chief?"

"It's not that," she insisted. *Not only that.*

"Then what?"

How could she explain? "I have this thing about putting right what's wrong and seeing the bad guys brought to justice."

"Ah. You're a do-gooder."

"If I am, that's fine with me."

Elena had lost her grandmother under terrible circumstances. Her death had affected Elena profoundly and was responsible, in part, for shaping her into the person she was today—someone determined to make the world a better place. She didn't talk about the tragedy with just anyone, not until she felt confident and comfortable in the relationship.

"It's more than fine," Ridge said.

She sat up straighter. "Your dad didn't deserve to be killed. Finding his murderer would vindicate him and see that justice is served. But I'll admit that yes, if it shows the chief and the others that I'm good at my job and deserving of their respect, that would be an added bonus."

Ridge reached across the table for her hand. "Elena. You're the first one to believe me. And the first one to offer help. That means a lot."

She quite liked the sensation his fingers enveloping hers evoked. So much for ignoring her response to him.

"I'm not the first person. People believed you, Ridge. That was the trouble. They discredited you to protect themselves."

"Thank you." He grinned in earnest. "Where do we start?"

"Start what?" came an unexpected voice.

They both looked up. Elena gave a small jerk.

Jake stood at their table. Beside him, Gracie stared, her eyes riveted on Elena and Ridge's clasped hands.

"Isn't this nice," she said. "We have the table next to yours."

Elena quickly reclaimed her hand, which only drew further attention to her and Ridge. Her cheeks heated with embarrassment.

Ridge acted as if nothing was out of the ordinary. Standing, he asked amiably, "What brings you here?"

"Lunch." Jake hadn't taken his eyes off Elena. "Same as you."

Their young server motioned. "Would you like me to push the tables together?"

"We're nearly finished," Ridge said.

At the same time, Gracie nudged her daughters forward and overruled him by proclaiming, "Perfect! Thank you."

Tables quickly joined, the server took the newcomers' drink orders. Moments later, Elena found herself sitting next to Gracie. Jake continued to stare at her from his seat next to Ridge. He looked like he might have guessed why they were here and wasn't happy about it.

Well, so be it. She and Ridge weren't doing anything wrong.

"You remember our girls, Lindsey and Laney?" Gracie asked. "Say hello, girls."

"Hello," the pair answered in unison before returning their attention to the video playing on their dad's phone.

"What are you two really doing here?" Jake asked, disapproval darkening his features.

"Biscuits and gravy." Ridge pointed to his almost empty plate with his fork.

"Why?" Jake addressed the question to Elena.

She deflected. "We were hungry."

"I don't buy it," he scoffed.

"Jake. Enough." Gracie sent Elena an apologetic smile.

"If you must know," Ridge said, "we were talking about movies and trying to pick one we both like."

"You're going to the movies?" Gracie pressed a hand to her heart. "Like a date?"

"We were discussing it."

Elena gaped at Ridge. He, in turn, sent her a reassuring head nod. She had to either trust him or cause a minor scene.

Their server returned with drinks. He refilled Ridge's coffee, then took food orders for the rest of them before disappearing.

"Be honest, Elena. What's it like working with my husband?" Gracie asked with pronounced glee.

Elena swallowed, telling herself she could get through this. "He's very good at his job. Thorough. Knowledgeable. I've learned a lot from him."

The remainder of their meal was an exercise in patience and endurance. Gracie's unabashed curiosity and Jake's relentless scrutiny knew no bounds. At last, she and Ridge were able to make their excuses—she was on duty in a few hours. He settled the tab, refusing to let her pay half or cover the tip.

"Bye. See you soon," Gracie trilled after them.

"Where's your car?" Ridge asked once they were outside.

"Over there." Elena indicated a compact hybrid, and they started walking. "Your family thinks we're dating now."

He chuckled. "Is that so terrible?"

"Yes. Because we're not."

"You have to admit, it's a great cover. No one will question us when we're together working on my dad's case."

She couldn't dispute that logic. At her car, she fished her phone from her purse and said, "We should exchange numbers."

"Good idea."

He gave her his, and she sent him a quick text.

"I'm thinking we should talk to the detective on your dad's case, assuming he's still around," she added. "I'll find out what I can and call you tomorrow."

"And I'll keep looking for the gold chain. It may have been buried with the gun and money, and I missed it."

"Okay."

"Thanks again, Elena."

She started to answer him when her phone pinged with a notification. Without thinking, she checked the display. The text was from a number she didn't recognize. The first few words were visible and jumped off the screen at her, striking like small daggers. Her finger automatically swiped to open the message.

"Elena, are you okay?"

Her face must have gone white for Ridge grabbed her by the arm to steady her.

She held out the phone to him, her blood running cold. "Read this."

Quit looking into Burnham's death or you'll end up dead like him.

Chapter Four

"You must be scared, Deputy. I want you to take a few days off."

"I'm not scared, Chief, I'm mad."

Elena sat across from her boss in his office. She'd reported the threatening text immediately after receiving it. Ridge, who'd been more upset than her, refused to let her out of his sight. He'd followed her home from the café and then insisted on accompanying her while she inspected every square inch of her apartment. She'd refused him, citing law enforcement policy, only to grudgingly let him in when her initial sweep revealed no evidence of an intruder or a break-in.

Reminding him that, between the two of them, she was the one trained for this type of situation had no effect. He'd remained adamant and conducted his own inspection.

When he'd finished, she called the unfamiliar number. No surprise, a message played after the first ring telling Elena she'd reached a number that had been disconnected or was no longer in service.

A burner phone, probably. She'd heard about ways to fake automated recordings.

Ridge left only when she promised to call him in an hour and again when she reached the station. She'd half-suspected that he'd remain in the parking lot, surveying her unit. She understood. He felt responsible for her receiving the threatening text even though she'd volunteered to help him.

Of course, he'd insisted they drop the investigation into his dad's case, and Elena told him they'd talk about it later. She wasn't easily intimidated.

The chief had called her into his office the second she arrived at work. They'd been chatting for the past twenty minutes.

"I don't like being threatened," Elena continued.

"You like being foolish?" he retorted. His chair squeaked when he rocked back. "Someone figured out what you're up to, and they're not joking around."

"Who?" she demanded. "And how?"

"There's a record of every keystroke you type on that computer."

"Are you accusing somebody within the sheriff's department of threatening me?"

"I'm saying you and your actions are visible. A lot of people saw you with Ridge earlier at the café."

And church, she silently added. Ironwood Creek wasn't so large that the news of a gun and money discovered on the Burnham Ranch hadn't spread like a gasoline fire. If someone had something to hide—say, for instance, that they were involved with Pete Burnham's death—they might conclude Ridge and Elena were trading information. Especially if they spotted the pair with their heads bent together in a serious conversation.

"What are you going to do about the text, Chief?"

"For starters, you're on desk duty for the time being."

"Chief!"

"Oscar's on his way in."

She groaned. "You wouldn't restrict me if I was a man."

The chief's expression darkened. "Your gender has nothing to do with this."

She didn't believe him. "What, then? I get to type reports and answer the phone?"

"Let's see what happens over the next day or two. You contact admin?"

"On the drive here." The sheriff's department took threats against their personnel very seriously.

"What did they say?"

"I filed a report. There's not much they can do under the circumstances. The threat is vague, and I haven't been attacked or approached. I called my phone company, but they won't tell me anything useful without a warrant."

"Speaking of a warrant, have you called the police? Because I think you should. In fact, I'm telling you to call them."

"I will." And she would. If only to create a record, should there be another threat. Sheriff's departments and local police had different jurisdictions, but they worked together to keep the peace and solve crimes. Besides, the person who threatened Elena may not be from Ironwood Creek. "They won't do much, either. Not unless something more happens."

Elena remembered Jake finding her and Ridge in the café and questioning them. Would he have sent the text? Not that she believed for an instant he'd hurt her, but he had warned her to steer clear of Ridge. This could be his attempt to scare her away.

An idea occurred to her. "You know, Chief, the text could be proof."

"Of what?"

"A connection between Pete Burnham's death and the drug trafficking. Whoever's involved is getting nervous."

"The person could also be a quack. Or pulling a prank."

"Some prank."

"People get their kicks out of toying with law enforcement, or they have an axe to grind."

"You really believe that?" she said.

"I'm not discounting anything."

"The gun and money most likely belonged to one of the drug runners. Maybe the guy Ridge saw arguing with his dad."

"We'll learn more when the lab forwards the test results."

Elena nodded. When she'd asked, Sage confirmed that the packages arrived on Friday. She'd also let Elena know that the chief had indeed requested a rush. That was unexpected, given how indifferent he'd seemed at first. Sage had gone on to tell Elena that rush requests seldom guaranteed quick results, which came when they came.

"What if Pete Burnham happened upon the drug runner burying the gun and money and was killed for it?" Elena asked the chief.

"That's doubtful." He opened his desk drawer, removed a bottle of antacid tablets and popped three in his mouth. "First of all, why would the drug runner have buried the gun and money on private property? Second, he wouldn't have bothered to take Burnham into the hills behind the ranch. He'd have offed him right there and left the body."

Elena had thought the same thing, but asked anyway. "Like the other two murders?"

"Exactly. Those men were shot right outside their backdoors. Burnham, on the other hand, was pushed off a ledge into a ravine."

"But they were locals like Pete Burnham. And the drug runners were using their land."

"Allegedly," the chief hedged.

"There were witnesses."

"There were people who reported seeing nighttime activity on the victims' properties prior to the murders. Not specifically on the nights of the murders," he emphasized. "No weapons were found. No evidence. Not a single lead uncovered in any of the cases."

"Until now," Elena said.

"Maybe." The chief returned the bottle of antacids to his desk drawer. "Assuming DNA evidence can be lifted from the gun and the money, and assuming it can be connected to someone in the system. Both are highly unlikely."

He was right. She and Ridge would just have to search elsewhere. And be discreet. One good thing about desk duty, she'd have time for research…except if the chief's earlier suggestion was correct, someone might be tracking her computer usage. She'd have to find another way.

The door to the station opened, and the chief craned his neck to see past her.

Oscar called out, "Hi, honey, I'm home."

Elena resisted rolling her eyes. The other deputy, twenty-seven years her senior, was biding his time until he could retire. Like her, he'd transferred from another part of the state and now called Ironwood Creek his home. He made no secret of wanting to return to the Flagstaff area one day.

"We'll be done here in a minute," the chief said.

They heard him cross to the breakroom,

where he'd stow his personal belongings and prepare to go out on patrol. *Him* instead of Elena. The thought left an unpleasant taste in her mouth. Desk duty felt like a punishment rather than the chief protecting her from danger.

"You going to be all right if I head home?" the chief asked. "My son and his family are coming for dinner."

"I'll be fine, sir."

"Call if there's a problem or you get another threat—or even if you're afraid. You don't have to act tough, Elena. You have nothing to prove to us."

His remark gave her pause. That was the only time he'd ever come close to acknowledging she received different treatment than the men. For a moment, and only a moment, Elena's hard shell softened.

"I will. Call, that is."

"Okay. Good." The chief stood and reached for his jacket laying on the credenza behind him. "I'll see you tomorrow."

She followed him out of his office and into the main room. Oscar sat at Elena's preferred desk, stroking his prominent mustache as he read. She swallowed down her annoyance and sat across from him. He'd chosen her desk solely to irritate her, and she wouldn't give him the satisfaction of seeing that his ploy worked.

After the chief left, she occupied herself with grunt work, pretending to be too busy to chat with Oscar. Sunday evenings were notoriously slow in Ironwood Creek. Just when Elena thought she might have to suffer Oscar's boorish company for hours on end, a call came in about a disturbance at Liberty Market, and he escaped. A relief, no doubt, to them both.

Rather than get on the computer, Elena went to the storeroom. She didn't hold much hope of finding anything interesting, since most of the sheriff's department's records were digitized. But there were some older paper records she'd noticed on previous research deep dives. It was worth a try.

While she was rifling through files, she called Ridge on her cell phone. He answered immediately.

"How are you doing?"

"I've been grounded. The chief put me on desk duty."

"Good."

Were all men alike? "I didn't call to talk about that," she said a little grumpily. "Are you near a computer?"

"I have a laptop."

"Can you do a basic search on the Bisbee detective assigned to your dad's homicide? His name was Frank Darnelly."

"I remember him. A tall guy. Imposing. Never cracked a smile."

Which would have intimidated a twelve-year-old.

"I don't want to use the station's computer," she explained, "in case someone is monitoring my usage."

"Is that possible?"

"It is for anyone with access to Cochise County's network." She pulled a new box from the shelf. "I'm just being extra cautious. Half the town knows I was the responding deputy to your ranch and that we went to lunch after church."

"That's true. Hang on a second."

She heard muffled noises in the background.

"Got my laptop open."

"Start by conducting a basic search with his name and a few other key words like Bisbee and police detective. Don't be surprised if you find nothing. People in law enforcement try not to be easily found."

"I think this is him," Ridge said a minute

later and read off the limited details. "How many Francis Darnellys could there be living in Bisbee?"

"Let's hope only one."

"There's no address or phone number. We could pay twenty-nine dollars for a background report."

"I have a better idea. My cousin's wife works for motor vehicles. She can probably get me Darnelly's address. He's retired now."

"Then what? Drive to Bisbee and knock on his door?"

"Actually, yes."

"When's your next day off?"

She replaced the lid on the box of useless files and pushed to her feet. There was nothing of value in the storeroom. "Tuesday."

"I'll pick you up after lunch. One o'clock?"

"Let's make it four-thirty. Bisbee is thirty miles away. He's more likely to be home at dinnertime. I'll meet you at Valley View Bank." The station phone rang then. "Gotta run."

She disconnected before he could say more.

Ridge sat on a plush visitor chair in the Valley View Bank lobby. Elena was supposed to have been here by now. In hindsight, they probably should have met at her apartment. But Elena had wanted to be careful should anyone be following them. Too late now.

Twice, he'd had to fend off a cheerful clerk who wanted to know if he could be of assistance. His mistake. He should have probably waited in his truck. Except someone just sitting in a truck tended to draw the wrong kind of attention. But so did a six-foot cowboy sitting in a bank lobby. Maybe he should ask about opening an account.

Fidgeting, he checked his phone again. Had something happened to Elena? Another threat? She'd sent a vague two-word text that hadn't relieved him.

Running late.

He was about to call her when the bank's glass doors swooshed open, and she entered, red-faced from either exertion or the freezing wind, a leftover from yesterday's nasty weather front. At least they wouldn't have to battle rain on their drive to Bisbee. The wind, for all its cold, had dispatched the clouds.

Ridge shoved out of the visitor chair and strode across the small lobby toward her. Customers, hurrying to complete their transactions before the bank closed stared briefly and then glanced away.

"Sorry I'm late," she said. "There was an accident on Ocotillo Street. Traffic had to detour. No one appeared badly hurt."

Ridge caught her by the elbow and escorted her back outside. "Let's leave before we draw too much attention."

"We should take my car," Elena said. "It's less recognizable in town than your truck with its custom license plate."

"Nah, I'll drive. If our cover is that we're on a date, it will appear less suspicious should someone spot us and we're in my truck." He didn't acknowledge her weary, sometimes-women-drive-on-dates expression. "There's a restaurant in Bisbee, Rusty's Steakhouse. I checked, and it's not far from where Frank Darnelly lives. We can say we had dinner there if anyone asks."

"I'm impressed." She smiled. "You're better at this covert stuff than I'd expected."

He opened the passenger-side door of his truck, and she hopped in. During the drive, they shared what they'd each accomplished during the last two days.

"I've turned the ranch upside-down trying to find the gold chain," Ridge said as they headed out of town. "Mom tossed or donated most of Dad's things after he died. She didn't want any reminders of him. I scoured every closet and drawer and cabinet in the house. Looked under mattresses. Flipped through the pages of books. Went through old boxes. I even called my mom and my uncle. Neither of them recalled anything about a gold chain."

"Other than potential DNA evidence and validating your story," Elena said, "I'm not sure what else locating it would prove."

"If we showed the chain around town, someone may recognize it and be able to identify the guy my dad argued with."

"That's a stretch, but it's not impossible," Elena conceded. "Still, I think we'll have better results focusing elsewhere. Like talking to Frank Darnelly and researching records. I went to the public library yesterday hoping to find some information on the other two unsolved homicides."

Ridge merged onto the highway leading to Bisbee. "Learn anything?"

"The only connection I found between the other homicides and your dad's was all three men owned land that sat between town and the mountains—land that accessed the landing strip."

"What landing strip?" Ridge asked.

"There's a long stretch of flat ground hidden behind Rooster Butte. I read about it in one of the reports. Small planes would meet the cartel's vehicles there and transfer their product. The planes then flew off to Phoenix or Vegas or whatever large city was their destination. The empty trucks returned to the border for another load."

"How did I not know this?"

"You were young," Elena told him. "Why would you know?"

Ridge decided to call his mom again tomorrow and ask her about the landing strip and their ranch's proximity to it.

"I spoke to the librarian," Elena continued. "She's lived in Ironwood Creek for over twenty years. She told me the drug trafficking and the landing strip were an open secret in town. Everyone knew, but no one talked about it."

"Because they were afraid," Ridge said.

"Or they benefited."

He thought once more of his parents. What was his mom not telling him?

The GPS voice on his phone advised him to take the next exit.

"How do you think the detective will react when we show up at his door?" He turned right at the stoplight.

"He won't talk at first." Elena shook her head. "Not without a lot of convincing."

"Do you have a plan?"

"I think you should take the lead. Appeal to him as a murdered man's son who's seeking closure. He'll act tough and indifferent, but he'll have a heart somewhere in there."

"Won't he respond better to you as a fellow law enforcement officer?"

"No." She glanced out the window. "He's old-school."

Ridge studied her profile. For a small woman, she was a warrior with the courage of David and the wisdom of Daniel. She knew when to fight and when to remain quiet and let others take up the sword.

Before long, they were passing rows of buildings and houses exhibiting Bisbee's iconic and eclectic architecture. Examples of the town's colorful mining history were evident everywhere. Shops and art galleries and coffee shops abounded. Tourists walked shoulder to shoulder on the sidewalks.

Ridge navigated the busy street, switching

from one lane to the other in an attempt to avoid delays and reach Darnelly's house before dinnertime.

More than once, he noticed a gray sedan in his rear-or side-view mirror. He asked Elena about it. She kept an eye on the car, which turned left two intersections later and didn't appear again.

Frank Darnelly lived in an attractive middle-class neighborhood. Ridge had found out that the retired detective was married and a proud grandfather, thanks to his wife who was very active on social media.

He parked on the street in front of the house rather than pull into the driveway. "Ready?" he asked Elena. She'd been quiet since her remark about Darnelly being old-school. Ridge didn't presume to understand what she went through, a young woman trying to make her way in a male-dominated profession.

She smiled at him. "Here we go."

At the front door, Ridge rang the video doorbell. He mentally rehearsed what he'd say if Darnelly answered or if his wife did. As it turned out, they were greeted by a disembodied voice from a tiny speaker.

"What do you want?"

Ridge swallowed, composing himself. Not what he'd been expecting. "Detective Darnelly?"

"Who wants to know?"

"My name is Ridge Burnham. I'm Pete Burnham's son. You were the detective assigned to his homicide investigation eighteen years ago."

A long silence followed. Finally, Darnelly repeated, "What do you want?"

"I found some potential evidence buried on my family's ranch. It may be connected to my dad's homicide. I was hoping you'd be willing to talk to me. To us."

"Who's your friend?"

Elena removed her badge from her jacket pocket and held it up to the smart doorbell's camera. "Deputy Elena Tomes with the Cochise County Sheriff's Department. I'm currently stationed at Ironwood Creek."

"Are you here in an official capacity?"

"No, sir. I'm the deputy who responded to Mr. Burnham's call when he discovered the potential evidence, but I'm here strictly as a friend."

Her answer was followed by another long silence.

"Detective Darnelly," Ridge said, deciding to appeal to the man's heart as Elena had suggested, "I've spent almost two decades living with uncertainty and anger and frustration. Struggling to put my past behind me. If there's anything you could tell us that might help find the person who killed my dad, or at least help me learn why he was killed, I'd appreciate it. As would my sister, Gracie. You may remember her."

More silence. Ridge exchanged a glance with Elena. He was about to give up and walk away when the door opened and a tall, lanky bald man stood glowering at them.

He retreated a step and motioned to them. "Come in. Wipe your feet first."

They did, and he ushered Ridge and Elena inside. His wife either wasn't home or had been instructed to stay out of sight.

"We're sorry to disturb you," Ridge started.

When he went to remove his jacket, Darnelly's brows drew together in a way that implied Ridge and Elena wouldn't be staying long enough to make themselves comfortable. He didn't offer them a seat. Instead, they stood awkwardly in the foyer.

"What did you discover on your property?" Darnelly asked.

"A handgun—a .40 caliber revolver. And a strongbox containing forty thousand dollars.

They were buried beneath my well house. From the looks of them, they were there a long time."

"Is the money counterfeit?"

Ridge drew back. He hadn't considered that possibility.

Evidently, Elena had for she said, "On inspection, the money appeared to be legit. The lab in Tucson will confirm."

The older man considered. "I doubt they'll find much trace evidence if the gun and money are eighteen years old. There's a lot of moisture under a well house."

Ridge refused to be deterred. "Is there anything you can tell us that wasn't in the report and could shed light on my dad's case?"

Again, Darnelly paused before answering. "For what it's worth, I always believed you about the stranger you saw arguing with your dad earlier in the day. I did investigate. Interviewed the neighbors and people in town. No one saw a bearded man with long shaggy hair that day or any day before or after. I checked arrests for the next year. Anyone remotely resembling the man you described had an alibi on the day of Pete Burnham's murder."

Ridge felt a rush coursing through him. Someone had believed him and made an effort to find his dad's murderer. He'd had no idea. "Thank you for telling me, Detective."

The hard edges of Darnelly's expression smoothed. "I'm sorry you lost your dad. That had to be rough. But there's nothing I can tell you that will help. Do I think the gun and money you found were buried by the man who shoved him over that ledge? Maybe. Likely not. I'd say your dad buried it, and if any DNA evidence comes back, it'll be his."

"Where do *you* think he got the money?"

"Where everyone in Ironwood Creek acquired large sums of cash in those days."

"The drug cartel?"

Darnelly shrugged.

Ridge wanted to believe his dad was innocent of any wrongdoing, but facts were beginning to pile up and point to the opposite. His dad had been arguing with a stranger who threatened him and his family. He'd gone back on an agreement. Even if Ridge could discover who'd murdered his dad, he wouldn't be able to vindicate him.

"My guess is your dad was receiving a kickback from the cartel," Darnelly said. "Or he stole the money."

"My dad was honest."

"Your dad had a drinking problem. He nearly ran that ranch of yours into the ground. Folks in a position like his don't always exercise good judgment. If the cartel came to him with a deal, he probably took it."

"He may have been trying, in his way, to provide for his family," Elena offered.

Ridge recognized her attempt to justify his dad's actions and fresh grief weighed on him. Less for his dad and more for the loss of a belief he'd held most of his life.

He caught Elena's concerned expression and tried to silently assure her that he was all right. Only he was far from all right. His world had shifted, and nothing would be quite the same after today.

The retired detective blew out a long, weary breath. "The cartel wielded a significant amount of influence and power back in those days. They still do. You need to be careful. Ask too many questions, and news will reach the wrong set of ears sooner or later."

"Whose ears?" Elena asked.

"You need to leave." Darnelly hitched his chin at the door.

Before Ridge could say more, Elena tugged on his arm. "Thank you, Detective."

Standing on the threshold, Darnelly issued them a final warning. "Take my advice. Let sleeping dogs lie. You might want closure or answers, but it's not worth risking your life. Or anyone else's." His glance cut to Elena before returning to Ridge. "Chances are good your dad got mixed up with the wrong people. Don't you make the same mistake."

With that, he shut the door in their faces.

Chapter Five

Ridge and Elena returned to his truck and drove the first mile in silence. He didn't want to admit how shaken the encounter with the retired detective had left him.

Avoiding Elena's concerned expression, he asked, "Do you think Darnelly was serious about the cartel still being active in Ironwood Creek?"

"He definitely believes it. Whether he's right or wrong, I can't tell you. I haven't seen any indication of their presence, but I haven't been a resident very long."

"And up until six months ago, I was gone a lot."

"They could be operating on the lowdown," she admitted. "Technology is constantly evolving. Makes it easy to carry out a sophisticated illegal operation under everyone's noses."

"In Ironwood Creek? How?"

"Drones. Hidden cameras and listening devices. Computer hacking. Spies."

"Spies?" Ridge scoffed.

"It's not that far-fetched. The cartel is a powerful and wealthy organization. Though it's more likely, in my opinion, they moved away from Ironwood Creek and went somewhere else." She scrolled through her phone. "I'll see what I can find out."

"Be careful, Elena."

"I will."

They crawled through the center of Bisbee, keeping pace with the other slow-moving vehicles. Evening had fallen while they were with Darnelly, coming early this time of year. Storefronts and office building windows glowed bright against an increasingly darkening sky.

"Are you hungry?" Ridge asked.

"A little."

"We can stop. What are you in the mood for?"

"I hate to ask, considering your regular diet of fast food, but can we get drive-through? I have an early morning dentist appointment before my shift starts and need to get home."

"Hamburgers or tacos?"

"Hamburgers." She pointed ahead. "What about that place we saw on the way into town?"

Ridge changed lanes. When he did, he noticed a pair of headlights changing lanes with him. He thought nothing of it until they stopped at the next light. Observing the car in his side mirror, he noticed the shape of it looked remarkably like the gray sedan that had stuck close to them during their earlier trip through town. Then again, the make and model were hardly unique.

He abruptly changed lanes and turned right at the next intersection.

"What are you doing?" Elena asked.

Ridge waited to answer until the sedan also turned. "I think we have a tail."

"Are you sure?" She cranked her head around.

"Don't look. You'll just draw attention to us."

Going faster wasn't possible, not with the congested traffic. Ridge did his best to outmaneuver the car, to no avail. It stayed with them, occasionally dropping back but always catching up again.

Elena opened the search app on her phone and began typing. "We could drive to the police station four blocks away. That'll lose them."

Without signaling, Ridge pulled into a fried chicken place. The car went past and continued up the road.

"Is he gone?"

"For now."

"Do we wait?" Elena asked.

"We might as well get something to eat."

She gaped at him. "You can eat after that? What if he comes back?"

"If someone was tailing us, they know we came here to see Darnelly and that we're heading home to Ironwood Creek. Us eating won't change anything. Besides, if they were going to shoot us, they'd have done so by now. Probably when we were leaving Darnelly's."

To Ridge's surprise, and, okay, his enjoyment, Elena chuckled. "Okay. Let's have some chicken."

"You're not scared?"

"I'm more cautious than scared. You're right, if their intent was to kill us, we'd be dead by now. In my opinion, they were gathering intel."

"I agree."

"They may have been watching Darnelly more than us. Or just making sure he didn't talk."

Ridge studied her. "You think he's covering up something?"

"He could be protecting someone. One of those higher-ups you mentioned."

"You may be onto something."

They opted to go inside the restaurant rather than hit the drive-through. Fried chicken wasn't the easiest food to consume while driving.

"Should we sit by the window?" Ridge pointed to a table after they got their orders. "That way, we can keep an eye out for the car.

"He realized we made him and that his intimidation tactics didn't work. He may not come back."

"Or if he does, he could be driving a different vehicle."

"Let's sit where we can see out the window, but aren't an easy target." Elena chose a table in the center of the small dining area. "We should also watch for a tail when we leave."

They dug into their meals. Adrenaline surges from being followed apparently worked up an appetite.

"Did you tell anyone where we were going today?" Ridge asked between bites.

"The chief and Sage, the station secretary. It's my day off, but I'm potentially on call if needed. I didn't mention what we planned or that we were seeing Darnelly, only that I'd be in Bisbee. What about you?"

"I didn't say a word."

"Even to Jake?" she probed.

"Especially not to him. Or my sister. I went so far as to sign out of the family tracking app we all have on our phones for emergencies."

"Will Gracie notice and question you?"

"Since she has no idea I left town, and I answered her when she texted me a while ago, no. At least, I don't think she will."

"Well, somebody figured out our plans."

"The same person who sent you that text?"

"Maybe."

"That leaves the chief and the secretary."

Elena furrowed her brow. "Actually, Sage keeps everyone's whereabouts on a daily log in case she's at lunch or something and one of us needs the information."

"Who has access to the daily log?" Ridge asked.

"It's right there on her desk for anyone to see."

He considered this information. "I'm worried about you, Elena."

"I'm more worried about you. You're a bigger threat to the cartel than me. I'm just a means to get to you."

"Still, you could get hurt. Darnelly's warning was no joke."

"I don't intimidate easily, Ridge. If I did,

I wouldn't have chosen law enforcement as a profession."

"Maybe you should be intimidated."

"Why don't we put this in God's hands?"

Ridge sat back. "I believe God gives us free will, and I choose to be safe."

"Not what I'm suggesting," Elena said. "Let's take a few days off from investigating. If nothing new develops, if the forensic tests on the gun and money are inconclusive, then perhaps God is giving you your answer. You're not supposed to know what happened to your dad. It won't serve you or the greater good. He wants you to move on."

"And if something does develop?"

"Then we continue investigating."

Ridge deliberated a moment. "All right. Fair enough."

Once they finished eating, they headed home. No one followed them as far as they could tell.

"Are you going to the winter picnic at church on Saturday?" Ridge asked, exiting the highway and taking the road leading into Ironwood Creek. "Gracie's twisting my arm."

"I am, unless I get called in."

"That's four days from now. We can check in with each other there, assuming nothing comes up beforehand."

"Will your sister be expecting us to go together? You did imply we were dating."

Ridge tried to read Elena's expression. How did she feel about their pretend arrangement?

"We could," he said. "Just to keep up appearances for the time being."

"Okay."

She didn't sound enthused. Well, this was business, and not a social outing. He needed to remember that.

"Okay," he echoed. "Pick you up at eleven-thirty? I'll bring the drinks." He strove to lighten the mood. "I make a mean lemonade."

"You have no kitchen."

"I will by then. And I've got to do something with all those lemons."

"That's right, I saw your trees. They're loaded with fruit."

"You're welcome to as many bags as you can carry."

"I may take you up on the offer." She smiled then. "I'm bringing pozole."

"Homemade?"

She feigned offense. "Yes, homemade."

"Elena Tomes. Are you saying you're a good cook?"

"A passable cook. My late grandmother taught me."

Ridge broke into a wide grin. "This I have to try."

Nothing amiss happened for the remainder of the ride home. Ridge pulled into the bank parking lot and drove to where Elena's car sat alone at the rear of the lot, bathed in the yellow glow from a light mounted to the building.

She climbed out of his truck. He did, too, and walked her to her car, relieved nothing awaited her other than a blanket of dried leaves, thanks to the earlier wind.

He couldn't help his sense of alarm when he remembered the text she'd received the other day. She may be well-trained, but she was still small of stature and vulnerable.

"Elena."

Without conscious thought, he drew her into a hug. She resisted at first, then relaxed, her palms resting on the front of his jacket. His arms went around her shoulders in a protective gesture.

"Be careful," he told her.

"I will."

He released her then, taking hold of her hands. "Do you mind if I say a quick prayer?"

"I'd like that."

He bent his head close to hers. "Dear Lord, if we are on the course that You intend for us, we ask that You take us under Your wing and watch over us while we search for answers. Grant us the strength we need to face our adversaries and overcome whatever obstacles lay ahead. We are now and forever Your humble servants. Amen."

"Amen," Elena repeated softly.

Ridge squeezed Elena's fingers. He had no reason to continue keeping her close, but he couldn't bring himself to let her go. Her hands felt right in his as if they belonged there.

All at once, a gray sedan rounded the bank building and came straight at them, headlights on high beam. Elena ripped her hands from Ridge's and spun to confront the intruder, not showing a single trace of fear. Ridge instinctively stepped in front of her, but she'd have none of it and moved out from behind him.

The car came closer and slowed to a stop. With the engine continuing to idle, the door opened.

"It's okay," Elena said, and exhaled in relief. "I know him."

The middle-aged man strode forward. When he entered the light cast by his car's headlights, Ridge also recognized him—though, without the uniform, it took a moment.

"What are you doing here, Oscar?" Elena asked, her tone a mixture of relief and apprehension.

The off-duty deputy offered an affable grin, his mustache twitching. "I was driving past and saw you and your car from the road. I wondered if you were okay." His grin widened. "I can see now you are."

"Yes. Ridge and I met up here a while ago. For…dinner. He was just dropping me off."

"Oh. Excuse me. Sorry if I interrupted."

"It's fine." Elena's confidence returned. "I was just leaving."

Oscar didn't move. His gaze narrowed on Ridge.

"We both were leaving," Ridge added, infusing a bite to his voice.

The standoff lasted another twenty seconds.

"Well, don't let me keep you," Oscar finally said. With a curt salute, he departed.

Ridge and Elena didn't talk until he'd vacated the parking lot.

Her expressive eyes met Ridge's. "Am I wrong, or did that whole encounter seem strange to you?"

"Very strange." He opened her car door. Once she was seated behind the steering wheel, he asked, "How well do you know him?"

"Not well." Elena buckled her seat belt. "Maybe I should do a little snooping."

"Be discreet," Ridge warned.

She reached for her door handle. "If I find anything interesting, I'll let you know."

Elena stood at the entrée table in the fellowship hall at church. She should have known better than to attend the winter picnic with Ridge. The hall had hummed with whispers when they entered. Elena could practically hear what people were saying. Two of Hillside Church's flock had found each other. She would hate disappointing them when the time came to confess that she and Ridge were pretending in order to divert suspicion.

She also hated lying. Did the end justify the means? She hoped the members and God would understand and forgive.

"That smells delicious."

Elena glanced behind her and smiled at old Mr. Harmon. "Do you like pozole?" She replaced the lid on her contribution to the lunch fare so it would stay warm.

"Indeed, I do. Please tell me you brought homemade tortillas to go with the soup."

"I'm sorry, no. Next time."

"Young Ridge Burnham is a fortunate man to be dating such a fine catch as yourself."

Elena cheeks grew warm, whether from Mr. Harmon's compliment or the reference to Ridge, she couldn't be sure.

"I don't know about that," she demurred.

"She's definitely a catch," Ridge said, joining her and the kindly gentleman. "Don't let her say differently."

"No need to convince me." Mr. Harmon winked. "Enjoy yourselves, you two."

"We will." Ridge placed a hand on Elena's shoulder.

She should have objected, but she didn't.

Every February, the church put on a winter picnic. The purpose of the event was to bring brightness to what was often a dreary time of year. The tables were covered with red-and-white-checkered cloths, and at the center of each sat an aluminum watering pot filled with white and yellow silk daisies. People had been encouraged to wear summer garb, and she saw an array of shorts, Hawaiian shirts and sundresses. The thermostat sat at a toasty seventy-six degrees, as opposed to the brisk fifty-eight outside.

Elena had dug out a pair of shorts and a neon green blouse. With her hair gathered in a ponytail, she did feel summery, especially standing next to Ridge in his "Fun in the Sun" T-shirt and flip flops.

They wandered over to the table that Jake, Gracie and the girls had claimed. There was no getting out of it. She and Ridge would have to sit with his family. Again. And this time it might be worse. Gracie continued to express her delight that her little brother was dating. Jake appeared less delighted. Much, much less.

Elena wondered if he'd give her any grief at the station. Probably—and mostly in retaliation because Oscar and the chief would give Jake grief. Jokingly, but not jokingly. Guys could be hard on each other.

"Hi, Uncle Ridge," the girls chorused when he and Elena sat down.

"Lindsey and Laney, say hi to Ms. Elena, too," Gracie prompted.

"Hi," they murmured, suddenly shy.

"Remember I told you she works with Daddy at the station?"

"Are you a sergeant deputy, too?" Lindsey asked.

"No." Elena smiled at the girl. "Just a plain old deputy."

"Is my daddy your boss?"

"Kind of. He's my immediate supervisor."

"What's the difference?"

Lindsey was pretty smart for a six-year-old.

"I can't fire her," Jake explained. "I can only tell her what to do."

Ouch. Elena hid her reaction by taking a sip of Ridge's excellent lemonade.

"Jake, be nice," Gracie chided. "Wouldn't you rather my brother date someone we like?"

"Who said I liked her?" He frowned, only to break into a grin when his wife elbowed him in the ribs. "Okay, okay. But how about we don't tell anyone at the station?"

Aha! He *was* worried about getting flak from the others.

They made small talk. Well, Gracie did most of the talking. When Elena snuck a glance at Ridge, his smile put her at ease.

From the front of the room, the minister called for everyone's attention. Midfifties and with a perpetually cheery countenance, he exuded warmth and compassion. "Welcome, welcome. It's wonderful to see so many familiar faces here today, and a few new ones. Glad our cloudy weather didn't keep you home."

After announcements, he said grace. The tables emptied one by one, and a line formed at the potluck buffet.

Lunch was a noisy, happy event. Everyone who got a bowl of Elena's pozole raved about it—Mr. Harmon more than anyone.

Elena patted his hand when he sat beside her. "Next time I make a pot, I'll bring you some."

"That would be splendid. I'm here most mornings."

He'd been given the title of custodian. For the most part, he puttered around the church, vacuuming the sanctuary, offices and classrooms, making minor repairs and running errands. The job made the widower feel useful and filled his lonely hours. Elena had heard his children didn't visit much. She couldn't imagine it. He was such a nice, sweet man.

At the end of lunch, Jake and Ridge were roped into assisting with a plumbing malfunction in the kitchen. Elena pitched in with the cleanup, a chore that didn't take long. One good thing about potluck functions with paper plates and plasticware, there was little washing.

"Come with me." Gracie linked arms with Elena when they returned from taking out the trash, escorting her to an empty table. The girls played nearby with a friend from Sunday school. "Let's chat."

Elena's guard shot up. The other woman's tone hinted at more than a casual conversation. Should she tell Gracie that dating her brother was a ruse?

She and Gracie sat, and the other woman wasted no time getting to the heart of the matter.

"I know you're helping Ridge with the investigation of our dad's homicide."

The revelation took Elena aback. Seemed she didn't have to confess. "You do?"

Gracie laughed merrily. "I do now. I wasn't sure. Don't ever get into acting, Elena. You're not very convincing."

So much for three years in high school drama club. A waste of time, apparently.

"Ridge is younger than me," Gracie continued. "I saw more of the damage our dad's drinking did to our parents' marriage and how it changed our mom. She wasn't always angry and bitter."

"He mentioned that."

Gracie nodded. "Dad was a jovial drunk. Which is better than a mean drunk, for sure, but Ridge remembers Dad as this big, lovable man who took him prospecting in the mountains and horseback riding and taught him about raising cattle. He doesn't remember Dad missing birthdays and holidays because he was drinking at the bar, or our truck being repossessed because the monthly payment money went to bail him out of jail."

"I think he's aware of those things," Elena ventured.

"He is. Here." Gracie tapped her head. "In his heart, he still idolizes Dad. That's why he's always pushing the police to solve Dad's case. And why, since finding the gun and money, he began his own investigation. There are still people in town who believe Dad was inebriated and his death was an accident. Proving he was murdered would earn him people's sympathies rather than their scorn. That's important to Ridge."

"Perhaps Ridge feels that when people look down on or speak ill of his dad, it's a reflection of him."

"Oh, that's exactly what he feels. Which is one of the reasons he bails on relationships before they get serious."

This was the first Elena had heard about Ridge's past romances. She had no reason to feel discouraged, yet she did.

"We're not in a relationship," she blurted, as much for Gracie's benefit as her own. Though after her and Ridge's hug in the bank parking lot the other night, their pretend dating didn't feel so pretend to Elena.

"You could be. I can see he likes you and you like him. Which is why I'd hate to see you hurt."

"We hardly know each other."

"Maybe I shouldn't have said anything about his unwillingness to commit. Please don't think poorly of him." Gracie's expression pleaded for understanding. "He isn't a player or a bad guy. Deep down, he believes he doesn't bring enough to the table."

"That's...ridiculous."

"I agree. He's done well for himself. Retired from rodeoing with multiple world champion-ship titles and money in the bank. He has every reason to be proud of himself. People respect him. But they also gossip about him. About us. Our dad, his drinking, his death. Ridge can't let go, and he's convinced he can't move on until he learns who killed Dad."

"Please don't take this the wrong way, Gra-cie." Elena chose her words carefully. "Is that how people feel, or how *you* feel?"

Rather than get angry, Gracie let her shoulders slump. "I won't say you're wrong, Elena. I want Ridge to let go of the past and move on. For many reasons. His safety. His peace of mind. His emotional well-being. And for mine. As long as he continues to search for answers, none of us can put what happened behind us."

Elena's heart went out to the other woman. She had experienced something similar when she lost her grandmother and then, barely a year later, her grandfather. She still grieved the loss.

Laying a hand on Gracie's arm, she said, "I'm sorry. Tragedy is ruthless and greedy. No one is immune to its clutches, and once it grabs hold, it doesn't let go."

"Maybe you can talk to Ridge?" Hope lit Gracie's eyes. "Convince him of the futility?"

"I doubt I can convince Ridge of anything. He's quite stubborn."

Gracie sighed again. "Yes, he is. Don't let that handsome face fool you." Her mood abruptly shifted. "I like the Ridge I see with you. I wouldn't mind if the two of you got serious. I'm just not sure that's possible."

Elena didn't have time to digest what Gracie told her before Ridge and Jake returned.

"Daddy, Daddy," Lindsey called. "Come see our drawings."

Jake stopped at the nearby table to inspect his daughters' artwork, compliment their talents and give them each a kiss on the top of the head. "That's the best picture of a horse I've ever seen."

"It's a dog," Laney said, insulted.

"You're right. My mistake." He tugged on her curls and then wandered over.

"Did you fix the garbage disposal?" Gracie asked as he dropped down beside her.

Ridge slid into the empty chair next to Elena and bumped shoulders with her as if they were indeed dating. Gracie's words about him bailing on previous girlfriends echoed in her mind.

"Ridge is the one who fixed it," Jake said. "Guess all those repairs at the ranch are paying off. His handyman skills are improving."

"That and his finding-money skills." Gracie's gaze scanned the group when her pun fell flat. "Okay, not funny?"

Jake cleared his throat and glanced at the girls before continuing in a lower voice. "I've been telling Elena she needs to steer clear of our troubles. I know. I was here when the cartel was active and the drug trafficking was at its peak. They're no one you want to mess with."

"He does know," Gracie chimed in. "When Jake first came to Ironwood Creek, he was young and fresh to the sheriff's department and determined to do his part cleaning up the town. He confronted more than one of the drug runners and was even shot once."

"Shot?" Elena blinked in surprise. "I had no idea."

"In the thigh, just a flesh wound. It wasn't serious." His demeanor changed. "But I realized what I was up against, and that I wouldn't win if I took on the cartel single-handedly."

"I was so scared." Gracie reached up and lovingly patted her husband's cheek. "I could've lost him."

"We're not taking on the cartel," Ridge said.

"You are," Jake insisted. "It's obvious. And they have long arms that still extend into Ironwood Creek. There's talk that if Sheriff Cochrane isn't reelected next year, his crackdown-on-crime program will lose its funding, and the cartel will return in full force."

Elena jerked upright. "Is that true? I haven't heard any rumors."

"Cochrane isn't a shoo-in."

"He's well-liked."

"Not by everyone," Jake said. "His programs, all of them, could be in jeopardy. That's what happens when leadership changes."

Unfortunately, he was right. And the thought bothered Elena. Had coming to Ironwood Creek been the right decision for her? While prepared to uphold the law, attempting to do that in a town under the thumb of a dangerous drug cartel hadn't been her plan.

God, is this the path You want me on? I need to know if I should keep helping Ridge and that investigating his dad's death is the right thing.

Her worries must have been reflected in her features, for Ridge reached for her hand beneath the table and gave her fingers a squeeze.

"Elena and I should get going," he said.

"Us, too." Gracie nodded at the girls. "Laney will need a nap after this."

Jake rose and stretched. "Me, too."

In the parking lot, Elena and Ridge said their goodbyes to his family and parted ways.

Alone at last, Elena asked, "Jake was shot? He never told me. I can't believe he didn't mention it when he was warning me to avoid you."

"He and Gracie were dating at the time. I was competing on the rodeo circuit."

"Getting shot is no small deal."

"It really wasn't serious. He was up and around in a week." They reached her car, where he continued. "I remember he got a commendation or an honor or something for being wounded in the line of duty. Of course, he milked it for all it was worth with Gracie. She waited on him hand and foot."

"Well, he was entitled." Elena pulled her coat closer around her to ward off the mild chill. "I've been shot at, but never hurt. It's scary."

He frowned. "I didn't mean to make light of his injury. He's a good deputy."

"He is," Elena agreed, giving credit where credit was due.

"What I remember most is the ceremony in front of town hall. I was in between rodeos and came home for it. Gracie was so proud. Sheriff Dempsey's predecessor presented Jake with the award. The mayor at the time and Olivia Gifford were on hand, too."

"The church bookkeeper?"

"Yeah. She used to work for the mayor back then. His administrative assistant, I think."

A lightbulb flickered to life in Elena's head. "Have you ever talked to her about your dad's homicide?"

"No. Why?"

"Because she worked for the mayor. She's bound to have information that didn't make it into public records."

Ridge flashed her a conspiratorial smile. "When are you free next?"

"Monday afternoon."

"That's great. Olivia always works on Monday, processing the collections from the day before."

This, thought Elena, was the answer to her earlier prayer; she was meant to be here and to keep helping Ridge. Why else would this lead appear?

Chapter Six

Ridge and Elena had decided not to call ahead and give Olivia Gifford any warning. Elena's idea. It wasn't that they didn't trust the church bookkeeper, but Elena said people automatically got defensive when questioned, even in a casual situation. When caught unaware, they tended to reveal more. That had made sense to Ridge.

On their way down the hall, they ran into Mr. Harmon. He pushed a mop and bucket on wheels toward the restrooms.

"Afternoon, sir." Ridge nodded.

The elderly man broke into a toothy smile. "What brings you two here on a Monday afternoon?"

"Is Mrs. Gifford in her office?" Elena indicated the partially open door.

"You bet, as usual."

"Thank you." She touched Ridge on the arm.

He got the message. Move along and say nothing.

"You have a nice day, sir," Ridge told Mr. Harmon.

"Same to you." The wheels on the bucket squeaked as he pushed it across the tiled floor.

At the office door, Ridge knocked. Mrs. Gifford alternated days with the church secretary. They shared a desk, computer, printer and copy machine. The congregation wasn't so large that two offices were required.

"Hello," a lilting voice responded.

He pushed open the door. "Mrs. Gifford?"

"Ridge. Hello. Come in." Her expression showed surprise when Elena accompanied him. "Oh, you brought company."

"I hope we're not disturbing you."

"Not at all." She removed her reading glasses and set them on a bank bag in front of her. "Would you like a water? And there're some leftover cookies from Sunday school yesterday."

Ridge and Elena both declined and sat in the twin visitor chairs facing the desk. He guessed the bookkeeper to be sixty-plus, based on how long she'd been a member of the church. But her flawless complexion and trim figure gave the impression of a much younger woman. If Ridge believed his sister's claim, Mrs. Gifford had had "some work done" a few years ago during a supposed trip to Southern California. He didn't care one way or the other about the rumored plastic surgery. To each their own. If she had the money and preserving her good looks made her happy, who was he to criticize?

Her glance traveled from him to Elena and back again. Ridge got straight to the point, another of Elena's suggestions.

"I'm sure you heard I found a gun and strongbox of cash on my property last week."

"I did!" Her brows rose, disappearing beneath the fringe of her fashionably styled hair. "Isn't that something?"

"I believe they're connected to my dad's homicide. Chief Dempsey sent them to a lab in Tucson for testing. We're waiting on the results."

"Really!"

"I asked Elena to come with me today and offer her advice."

"Amateur sleuths. I love it." She covered her mouth with her hand and looked embarrassed. "I listen to some of those true crime podcasts. You know the ones. Promise you won't tell anyone. I would die. My husband is always making fun of me."

"We won't tell."

"We promise," Elena added.

Ridge noticed she sat quietly, listening and watching. Just like she had that first day in his kitchen. Did Olivia referring to her as an amateur sleuth bother her? Ridge didn't think so.

"What have you found out?" the bookkeeper asked.

"Not much." He didn't mention the text Elena had received, the warning from Detective Darnelly or that he and Elena were followed. "That's the problem, which is why we're here. We're hoping you might provide some insight."

"Me?" She drew back, her hand dropping to rest above her heart.

"You worked for the mayor around the time my dad was killed."

Elena had been right. Instantly, Olivia's demeanor changed from friendly to wary.

"Yes, but what does that have to do with anything? Mayors aren't involved with police investigations."

"They do work together, though, right?" Ridge asked. "Mayors are kept abreast of investigations into local homicides."

"Yes," Olivia acquiesced. "From what I re-call about your dad's case, however, there wasn't much to investigate. No witnesses or DNA. No legitimate leads."

At her dismissive tone, Ridge felt his irrita-tion rising. He took a calming breath.

"I've read the police reports. Not much ef-fort was put into the investigation. Maybe you heard or saw something while you were at the mayor's office."

"No, I didn't."

"Please. It's important."

Olivia shook her head. "I can't help you."

Ridge hated accepting defeat, but he saw no other option. For whatever reason, the book-keeper refused to discuss her experiences. But then, Elena appealed to her in a voice both com-passionate and pleading.

"Mrs. Gifford, I understand you lost your sis-ter in an automobile accident when you were a teenager. The driver of the car that hit her fled the scene. They didn't find him for almost four months."

Olivia gasped. "How do you know that? I never talk about her."

Ridge wondered, too.

"You made a Christmas cactus donation in her memory. It was in the church program."

Ridge wondered if Elena had used her access to official records to research the accident.

Olivia's eyes filled with tears. "It was a terrible time for my family. Her death nearly destroyed us."

"I'm sorry to bring up such unhappy memories." Elena paused. "I imagine you and your family had unresolved feelings about what happened to your sister. Perhaps even some anger. Certainly, you suffered all those months you waited to learn who had caused the accident and were relieved when the person was taken into custody."

The other woman sniffed and snatched a tissue from the box on her desk. "I've forgiven the driver. That's the Christian thing to do."

"Which is very kind of you. There are people in your shoes who couldn't or wouldn't."

"I'm not sure what this has to do with Pete Burnham's death."

Ridge worried that Elena's tactic may have the opposite of its intended effect. Olivia seemed to be shutting down. They needed to win her over.

"Surely," Elena said, "you can understand

how Ridge feels. To go all these years, having no idea what really happened to his dad and knowing the person responsible got away free and clear."

A small crack seemed to appear in Olivia's invisible armor. She released a wobbly breath.

"That must be hard."

"It is," he agreed.

She thought a long moment, her fingers fiddling with the stem of her reading glasses. At last, she raised her chin.

"I don't *know* for certain, but I did overhear some conversations. One-sided, mind you. Once, the mayor was on the phone with Ironwood Creek's then–deputy chief. I put the call through myself, so I know that for a fact. The mayor said something to the deputy chief about the Bisbee police pressuring the investigating detective to…" She squinted as if searching her memory. "Let the case rot. I'm pretty sure that's an exact quote."

A surge of excitement wended its way through Ridge. "Are you sure he was talking about my dad's homicide?"

"Yes. The mayor mentioned him by name."

"What else can you tell us?" He braced his hand on the desk. Elena sent him a don't-scare-her-off look, and he sat back in the chair. "Even the smallest detail would be helpful."

"I... I..."

"Please, Mrs. Gifford," Elena coaxed. "You'd be doing us a great service."

"I don't like to gossip about people behind their back."

"You're not gossiping. No one is accusing you of that. Not for one second."

After more fiddling with her reading glasses, she said, "I'm telling you this only because I think highly of you, Ridge, and your sister. Your mother, too. She did her best under difficult circumstances."

"I appreciate that, ma'am." He waited, anxiety gnawing at him.

"I suspected the mayor was taking a kickback from the cartel. There were phone calls that came into his office from rough-sounding individuals who were quite rude to me. And visitors who gave me the chills." She shivered. "They always came in with these canvas satchels and left without them. The mayor stayed late on those days. I'd think, how stupid and obvious. They didn't even try to hide what they were doing. But I suppose the cartel had no fear. They ran this town and most of the people in it." She started to cry and dabbed at her nose with the tissue.

"Tell us about that," Elena said.

"You were young, Ridge. You probably don't remember."

"I used to watch the drug runners driving across our property."

"No one did a thing about it," Olivia continued, composing herself. "We were afraid of the cartel, and our sheriff's deputies."

"The deputies?"

This was news.

After a moment and another dabbing of the tissue, Olivia said, "They were on the cartel's payroll. If not willingly, then they were scared into compliance."

Like his dad, Ridge thought, remembering the stranger in the barn threatening his dad.

"Were local landowners also receiving kickbacks from the cartel?" he asked.

"Without a doubt," Olivia said. "Those were some lean times economically. Folks were hurting. Out of work or reduced hours. The mayor was under a great deal of pressure to respond. The cartel took advantage of that by offering money."

"To people like my dad."

"I'm afraid so, Ridge."

Old anger rose anew. "If my dad's involvement with the cartel was common knowledge, why did people insist he fell because he was drunk?"

Olivia spoke after a long pause. "Admitting the cartel murdered those who stood in their way was not only frightening, it risked incurring their wrath. Denial was safer. That's still true even today."

What if his dad had undergone a change of heart like the argument with the stranger implied? Ridge wondered. If Olivia was to be believed, the cartel would have sent an operative after him. It made sense.

"That's why I quit my job with the mayor." Olivia drew in a shaky breath. "I couldn't take it anymore. All the stress and worry. I didn't want to hear or witness something and then have to fear for my life."

"I don't blame you," Elena said.

"Did my mom know?" Ridge asked, wanting and not wanting to hear the answer.

Olivia faltered. "I... I can't say for certain. But I believe she did."

Pain tugged at his heart. Why hadn't she told him? He'd questioned her enough over the years.

"Did you ever hear of anyone called the Hawk?" Elena asked.

Olivia jerked and then tried to cover it by smoothing the front of her sweater. Ridge noticed. Elena, too. Her sideways glance telegraphed as much.

"No." Olivia feigned ignorance. "Is that a real name?"

"It is. And are you sure?" Elena pressed.

The bookkeeper stiffened, in either offense or avoidance of the subject. "I need to get back to work. I leave at three."

Ridge chose not to pressure her. She'd clearly made up her mind. Whatever she knew about the Hawk, she wasn't telling. Because of that same fear she mentioned earlier? Did Olivia believe, like Jake and Frank Darnelly, that the cartel was still active in Ironwood? Maybe she worried she'd said too much, and there would be repercussions.

"Thanks for your help, Mrs. Gifford." Ridge stood. He still had questions for her, but they would have to wait for another day.

Elena also rose. "See you on Sunday."

"Have a good week." The bookkeeper slipped on her reading glasses and returned her attention to the computer, effectively dismissing them.

★ ★ ★

Mentioning the Hawk had definitely touched a nerve with Olivia Gifford. As a deputy sheriff, Elena had questioned plenty of guilty people who lied about what they'd done. She didn't need to be an expert in reading body language to spot the obvious signs: a nervous twitch, a change in speech patterns, fidgeting, putting up walls and presenting false smiles. Olivia had exhibited all of those and more.

At the door, Elena paused before exiting the office. She couldn't bring herself to leave, not without making one last attempt. When Ridge gave her an inquiring glance, she offered a reassuring nod.

Turning back to face Olivia, she asked, "By the way, does anyone else in town know about the former mayor's alleged involvement with the cartel?"

Again, Olivia hedged. "Probably."

"Who?" Ridge demanded before Elena could get the question out.

Olivia firmed her lips into a flat line. Elena expected the bookkeeper to send her and Ridge packing. She was wrong, though. After a moment, Olivia answered.

"If I were to hazard a guess, Chief Dempsey.

He was the sergeant deputy at Ironwood Creek station in those days. Before his promotion. He and the former chief were close." She held up her hand and twined her first and second fingers together. "If the former chief was on the take, rest assured Dempsey was either complicit or uninvolved, but keeping quiet about it. Protect the sinner and you are equally guilty of sin, isn't that what they say?"

The accusation hit Elena like a dunking in ice water. She'd gone back and forth on Chief Dempsey's involvement with the cartel, only to decide that, for all his gruffness and imperfections, he was an upstanding officer of the law. To have someone else accuse him of misconduct, if not out-and-out lawbreaking, forced a rush of air from her lungs. Ridge was equally struck by Olivia's proclamation, given his astonished expression.

"What happened to the former deputy chief?" Elena inquired in a tenuous voice.

"He resigned shortly after Pete Burnham's homicide and died rather suddenly."

"How?"

"Something to do with his heart." Olivia lifted a narrow shoulder. "Apparently, he had a previously undiagnosed condition."

That sounded rather convenient to Elena. Retiring soon after a local was killed and then suddenly dying?

No. She was letting her imagination run wild, fueled by her disarming conversation with Olivia.

"What about the former mayor?" she asked. "Does he still live in the area?"

Olivia shook her head, her manner brusque with impatience. "He retired and moved to Florida."

"Is he still alive?"

"I have no idea. He never kept in touch with anyone in Ironwood Creek."

"Okay. Thank you again, Mrs. Gifford." Elena could probably find out that information on her own. Just not at the station in case someone was tracking her activity on the computers.

Outside, in the hall, she put a finger to her lips, alerting Ridge not to talk until they were out of earshot. She wouldn't put it past the bookkeeper to jump out of her chair and attempt to listen at the door.

In the church lobby, they headed toward the double glass doors.

Ridge pushed on the lever, and they stepped outside. "I hate to say this, but I think she was hiding something."

"Agreed. She's heard of the Hawk, that's for sure."

"Don't you think it's coincidental the former deputy chief and mayor both left their jobs soon after my dad was killed?"

"Very. Especially since, according to Olivia, the mayor and perhaps the former chief were taking kickbacks."

"Did the cartel get rid of them?" Ridge asked.

"They may have left because they were targeted."

"A sudden heart attack and a previously undiagnosed condition? That sounds pretty fishy to me," Ridge said.

His thoughts mirrored her own. "There's no way we can prove anything," she said.

"Sounds like Olivia left her job in the nick of time."

"I'd have kept my mouth shut, too, if I was her. Three people have died over the years, including your dad. I'm surprised she didn't move to the other side of the country."

"What about Chief Dempsey? It sounds like he was involved."

Elena felt renewed shock as she and Ridge hurried across the concrete walkway toward the parking lot. Rain was in the forecast, and the temperature had dropped several degrees. She pulled her coat more tightly around her.

"That's a tough one," she said, still grappling with this new knowledge concerning her boss. "I respect the chief, and I like him. I hate entertaining the possibility that he's involved in any way. But he's one of the people who knew I was going to Bisbee the other day. And he could be tracking my activity on the station computer, though if he were, why would he have warned me about it?"

"What about Oscar Wentworth? Him just showing up the other night when we were in the bank parking lot? I didn't buy his story about driving by and seeing your car. Plus, his sedan looks an awful lot like the one that tailed us."

"I didn't buy it, either. And he's been at the station a long time. Part of that during the cartel's heyday."

"Did you ever find out anything more about him?"

"Yeah. He had a couple of personal judgments against him years ago for loans he defaulted on. They were eventually paid off."

"When?" Ridge asked.

"Right before Sheriff Cochrane was elected and launched his anti-crime campaign."

"Another coincidence?"

"They're adding up."

As they neared Elena's car, they heard Mr. Harmon hailing them. They turned and waited for the older man to catch up.

"I think you dropped these in the hallway." He held out a set of keys. "I found them outside Olivia's office."

Ridge patted his jacket pockets and then took the keys. "Thanks. I didn't realize I'd dropped them."

"You'd have figured it out."

"You saved me the trouble."

"Happy to oblige." Instead of leaving, he asked, "Did you get everything squared away with Olivia?"

Elena suspected Mr. Harmon was fishing for information. He wasn't so much a busybody as he was a bored old man. Not much went on in his life. Her and Ridge visiting the church bookkeeper had probably been the highlight of his day, if not the past few days.

"She was very helpful," Ridge said.

"She's a good person. Volunteering like she does."

"I thought the bookkeeper was a paid position," Ridge said. "Like the secretary."

"The secretary, yes. The bookkeeper, no. Olivia does the work for free."

"That's very generous of her," Elena added.

"She'd be the first to tell you she doesn't need the money." Mr. Harmon chuckled. He appeared in no hurry to get back, relishing the chance to chat with people. "And I reckon that's true. She never took another job after quitting the mayor's office. No need after she came into all that money."

Elena's ears pricked up. She hadn't heard this about the church bookkeeper. "What money?"

"Some relative died and left her a windfall." Mr. Harmon winked. "That's how she paid for all those 'spa treatments,' if you catch my drift."

Evidently, the stories about her having a face lift and other procedures weren't mere rumors. Elena and Ridge exchanged glances. Were they thinking the same thing?

"I'd love to stay and chat longer," she told Mr. Harmon. "But I'm on duty in a couple of hours. I need to go home first and change."

"Of course, of course. Didn't mean to keep you. I've got to finish up here for the day." He gave them a wave before shuffling off, his gait stilted.

"Olivia came into a windfall right after leaving the mayor's office," Elena said to Ridge the moment they were alone.

"Is there a chance she was receiving a cut of whatever was in those satchels the cartel delivered to the mayor?"

"She was in a position to hear and see a lot. The cartel may have bought her silence."

Ridge looked uncertain. "If she was in on it, then why would she tell us as much as she did?"

"That's a good question." Elena met Ridge's gaze. "As is why didn't she leave town or have something untoward happen to her like the former mayor and chief?"

"She does know more than she's admitted."

"Absolutely," Elena agreed, mentally adding Olivia to her list of suspicious people to research.

"Let's meet again. At the ranch this time?"

"I'll call you later when I know my schedule for the next few days. Jake asked for personal time off tomorrow. We're scrambling to cover for him."

Ridge frowned. "Gracie didn't mention anything."

"He didn't say what for, and I didn't ask." In Elena's opinion, personal time off was just that. Personal.

"I'll wait to hear from you. But for now, we

have a plan." Ridge squeezed her arm before walking briskly to his truck.

Elena climbed in behind the wheel, deliberating a moment before starting the engine. Since coming to Ironwood Creek, she'd been worried about fitting in with the good old boys' club, being taken seriously and proving her worth.

Now, it seemed, she had something else to worry about. The possibility that the men she worked side by side with were accessories to murders, if not the ones who carried them out.

Chapter Seven

Elena wandered into her living room, cradling a cup of herbal tea and stifling a yawn. She should hit the sack. She'd been up all night on duty, responding to one call after the other with no downtime in between.

There'd been another theft at the Creekside Inn. This time, a room was broken into and ransacked. The guest admitted to not realizing her key card was missing. During the ninety minutes she spent having dinner with a friend at The Smoke Shack, the burglars—presumed to be the same two men from before, wearing hoodies and ski masks as revealed on security footage—had recovered her key card from where she dropped it in the parking lot and entered the room, stealing a pair of expensive earbuds, designer sunglasses, an electronic tablet, four hundred dollars in cash and several bottles of prescription drugs.

No, the guest hadn't availed herself of the complimentary room safe. No, she wouldn't make that mistake again. And, no, the manager hadn't the faintest idea how the burglars were casing the inn without being spotted.

Mere moments after Elena returned to the station, she'd been dispatched on another call. The cat lady's neighbor, a single mom, had reported a prowler in her backyard. She was home alone with her small children, and she was nervous. When Elena arrived, she'd heard the dog with the curly hair barking furiously from inside the house. Obtaining the mother's consent, she'd checked the entire yard, her flashlight beam zigzagging across the lawn. Near the fence line, she discovered a paper bag. Opening it up, she grimaced at the offensive smell and averted her face before retching. The bag was filled with rancid meat.

She suspected the cat lady of attempting to poison the dog but, without proof, had made no outright accusations. The mom instantly came to the same conclusion on her own and had burst into tears. All Elena could do was advise her to repair the fence, install security measures and keep her dog inside as much as possible.

"I'll talk to my ex-husband," she'd said. "See if he will help."

"If not," Elena had told her, "call me. My number's on that card. Hillside Church has a community assistance program run by volunteers."

The mom had cried again and hugged Elena.

"Good fences make good neighbors," she'd said, right before her radio went off and she was driving to the next call—reported trespassers in the abandoned pecan grove. After the recent rain, the grove was a mud pile. Elena had managed to get covered in grime from head to toe.

When she arrived home at 7:00 a.m., she'd immediately jumped into the shower. The hot water had felt wonderful and also revived her. She needed to sleep; she'd be reporting for duty at six this evening. But she also needed to wind down first; otherwise, she'd toss and turn. The tea would make her drowsy. So would reading a book or magazine, especially in bed. Except Elena's mind refused to stop churning.

She'd been thinking about Ridge and their conversation with Olivia every free minute since they'd left the church. Also, what Mr. Harmon had said. On the surface, the facts of the bookkeeper resigning her job with the mayor and then coming into a substantial amount of money from a distant relative had nothing to do with each other. Elena's gut insisted differently.

Too many things had happened in the wake of Pete Burnham's death to write them all off as coincidences. Add to that Ridge finding the gun and money. What was the common thread? Or person? There had to be one.

Olivia Gifford had lived in Ironwood Creek during the peak of the cartel's drug trafficking. She'd also worked for the mayor, who in all likelihood had received kickbacks from the cartel, and she had remained in town when others had fled or died under mysterious circumstances. Wasn't she worried she'd seen too much and was at risk?

Elena needed to learn more about the bookkeeper. Then, she and Ridge could visit her again with additional hard-hitting questions. Elena knew they wouldn't catch her unaware this time. She'd clam up the instant they stepped into her office. Because of that, a plan was in order.

There was that word again. *Plan.* She and Ridge were making them frequently of late.

She sat down at her dining table and booted up her laptop. She sipped her tea and stared out the glass patio door at the nearby mountains. Ridge had a similar view of the same mountains from his ranch. What were the chances he was enjoying a morning beverage and staring at their rounded peaks?

Enough, she told herself. *Stop relating every thought and action to him.*

Great view aside, she did like this apartment. Being on the first floor was a big plus. Rather than a balcony, she had a patio. On nice days, she sat in her chaise longue and watched the wildlife through the wrought-iron fence surrounding the complex. She frequently saw quail, rabbits and lizards, and a pair of bonded owls lived in the nearby stand of saguaro cacti. She didn't even mind the periodic coyote and javelina who visited, mostly at night.

If Elena wanted, she could exit through a gate and access a network of walking trails in the ten-acre natural area adjacent to the complex. On her days off, sometimes she hiked or jogged the trails, along with her neighbors, many with their dogs.

Her dad was less fond of her proximity to the natural area, citing a security risk. Elena would kiss him on the cheek, count her blessings that she had parents who loved and cared for her, and then assure him that, along with her state-of-the-art locks, the apartment complex utilized high-tech cameras and employed a security service who patrolled every four hours.

Her argument had made no difference. Her dad purchased and installed a home security system for her that included cameras mounted outside her front and patio doors. Elena checked them regularly from the app on her phone and received notifications whenever movement was detected.

While it was on her mind, she glanced at the app on her phone. No alerts during the night while she'd been gone.

She then returned to her laptop and checked her inbox. Scanning the senders and subject lines of incoming emails, she answered a few and decided the rest could wait. Opening a search engine, she typed in Olivia Gifford's name. The results were mostly links to church and civic activities, nothing out of the ordinary. Olivia had served for a few years on the town council after leaving her job at the mayor's office. Not unusual for someone with a strong interest in town politics.

Elena clicked through various links, discovering an old photograph of Olivia at a fundraising dinner. She stood alongside her former boss, the mayor. Also included in the photo were the then chief of police and a man identified as Ironwood Creek business entrepreneur Marcus Rivera. Elena leaned closer to the laptop screen and scrutinized the photo. Did secretaries usually attend fundraising dinners? Perhaps Olivia had gone with her husband, but he hadn't been included in the photo. The mayor's wife wasn't in the photo, either.

Something in the photo suddenly caught Elena's eye, and she squinted, only to draw back. Was that a young Chief Dempsey standing behind the mayor? She looked again. It *was* him. He would have been the sergeant deputy in those days.

She read the accompanying article. It was neither long nor informative. A fluff piece for the paper. But who was this Marcus Rivera?

A search of him revealed almost nothing. Elena found his name listed as the chairman of M.R. Investments, Inc., a company that operated about twenty-five years ago, then seemed to disappear fifteen years ago. She didn't have the experience or resources to learn more.

She next did what any investigator would— she scoured social media. Olivia had the kind of presence you'd expect from someone with children and grandchildren and who took annual vacations. Lots of posts about birthdays and holidays and trips. Elena quit skimming her pages after ten minutes. She found absolutely zero on Marcus Rivera. At least, no Marcus Rivera that could be the same man who'd attended the fundraising dinner.

Who was he, and what role had he played in Ironwood Creek's unsavory history? She considered asking Chief Dempsey. He'd been photographed with Marcus Rivera and might know more about the local businessman. Olivia Gifford no doubt did. But would she just clam up again if asked?

When Elena's phone abruptly rang, she gave a start. Her nervous reaction turned into a smile when she read Ridge's name on the display.

"Hi, how you doing?" she asked, leaning back in her chair.

"I was afraid I might wake you."

She liked the warm tone of his voice when he talked to her. "I'm heading to bed soon. I got sidetracked. Researching Olivia online."

"Find anything interesting?"

"Maybe." She told him about the old photo at

the fundraiser dinner and Marcus Rivera. "Ever hear of him or M.R. Investments, Inc.?"

"Not that I recall. I was a kid at the time. If anyone mentioned him, it would have gone in one ear and out the other."

"What about your mom or sister? Maybe you could ask them if they ever heard of the Hawk."

"I will."

Elena's gaze drifted to her laptop. Did Ridge have a social media account? Gracie probably did. And she'd have pictures of Ridge.

Elena refused to type in either his or Gracie's name. She would not be that kind of person.

"We should also ask Olivia about this Marcus Rivera," Ridge said.

"Agreed." Elena let out a breath, glad to be back on track. "I also have a friend from the Maricopa County Sheriff's Department, Phoenix station, who has much better computer skills than me and owes me a favor."

"Okay. And I can pump Jake for information," Ridge offered. "He was around in those days. I just need to figure out a way to work it into conversation without alerting him."

"That won't be easy."

They discussed more strategy before deciding to meet at Ridge's ranch the following afternoon at four. Elena would be off work and able to catch six-ish hours of sleep after her shift and before leaving for Ridge's. That would also allow her time to call her friend from her old job in Phoenix.

"I'll make dinner," Ridge said. "In my brand-new kitchen. Save you the trouble."

"You don't need to do that." Dinner sounded a lot like a date to Elena. As had breakfast at the café and the winter picnic.

"No trouble. I'll just throw together a pot of chili and a pan of cornbread."

"Throw together?"

"That didn't sound appealing." He laughed. "It'll be edible, I promise."

She was about to comment when her phone buzzed with a notification from her security system. There was motion on her patio. She opened the app and saw an indistinguishable shape moving through the vicinity of her shadowed patio area.

"Ridge, I've got to go."

"What's wrong?"

"Probably nothing. My security system giving me a notice. I'm going to have to look."

"Elena." Alarm filled his voice. "I'll stay on the line with you."

She decided not to argue. "Okay."

Grabbing a jacket hanging from a hook on the wall, she stuffed the phone in her pocket then started for the Arcadia door, her heart racing.

Outside, she found an empty patio and saw nothing in either direction. Not so much as a spider climbing the patio wall.

"Elena?" Ridge's voice called to her from her pocket.

She took out the phone. "Yeah. I'm here. All's clear. Hold on while I check the app."

Sitting on the chaise lounge, she watched her phone screen, studying the dark shape rolling by. It could be a person crouched over. It could also be a large plastic trash bag floating on the wind. A big black dog. She rewatched the footage twice. At this time of morning, her west-facing patio lay in shadows. Between that and the black-and-white video, there was just no telling what had traveled past.

"I don't know what it is," she told Ridge and pushed to her feet. "I'll look again later when I'm not sleep-deprived."

"Are you sure you're going to be okay?"

"I'm sure." She went back inside and engaged her locks. She'd also sleep with her gun on her bedside nightstand rather than in the safe. "I have an alarm system."

"Call me when you wake up."

"I will." His concern for her brought a smile to her face. "And I'll see you tomorrow."

They disconnected, and Elena made for her bedroom. At the last second, she remembered her laptop. She'd left it on and with several tabs open, including her social media account.

When she leaned over the computer, she noticed a small box in the corner of her screen. Someone had sent her a direct message. Elena didn't recognize the sender's obscure name or the tiny cartoon character avatar and was about to delete the message when she flashed back on the threatening text she'd received. She clicked open and felt her pulse kick into overdrive as she read the sender's message.

Back off now or you and your family will regret it.

"Sorry, kiddo," Trudy said. "Wish I could be more help."

"Me, too." Elena sat at her dining table and rubbed her temples. "But I appreciate you trying."

"Without an IP address, it's hard to find out

who's behind a fake social media account. And now that the person who sent the message has deleted the account, you're going to need a friend in the FBI rather than the sheriff's department to trace it."

Her former coworker and mentor from the Phoenix Sheriff's Department had done her best to assist Elena in identifying the person behind the threatening direct message. She'd walked Elena through the steps over the phone, but to no avail. The account had disappeared into cyberspace.

"Have you told your friend Ridge yet?" Trudy asked.

"Yes. About the object picked up by my motion detector. Not the direct message. Not yet." She swallowed. "I will. Today."

"You'd better."

"He's worried, even though I downplayed it." Elena had filled her in on Ridge and their relationship at the start of their phone call. "I said it was just a trash bag."

"He's right to be worried. This is the second threat you received."

"I was hoping to have good news to tell him after we talked."

"And now that you don't?"

"My guess is he'll go a little off the deep end."

"Elena, this person specifically mentioned your family. Please tell me you alerted them. They need to be on the lookout."

"I called my dad."

"That's a relief. What did he say?"

"You've met him. He wants me to quit my job here, move back home and stay barricaded in my old room for a year."

"Maybe you should. This is serious business."

"You're right." She sighed. "Dad was also understanding. He said he'd want to help out a friend, too, if he was in my shoes. That it's the Christian thing to do."

"I agree—to a point. As long as it doesn't endanger you or anyone else."

"The thing is," Elena said, "I feel sorry for Ridge. Pete Burnham was likely killed to silence him or prevent him from testifying against someone high up in local government."

"You don't want the same thing to happen to you and Ridge," Trudy warned.

"No, but I also hate the idea of a killer getting away scot-free. Not once but three times." She'd told her friend about the other unsolved homicides. "There was a serious criminal element in Ironwood Creek at one time that got away with a lot. They should be exposed."

"Be realistic. They're long gone. You said yourself you've seen no evidence of them now, which means someone else is behind these messages."

She was sure it was someone who used to be in cahoots with the cartel. Elena mentally ran through her list. Olivia Gifford. Chief Dempsey. Oscar. Jake. Marcus Rivera. The man who'd argued with Ridge's dad. Who else? Who hadn't they thought of yet?

"I have to find out who's sending me those threatening messages."

"Don't be foolish, Elena. No need to risk your life and that of your family. Tell Ridge about this latest message and then drop out of the investigation. If he wants to continue on his own, that's his business."

"I'm just trying to help a friend get the answers he deserves."

"A friend or a *boyfriend*?"

"It's not like that," Elena insisted, even as she remembered the sensation of Ridge's arms around her during their brief hug and the warm timbre of his voice on the phone. "You know me. Career first above all else."

"I used to say that." Trudy's voice became wistful. "Until I met Richard and was convinced otherwise. You know it's possible to have both a career and a personal life."

"Two step-kids. One of your own. A demanding job. A mother-in-law with health issues. I honestly don't know how you do it."

"A lot of love and a lot of patience."

And a lot of sacrifices, thought Elena. She'd seen that firsthand. Her mother and grandmother had given up so much to run the family in order that their husbands could dedicate themselves to their jobs. College. Travel. Friendships. Her mother had abandoned a job she loved when she became pregnant with Elena's older sister.

Elena was certain her mother didn't regret a single decision she'd made or a moment of her life. But could Elena ask the same of her future spouse? To give up something they loved for her and her career?

Ridge had a ranch and a dream of raising cattle. Would he be willing to sell and move if a transfer benefited her? Stay home with the children? Not object to her intense and ever-changing hours? Sympathize with and be supportive of her bad mood when she had a grueling day? It was a lot to expect and not the life for everyone.

There was also the other question to consider. Would she be willing to make sacrifices for her husband? Because isn't that what married people did? Give and take?

It was all so complicated. Elena wanted what her friend Trudy had achieved. A serious, loving relationship and a family. When the time was right, she prayed she'd meet the right person and that the circumstances would fall into place.

She thought again of Ridge. To be honest, she had no idea what he was looking for down the road. Assuming he even wanted a wife and family, how long would he be willing to wait for the right woman? More than likely, once she finished helping him with his dad's homicide—which might be today after he learned about this latest message—they'd go back to being acquaintances at church. The idea of that caused a small prick of pain.

Elena glanced at the time on her phone. She needed to hurry. She was supposed to be at the Burnham ranch in less than an hour. "Any chance we can meet for coffee or lunch next time I'm in Phoenix?"

"I'd love nothing better," Trudy said. "And if you need anything else, give me a holler."

"Thanks."

Elena went to her bedroom and studied the contents of her closet. What did one wear to a strategy session that might turn into a not-seeing-each-other-again get-together? Jeans, she decided. And a sweater.

She and Ridge had talked on the phone several times since yesterday morning when her security camera had detected motion. Elena replayed the events in her head. She'd been distracted by a motion notification on her phone app. Then, when she returned to her computer a few minutes later, a threatening message awaited her.

The events were too coincidental for her comfort level. But how could the person who sent the message know she'd be away from her computer unless they were the cause of the distraction? Then again, what did it matter if she was at her computer when the message arrived?

At Ridge's insistence, she'd gone to the apartment complex office and spoken to the assistant manager. The woman checked with the security company who serviced the complex. Their guard reported no suspicious activity at the time

Elena's phone alerted her or all week, for that matter. She was the only resident to contact the office. Additionally, a review of the surveillance video showed nothing of concern.

"Could have been a tumbleweed," the assistant manager had suggested. "Or a raven. They can be such pests. Or a drone. They're popular now."

At least it wasn't a person. That was what had mattered to Elena.

Regardless, Trudy was right. Maybe Elena should tell Ridge about the new message and take a step back from the investigation into his dad's death. Her own safety aside, she refused to put her family in jeopardy. Except, quitting on a friend didn't come easy for her. That do-gooder personality again.

As she brushed her hair, she contemplated a way to continue helping Ridge that didn't make the cartel—or whoever was menacing her—nervous. The two of them could discuss it over dinner.

Elena checked her rearview mirror every couple of minutes during the drive. As she pulled into the Burnham Ranch, she was reminded of her visit there the day Ridge had found the gun and strongbox. They were still awaiting test results from the lab. Sage had been right, requesting the tests be expedited had made no difference.

Additionally, Elena had yet to find the right moment to speak to the chief about the photo from the fundraiser and Marcus Rivera. He'd either been busy with paperwork, on the phone, going over the schedule with Sage, or not at the station the same time as Elena.

In light of the threatening social media message, she considered not speaking to the chief. He may have been involved with the cartel and Pete Burnham's murder, much as she disliked the notion.

Ridge had texted her before she left her apartment, telling her to come directly to the barn when she arrived. She'd assumed he was working on repairs or renovations. She parked in front of the house and walked over to the barn, noting some improvements in the two weeks since her last visit. The pasture and round pen fencing had received a fresh coat of white paint. Missing shingles and side panels on the barn had been replaced, and a rooster weathervane perched atop the roof ridge, transforming the structure from rundown to quaint.

Ridge had been busy. Elena was impressed.

Nearing the large opening, she called, "Hello."

"In here."

She entered the barn, pausing a moment to let her eyes adjust to the dim lighting. The interior appeared noticeably tidier. Junk had been hauled away. The barn floor was swept clean and thick rubber mats lay along the center aisle. Tools hung from pegs on the walls, grouped by type. The storage room door sat ajar, revealing a pair of racks holding saddles, bridles and other horse tack.

The sweet smell of straw filled the air. It came, she realized, from several bales stacked alongside the row of stalls.

"I've got something to show you." Ridge beckoned her from where he stood in front of a stall.

The seriousness of his tone turned her curiosity into concern. Had he found something, perhaps the gold chain?

"Ridge, what is it?"

"You'll have to come here and see for yourself."

Ridge watched as Elena walked slowly toward him, well aware he was causing her unnecessary anxiety. Her features, usually controlled, telegraphed her anxiety. But he couldn't resist having fun with her. They were always so serious.

"Did you find the gold chain?" she asked, approaching the stall.

"I wish. But not yet." He hadn't given up hope. "Something else. It seems I've acquired some livestock."

"Cattle?" Her worry transformed into excitement. "You said you were going to get some once the ranch was in shape. I saw the improvements on my way in."

"Not cattle. Think smaller."

"Calves?"

"Wrong animal. And there's only one."

"Ridge." She groaned with frustration and then joined him at the stall. Peering over the door, she let out a surprised gasp. "Oh, my goodness. A miniature donkey. How cute."

"Meet Minnie Pearl." He gestured to the diminutive gray animal standing amid an abundance of fresh straw. "She's going to be staying with me for a while."

"Minnie Pearl?"

"I'm told she's named after an old-time comedienne. Apparently, the real-life Minnie Pearl used to greet audiences with a loud howdy when she stepped on stage. And this Minnie Pearl is not only a miniature donkey, she has a bray that will rattle your bones. Wait until you hear her."

Elena laughed, a sound Ridge had grown fond of hearing.

"Come on." He unlatched the door. "She's friendly."

Elena followed him into the stall. Minnie Pearl lifted her disproportionately large head in a plea for attention. Elena obliged and scratched the donkey between the ears. Minnie Pearl closed her eyes in contentment.

"Aren't you a sweetheart," Elena crooned. When she stopped scratching, Minnie Pearl nudged her for more. "And tiny."

"She's just eight hands." Ridge removed a piece of carrot from his jacket pocket and passed it to Elena. "Here. Give her this."

"What's eight hands?"

"Hands are how equine height is measured. An average horse is fifteen or sixteen hands. So she's half their height."

"Pony size."

Minnie Pearl gobbled the carrot, crunching loudly.

"She wants more," Elena said.

"Sorry, girl." Ridge patted her neck. "That was the last."

Stamping a delicate hoof, Minnie Pearl drew back, opened her mouth and emitted a high-pitched, ear-splitting sound that gained volume as it reverberated off the barn walls.

Elena stared in shock. "Did that big sound really just come out of her?"

"Now you know how she got her name."

"She's too small for you to ride. What are you going to do with her?"

Ridge gave Minnie Pearl another pat. "She belonged to an old rodeo buddy of mine. He was in a bind and couldn't keep her anymore. I said I'd take her in and try to find her a home." He checked the waterer, which he'd repaired before Minnie Pearl's arrival. It had been fifteen years since the stall was last occupied. "Who knows, I may keep her. She's doesn't eat much, and I kind of like having something else on this ranch besides me. I'm tired of talking to myself."

"Not that you aren't good company, but won't she get lonely in this big barn by herself?"

"I was thinking of getting a horse, though horses and donkeys don't always get along." He rubbed a knuckle along his chin. "I should probably adopt a wild burro or two at the Bureau of Land Management auction next month. They never have enough homes for the hundreds they round up every year."

"Seriously, burros? I thought you wanted to raise cattle."

"I can do both."

She smiled tenderly at him. "You have a soft heart."

"Don't tell anybody."

"Your secret's safe with me." She returned to scratching Minnie Pearl between the ears. "When I was a little girl, I dreamed of owning a horse. Read every Walter Farley and Marguerite Henry book ever published."

Ridge smiled and shifted, closing the distance between them. "I could teach you to ride if you're interested."

She raised her wide, dark eyes to his. Ridge lost himself in their brown depths.

"But you don't have any horses," she said. "Not yet."

"I could borrow a pair. I know plenty of people I could ask."

"Um, we'll see."

"We won't always be investigating my dad's homicide. If you're worried about there being a conflict of interest..."

His gaze connected with hers and held. Ridge

knew there was no reason for them to continue standing there in the stall. She'd come to the ranch so they could talk strategy. Only right now, standing close to Elena, that seemed like a million miles away.

"Ridge." The hesitancy remained.

He steeled his resolve. His intention wasn't to pressure her, but rather convince her of his sincerity.

"I won't lie," he said. "I'd like to spend more time with you and get to know you better. For real, not as some cover story. Horseback riding strikes me as a good way to accomplish that. If we both decide we like each other, we can go from there."

She didn't say yes. She didn't say no, either, which gave him the confidence to continue.

"But if that were to happen," he said, "there are some things you need to know about me first."

"That sounds ominous."

"Just full disclosure."

"Ah. I see."

He opened the stall door. Elena couldn't leave without giving the donkey's fluffy head a final scratching. He closed the stall door quickly before Minnie Pearl escaped and slid the latch in place. He'd come back later and give her some grain.

He and Elena ambled over to an old metal folding chair near the tools. Ridge gestured for Elena to sit, and he flipped over a plastic bucket to use as a stool.

"I wasn't always a believer," he began as they got settled. "We attended church when I was a kid, but after my dad was killed, well, Mom had a falling out with God, I suppose you could say, and we stopped going. Honestly, I didn't mind and spent my Sundays practicing roping and, later, bull riding."

"I can see how losing your dad in such a tragic way caused your mom to struggle with her faith."

"When I started rodeoing professionally, a few of the guys introduced me to the Cowboy Church. I attended at first only because a good friend was trampled by a bronc and seriously injured. He was in the hospital for days, hanging on by a thread. A bunch of us went to a Cowboy Church service and prayed for him. I tagged along just to be supportive. The next morning, my friend was upgraded from critical to stable. I told myself the power of prayer couldn't have accomplished such an amazing turnaround. But the possibility intrigued me, and I attended another service the following week in a different town. A year later, I became a member of Cowboy Church."

Elena's features softened. "That's an incredible story."

"When I moved back to the ranch, I started going to Hillside, which is where I went as a kid. They welcomed me as if I'd never left."

"They welcomed me as if I'd always belonged."

"Faith is an important part of my life."

"Mine, too," she said.

"I'd hoped it might repair the rift between my mom and me. That if I believed hard enough, we'd find common ground on which to build." His chest grew tight with emotion. "Hasn't happened."

Elena reached out and touched his arm, the gesture saying more than words could.

"My dad's choices hurt my mom and disappointed her and sucked every ounce of joy out of her. She hasn't forgiven him, and she doesn't understand how I have. Me living here has stirred up a lot of unpleasant memories for her."

"You said she married a great guy."

"She did. Ben is perfect for her. She has every reason to be content—a good husband, two beautiful granddaughters, and Gracie and I are

doing all right for ourselves. But Mom strug-
gles to let go of the past." He tried to chuckle.
"I inherited that from her."

"I'm not sure learning what happened to your
dad is the same as refusing to let go of the past.
You're seeking justice."

"You work in law enforcement. You understand that. Not everyone else does."

"I understand, but not because of my job."
Elena swallowed, her thoughts appearing to turn
inward. "My grandmother was killed three years
ago."

He reached for her arm and squeezed it. "I'm
so sorry."

"She was a wonderful person. She was kind
and gentle and good, and I loved her to pieces.
One night, she was walking the dog when
she was attacked and beaten. In her own quiet
neighborhood. She didn't survive her injuries.
Her assailant wasn't found for seven months,
until he attacked another person. That time, he
was caught. DNA evidence connected him to
my grandmother's assault. Three days after he
was sentenced, my grandpa died, I believe from
a broken heart. It was the worst time of my life."

Ridge longed to pull her to her feet and into

a hug. He'd suspected she'd suffered a grave loss, and now he had confirmation.

"Thankfully, the second victim survived," Elena continued, her voice steely. "The assailant was homeless and a drug addict. It took a long time for me to forgive him. I wasn't sure I could. Then, later, we learned about his own sad family history. Our family pastor counseled us on the power of forgiveness. I was finally able to let go of my anger." She paused. Inhaled. "So, I get how your mom feels about your dad. Loss can be an open wound that never heals."

Ridge studied Elena with new eyes.

"You're amazing. Thank you for teaching me that I should be more tolerant of my mom. And for sharing your story. That couldn't have been easy."

"I always wanted to go into law enforcement like my dad and grandfather. I didn't grasp how truly important the work is until my grandmother's attacker was on the loose those many months. Going the rest of my life without ever knowing, without closure, I can't... I can't imagine what you've gone through."

The bond Ridge had felt with her strengthened tenfold. They were a lot alike, especially in the ways that counted. Without much effort, she could win his heart.

"I tell myself the timing's wrong for me to date." He leaned in, took a lock of her hair and twirled it between his fingers. "That the ranch comes first."

"I tell myself that, too." She leaned in ever so slightly. "My career comes first."

He nodded and tucked the hair behind her ear. "Have you ever asked yourself why God brought us together, if the timing wasn't right for either of us? He could be telling us something. Maybe we should listen."

"What would that be?" Her words came out on a whisper.

"That our paths aren't meant to merely cross, but converge?" He hurried on before she could protest. "I like you, Elena. And I think you like me. We may be pretending to date, but there have been moments when it felt real to me. Moments, if I'm to be honest, when I wanted it to be real."

"I enjoy being with you, too."

He smiled. "Not just when we're crime-fighting?"

"What if God brought us together so that we could learn who killed your dad, not to date?"

"He could have more than one reason in mind."

"You're an optimist, Ridge, as well as a softie."

"There's always one way we can find out."

"How's that?" she asked.

"This."

He leaned in and brushed his lips across hers.

Chapter Eight

Elena hesitated for only a moment before letting go and responding to Ridge's oh-so-wonderful kiss. When he cupped her cheek with his palm, she melted into him as naturally as if this moment was always meant to be. And perhaps it was.

Time slowed. It may have stopped altogether. She knew she wanted their kiss to last...and last.

Eventually, they drew apart. Ridge stroked her jawline with his thumb before letting his hand drop.

"I don't regret that. I hope you don't, either."

"Not in the least."

He smiled, his gaze roving over her face. "Tell me there's a chance for us."

Elena sat back in the chair, reality returning with an unwelcome rush of cool air filling the empty space between them. She didn't like that, much preferring the warmth when they inhabited each other's personal space.

"What's wrong?" Ridge asked, his demeanor changing when she didn't immediately answer.

She hated causing him distress and shouldn't have waited to mention the threatening message. Minnie Pearl had been a temporary distraction, but not an excuse.

"There's something you need to know," she said, gathering her resolve. "Something I should have told you when I first arrived. Before you… before *we* kissed."

"What happened?"

She sighed. This was way harder than she'd anticipated. She'd liked their kiss, liked the prospect of them dating one day in the future. That would all end in the next few minutes.

"Elena. Tell me."

"I received another message, right after I hung up from talking to you."

"And you didn't tell me?" Storm clouds darkened his features. "What kind of message?"

"It was another threat, Ridge. This one against my family."

"Good Lord. Are you all right? Are they? What did the message say?"

"'Back off now or you and your family will

regret it.'" The fear she'd been holding inside uncoiled. Here was the reason she'd avoided mentioning the message to Ridge. Then she'd have to admit how much it had shaken her.

"Is everyone okay?" he repeated.

"Yes. I called my dad right away. He and the family are taking precautions. Actually, he's handling the news better than I expected. That could change once it sinks in." She'd spoken to her family again this evening. "He knows the drill. He's received threats before, once when he arrested a dangerous gang member leader."

"That doesn't minimize the threat."

"No. Of course not. They're getting a hotel room for a couple nights."

"I'm glad to hear that." Ridge took hold of Elena's hand. "Are you okay?"

His concern touched her, and she found herself opening up to him. "I'm scared, at least a little. I'm mostly angry. I don't like being threatened, and I hate that my privacy has been invaded." She hated feeling vulnerable worst of all.

"What did the chief say?"

"I haven't told him yet."

"Elena! Why not? You and your family are in danger."

"I'll tell him when I report for duty tonight.

He's going to advise me to inform admin and call the police like the last time."

"Which you should."

"We're not going to be able to trace the sender of the message. It was a DM on social media and the sender's account has already been deleted. There isn't much they or anyone can do. It's frustrating. And what if the chief is involved?" That concern, as much as her conviction that nothing would be done, had her waiting.

"If he is involved, you don't want him thinking you suspect him. Act normally. Tell him about the message and write up a report."

"Okay. Good idea. I will."

"You shouldn't be alone." His tone softened. "Do you have a friend who can stay with you? Or maybe you should get a hotel room like your parents. One in another town a hundred miles away."

"My dad suggested that, too. I'm considering it, but I hate the idea of hiding."

"Consider it hard, Elena. This is the second threat you've received."

"Yes, but I'm convinced whoever is sending me messages is using me to get to you. They believe, because I'm a woman, I'll frighten more easily, and you'll give up investigating your dad's homicide to protect me."

"They're not wrong, at least about the last part."

"We can't let them win," Elena argued.

"Oh yes, we can," he insisted. "Your safety and your family's are too important."

"Your dad deserves justice."

"This isn't your battle to fight."

She changed tactics. "What if we figure out a discreet way to keep investigating?"

The corners of his mouth rose in a reluctant smile. "Do you ever give up?"

"We're onto something," she insisted. "We just don't know yet what that is or how everything relates to your dad's homicide."

He closed his eyes and released a long breath. "You said the sender of the message can't be traced?"

"I called a former coworker of mine in Phoenix from the Maricopa County Sheriff's Department. She's a tech whiz." Elena explained how Trudy had walked her through the process of tracking the message's origin. "We couldn't find anything."

"It has to be the same person who sent you the text. Nothing else makes sense."

"How do they know what we're up to?" Elena rubbed her palms along the tops of her thighs, trying to release her pent-up energy. "That's what really bugs me. Even if someone close to me is keeping tabs, I haven't said anything to anybody. Have you?"

Ridge shook his head.

"I've been thinking. We can—"

"You're done helping me," Ridge said firmly.

She pretended not to hear him. "I should still talk to the chief about that fundraising photo. Marcus Rivera was involved with the cartel. I have no doubt. And the chief could confirm that. He was at the event."

"What if he's the one keeping tabs on you? You just said you don't trust him."

"I don't trust him, but I'm sure he holds the answers. He may not have been involved in your dad's homicide or with the cartel, despite what Olivia Gifford says, but he knows things. He was sergeant deputy under the previous corrupt chief. And we know for sure that *he* was in cahoots with the mayor and the cartel."

"Assuming Olivia wasn't lying to protect herself."

She shook her head. "I don't think she was. Not about the former chief and mayor. I watched her carefully. She was genuinely distraught when she described cartel members visiting the mayor."

Ridge stood. "I'll talk to the chief myself and figure out a way to continue investigating on my own."

"He won't tell you anything."

"Fine, but Jake might."

Elena also stood. "He doesn't want you involved any more than he wants me to be."

"He'll be more open if he thinks you and I aren't working together anymore."

"Maybe not. He wants you to stop pressuring the police about your dad's case because Gracie's afraid she'll lose a brother as well as her father."

"What if he sent you the messages? To scare you off, which would scare me off? For Gracie's sake."

"I wondered that at first," Elena said. "I mean, anything's possible. But Jake strikes me as someone who takes a more direct approach. And what about when we were followed to and from Bisbee? He was on duty that night."

"That's true. However, he might know about Marcus Rivera. He was a deputy during those years."

"I'll ask him."

Ridge had become a brick wall. Elena realized she wasn't going to get any further with him. Not today.

"Be careful, Ridge." She surprised them both by suddenly throwing her arms around his waist. "I couldn't bear it if you were hurt."

His hands settled on her shoulders. "Same here."

"Are you sure I can't convince you to let me keep helping?"

"Are *you* sure I can't convince you to stay in a hotel?"

"Maybe."

She pressed her face into his jacket as tears pricked her eyes. The feel of the rough material tickling her face felt nice. Too nice. His strong hands comforted her.

Wait. Weren't they just discussing the timing of things and it being off? Yet, God had bought them together. He must, as Ridge had suggested, have a purpose in mind. If not to learn who was behind Pete Burnham's murder, maybe God meant for Elena and Ridge to explore dating.

Ridge was someone her parents would truly like. She could picture him and her dad talking sports. Imagine her mom insisting Ridge have seconds of her delicious cooking. And she was fond of Ridge's family, even Jake when he wasn't being overprotective and bossy.

Which reminded her, there was more to consider than her and Ridge when it came to their dating. She had to go into the station every workday.

"I'm not sure how Jake would feel about us. If we were to consider dating." Elena gazed into Ridge's ruggedly handsome features. "He is my immediate supervisor. Things could get awkward."

"Is there a policy against deputies fraternizing with in-laws of coworkers?"

"No, but—"

"Then don't worry about Jake. He acts tough, but he's not all bad."

"Says you."

Elena marveled a little at how easily they could discuss dating. It seemed they were no longer partners investigating crime. Now, perhaps they were potential romantic partners. How was it possible to feel bad and happy at the same time?

"I'd also hate for the chief to think I'm using you as a way to make points with my immediate supervisor," she added.

"The chief's smarter than that."

"It's something to think about before we... commit."

"No need to feel rushed, Elena."

She appreciated him recognizing and considering her concerns.

"I promised myself I wouldn't consider getting involved with anyone until I finished renovating the ranch. I'm still a ways away."

"We start slow then," she said. "See how things go."

"Slow and steady."

That had a nice ring to it. Dating was complicated. And risky. And full of potential pitfalls. She, too, had made promises to herself that seeing Ridge romantically would break. Yet, somehow, he'd breached the barriers she'd carefully erected.

No, that wasn't true. If she were honest with herself, she'd admit she'd lowered those barriers in the first place—for him. She hadn't done that before. Hadn't allowed it. There must be a reason.

Ridge was different. What she felt for him was different. And he had feelings for her that he openly admitted. Could he be the right man for her?

"You free this weekend?" he asked. "We could go to a movie."

She smiled at the shift from their pretense of fake dating to this request for a real date. "I'd love to see a movie with you."

Ridge held her chin between his forefinger and thumb and dipped his head. She let her eyes drift close, waiting for his lips to find hers.

All at once, the sound of shattering glass split the air. Elena's eyes flew open, and she spun. "What was that?"

Ridge pushed her away. "Get out of here," he shouted.

She disobeyed and instead moved toward the sound. Her heart seized inside her chest at the sight of broken glass shards lying in a pile not fifteen feet away from where they stood. Flames erupted from a puddle of liquid and, within seconds, spread along the barn floor.

"Oh no!" She turned and grabbed Ridge by the arm, acrid smoke starting to fill her lungs. "We have to extinguish the fire. Do you have a water hose?"

"In front of the barn. I'll get it." He pushed her again. "You head to the house. Call 9-1-1."

She saw the reason for his urgency. The flames were already engulfing the bales of straw, consuming them with the ferocity and speed of an enraged beast. In another moment, the old wooden stalls would catch fire, and the barn would go up like a tinderbox.

Above the crackle of the fire, she heard a loud, panicked braying.

"Minnie Pearl!" Elena started running toward the little donkey's stall, the flames now precariously close.

"Elena, no! Come back."

A jagged arrow of fear cut through Ridge and launched him into motion. Someone had thrown what appeared to be a Molotov cocktail through the barn window. Whatever flammable liquid they'd used had instantly ignited and spread at an alarming speed.

She either hadn't heard him or refused to listen. Darting along a narrow space between the fire and the stalls, she headed straight toward Minnie Pearl.

"Wait!" He chased after her, his only thought of protecting her from harm.

In a matter of seconds, the fire had tripled in size. Ridge had never seen anything like it.

The stack of hay bales burned like a giant bonfire, the flames reaching ten feet high. Heat blasted him in the face. It must be worse for Elena who was closer.

Terror drove him ahead. At last, he reached her. "Elena!"

She didn't turn around, not even when he grabbed a fistful of her jacket and pulled. Flames closed in on all sides. The only avenue of escape was forward.

Releasing an anguished cry, she wrenched free of his grasp.

"Elena!"

Somehow, she reached Minnie Pearl's stall unscathed. Sliding the latch, she threw open the door and tumbled in, Ridge on her heels. Minnie Pearl stood in the corner, her long ears pinned back, her eyes wide and glassy with fright. Rather than greet the two humans as her rescuers, the donkey cowered and shrank farther into the corner.

Outside the stall, the fire continued to grow. The air sizzled, searing Ridge's lungs. Smoke absorbed every molecule of oxygen, making breathing difficult. He considered shutting the door, but then they'd be trapped inside with no avenue of escape. Burning embers, glowing red as a hot poker, floated up and away, landing several feet away where they ignited new fires.

Please, Lord. I beg You. Guide us away from this inferno and lead us to a safe haven.

"Elena, if we don't get out now, we'll die."

"We have to save Minnie Pearl."

She locked her arms around the donkey's neck and attempted to pull her from the corner. Minnie Pearl was living up to the reputation of her species and refused to budge.

Ridge admired Elena for her bravery and her compassion. He was equally annoyed at her complete disregard for their well-being.

"She's not going anywhere," he said.

"And neither am I."

Good heavens, she was as stubborn as the donkey. He also thought he could fall in love with her, given half the chance.

The revelation was like a kick in the pants. "Hold on," he hollered and squeezed himself between Minnie Pearl and the wall. "Get ready," he told Elena.

She braced her legs.

Ridge planted his palms on Minnie Pearl's rounded rump and shoved with all his might.

Elena tugged. The diminutive donkey was remarkably strong and remained rooted in place. Resting wasn't an option. Ridge shoved again, encouraging Elena.

Minnie Pearl let out a strangled squeal and then lunged forward. Once going, she didn't stop and rocketed out of the stall, knocking Elena to the ground.

Ridge rushed to her side and knelt. "Are you okay?"

"I'm fine."

"Can you walk?" He stood and yanked her to her feet, one eye on the nearby flames. "We need to get out of here."

She took a step and another, with more confidence. "What about Minnie Pearl?"

"She's long gone."

Holding her hand, Ridge approached the open stall door. The flames blocked their way, dancing high above their heads. He assessed their options. There was only one.

"Head left toward the back of the barn and out the door we went through that day I took you to the well house. Remember?"

"Yes."

"Cover your nose and mouth with your arm and duck your head." He squeezed her fingers. "Ready?"

She nodded.

Together, they rushed out of the stall and sprinted left through the flames. They were fast, and nothing caught fire. Even so, the intense heat struck them with a force that had Ridge remembering scary stories from Sunday school when he was a child. His eyes stung and watered. His vision blurred. His heart pounded.

Once they were past the flames, they hurried through the barn's rear door. Outside, they stopped running and coughed until their lungs cleared. Then they were on the move again.

"Call 9-1-1," Ridge shouted as they ran along the side of the barn to the front. "I'll get the hose."

At the hose bib, he flipped the spigot. Water flowed in a steady stream. He unfurled the hose and dragged it inside the barn. Using this thumb to create a spray, he aimed the water at the flames, moving his arm in a wide arc to cover a larger area.

Elena stood just outside the barn, her phone pressed to her ear. Did she never listen? He'd told her to go to the house.

While Ridge continued dousing the flames, she appeared beside him. "The fire department's on their way."

"Good." He inclined his head. As long as she refused to listen, she might as well be useful. "There's a fire extinguisher in the tack room."

She went to fetch it, returning a half minute later.

"Can you operate that?" he asked.

She pulled the pin and aimed the nozzle toward the fire. White foam sprayed out.

"Hit the flames from that side. Spray along the stall doors. I'll get this side."

Together, they succeeded in impeding the fire's progress. When the fire truck arrived five minutes later, the fire was a quarter contained.

"Stand back," the captain instructed Ridge and Elena.

They watched from the sidelines as, with their superior equipment, the fire crew extinguished the remaining blaze in a matter of minutes. When they were done, all that remained was a huge smoldering, blackened patch covering half the barn floor.

Ridge surveyed the damage. The scorched stall doors could be repaired or replaced. His new rubber mats were a lost cause, however. The generator and compressor were questionable. Water damage was extensive.

"You all right?" he asked Elena.

"Yeah." She wiped a black smudge from her forehead. "Minnie Pearl's standing by the house. She looks unharmed."

"Good. I figured she'd run to safety once she got away from the fire."

"What are you going to do with her? She can't stay in the barn."

"Put her in the round pen for a week until the barn airs out," he said. "She'll be fine with a bucket of water and another of grain, and that'll give me time to make the repairs."

"You need help?"

"You offering?"

"Maybe." She tendered a weak smile. They'd been through a lot the past hour, and her fortitude impressed him. "I'm sure there are members of Hillside Church who will volunteer the minute they hear what's happened."

"You can always count on your church family to step up in a time of crisis."

The fire captain joined them. "You're very fortunate," he said. His crew was giving the barn floor a thorough soaking to be on the safe side. "All in all, this could have been much worse."

"I agree." Ridge wiped his grimy hands with a handkerchief from his jeans pocket. "Very fortunate." *Thank You, Lord.* "Glad my insurance policy is paid up."

At that moment, two sheriff's SUVs arrived. Chief Dempsey climbed out of the first one and

Jake the second. Elena hadn't needed convincing to call the chief this time. The fire was no small threat or scare tactic. Someone had tried to hurt, if not kill them and nearly succeeded.

Ridge would have nightmares for weeks, if not for the rest of his life. He could still see Elena running through the flames and feel his terror that her clothes would catch fire.

"Captain Gates." The chief acknowledged the fire captain.

"Chief Dempsey."

The two men shook hands and chatted briefly before the fire captain turned to Ridge. "We're almost done here. We'll leave as soon as we put our equipment away."

"Thanks again for your help."

"Glad you and the deputy are all right and the damage wasn't worse." He walked off to rejoin his crew.

Amen to that, thought Ridge.

Jake clasped his shoulder. His usually tough exterior had given way to deep concern. Ridge rarely saw his brother-in-law unnerved.

"How you doing, pal?" Jake asked.

"Honestly? I've had better days."

"Man, this is awful." His brother-in-law's

gaze explored the damage. "Gracie's worried about you."

"I'll call her in a little while."

"Elena, you hanging in here?" The chief scrutinized her. "You look pale."

"I'm fine." She nodded stoically. "The paramedic checked us over, said our oxygen levels were good. Real good, in fact."

"Heard you're pretty handy with a fire extinguisher."

"She rocks." Ridge smiled fondly at her and placed a hand on her shoulder.

His actions didn't go unnoticed by Jake. This time, however, he didn't appear annoyed or suspicious. Just relieved.

"She does," the chief agreed, then looked around. "Which window did the incendiary device come through?"

The four of them walked into the barn and across the sodden, blackened mess on the floor. The acrid smell irritated Ridge's nostrils and stung his throat. How long would it linger?

"Here." He pointed to the small, broken window next to the storage room. "Elena and I were standing by the generator."

Jake took pictures with his phone. Ridge would, too, later, for the insurance claim.

"Any closer," the chief observed, "and you might have gone up in flames instead of the straw bales."

"True."

"I wonder if the person who threw the bomb knew where you and Elena were standing." Jake studied the window. "I'm going outside to have a look."

"Did you see anything at all?" the chief asked after Jake left. "Anyone?"

"No." Ridge shook his head.

"Nothing, Chief," Elena concurred.

"What were you doing when the bomb came through the window?"

She tensed, not wanting her boss to know that she and Ridge had been about to kiss.

"We were talking," he said. "We had our backs to the window and didn't notice."

Had the person who'd tossed the Molotov cocktail at them known they were distracted? Had they been watching Ridge and Elena? It was possible.

"The person must have walked onto the ranch," Elena said. "We'd have heard a vehicle."

The chief wrote an entry in his notebook.

Jake returned, huffing slightly. "Can't see the entire barn through the window, but you three were visible. The person could have aimed right at Ridge and Elena if they'd wanted to. I'm guessing they were either in a rush and blindly tossed the bomb or didn't intend to kill you."

"Notice any footsteps?"

"The ground is covered with them. Along with tire tracks and coyote tracks."

"Elena and I ran past there during the fire," Ridge said. "I walk the barn perimeter at least once a day."

Jake wiped perspiration from his damp brow. "You'd need a team of experts to make sense of that many footprints. There's no way we'll get approval for that."

The chief stuffed his notebook and pencil in his jacket pocket. "Come on, Jake. Let's pay the neighbors a visit. It's dinnertime, so most people will be home. With any luck, one of them noticed an unfamiliar vehicle parked down the road or a stranger on foot traveling in the direction of the ranch."

"Call me if you learn anything important," Ridge said.

"I'll be in touch. I may have more questions when I write up my report. In the meantime, you be careful, Ridge." He turned his attention to Elena. "You take the night off."

"But Chief—"

"No arguments. I'll see you in my office to-morrow morning. Bright and early."

"Yes, sir." Elena met his eyes briefly. She looked as if she knew what the chief wanted to talk to her about.

Ridge thought he knew, too. And if he was right, Elena wouldn't like it.

Chapter Nine

Elena sat at Ridge's kitchen table, trying to eat the chili and cornbread Ridge had prepared and having to choke down every bite. The Molotov cocktail and resulting fire had frightened her more than she cared to admit. More than she'd allowed him to see. She'd been running on pure adrenaline for the last two hours and had yet to calm down.

She'd never been that close to such a large fire. At first, she'd been convinced the hose and extinguisher would be useless. The flames had spread at an incredible rate, faster than she and Ridge could douse them. They might as well have been fanning the fire with pure oxygen rather than dousing it with water and retardant chemicals.

Finally, though, God had answered her fervent prayers, for her and Ridge's efforts began to have an effect.

Poor Minnie Pearl. Elena's chest ached at the thought of that sweet, gentle creature coming to harm. Another prayer answered. The donkey now resided, temporarily, in the round pen. Ridge had even found an old pony-sized horse blanket for Minnie Pearl to wear so she wouldn't get too cold at night.

He'd scolded Elena after the chief and Jake had left for rushing into the fire to save the donkey. She'd insisted she would do it ten times over, if necessary. He hadn't argued that point. And she'd understood he wasn't mad at her, but rather scared for her.

"Can I get you seconds?" Ridge asked.

How he'd managed to eat a giant bowl of chili and two generous portions of butter-slathered cornbread amazed her. Perhaps, for him, adrenaline increased his appetite rather than diminished it.

"No, thanks. It was delicious, though. You're right, you're a decent cook."

He smiled. "I did mean what I told the chief earlier. You rock, Elena."

She attempted a feeble smile. "I don't feel that way now."

"Most people would have panicked. Bolted or

froze. You keep your head under pressure. Except for when you ran into the fire."

"If not for my training, I might have bolted or froze, too."

"I was impressed."

She let her gaze wander the kitchen, noting small details. She hadn't been inside Ridge's house since the day he'd found the gun and the strongbox. Since then, the new cupboards and cabinets had been installed, along with new appliances. "The remodeling came out great."

"Thanks. I'm happy with the results."

"Bathrooms next? Are you getting water-saving fixtures?"

He set down his spoon, propped his forearms on the table and studied her. "I think we can skip the rest of the small talk."

She'd been anticipating a more serious discussion and was surprised he'd waited until the end of their meal. "I've been thinking of ways to find out who threw the Molotov cocktail. The captain mentioned a fire investigation to determine what accelerant was used. Once that's—"

Ridge cut her short, his tone grave. "I want to talk about what happened today with us. Not a fire investigation and what accelerant was used."

A flurry of pinpricks raced along Elena's spine. She hid her anxiety by schooling her features into a neutral mask.

"Okay. I'm listening."

"You could have been hurt or killed today. That was the intention of whoever threw the Molotov cocktail."

"I disagree. You heard Jake when he checked the barn window. The bomber could have hit us if they'd chosen. Instead, they aimed a distance away. It was a scare tactic, Ridge."

"And I'm plenty scared. Had things gone differently, we'd be having this conversation in a hospital room—or worse, not at all."

"We're fine now. I'm fine." She stopped herself from reaching across the table for his hand to reassure him, convinced he didn't want or need that. He had a different reason for this conversation.

"I don't want your help anymore with my dad's homicide," he said.

Oh. They were back to this again. "Even discreetly?"

"It's too dangerous, and I won't be responsible for something bad happening to you."

She sat still, organizing her thoughts before speaking. "I get where you're coming from."

"Good. We're in agreement."

"But you won't make any headway on your own."

"I don't have to. After today and the fire, I'll have the sheriff's department behind me. They can't continue to ignore me. I'm going to talk to the chief about Marcus Rivera and the old photograph. And I'll tell him what we learned from Olivia Gifford. When the test results come back on the gun and the money, I'll have enough to go to the Bisbee police and demand they reinvestigate. Like they mean it this time. If they refuse, I'll go higher. The mayor's office. The newspaper. TV stations. Whatever I have to do."

Jake hadn't been joking when he told Elena that Ridge could make problems.

"What if the test results come back inconclusive?"

"I'll still have enough to apply pressure."

"I can help. I know the ins and outs of the sheriff's department. Their inner workings. I have friends like Trudy and my cousin who can come in handy."

Ridge shook his head. "Absolutely not. Someone wants us stopped. So far, they've settled for warnings. Next time could be different. But if the Bisbee police are investigating Dad's homicide, that will change the game. Whoever's after us won't dare endanger the detective currently on my dad's case."

"They will, Ridge. They did before. If not with gun and bullets, then money. We don't have proof, but according to Olivia, the former police chief was likely taking bribes, along with the mayor. Whoever is behind this has power and influence and they aren't easily intimidated."

"All the more reason for you to stay out of it. I won't meet your family for the first time at your funeral."

Her heart responded to the emotion flaring in his eyes. His words were coming from a place of caring, greater than any of her previous suitors had shown.

She suddenly wanted to stay safe. For Ridge and for their potential future.

Yet, she couldn't simply walk away from a grave injustice. It wasn't in her. "I can handle myself. You said so yourself, I keep my head under pressure."

"No. I've made up my mind."

He had, and she could see there was no changing it. Not today.

"Like I said before, Elena, this isn't your battle to fight." His voice had lost its harsh edge. "It's mine."

"I thought it might be ours."

"That's...that's not possible." He squared his shoulders as if steeling himself for something he didn't want to do. "I was wrong to have accepted your offer to help me at the start."

She winced at a sharp pain in the vicinity of her heart. Until now, she hadn't seen his decision to exclude her as a rejection, but it was. She'd been wrong all along, and his feelings for her weren't as strong as she'd believed. Neither were they as strong as her feelings for him.

"I appreciate everything you've done," he said, seeming oblivious of her internal struggle. "But I'm moving forward alone from this point on. The chief and Oscar are untrustworthy, until proven differently, and you work with them. They have eyes on you. One of them has to be the individual tracking your computer activity at work. Or the station secretary. We haven't talked about her much, but she's in the perfect position to monitor your every move."

Elena couldn't bring herself to let go. She was stubborn, yes. More than that, fear prompted her to action. There were two types of people: those who avoided danger and those who faced it head-on. She was the latter. She took matters into her own hands and would never be a helpless victim.

"You're right," she said. "We haven't considered Sage, which is why you need me. I can monitor her just as easily as she can me. And no one will be the wiser. At the very least, I can be your sounding board. I'm good at giving advice."

"Someone will see us together and become suspicious."

"No, they won't. We're dating. Couples who date spend time together."

Ridge hesitated, his expression changing. "We have to stop seeing each other."

Elena had anticipated resistance, but not this... this complete dismissal. One bump in the road and he called it quits? The sharp pain of rejection from earlier returned. Well, that was what she got for lowering her defenses, opening her heart and letting Ridge in. A man who wouldn't stick with her through thick and thin.

"I think you must have set a record," she said, her hurt taking the form of anger. "Two whole hours after we agreed to try dating, you kick me to the curb."

"It's not like that, Elena."

"No? Then what's it like? You were the one who insisted we test the waters, not me. I wasn't sure."

Contrition filled his features. "I'm sorry. I should have said we need to stop seeing each other for now. Once this has blown over, we can go back to the way things were before."

"That's worse, Ridge." Her throat closed, making her voice choppy. "I'm not something you can put down and pick up whenever the mood strikes."

"I'm not saying this well." He rubbed his forehead and started again. "Elena. You're amazing. Incredible. Smart and brave and capable. You're close to your family, have a strong faith, love your job, and you're trying to make a difference in the world. You're exactly the kind of woman I've been looking for and never thought I'd find." His dark eyes begged her to put her hurt aside and listen. "I'm trying to protect you, not cause you pain and certainly not diminish what we have. If I've done either, I regret it."

She let his declaration sink in and soothe the wounds his earlier words had inflicted.

"I'm not a delicate flower," she said. "I'm capable of protecting myself." She stopped him with a raised hand when he opened his mouth to speak. "But I do appreciate you not wanting to put others in jeopardy. That's admirable, and I respect you for it. As much as I want to join you on your journey to find the truth about your dad's death, I will abide by your wishes and back off. That's your call, Ridge."

His shoulders relaxed in relief. "When you ran into the fire today, I was terrified. I couldn't think. Couldn't function. Couldn't make my legs run fast enough. I never want to experience that again. And I can't be the one who puts you in danger's path."

"I didn't mean to scare you. Minnie Pearl... I was worried. The fire. It was headed straight for her."

"I know. I wouldn't have wanted to see her suffer. But it was hard watching you."

Elena nodded, still struggling to process her feelings. So much had transpired in the last two days. First, there had been the threatening direct message. Her stressful conversation with her dad and her family seeking safety in a hotel. Then, the kiss she'd shared with Ridge, their mutual wish to date. Next, the fire. Now this, Ridge wanting to take a break when they'd barely started. She was entitled to feel uncertainty and confusion.

"I'm going home." She rose, desperate for solitude and an opportunity to reflect. "But let me help you clean the kitchen first."

"Elena." Ridge also stood. "I don't want you to leave like this."

His statement hit her wrong. He'd squashed all her romantic hopes for them, and then didn't want her to "leave like this," as if she was the one at fault.

"What other way is there?" She glanced around for her jacket, forgetting she'd left it draped on the recliner by the back door. "We're not working together on your dad's case. We're not dating. We're not even friends."

"We can be."

"No, we can't." Since he clearly didn't want her help with the investigation, or even with cleaning up after their meal, she headed toward the back door. "And you know that, even if you won't admit it."

"Elena."

"You can't deal me a huge blow and then expect me to be fine."

"You're right. That was…insensitive of me."

"You want space, you got it."

Seeing him at church and around town would be difficult enough. She wouldn't make it harder by pretending they were friends or holding out for a future with him that would never happen. Let the gossipers talk when they saw her and Ridge keeping their distance and noticed their cool demeanor when in each other's company. Elena couldn't care less.

Tears filled her eyes. She had to get out of here. Ridge could not, would not, see her fall apart. The reason didn't matter. Pride or embarrassment or fury. She simply knew that him witnessing her vulnerability was more than she could endure today. Tomorrow, when she'd come to terms and composed herself, would be different. Then she could talk to him.

Ridge accompanied her outside. She stood on the porch a moment, ruthlessly thrusting her arms into the sleeves of her jacket.

"I'm going to follow you home," Ridge said, donning his own jacket.

"That's not necessary."

"It is."

He was doing it for himself more than her. She supposed she could let him. Besides, what would denying him achieve? Certainly not any satisfaction. Not for her, anyway.

Ridge walked her to her car. Of course he did. She opened the door, unable to look at him.

"Take care, Ridge."

He didn't let her escape and pulled her into his embrace. She pressed her palms to his chest, intent on pushing him away. Only she didn't. Instead, she buried her face in his jacket.

"I wish I hadn't been the one to come out here the day you found the gun and strongbox," she whispered.

"Is that really true? Because I don't wish that."

She shook her head and sniffed.

"God has a plan for us, Elena. I'm sure of it. We have to be patient. We'll be together when the time is right. I've waited this long to find you. I can wait a little longer."

Elena recalled Psalm 5:3. *My voice shalt thou hear in the morning, O Lord; in the morning will I direct my prayer unto thee, and will look up.*

"What if you never find out what happened to your dad and who's responsible?" How long would he expect her to wait?

"Can we cross that bridge when we come to it?"

She didn't answer. His ambiguous answer disappointed her, and she retreated.

"Goodbye, Ridge. Follow me if you want, or not. Your choice. Makes no difference to me."

She got into her car then, not waiting for him to answer.

The tears didn't come. Elena refused to let them. She was made of sterner stuff, she told herself as she drove home, all the while checking the rearview mirror and seeing the headlights of Ridge's truck.

Nothing had changed. She was in the same place she'd been a few weeks ago. A deputy sheriff with a promising career. A loving, close family. A nice, if small, apartment. A church home. A bright future.

Except now she felt an emptiness inside her. A giant hole with a cold draft blowing through. How could losing something she'd never quite had leave her with such a gaping wound?

Minnie Pearl stopped in front of the barn door and stared as if assessing the damage from the fire. Ridge came up to stand beside her and placed a hand on her withers. He'd been letting the donkey roam the grounds for a little exercise. She'd already attached herself to him and the ranch and wasn't the least inclined to wander. She followed him around like a puppy as he shoveled debris into a wheelbarrow and hauled it to the dumpster.

Opening her mouth wide, she let out an enormous bray.

Ridge gave her head a scratch. "I couldn't agree more. It's a mess."

Along with the rest of his life.

He'd spent the night punching his pillow and getting almost no sleep. As a result, he was downing coffee this morning like it was water and regretting almost everything he'd said to Elena the previous day.

Ridge was hardly an expert in relationships, especially when it came to breakups. He hadn't had enough practice, not with women he'd truly cared about. A professional rodeo competitor spent more than half their life on the road. That strained any relationship. A guy could only miss so many birthdays and holidays and dinner dates before a gal grew tired and gave him his walking papers.

Had his chosen career been all that dissimilar to his dad's drinking? They were both gone much of the time. How had he not seen that before?

His relationship with Elena had been different, however. He wasn't rodeoing anymore. He'd returned to Ironwood Creek with the purpose of settling down. Trying to find out who'd murdered his dad might have put off some women, but Elena understood and supported him. More than that, she'd been willing to help him. Too willing, to the point she'd wound up in danger.

All night long he'd asked God why. One moment, Ridge had been holding Elena in his arms, imagining their future together and all the amazing possibilities. The next moment, a bomb had exploded, and they were battling a fire. Then, he was telling her they couldn't see each other anymore.

He'd been intent on protecting her, refusing to be the one responsible for her coming to harm and drowning in guilt that she almost had.

But that was about him and his feelings. What he should have done instead was consider *her* feelings. Ask *her* what *she* was going through and how he could help her. Respected *her* wants and wishes.

Ultimately, he and Elena would have ended up in the same place—parting ways. There was no doubt in his mind, the danger had been too great. But the decision would have been mutual, not just his, and she'd have landed gently rather than like a fall from a three-story window.

Minnie Pearl brayed again. Ridge swore there was a harsh reprimand in the loud reverberations.

"I know, girl. I'd take it back if I could. Do you think Elena will answer the phone if I call?"

Minnie Pearl meandered off toward the house.

"You're probably right. Guess I should give her a few days."

The donkey kept going, her stubby tail swishing. She found a patch of early-blooming wildflowers beneath the ironwood trees along the driveway. Like goats, donkeys would eat most anything that sprang from the earth, as long as it wasn't poisonous.

Ridge headed into the barn where the tools hung. They had escaped damage from the fire. Yet, only a few feet away, the severely scorched storage room door would need replacing.

He traded the shovel he'd been using for a rake. As he lifted the tool off its hook, the gravity of the last twenty-four hours hit him like a one-two punch. His strength left him in a rush, and his knees weakened. Leaning his back against the wall, he closed his eyes.

"Dear Lord. Please watch out for Elena. Take her into Your care and safeguard her from danger. She may not think she needs protection, but she does, but she needs Yours. Help heal the hurt I caused her and let her be receptive to an apology from me. I know I've ruined any potential future with her, and that's on me. But I hope she and I can at least reach a point where she can stand to be in the same room with me." Ridge tried to chuckle, but the mirth wouldn't come. "If I'm not meant to learn the answers about what happened to my dad, give me the ability to accept that as Your purpose for me. But if I am supposed to learn them, please guide me on my quest. Thank You, Lord, for Your unfailing love. Amen."

The prayer restored him. He walked over to the barn aisle and began raking with a vengeance, mingling the ash and soot in with the dirt. A glance across the yard assured him that Minnie Pearl was happily munching on flowers. He might have to do something about that. He liked the flowers. They added to the ranch's hominess.

Just as he was working up a sweat—and working off his frustrations about him and Elena—his phone rang with his mother's favorite Blake Shelton song. He stopped and leaned on the upright rake. Gracie must have told their mother about the Molotov cocktail and fire. His sister had spent thirty minutes on the phone with him last evening, alternating between crying and insisting he quit being so stupid and abandon this foolish notion of his to get justice for their dad.

He put the phone to his ear. "Hi, Mom. How are you doing?"

"Ridge. Honey. Why didn't you call me? I had to hear about what happened from Gracie."

"Sorry, Mom. I was going to call tonight. I haven't had a free minute, with the sheriff's department yesterday and then with the insurance company and filing a claim this morning. Had to take a bunch of pictures and email them off. I'm in the barn now cleaning. There's a ton of repairs. I'm going to be busy for a while."

He had no doubt she'd called to pressure him again about selling the ranch. Here was the perfect reason, in her opinion. Someone had nearly killed him. He'd be better off getting away from the ranch and out of Ironwood Creek altogether. Drawing in a breath, he readied himself for the confrontation.

"I'm so glad you're all right." Tears thickened her voice. "And the young woman who was with you. The deputy sheriff. Gracie told me about her. Said she's a nice person and was helping you with your dad's case."

"Yeah, she is nice. But she's not helping me anymore."

"Oh?"

If Ridge admitted he sent Elena away because of the danger, his mom would use that to apply more pressure to sell the ranch.

"It was for the best," he said. "I didn't feel right involving her."

Not a lie, not really.

"I hope after what happened, you're giving up. Gracie said whoever was behind the bomb is sending you a warning. You have to listen, Ridge." Her voice cracked at the end.

"His murderer needs to be brought to justice."

"Do they? I know you're tired of hearing me go on about your dad, but even if you were to discover who killed him, would your life change?"

"I'd find some peace."

"Peace comes in many forms. One thing your dad wouldn't want is for you to miss out on what makes you happy because you're obsessed with a vow you made to yourself when you were a boy."

How did she know about that?

His mom and sister both accused him of being emotionally stuck. Were they right? And if he let go, what then?

Elena's face appeared before him, and he heard again his mom's words: "What makes you happy."

"I say this because I love you," she said with unaccustomed tenderness. "We haven't always gotten along, and I wish that were different. Before you say anything, I take full responsibility. I allowed my anger at your dad to bleed into every part of my life, including my relationship with you. That was wrong, and I'm sorry, honey."

Ridge needed a moment before answering. "I never expected to hear you say that, Mom."

She sobbed quietly before collecting herself. "I should have. I fell into a horrible habit I couldn't break. When Gracie told me about the bomb and the fire…all I could think of was that I had every chance in the world to be a better mother to you and never took it. You deserved more. You lost the father you loved. And you lost your mother, too, because I was driving you away. I realize it's a lot to ask, but…can you forgive me?"

"Mom…"

"Think about it. You don't have to answer me today."

Ridge dragged in a breath, the concrete block in his chest shifting to make room for something he hadn't felt in a long time: optimism for an affectionate and supportive relationship with his mom. He hadn't realized how desperately he craved that until this moment and how grateful he was for the prospect.

God had given him an opportunity to heal at least one part of himself. It was a blessing. He'd be a fool to reject it.

"When I was younger, after Dad died, I was a real jerk. I admit it. In a constant state of anger. Moody. Withdrawn. Raising me couldn't have been easy."

"You turned out great, in spite of me."

"In spite of *me* and because of *you*, Mom. And that's why there's nothing to forgive."

She sniffed. "You're my favorite son."

He laughed. "I'm your only son."

"That, too." Her smile reached across their connection. "I'd love to see you soon. Maybe I'll come for a visit. I miss the girls and Gracie."

"You can stay here, if you'd like. Ben, too," Ridge said. "I have plenty of room if you want to bring him along."

"I'll ask him. Thanks, honey."

He waited for her to mention selling the ranch. She had a surprise in store for him, however.

"I can check out the new kitchen. Gracie says it's gorgeous."

"Okay. Not the response I was expecting."

"Look, honey. I won't lie to you and tell you I think you should keep the ranch. But if Gracie's all right with your decision, then so am I."

"I'm hoping to buy her out soon."

"She mentioned that."

"Start buying her out, I should say, if she's willing to take payments."

"I'm glad for you, Ridge. Perhaps I've been wrong all these years and the best way for you to move forward is remodeling the ranch and raising cattle like your grandfather. Not selling it."

Moving forward. Restoring the ranch. Raising cattle. Giving up his boyhood vow to find his dad's murderer.

If he did all that, maybe he and Elena could start fresh. The idea appealed to him. If she was willing. That remained to be seen.

Dear Lord. What do I do? Please show me the path. Do I continue searching for the answers I seek and the peace I crave, or abandon it all and choose a new path?

Ridge needed to ruminate for a while. Search his heart and converse with God. And, it seemed, he had a visit from his mom to prepare for, one he was looking forward to.

"Mom, I need to finish up here in the barn and then head to the hardware store."

"Of course. I...just... It's..."

"What?"

"Nothing," she said airily. "I'll tell you when I see you."

"Tell me now."

"It's, um, about the strongbox of cash you found."

Ridge forgot all about his chores and errands. "What about them?"

"If you're not sitting down, you should."

Chapter Ten

Ridge didn't consider himself a wimp. He didn't fall apart when receiving bad or shocking news. His mom knew that about him. If she thought he needed to be seated when he heard what she had to say, there must be a good reason. She was about to turn his world on its side.

He made his way to the metal chair where he drew in several calming breaths before sitting.

"Go on," he told his mom.

She paused. "I... I'm almost certain your dad is the one who buried the strongbox beneath the well house. And that the money inside it was payment from the cartel for letting them transport drugs across the back side of the ranch."

Ridge had recently concluded as much and disliked what it implied—that his dad had been as much a criminal as the people who'd been paying him off. But to hear his mom all but confirm it...

His heart sank. His dad really had been nothing like the man he remembered.

"Why didn't you ever tell me?"

"I'm sorry, honey. Please don't be mad. I was sure you'd take what I said and go on a rampage."

"I might have. I still might."

"And invite another attempt on your life? You're smarter than that. And you don't want the deputy sheriff to get hurt."

His mom had that right.

"Listening to you," she went on, "I'm confident you'll make the best decision, which is passing what I'm telling you on to the authorities and letting them do their job instead of you trying to do it."

Ridge was glad his mom had suggested he have a seat because he felt as if the ground beneath him were shifting.

"If that money came from Dad, why did he bury it rather than use it for the family and the ranch? Why didn't you insist on it if you knew he was taking a kickback? And more importantly, why didn't you dig up the money years ago?"

Her sigh said he was asking a lot of questions. "First of all, in the beginning, I wasn't entirely sure he was on the cartel's payroll. Of course, I had a strong suspicion. But whenever I asked, he denied it. In hindsight, I think he believed he was protecting us. You and me and your sister. The less we knew, the less danger we'd be in. And, frankly, part of me resisted knowing the truth. As long as I was ignorant, I could pretend all was well. Then one day, several weeks before he died, I overheard your dad talking on the phone with the auto repair shop about having my car repaired. It had been sitting in our garage for two months, not drivable."

"I remember," Ridge said.

"They wanted eight hundred dollars. If your dad had that kind of money, he wouldn't have spent it on repairing my car's transmission."

"Unless there was more where that came from."

"Right," his mom agreed. "After he mysteriously produced the money to repair my car, I couldn't pretend any longer. We argued all the time. No amount of money was worth the risk. There'd been one murder by then. Everyone knew the cartel was behind it, even though there was no proof. I was scared for all of us."

"I don't blame you, Mom."

"I decided then and there to find the money,

if it could be found, and leave town with you kids. Believe me when I say, I searched the house and barn from top to bottom. I never found anything, which made me all the more angry and fearful. I became convinced people were following me whenever I left the house."

"Were they?" Ridge couldn't imagine his mom's terror.

"Maybe. I think so. When your dad died, I searched again for the money and again found nothing. I'd decided either someone had scammed him out of it, he drank it away or his murderer stole it. I was so furious at him. For dying and for dying without giving me the money we desperately needed."

Ridge could see how his mom would come to those conclusions and how she could have carried a grudge against his dad, both while he was alive and after his death.

"There's something I don't understand. Why did he keep lying to you about the money? Obviously, your ignorance wasn't keeping you safe."

"Shame, is my guess," his mom said. "Not the taking of the money, that didn't bother your dad, but that he frittered it away instead of giving it to his wife and children who, at times, were living on the brink of poverty."

Ridge wondered if shame was what had driven his dad to take money from the cartel in the first place. Except forty thousand dollars seemed like an awful lot. And his dad cooperating with the cartel didn't explain the argument with the stranger in the barn and the accusations the man had made.

"Did Dad have any morals whatsoever?"

"Don't be so hard on him, son. He was hardly the only one on the take. There's no excuse for what he did, of course. But sometimes, when it comes down to providing food and clothes for loved ones or going hungry, the choice to look the other way is easy. Not to mention the cartel didn't accept no for an answer. They hurt people to get what they wanted."

"That's true." Ridge wouldn't have wanted to be in his dad's shoes.

"Unfortunately, for us, money burned a hole in your dad's pocket. I often ask myself, if he hadn't partnered with the cartel, would he have quit drinking and gotten his life together."

"He may not have had a choice," Ridge said.

"Things certainly ended badly for anyone who went against the cartel." His mom released a trembling sob.

"I don't remember any of this."

"I'm surprised. Your dad and I bickered constantly. I hated that he was more than likely aiding the drug trafficking. I hated worse that he drank up most of the money. Most of all, I hated that there was nothing I could do to change those circumstances. Not without putting myself and my children in danger."

Guilt squeezed Ridge's chest. As a boy, he'd tuned out his parents' arguments, believing they were about only his dad's drinking. If only he'd listened to their words, maybe he could have stopped his dad. "I'm sorry you went through all that."

"When I'd ask you not to stir up trouble by digging into your dad's death, it's because I saw what happened to people who crossed the cartel."

He saw that now. "I was wrong to cause you so much worry."

"It's not your fault. Your dad is responsible."

The last vestiges of the unrealistic image Ridge held of his late father evaporated into thin air. "He really was a terrible person."

"No, he wasn't," his mom insisted. "Please don't think that, honey. He was an alcoholic. He had a disease. I wish he'd tried harder to fight it because he had a beautiful spirit and an amazing capacity to love, which you know because he showed you that every day. For me, I should have been a better wife."

"You're not to blame."

"No one is. We were all victims and in a situation beyond our control."

"Were we? Couldn't we have moved?"

"It wasn't that simple. Your dad refused to sell the ranch his father had built from the ground up. He was determined it remain in the family. Then, after your dad was killed, the cartel had eyes on us. If I had said or done anything that put them or their operation at risk of discovery, they'd have me killed, too. By staying, allowing them to watch my every move, I protected you and Gracie."

"There's one thing I don't understand. If you knew how Dad really died, why did you always tell me you thought he'd been drunk and fallen?"

"Again, to protect you and Gracie. As long as you both were ignorant of the cartel, you remained safe. I escaped Ironwood Creek as soon as I could."

"After I left home to rodeo."

"Gracie was married to Jake, a deputy sheriff who knew about the cartel and would safeguard

her with his life. You were on the road most
of the time. Years had passed during which I'd
shown the cartel I could be trusted. And then,
Sheriff Cochrane was elected. Right from the
start, he made it his mission to drive the cartel
from Ironwood Creek with his crack-down-on-
crime program. The town went from being the
busiest drug route in the southwest to a quiet
and safe community that attracted tourists."

Ridge rubbed his forehead, struggling to absorb all the information his mom had told him.
This had to be the most incredible conversation of his entire life. Not only had he mended
an eighteen-year-old rift between him and his
mother, he'd learned astonishing details about his
hometown and neighbors and parents. It was as
if his mom were describing complete strangers.

He forced himself to refocus. Too many unanswered questions continued to plague him.

"Forty thousand dollars is a huge sum. Dad
obviously didn't drink up all the money the cartel paid him. Do you think it's possible he stole
it?"

His mom hesitated before responding. "I've
considered the possibility. In a way, it makes
sense."

"Except, not to malign Dad or anything, but

he never struck me as being stealthy and the type to construct elaborate plans."

"He could have robbed one of the drug runners. Lain in wait for him along the route and pulled a gun on him."

Ridge envisioned his dad stepping in front of the drug runner's four-wheel-drive vehicle in the middle of the night and pulling a gun on the driver, his face covered by a mask. "That would have been incredibly dangerous, if not insane."

"And something your dad might have done."

"He might have." One thing didn't make sense to Ridge, however. "Except why would Dad have stolen money if he was being regularly paid by the cartel to let them use the ranch?"

Again, his mom's voice filled with sorrow. "You know how your dad was. A dreamer. Head in the clouds when it wasn't in the bottom of a whiskey bottle. He used to take you prospecting into those hills. Twice he invested small amounts of money in get-rich schemes that went nowhere. He had this idea of turning the ranch back into a cattle operation, which made no sense as he was the one who sold off all the cattle we had. I couldn't talk any sense into him. He was determined to buy some calves and repair the barn."

"He was?" Is that where Ridge had gotten the idea? Had he heard his dad talking about it to his mom and the seed had been planted? It was possible.

"If I'd suspected for even a second that he was planning to rob a drug runner," his mom said, "I'd have knocked him unconscious rather than let him go out." She started to sob. "I didn't think he was serious about the cattle."

"Who would?"

"I've spent years either dodging responsibility or letting myself drown in it. Ben couldn't be more supportive and understanding. I don't know what I'd do without him. That's not to say I didn't once love your dad," she added.

"I know that. I also know he didn't make loving him easy for you."

"I regret so many things."

"You and Dad were in an impossible situation. You had no choice but to work with the cartel. I'm amazed you kept it together as well as you did.

"I had you kids to think of and protect. Everything I did was for you."

With sudden clarity, Ridge realized what he'd perceived as his mom's bitterness, anger and misery from living with an alcoholic husband was, in fact, her fear, worry, frustration and resentment from their forced partnership with the cartel.

How could he have been so wrong all these years? Being young wasn't an excuse. He hadn't been twelve for a long time.

"I wish you had told me all this sooner," he said.

"I probably should have," she admitted, her tone despairing. "Your constant pressuring of the authorities about your dad could have put you all in danger—not just you but Gracie and her family, too."

Ridge felt the impact like a punch to the solar plexus. He'd been selfish and single-minded, never taking his sister and nieces and even Jake into consideration, especially after Elena received threats and the bomber had set the barn ablaze.

His mom was worried about not being a good mother? She had nothing on Ridge, who hadn't been a good son, brother, brother-in-law or uncle.

"Please, honey," his mom said. "I beg you. Walk away from all this. Nothing good will come of it."

He was starting to think she was right.

"Isn't Dempsey the chief now? I always liked him. And, once you've put this quest of yours behind you, ask that nice deputy sheriff out on a date, work on the ranch and do whatever puts a smile on your face."

Her advice had merit.

"Pray on it," she added. "You have such a strong relationship with God, I'm sure you'll reach the right decision."

Ridge closed his eyes, his thoughts continuing to race. "I have a lot to think about." And he would pray on it. "Thank you for telling me, Mom."

"If you want to talk again, call me. Or we could find some time alone when I visit."

"I'll probably have more questions."

"I'm always available."

"Before I let you go—" He paused. "Have you ever heard of Marcus Rivera?"

"Hmm." She went quiet while she pondered. "He had a business in town. Investments or something."

"Ever meet him?"

"No. Why?"

"Elena, the deputy sheriff, found an old photo of him with the former mayor at a fundraising dinner. We were wondering if he had a connection with the cartel."

"I wouldn't be surprised. The cartel had plants."

That got Ridge's attention. "What do you mean by plants?"

"People placed in positions that would benefit the cartel."

"Like spies?"

"Kind of. There were rumors about the former mayor," his mom said. "And others. A councilman, as I recall. And a banker."

Marcus Rivera, too, perhaps, a prominent local businessman who dealt with finances.

"One last question, Mom. Did Dad or anyone ever mention the Hawk?"

"I remember *you* telling the police detective about overhearing your dad and the stranger arguing, and the stranger mentioning the Hawk."

"But that's all?"

"Once when your dad and I were arguing, he mentioned the Hawk. When I called him out on it, he got mad and told me I was mistaken."

"Did you inform Detective Darnelly?"

"No. Only because I didn't want to alert them about the money in case the cartel came after us." She hesitated. "I had the impression Hawk was a code name."

"For a plant?" Ridge asked.

"For the plane that met the drug traffickers at Rooster Butte. Do you remember Mr. Vasquez who owned the market? Once, I overheard him talking on the phone to someone about the Hawk and that it was landing at midnight. We all knew about the plane. It was just another of those things we didn't discuss."

Of course. The Hawk was the plane. All the pieces suddenly fell into place.

He needed to tell Elena.

"Mom, I have to run."

"Call me soon. I love you."

"I love you, too. Bye."

He didn't hurry off to the hardware store after disconnecting. The conversation with his mom had not only lifted a weight from him, it had provided clarity. He needed a moment to reflect.

His mom had forgiven his dad. That felt good to know, and it gave Ridge an optimism for the future he hadn't had before. Maybe it was possible for him to have a good marriage and not make the same mistakes his parents had.

With renewed determination, he dialed Elena's number, praying she'd pick up. As one ring followed another, he told himself she might be busy at work and unable to answer.

He was mentally composing the voice mail message he'd leave when the ringing abruptly stopped.

"Hello." Her neutral tone gave nothing away.

"Elena. Hi. Sorry if I'm interrupting you. It's important."

"What is it?" she asked, still neutral.

"I just got off the phone with my mom. She told me things about my dad and the money and the cartel that she'd been keeping secret all these years. It gives some insight into my dad's case."

"Ridge." She spoke slowly and with a trace of weariness. "You said yesterday you didn't want me involved in your investigation."

"I'm not investigating anymore." It wasn't until the words were out that he realized he'd made his decision. "I'm going to pass this information on to law enforcement."

"Really?"

"The problem is, I'm not sure who to trust. I'd like to meet with you and tell you what my mom said. Get your input." He swallowed. "You once offered to be my sounding board, and I need one right now."

She didn't immediately answer, forcing him to wait.

At last, she said, "Okay. I'm off duty in an hour. I'll come to the ranch. I just need to stop at home first." And then she hung up on him.

Elena ended the call with Ridge and sat with her chin in her hand, replaying their conversation. He'd sounded anxious. Her first thought had been that he was concocting an excuse to meet with her and convince her to give their relationship a second chance—not that she would. But then she'd changed her mind. He'd learned something. Whether it would shed light on his dad's case or not remained to be seen.

Ridge had said he didn't know who to trust. She concurred, having her own doubts about the chief and Oscar and even Jake, for that matter. Not because Jake was out to get her. Rather she speculated he might have sabotaged her and Ridge's efforts in order to protect Ridge.

There was no way he was the one behind the Molotov cocktail. Someone close to Jake could be, however. Someone else besides the chief and Oscar. Was it Sage? Olivia Gifford?

Elena's head throbbed and her heart ached,

ever since she and Ridge argued yesterday, and he'd sent her on her way.

What was wrong with her? She and Ridge hadn't really dated. A few meals, evading the mysterious vehicle trailing them to and from Bisbee, strategy sessions, digging into old records together, and escaping a treacherous fire. Those things didn't count as courting.

Kisses did, though. She and Ridge had grown close in a very short time. That must mean something.

Dear, sweet Lord. I did come to care for Ridge. Do care for him. Should I see him today or call him and cancel? Am I the means for him to find out who murdered his dad? The one who can help him? Will I be hurt again?

The station door opened, and Oscar burst in with his usual reporting-for-duty energy. He took one look at her and stopped in his tracks. "What happened to you? You're a mess." He grimaced. "And you smell."

Elena sat up and shook off her ruminations, which had been getting her nowhere. Her current disheveled state was the reason she'd told Ridge she needed to go home first before meeting with him. Despite having washed up as best she could in the station restroom and running a wet comb through her hair, her skin itched and dark splotches stained her uniform. She couldn't wait to shower and change clothes.

"I fell into the dumpster behind the Gas Up and Go," she admitted.

"Fell in or went dumpster diving?" Oscar chuckled at his joke, his mustache twitching.

She looked away.

From her desk on the other side of the room, Sage tsked and rolled her eyes. She'd been sympathetic when Elena returned to the station, offering to help her clean up and producing a package of wet wipes from her purse.

"Leave it to a rookie girl deputy." Oscar shook his head.

Elena paid him no heed. This was just another pathetic example of how her fellow deputies didn't respect her or treat her as an equal.

"The Gas Up and Go was robbed."

"No fooling?" Oscar sat at the empty desk across from her. "What happened?"

"A young man, twenty-two years old, pulled a knife on the clerk. Demanded all the cash in the register. The clerk handed it over, which was the smart thing to do. Better than being stabbed. A customer in the back ducked into the bathroom and called 9-1-1. Thank God the perp didn't notice her. I happened to be only a few blocks away when the call came in."

"And you found him in the dumpster?" Oscar snorted, clearly finding the situation hilarious.

Elena squared her shoulders. "Yes, I did."

"What? No way!"

"Don't you have work to do, Oscar?" Sage asked.

Elena appreciated the support, but she was capable of handling Oscar herself.

"He was already wasted," she said. "Obviously not thinking straight. He grabbed a bottle of beer from the cooler before running out of the market, only to stop behind the building to drink it. When he heard my siren, he hid in the dumpster. Figured I wouldn't look there."

"He was wrong," Chief Dempsey said. He stood in the doorway between his office and the main room. "Elena did all right. She got her man, and the Bisbee police collected him an hour ago and took him into custody. Guy had a half dozen priors there. He'll have a nice stay at the city jail until everything is sorted out and he goes before a judge."

"By falling into the dumpster and getting covered with...is that horse manure?" Oscar's amusement rang in his voice and shone in his eyes.

"Sawdust," Elena said. "They use it to clean up spills."

"Well, I hope whatever spills they cleaned up come out of your uniform." The other deputy couldn't hold back any longer and erupted in laughter.

"That's enough." The chief's brusque tone quieted Oscar.

"I'm just having a little fun with her, Chief."

"Let's get to work. Elena, your shift's almost over. If you want to leave a little early, go ahead."

"I wouldn't mind. Thank you, Chief." She rose and went into the breakroom to collect her purse and personal items.

When she reentered the main room, the chief hailed her from his office. "You have a second before you leave?"

She made the mistake of glancing in Oscar's direction. He pinched his nose and squeezed his eyes shut as if being assaulted by a strong stench.

Ignoring him, she walked head held high into the chief's office. He sat at his desk, shuffling through a stack of papers. In her grimy state, she stood rather than soil a visitor chair.

"Yes, sir?"

He set the stack of papers aside. "Wanted to let

you know, the results from the gun and strong-box are in."

"Oh?"

"Unfortunately, the lab director called while we were with the Bisbee police officers, handing over your perp. When I returned the call, the director wasn't available. No one else could help me. I'm waiting to hear back."

"Okay. Well, that's good."

"They found something, Elena."

"What?" She reached for the back of the visitor chair.

"The director didn't say what. Likely the information is too sensitive to leave on voice mail message."

Too sensitive. She wondered what that meant.

"Will you let me know the results as soon as you hear?" she asked.

"That's why I'm telling you."

"Thanks, Chief." She considered informing him that she was on her way to meet with Ridge, and he claimed to have new information on his dad. Her instincts cautioned her to remain quiet. Trust issues aside, the news was Ridge's to impart.

"See you tomorrow, Elena." He dismissed her with a nod.

"Stay safe," Sage called out as she passed by the secretary's desk.

Oscar was on the phone. From the conversation, it sounded as if he was about to head out. A Jeep had gotten stuck while attempting to cross Ironwood Creek. He didn't acknowledge her as she left.

On the walk to her car, Elena thought about seeing Ridge in an hour. She tried convincing herself that the knot of anticipation in her stomach was from the new information he had on his dad and had nothing to do with their personal situation.

Questions assaulted her all during the drive to her apartment. Should she tell Ridge about the lab results, or would Chief Dempsey? More urgently, did she even trust the chief? Granted, he'd told her about the lab director calling. But, in the larger scheme of things, that meant very little. He could be onto her and feeding her information to give her a false sense of security.

Her head ached worse than before. Ridge sending her away yesterday made no difference. She was still up to her neck in Pete Burnham's unsolved homicide.

Chapter Eleven

Ridge poured a scoop of pellets into Minnie Pearl's bucket and checked the bungee cord securing it to the round pen railing. Minnie Pearl liked to knock over her water and grain buckets, spilling the contents, which likely meant she was bored. He let her roam the ranch as much as possible, but she had to stay in the round pen for her own protection at night and when he was gone. Coyotes and mountain lions were known to attack small donkeys. Maybe next time he was at the feed store, he'd buy one of those equine enrichment toys she could bat around with her nose.

Finishing his chores, he made for the house, intending to wash up and change into a fresh shirt before Elena arrived. He was still grappling with everything his mom had told him about his dad, along with his eagerness at seeing Elena again. Common sense warned him to proceed with care. Nothing had changed overnight. She'd likely be reserved, if not hurt and angry.

He would only discuss his dad and avoid the subject of *them*. Now, if *she* raised the subject, he'd attempt to apologize for his poor behavior yesterday and to explain. But only if.

He entered the house through the back door, his glance darting right to the remodeled kitchen and then left to the new large screen TV dominating the great room. He'd believed the renovations and redecorating would erase the bad memories of his childhood and enable him to create positive ones. He'd been only partially right. The rooms were empty and too large. What was the point of a fancy new kitchen and new bathrooms and new furniture if he didn't enjoy them?

He'd have visitors soon—his mom and Ben were coming—and he wondered if that would make a difference. But Ridge wanted more than that. He'd refused to consider dating and falling in love for so long, waiting until he'd restored the ranch to its former glory. He was wrong about that, too. This house deserved to be a home, filled with a boisterous, joyous family.

Ridge deserved that, too. He'd denied himself the opportunity for happiness, afraid if things weren't perfect, his marriage would end up a train wreck just like that of his parents'. Except, look at his sister. She'd built a wonderful life for herself. Why couldn't Ridge trust himself to do the same?

"Lord," he said as he fastened the buttons on a clean shirt. "Once again, I'm asking for Your help. Which is the right path for me? I came home hoping to rebuild my life as well as restore the ranch. As if that would bring me the peace I desperately crave. Perhaps I'm looking in the wrong place. Is Elena the one for me? I think she could be. I'd like to find out. I ask You to provide a moment while she's here for me to tell her I'm sorry. If she isn't moved, then I'll—"

Ridge's prayer was interrupted by the ringing of his cell phone. He grabbed it off the dresser, experiencing a hitch in his breathing when he saw the name on the display.

Putting the phone to his ear, he said, "Afternoon, Chief."

"Ridge. Did I catch you at a bad time?"

"No. I'm waiting on…" He started to say Elena only to clamp his mouth shut. Revealing he and Elena were meeting might not be a good idea. "I have a few minutes to spare."

"Good. I wanted you to be my first call. I just

got off the phone with the director of the lab in Tucson. The tests results are in on the gun and strongbox."

The bottom dropped out of Ridge's stomach. He stumbled his way to the bed and sat down on the edge of the mattress.

"The director went over the report with me," Chief Dempsey continued, "and emailed me a copy. It just hit my inbox."

"What does it say?"

"There was no usable DNA evidence on either the gun or strongbox. Both were in the ground too long."

Ridge let out a breath. "I was hoping for more."

"They were able to lift some fingerprints from the inside of the strongbox and from the plastic wrapping on the hundred-dollar bills. Before you ask, they found only your dad's."

This was consistent with what his mother had told him. His dad must have stolen the money from a drug runner and buried it. That part of what happened to his dad, at least, was solved. Just not who'd killed him.

"Well, Jake was right. That was a complete waste of time."

The chief cleared his throat. "Actually, that's not true. They did find something of interest."

Ridge straightened. "What?"

"There's a false bottom in the strongbox, which was discovered once all the stacks of money were removed."

"A false bottom!" He hadn't bothered to look beneath the stacks of money. There had been no reason. "Did it hold anything?"

"There are pictures attached to the report. I'll email you a copy."

"Just tell me."

"They found a gold chain. It fits the description of the one you gave the police eighteen years ago. The one you said you found in the barn after your dad and the unidentified man argued. They're running a DNA test, but that's going to take a week or two."

Ridge began to pace, his heart galloping. Here it was, proof he'd been telling the truth. Between what his mother had told him and this, the Bisbee police would have no choice but to restart the investigation.

"Thank you, Chief."

Without another word, he disconnected, his excitement diminishing as quickly as it had escalated. Should he have advised the chief to keep the test results under wraps? Which, on second thought, would be a waste of breath if the chief was in cahoots with the cartel or one of the plants his mom had mentioned.

He had to talk to Elena. She couldn't get here fast enough.

Elena closed the lid on her washing machine and pressed the start button. She'd opted to wash her soiled and smelly uniform separate from her other clothes and use double the laundry detergent. Even then, she worried the dirt and odor wouldn't come out. She may have no choice but to replace the uniform with a new one.

Oscar's reaction to her disheveled state annoyed her. Had she been a man, he might have poked fun at her, but in his next breath he would have congratulated her for successfully apprehending the thief and on a job well done.

Would she ever fit in and be accepted? It didn't seem likely, not in Ironwood Creek. Perhaps she'd been mistaken and hadn't found a home here after all. Her uncertainties grew when she recalled what happened yesterday with Ridge.

What an idiot she'd been. That was what she got for letting her guard down and developing feelings for him.

Had he been using her all along just to advance the investigation into his dad's murder?

No, he wasn't a duplicitous person. Not in the slightest. And how often had he tried to convince her to quit helping him, for her own safety, and she'd refused?

Still, her broken heart ached. He may not have intentionally used her, but she had let herself be useful to him. And that had clouded their breakup, if one could call it a breakup. More like an end to their friendship.

For a moment, she considered phoning Ridge and canceling their meeting. Whatever he had to tell her, he could surely accomplish on the phone.

Unless she *wanted* to see him again.

Elena squared her shoulders. Nothing could be further from the truth. She was done with Ridge Burnham. He'd rejected her. Elena possessed enough self-awareness to admit that. She wouldn't talk about it with anyone or admit her embarrassment, but she'd be honest with herself. Her beloved *abuela* had taught her that, along with many other important life lessons. The most meaningful lessons Elena had learned next to those she heard from the pulpit on Sundays.

With the washing machine running, she returned to the kitchen where she slipped into her favorite bulky sweater. Collecting her phone from the counter, she dropped it into the side pocket of her purse. Just then, her doorbell rang.

Elena's first thought as she walked across the living room was of her gun, locked securely away in the bedroom closet safe. Normally, answering the door didn't panic her. That was before she'd received threats and might have died in a fire if God wasn't watching out for her and Ridge.

"Don't be ridiculous," she mumbled under her breath. No one intending harm would come to her front door and ring the bell. They'd sneak around back and break in through her patio door.

She pressed her eye to the peephole before disengaging her deadbolt. Her taut nerves instantly relaxed at the sight of Jake. Nonetheless, she didn't immediately open the door. Why was he here, and what did he want?

"Hey, Elena." His muffled voice called to her through the door. "If you're in there, open up. I heard about what happened. Just wanted to check on you. Make sure you're all right."

She relented, disengaging the deadbolt and opening the door. "Hi, Jake."

"What?" He flashed a jovial grin. "You aren't gonna invite me in?"

"I'm on my way out, actually." She didn't mention her destination. He'd get the wrong idea, which he'd then pass on to Gracie. "And, as you can see, I'm just fine."

"I won't keep you long." His grin turned serious. "You've been through a lot, collaring that perp. Anyone would be shaken up."

Elena hesitated. It seemed he was here to extend an olive branch and was treating her like he might Oscar or any other deputy.

As she debated with herself, the door of her closest neighbor opened and a middle-aged woman emerged from her apartment wearing yoga pants and a sweatshirt. Her brows rose seeing Jake standing there, out of uniform. Did she assume Elena was entertaining a gentleman friend?

"Ma'am." He saluted the woman.

"Hello." She didn't bother disguising her avid curiosity.

"Afternoon, Beth," Elena said, forcing a casual tone.

"Um, see you later." After a few awkward seconds, the woman continued on her way, her gym bag slung over her shoulder.

"Come on in, Jake, but I've only got a minute." Elena spoke loud enough for her neighbor to hear. She wanted no misunderstanding. While nice, Beth very much liked to mind the other residents' business and talk about them behind their backs.

Inside Elena's apartment, Jake stood in the middle of her living room, his gaze roaming. "Nice place you have here."

"Thanks."

"Real homey." He nodded with approval. "Not what I expected."

She almost asked if he'd thought she used wooden crates and beanbag chairs for furniture.

"I appreciate you stopping by..." She glanced at her watch, hoping he'd get the hint and leave.

He cleared his throat. "Look, kid, I—"

"Kid?" Elena walked to the kitchen.

Jake followed her. "Sorry. Gracie's all the time nagging me about my inability to communicate well, as she says."

Elena leaned on the counter and waited for him to continue.

"You're a good deputy. I don't tell you that very often."

She didn't let her surprise show. "You don't tell me that ever. None of you do."

"We're a boys' club at Ironwood Creek. No denying that. We'll get better. We just need a little time."

She said nothing, thinking of Oscar's taunts an hour ago.

"We'd like that time, Elena. You'll see, things will improve." His features shone with sincerity. "Especially if you keep proving yourself like you did today."

Elena couldn't help smiling. They were boys, the whole lot of them. But maybe she, the only woman, could teach them and make them better at their jobs as much as they were supposed to teach her and make her better at her job.

"As far as apologies go," she said, "that wasn't the worst one I've heard."

"Good." He shrugged. "I'm also sorry about you and Ridge."

Elena stiffened. She'd told no one and didn't appreciate the personal remark. "I'm not sure what you mean."

"You and him. My mother-in-law called Gracie. She mentioned you and Ridge had a falling-out."

Elena almost asked Jake to repeat himself. Ridge had told his mom about the two of them? She hadn't realized he and his mom were close enough to share personal information. Not from what Ridge had said. And now it appeared Elena's name was on every Burnham family member's tongue.

Her stomach rolled. Here she'd been worried about her neighbor. This was much worse.

Jake reached out and patted her shoulder. "If there's anything you need, just give me a shout. I'm serious, Elena."

She couldn't bring herself to answer him. Jake might mean well, but he was her immediate supervisor and contemporary. They were law enforcement officers. She detested appearing weak or emotional in front of him.

Getting involved with Ridge had been a mistake for yet another reason. In hindsight, the last few weeks had been like a roller-coaster ride, filled with emotional highs and lows, excitement and fears, joy and pain, hope and disappointment. That was no excuse, however. She should have known better and stayed far, far away from him.

She hated missing church for any reason other than work, but maybe she should skip the next few weeks. Give her and Ridge some space. She could always attend the Wednesday morning bible study if she wasn't on duty. Except that would also give people like Jake and Gracie more reason to talk and possibly fuel the rumor fires.

Elena sighed. "Sorry, Jake. I'm running late for my appointment."

"Sure. I'll get out of your hair. Let me walk you to your car."

She turned and reached for her purse on the counter. "That's not necessary."

"It's getting dark. And someone threw a Molotov cocktail at you yesterday. You can't be too safe."

He said the last part from behind her.

Right behind her.

The hairs on the back of Elena's neck prickled. Her hand went to her side, seeking her gun that wasn't there. Every one of her senses urged her to run. Run now!

She ducked and moved to her right. Twenty-five feet away, the front door and safety beckoned.

Jake was quicker. He caught her arm in his vise-like grip and wrenched ruthlessly, nearly dislocating it from her shoulder and throwing her off-balance. She stifled a sharp yelp.

"Bad news, kid," he growled in her ear. "You're not going anywhere."

A knock sounded at her door.

Jake's meaty hand over her mouth muffled Elena's cry for help.

"Not a peep from you," he growled in a voice she'd never heard before. "You hear?"

She nodded, though she was tempted to bite his fingers. Better sense prevailed. The person standing at her door could be a cohort of Jake's. With everything that had happened to her and Ridge, the sergeant deputy couldn't have been working alone.

He abruptly thrust her into the counter. Hard. Before she could catch her breath, a blinding pain exploded in the back of her head. A shower of bright zigzagging lights erupted behind her eyelids. The floor rippled and rose up to crash into her an instant before her world went black.

Ridge tried Elena again. Four rings. Five rings. On the sixth ring, the call went to voice mail.

He disconnected and tossed his phone onto the kitchen table without leaving another message. Two were sufficient. A third wouldn't make her return his call any sooner.

Worry ate a hole in his gut. Elena wasn't one to play games. If she'd decided not to meet him, she'd have called or texted and not left him hanging. Same if she'd gotten held up at work, stuck in traffic or had car trouble.

Something was wrong. His instincts rarely led him astray, and right now, they were shouting at him.

"Where are you, Elena?" Anxiety coursed through him. In his next breath, he sent a prayer to God, asking Him to watch over her.

Pacing, he tried to calm himself with a dozen plausible reasons why she wasn't answering. Her phone was on mute. She was on her way and accidentally left her phone at home. Her carrier was experiencing a service problem and calls weren't going through. She'd dropped her phone, breaking it. Her battery had died. The list went on and on.

Ridge didn't relax. If anything, his anxiety escalated to the point he wanted to punch his fist through his newly painted kitchen wall.

He should have suggested she download the same locating app he and his family used, at least while they were investigating his dad's homicide. Why hadn't he?

When his phone rang, he dived for the table and grabbed it, his heart grinding to an agonizing stop when he saw the chief's name and number on the display. His fingers fumbled and refused to cooperate as he attempted to answer.

"Hello. Hello."

"Ridge? Are you all right? You sound out of breath."

"Is Elena with you?"

"No. She left the station a while ago. She said she was going home."

"She's not answering her phone."

"I know," the chief concurred. "I've been trying to reach her. I'd promised to call her with the lab results on the gun and strongbox. I thought maybe you might know where she is." Whatever suspicions the chief harbored about Ridge and Elena's personal relationship, his demeanor revealed no judgment.

"She's supposed to be on her way here." Ridge didn't explain why. "She's late."

"That's not like her."

"Neither is not answering her phone." Ridge resumed pacing. "Can you contact her phone carrier? Have them track her phone?"

"Not usually without a warrant."

"Can you get one?"

"That would take time," the chief explained.

Or was he intentionally stalling? Ridge wished he knew for certain.

"We don't even know that she's missing," the chief continued. "She's only been out of contact for an hour or two. There could be a very rational explanation."

"If there was evidence of foul play, would you get that warrant?"

The chief lowered his voice. "What are you planning, Ridge?"

He was already shoving an arm into his jacket. "I'm on my way to her place. I'll let you know what I find out when I get there."

"You do that."

Ridge hung up. He may not trust the chief, but for now, he had no other choice. Grabbing his keys, he remembered to look up Elena's address in the church directory before bursting through the door like a bull released from the bucking chute.

His truck tires showered dirt and pebbles into the air as he sped away. He mentally calculated the time required to drive from his place to Elena's and any available shortcuts. At every stoplight and every delay, he pounded the steering wheel or squeezed it until his fingers cramped. When her apartment complex came into view, his concern waned. Finally, he was here. Just as quickly, his worry returned when he drove past her parked car beneath the metal canopy.

She was home. So, why wasn't she answering her phone?

Please let her just be mad at me and ignoring my calls. I'll take that any day over her being in trouble.

Ridge pulled into a visitor parking space and jetted from his truck. Evening had fallen by this time. It blanketed Elena's complex in a blue-gray haze dotted by the lighted walkways, exterior door lights and illuminated apartment windows. Except for Elena's. Her apartment was dark and eerily silent.

No, not entirely dark, Ridge noticed as he passed the living room window. A dim light was visible through a narrow slit in the drapes.

He knocked on the door. When she didn't answer, he knocked again. Pressing his ear to the door, he listened. No footsteps. No one calling, "Coming."

"Elena!" he hollered through the door and then pounded on it. Next, he tried the doorknob. Locked. "Elena, it's Ridge. Are you in there?"

A door opened. Not Elena's but rather her neighbor's. A middle-aged woman in workout clothes stepped outside. She paused, clutching a canister in her right hand, probably pepper spray or mace.

"Who are you?" she called, none too friendly.

"I'm Ridge Burnham. I'm a friend of Elena's. I'm worried about her. She was supposed to meet me and didn't show. Have you seen her?"

"About an hour ago." The woman stepped forward. "I was heading to the complex's gym. She was standing there at her door talking to a man."

A man? Ridge's alarm spiked. "Did you recognize him?"

"Never seen him before."

"What did he look like?"

"Just a guy. Thirty-five or forty. I'm not good at telling ages."

"What was he wearing? Did he have any facial hair or distinguishing features?"

"I don't recall any facial hair." The woman became flustered. "I... I think he was wearing a dark jacket and a ball cap."

Ridge fumed. She'd described anyone and everyone.

"I'm pretty sure she's gone," the woman said. "I forgot my key card to the gym at work. I came back here to see if I could borrow Elena's. When I knocked, no one answered."

"Did she leave alone or with the man?"

The woman shook her head, her disconcert-ment increasing. "I just said I left and when I came back, she wasn't here. I had no idea any-thing was wrong. The guy was smiling. She acted like she knew him. They weren't argu-ing or anything."

Ridge moved to the living room window, startling the neighbor who squealed and scooted backward. He pressed his face to the glass and peered through the slip in the drapes. Scanning the apartment's dim interior, he noted nothing out of the ordinary.

Where are you, Elena? What happened to you? God, please. Help me find her.

He saw it, then. A dark rectangular shape. Her purse! It sat on the kitchen counter. Elena wouldn't have left without it. Not willingly. And if her phone was in the purse, that would explain the unanswered calls.

Ignoring the neighbor, he dug his phone out of his pocket and dialed Chief Dempsey, who answered on the second ring.

"Chief. I'm at Elena's apartment. She's not here." He explained the details in a rush.

"I'm going to call the complex manager," the

chief said. "Have them enter the apartment in case she's in there and unconscious."

Something about the situation and the man in the ball cap sat wrong with Ridge. He feared Elena was in serious trouble, and time was wasting.

"Chief, who else knows about the lab test results?"

"Our station secretary, of course. Oscar, maybe. He was here when I told Elena. He's out on a call now."

"Anybody else?"

"Detective Stewart with the Bisbee police."

The detective currently assigned to Ridge's dad's case. "What about Detective Darnelly?"

"Doubtful. He's retired."

"He could still have connections," Ridge countered.

"What are you getting at?"

"I'm just trying to figure out what happened to Elena."

"You wait there," the chief told him. "Let me get off the line and call the apartment manager. Once we establish whether or not Elena is inside, we'll determine our next step."

They disconnected. Ridge glanced around.

The neighbor still stood near her door, watching him warily.

"Aren't there back entrances to these apartments?" he asked.

"Yes. We all have patios."

Ridge was about to go around to the rear of the building when he paused, still bothered by the man who'd visited Elena. "How tall was the guy talking to Elena?"

"Average. Not short. Not as tall as you."

"Thin? Fat?"

"Neither. Maybe a little stocky."

Detective Darnelly was every bit as tall as Ridge. It couldn't have been him. And Oscar sported a large mustache. The neighbor hadn't recalled any facial hair.

"What kind of ball cap was the guy wearing?"

The neighbor thought a moment. "Arizona Cardinals?"

Average height. A little stocky. Jake's favorite football team. The shock nearly felled Ridge.

He spun to face the neighbor. "The manager is on their way to check Elena's apartment. Can you stay and meet them?"

She nodded. "Okay."

He sprinted off, racing to his truck. If the manager found Elena, the chief would phone

Ridge. And while he prayed that was the case, he didn't believe it.

Someone had Elena. That someone was either Jake or a partner in crime. Ridge just had to figure out where they'd taken Elena before something bad happened to her.

Chapter Twelve

The instant Ridge started his truck, he dialed his sister. As he reversed out of the parking space, his Bluetooth kicked in.

Gracie answered with a bright "Hello there, brother."

In the background, the girls were chattering.

"Where's Jake?" Ridge asked without preamble.

"He's at church. There's a men's fellowship meeting."

"When's the last time you spoke with him?"

"Why? What's going on?"

"I need to know, Gracie. Have you talked to him since he left for the meeting?"

She hesitated. Covering the mouthpiece, he heard a muted "Girls, be quiet. Mommy's on the phone with Uncle Ridge. Go play in your room."

There was an indistinguishable verbal objection, but then the noise level diminished.

"He called me about an hour ago. Said the guys had a lot to discuss, and he might be home late." Gracie paused. "To be honest, he sounded a little off."

She had Ridge's full attention. He barely noticed the traffic as he sped out of town and toward the outskirts. "Off how?"

"Stressed. But not like work stressed. It's hard to explain. I didn't pay much attention, my mind was only half on the conversation. The girls have been testing my patience all day."

"I need you to be more specific, Gracie. It's important."

"What's wrong?"

Now it was Ridge's turn to pause. He debated whether he should level with his sister or continue to keep her in the dark.

"Elena's missing," he finally said. "It's possible, but not for certain, that Jake was the last person seen with her."

"Missing? Oh, my gosh. I hope she's all right."

"I need you to tell me everything Jake said to you."

"I already did. Well, other than he told me he loved me. But he says that all the time," she insisted.

Could Ridge be wrong suspecting his brother-in-law of foul play? He had no proof.

"Except…"

His sister's voice yanked him back to their conversation. "Except what?"

"He didn't just say he loved me. He said he's always loved me and the girls and that everything he did was for us. I thought he was talking about his job and volunteering so much at church. I told him I've always loved him, too." Gracie made a soft sound of distress. "You're scaring me, Ridge. Jake would never hurt Elena. He likes her. Besides, he's not that kind of person. He's good and thoughtful and caring."

Ridge had always thought so too, and he wanted to be wrong, if only for his sister's sake.

"Dial him and put us on a three-way call," Ridge instructed. "Let's find out where he is."

"Is that really necessary?" Gracie had become defensive.

Not unexpected. She loved her husband and was loyal to him.

"Please, Gracie. Just ask him if he's talked to Elena or seen her today."

"Fine."

A few seconds later, he heard ringing. She'd added Jake to their call. *Thank You, Lord.* Ridge waited, his jaw clenched.

Five rings later, Jake's voicemail greeting filled the line.

"That means nothing," Gracie said as the greeting played. "He could be busy."

"True."

After the beep, she left a message. "Hi, sweetie. Call me back when you have a second. Love ya. Bye." When she disconnected from Jake, she asked Ridge, "Happy?"

"Who else attends the meeting?" Jake asked.

"What?"

"Doesn't Mr. Harmon go? Call him."

"Ridge."

"I wouldn't ask if it wasn't important."

"Okay, okay."

She did as he requested, including Ridge on the call. They didn't talk for long. Once Mr. Harmon confirmed Jake never showed, they thanked him and said goodbye.

"There could be a very good explanation," Gracie said.

He hated hearing her insecurity, as he was sure she did, too. No one wanted to believe for one second the person they'd loved for years was capable of dastardly deeds.

"Have you checked the location app?"

"Hold on. I will." After a moment she said,

"He's not appearing anymore." Her voice rose. "Ridge, what does that mean?"

"He may have disabled the app."

"Why?"

"I don't know." He wasn't about to admit what was going through his mind. "Call me the instant you hear from him." Ridge pressed his foot down on the gas pedal, accelerating.

"I will. And you call me when *you* hear from Elena."

"Will do." He phoned Chief Dempsey at the next intersection.

"Did Elena contact you yet?" the chief asked.

"No. What about the complex manager? Were they able to get into her apartment?"

"She wasn't there."

"I'm worried, Chief. I spoke to my sister. Jake never showed up at the church meeting he was supposed to attend. And my sister said he sounded a little off when they spoke earlier."

"What are you driving at?"

"I think Jake may have taken Elena."

"Jake? Are you nuts?"

"Have you heard from him recently?" Ridge asked.

"He's off duty."

"Would you try calling? See if he'll answer you?"

The sheriff grumbled but obliged. "Sage," he hollered. "Get ahold of Jake for me. Yes, now. Yeah, I know." An anxiety-filled minute of silence passed while they waited on the station secretary. "Okay, thanks." To Ridge, the chief said, "No answer. Which means nothing, Ridge. He could be out of range."

"Elena's neighbor described the man she saw at Elena's door. He fits Jake's description."

The chief cut him short. "Until I have a good reason to believe otherwise, I'm going to assume Jake's the fine and upstanding deputy and citizen he is and has always been."

Ridge wasn't deterred. "Is he driving his SUV? Can you locate him using the GPS device?"

"That's a stretch, don't you think?"

"What I think," Ridge answered, his jaw tight, "is that shortly after the lab contacts you with the news they found a gold chain in a false bottom of the strongbox, Elena mysteriously disappears without her purse and phone, my sister receives an odd phone call from Jake, who then goes off-grid, and a man matching his description was seen at Elena's door. All of that can't be a coincidence."

He turned onto the road that would take him

to his ranch. He couldn't say why he was driving there, only that it was where his instincts were leading him.

The chief had yet to answer Ridge. Apparently, the man took a long time to consider. Or he had been in on the conspiracy behind Ridge's dad's murder from the beginning and was devising a plan on how to get away without attracting notice.

At last, the chief spoke. "All right. I'll see what I can find out."

Fortunately, no other vehicles were on the road when Ridge's truck momentarily swerved, the result of relief pouring through him. He immediately regained control and straightened the steering wheel.

"Thank you, Chief."

"I'll be in touch." The line went dead.

Ridge drove onto the ranch and parked behind the house. What should he do? Go inside, or maybe head to the barn? Waiting would be excruciating.

Stepping out of the cab, he heard Minnie Pearl braying from her temporary home in the round pen. He realized she must be hungry. Had he forgotten to feed her? Jogging toward the barn, he remembered he *had* fed her. Why the ruckus then?

She trotted back and forth across the pen, her large ears flopping. At the railing, she stopped and brayed again. Something had her riled. Coyotes? A rattler? A trespasser? Donkeys had excellent memories. Had the arsonist returned?

An investigation of the pen yielded nothing. But as he did his instincts, Ridge trusted Minnie Pearl.

Unable to keep still, he continued looking. In the barn, the remaining damage reminded him of the Molotov cocktail and fire. He sat in the metal chair and tried to read the lab report the chief had forwarded him on his phone, but he couldn't concentrate. Twice he started to call his sister, only to change his mind. She'd phone if she heard from Jake.

There was only one thing he could do. Letting his head fall into his hands, he prayed harder than he ever had before.

"Dear Lord. I beg You to keep Elena safe from harm. I shouldn't have put her at risk. Please don't let her pay for my mistakes. And if I've mistakenly believed Jake guilty of wrong-doing, I ask Your forgiveness and his. But if I'm right, and he's involved, please lead me to him so that I can save Elena. She's Your devoted servant, as am I. We need Your protection."

Before he could finish, his phone rang.

"Yeah, Chief. What have you heard?"

"I have a location for Jake's vehicle."

Ridge's chest seized. "Where?"

"I'll be at your place in five minutes. Meet me behind the house. Have your ATV gassed up and ready to go."

"The ATV? Why?"

"Tell me you remember the spot where your dad was killed."

"I do." He'd never forget.

"Good." With that, the chief disconnected.

Pain. It had taken the form of a pickax chipping away at the back of Elena's head. The tiniest movement on her part caused excruciating agony.

She moaned. Her mouth felt dry, and her jaw refused to work properly. Something big was lodged in her throat, and she couldn't swallow. Continued attempts caused her to panic. Forcing herself to relax, she inhaled through her nose until her racing heart slowed enough that she could focus.

Bit by bit, she became aware of her surroundings. A small stone dug into the right side of her face and something sharp—a stick?—jabbed her calf. Nearby, an owl hooted. Concentrating gave recognizable shapes to the inky forms surrounding her. Boulders. A bush. Cacti. She must be lying on the ground. But where?

A shiver ran through her. From shock? Pain? Fear? The cold? All of the above? The sweater she'd chosen earlier in her apartment provided inadequate protection now that night had fallen.

Her apartment. She'd been readying to meet Ridge at the ranch. And then… And then… there'd been a knock on her door. She fought to grab hold of the blurry memory floating on the fringes of her mind.

Jake.

She suddenly remembered a brilliant pain followed by blackness. He…he must have knocked her unconscious and kidnapped her. But why?

Because she and Ridge had gotten too close to the truth. And Jake was somehow involved.

Ignoring her agony, Elena tried to sit up— only to discover her hands were bound behind her back. A scream escaped, muffled by the rag shoved in her mouth and the gag holding it in place.

No! No, no, no! This couldn't be happening. Had Jake dumped her somewhere in the desert or mountains where no one would ever find her to die?

Her stomach clenched. She was going to be sick.

Elena fought against the nausea. If she vomited, she might aspirate and choke to death. Squeezing her eyes shut, she felt tears slide down her cheeks.

Dear Lord. I don't want to die like this. Not alone. Not without saying goodbye and I love you to my family or telling Ridge how I really feel about him. Help me find a way to save myself.

Sit up. She had to sit up and then stand. She tested her legs, ecstatic to find that her ankles weren't bound. Neither was she blindfolded. Once on her feet, she could get her bearings and walk for help. Wherever Jake had left her, there must be a road nearby. He wouldn't have carried her that far. He was strong, but dead weight was heavy and unwieldy.

Gritting her teeth, she ignored the dizziness and fiery jolts crisscrossing through her and tried to sit up.

"Here. Let me help you." Jake materialized above her. His voice held a combination of exaggerated mirth and cruelty.

She froze, terror invading her bones. She'd made a grievous error in judgment. Jake hadn't abandoned her. He'd been right beside her the entire time.

Without any warning, he grabbed her by the arm and jerked her upright.

Streaks of red and blue flashed in front of Elena's eyes. She screamed into the rag as the invisible pickax split her head in two.

"On your feet." Jake unceremoniously hauled her up by the waist.

A wave of dizziness tried to knock her sideways. She had almost no time to steady herself when Jake leaned close and growled in her ear.

"Don't move."

She felt a sharp jab in her ribcage. His gun!

When he reached for her, she averted her head.

"I said, don't move."

Taking hold of the duct tape covering her mouth, he ripped it off in one swift move. Elena gave a yelp and then spat out the rag. Blessed air filled her lungs as she bent forward and succumbed to a coughing fit.

Jake chuckled. "Being a bit dramatic, aren't you?"

A moment later, her fit subsided. When she

could finally talk, she croaked out a one-word question. "Why?"

"I think you know the answer to that. You and my brother-in-law are too nosy for your own good."

"Why are you doing the cartel's dirty work?"

"Ah." He shifted.

Elena began to panic again and fought her restraints. What was he doing? She tried to turn her head to see behind her. The jarring pain from her head injury stopped her.

She felt her hands jerk and heard a ripping sound. The next second, her arms fell to her sides like those of a rag doll. He'd cut the duct tape binding her wrists. Her hands tingled as blood flow resumed.

"Given the choice, I'd have left those and the gag. But my instructions are to make your death look like an accident, though I can't imagine we'll fool anyone. Duct tape leaves residue." He sighed with mock disappointment. "You'll just be another unsolved murder. Like Pete Burnham and the others."

Keep him talking, Elena told herself. *Buy time.* Ridge was expecting her at the ranch. When she didn't show, he'd attempt to reach her and then, God willing, go in search of her. Given the recent danger they'd been in, he'd be worried.

Please, Lord. Send Ridge. Let him find me.

Jake shoved the gun harder into her side. "Start walking."

She stumbled before gaining her balance. "Where are we going?"

"You'll see. It's not far."

They started climbing a rise, Elena in front and Jake behind her, his gun pressed against her back. They were in the hills, but where? Between her head injury and the darkness, she couldn't be sure of their location, but something about the area struck a chord with her. Glancing at the moon, she guessed it to be about seven or eight at night. She scanned the area for headlights. Those she saw were too far in the distance to notice her and Jake, much less come to her rescue. She was on her own.

"When did the cartel recruit you?" she asked. "After you first came to Ironwood Creek?"

"Oh, long before then. I was twenty and serving time for a burglary conviction."

"How did you get to be a deputy sheriff with a felony record?" She stepped carefully, not wanting to trip.

"Come on, Elena. You're smarter than that,"

Jake said. "The cartel gave me a new identity and sent me to police academy. I was their man on the inside from the very beginning." He sighed. "Ah, those were the good old days. Before Sheriff Cochrane was elected and forced us to...retreat. Now, we're just waiting for the next election."

"What happens then?"

"Cochrane won't win."

Jake's breathing became labored the higher they climbed. Elena's, too. They hadn't traveled far, but the grade was steep and the ground uneven.

"You can't know the outcome of the election," Elena said.

"But we can. Sadly, poor Sheriff Cochrane will become the subject of a very embarrassing scandal right before he announces his plan to run for another term. He'll not only decide to drop out of the race, he may even face some very serious charges."

"A real scandal or one your people fabricate?"

"Does it matter? The results will be the same. We'd have done it sooner, but the timing wasn't right. We didn't have our candidate in place."

Elena stubbed her toe on a rock and let out a low "Oomph" as she teetered.

Jake was less quick responding than before. Was he tiring? Could she use that to her advantage? He outweighed her by eighty pounds. But she was nimbler than him and in better shape. She could also outrun him, and the darkness provided cover. At least, she could under normal circumstances. When she hadn't been clobbered on the head.

One thing for sure, she couldn't outrun a bullet, and Jake was a good shot.

They reached the top of the hill. Elena saw the lights of Ironwood Creek in the distance. To her right, more lights dotted the landscape below, marking the location of houses and ranches.

"Keep moving," Jake barked. "A few more feet."

Elena obeyed, fear increasing with every step as coal-black emptiness appeared not five feet in front of her. Cold air rose from the depths to swirl about her and brought with it a message: she wasn't long for this world.

No, no! I'm not ready.

"We're here," Jake announced, huffing and puffing.

Elena started to tremble. Hugging herself did nothing to ease the violent quakes.

"Don't you recognize it?"

She stared as a fresh wave of terror consumed her. She should have known where he was taking her, but her thoughts had been too fragmented to put in any kind of order.

"Come on, Elena." He pushed the gun into her back. "We're at the ledge. The same one I pushed Pete Burnham off."

Her voice quavered when she spoke. "You k-killed him?"

"I didn't want to. I liked him, actually. Pete was a friendly drunk. But I was under orders. He stole money from us. I gave him a chance to come clean. He lied. Claimed he'd give it back. But he didn't. He wasn't very bright."

"You were the man in the barn Ridge saw arguing with his dad."

"I was worried he'd recognize me when we first met. Apparently, the passing years dulled his memory. Plus, I'd cleaned up. A shave. A haircut. He wasn't looking for his dad's killer in the deputy sheriff dating his sister. It was a perfect cover."

Keep him talking. As long as I'm alive, I have a chance.

How far down to the ravine bottom? She tried to remember if she'd read that in the police report. If she jumped, would she survive? She was a dead woman if she continued to stand here.

"You'd have killed Pete even if he returned the money."

"That's true. Burnham sealed his fate the moment he robbed our man. The cartel doesn't tolerate disloyalty."

"The cartel being Marcus Rivera?"

"You are clever, aren't you?"

"Where is he now?"

"He left the country. He'll return after the election."

"The new sheriff may take the same zero tolerance stance on crime and the cartel as Sheriff Cochrane," Elena said.

"Our candidate will have a lot of money behind him. And money is what wins elections."

"Dirty money."

"You're taking this personal," Jake said, weariness in his voice. "It's business."

"Murder is business?"

"Murder is the cost of doing business. You'd come to learn that if you'd been a deputy longer." He shoved the gun barrel into her back. "I'm tired of talking. I need you to turn sideways so it looks less like you were pushed and more like you fell."

An icy spike of fear pierced her heart. This couldn't be the end. She didn't want to die this way.

"I want to say goodbye to my family. Will you let me call them?"

"Oh, good grief. You aren't serious."

"What about Gracie? And your daughters? You're going to kill me and then return to them as if nothing happened? My neighbor saw you. Eventually, they'll figure out it was you."

She sensed a shift in him. "I'll miss Gracie and the girls."

"You're leaving?"

"No choice."

Elena swore she detected regret in his voice. "Why?"

"Marrying Gracie was a way for me to be accepted into the community."

"Except you fell in love with her. And you love your daughters, too."

"Shut up."

"What's going to happen to them after you're gone? No one will believe Gracie's innocent. She could go to jail. Your girls will be raised by someone else. Possibly a stranger."

"I said, shut up." He slapped her on the side of her head with the hand not holding the gun.

Elena cried out as her legs went out from under her. He hooked her by her sweater collar before she fell.

"Let me go, Jake," she said, whimpering. "Let me go, and I won't tell anyone. You can return to Gracie and the girls and your job, and everything will go back the way it was."

He laughed, a sharp, ugly sound. "If I let you go, I'm as good as dead. Rivera will see to that. I'm better off leaving. The cartel will take care of me. Give me another new identity and set me up in a new location. More importantly, they'll protect Gracie and the girls. If I *don't* do my job, their lives will be in danger."

"The cartel would kill a woman and children?"

"You don't understand. Theirs is a multi-billion-dollar business. Everyone is expendable. Including your boyfriend."

Tears blurred Elena's vision. "What will happen to him?"

"You two should have quit when I told you to. You were threatened. You were followed. But you didn't heed the warnings and kept sticking your noses in where they didn't belong. And now look. You're both going to pay with your lives. The next bomb won't miss Ridge by fifteen feet. It will land inches from him. Maybe while he's in bed, asleep."

Elena stifled a desperate sob. "He's Gracie's

brother. The girls' uncle. If you care about her at all, you won't take him from her and your daughters. They'll need him after you've disappeared."

Jake didn't answer immediately. She thought, hoped, prayed she'd gotten through to him. That somewhere, deep down, he wasn't all bad.

"I've heard enough," he grumbled and knocked her in the shoulder. "Turn sideways. Let's get this over with."

"No, Jake. Please. Don't." Her bones dissolved to jelly. She reached out in a helpless gesture, only to drop her arms. Her life, her future, was slipping away. She believed with all her being that heaven waited for her, and she would gladly enter God's kingdom when it was her time.

Am I wrong, Lord, not to want to go yet?

She broke into sobs.

"Enough blubbering."

Jake pushed her the last few feet toward the ledge. Elena sensed the drop-off more than saw it. Shadowy shapes moved in the blackness below as if alive.

Would it hurt when she fell? Would her last earthly memories be of pain and fear?

"See you around, rookie."

Elena squeezed her eyes shut, every muscle in her body tensing in anticipation.

And then a sudden noise filled her ears, one that didn't belong there. One Jake hadn't expected to hear given his reaction.

"Son of a—"

He turned away from her, shoving into Elena as he did. She momentarily teetered on the edge of the precipice before regaining her balance at the last second. Her breath fast and ragged, she dared to look and saw what had angered her captor.

The unexpected sound belonged to an engine, and a pair of headlights coming up the rise straight toward them.

Chapter Thirteen

Every cell in Ridge's body had turned to red-hot fury at the sight of Elena standing at the ledge in the same spot his dad must have fallen and his brother-in-law, a man Ridge had once trusted, about to push her off.

She was alive. Jake hadn't succeeded.

Thank You, Lord, for leading us to her in time.

"Wait here," the chief said and climbed off the back of the ATV.

Wait? Was the man serious?

Brandishing his weapon, the chief approached Jake and Elena.

Ridge was right behind him, disobeying orders. "Elena, are you all right?"

She and Jake stood in the twin beams of the headlights. Fear distorted Elena's features. Anger, Jake's. In the harsh glow, he didn't resemble the man Ridge had known all these years.

A memory tugged. The barn. His dad and the stranger.

"Step away from her," the chief ordered, "and drop your gun."

Jake stared directly at Ridge, ignoring the chief. "You always were a smart one. That's why you did so well rodeoing. You had good sense when it came to assessing the bulls and your competition. And now, it seems, you figured me out."

Ridge saw it then. The resemblance to the stranger in the barn who'd argued with his dad hours before his death. How could he have missed it? If he'd noticed, they wouldn't be here now, and his sister wouldn't have married a cartel operative.

"I'm taking you in, Jake," the chief said.

"We'll see about that."

Jake spun and reached for Elena. She shrieked as he pulled her roughly against him, using her as a shield. His gun moved from her side to her head, and she froze, not daring to move.

Ridge didn't realize he'd taken a step forward until the chief growled, "Stay put, Ridge. Don't make things worse."

It required every ounce of his willpower to

grind to a halt. "Elena," he called out, his voice choked. "Are you all right?"

She nodded shakily. She was anything but all right. A man with no regard for human life held her hostage.

"Be reasonable, Jake," the chief said with remarkable calm. "You won't get far."

"I don't have to." He sneered at the chief. "There's a pickup point less than two miles from here. The ATV should get us there no problem."

"Us?" Ridge demanded.

"Can't leave my insurance policy behind now, can I?" He lifted one shoulder in a casual shrug. "If you and the chief agree to cooperate, I'll leave the two of you here tied up. I'm pretty sure you have some rope in that storage case on the ATV. Someone will find you in a day or two."

Ridge's fists clenched at his sides. "What about Elena?"

"There's collateral damage in every negotiation."

A vile taste filled Ridge's mouth. How could he have treated Jake like family? Considered him a friend? Spoken highly of him? How could this monster hold his daughters in his lap, profess to love them, and all the while be plotting how to execute his next crime or kill his next victim?

"Leave her with us," Ridge said, his heart being ripped from his chest. He'd yet to tell Elena his true feelings for her or describe the bright, happy future they could have together. What if he never got the chance? "You don't need her."

"But I do," Jake insisted.

"This is your last chance, Jake," the chief reasoned. "If you let her go, there's a possibility things will go a little easier on you."

"Easier on me?" He laughed only to abruptly stop at the distant sound of an approaching siren. Anger morphed into the first signs of panic as reality sank in.

"You didn't think we came alone?" the chief asked. "Oh. You did. That's on you. All these years of us working together, you have to know I'm better at my job than that."

Just as Ridge wondered how he could have been fooled by Jake for all these years, he wondered why his instincts hadn't told him to trust Chief Dempsey.

Jake glanced around, his expression wild and his brow shining with sweat in the glow of the headlights. "This does change things." He craned his neck and peered over the ledge, all the while holding the gun to Elena's head.

Fright widened her eyes, and she visibly trembled, no doubt due to Jake's growing agitation and recklessness. He was cornered with nowhere to go. Ridge didn't believe the man would give up easily.

"Don't be a fool, Jake," the chief warned. "You won't get away with this."

"We'll see about that."

"What about Gracie and the girls?" Ridge made a desperate attempt to reason with the man. "They'd want you to surrender. At the least, they'd want you to release Elena."

Jake hesitated, but only for a moment. Whatever evil had a hold of him refused to let go.

"I'm going to walk away." He shuffled a step to the side. "And I'm taking Elena with me. If you come after us, she dies."

"I won't let you," the chief said. "I'll shoot first."

"You won't risk hitting Elena."

By then, the vehicle had arrived, its loud siren piercing the night air. The occupant—Oscar?—wouldn't be able to make it up the hill. The rugged trail barely accommodated the ATV. He would have to park at the bottom and travel the remaining distance on foot, giving Jake a five- or ten-minute head start.

"Tell Gracie I'm sorry," he said and began backing away, dragging Elena with him.

"No," she cried out, resisting.

God, don't let him take her, Ridge silently begged.

The next moment, the recognizable *thump-thump* of helicopter blades sounded, growing closer with each passing second. As the copter neared, a giant beam of light shot down from its underside. It cut a zigzag path through the brush and cacti until it found Jake and Elena. There, the helicopter hovered in the sky above them, shining its beam directly on them.

Ridge looked up and read the writing on the helicopter's side. Bisbee had sent a medical rescue team.

Jake squinted, blinded by the bright light. His hand holding the gun wavered as the gravity of the situation played across his features. And then, desperation filled his eyes.

Panic consumed Ridge. The situation had become desperate. There was no telling what his brother-in-law would do.

The chief took aim.

"Elena," Ridge hollered.

Her gaze met his across the distance separating them. He didn't know if she could see his face so he moved into the ATV's headlights.

"You can do this," he told her, hoping and praying she understood his meaning. "You can get away."

All at once, her expression changed to one of calm determination. And then, she elbowed Jake viciously in the stomach. With the swiftness of someone trained in self-defense, she twisted and threw herself to the ground where she rolled out of the way.

Jake spun and leveled his weapon at the chief.

A shot rang out, echoing in Ridge's ears.

"Elena!"

He dove toward her just as Jake dropped his gun and staggered backward, a dark circle appearing in the center of his jacket.

Complete chaos erupted. Deafening sounds and frenzied actions all occurring at once. The helicopter. Shouting. Lights. The sledgehammer inside Ridge's chest slamming into his ribs.

"Stay back!" the chief yelled.

He heard the other man as if from a distance. Reaching Elena, he dropped to his knees and scooped her into his arms. "Elena! Sweetheart. Are you all right?"

"I'm fine." Her voice shook, and her limbs trembled. "I'm fine."

"Thank God."

"What about Jake?"

Ridge looked up just as Jake, his expression crazed, hurled himself over the side of the ledge. Squeezing his eyes shut, Ridge pulled Elena closer and said a silent prayer for his sister and nieces.

Shouting preceded the arrival of Oscar, who'd parked at the bottom of the hill. The beam from the helicopter swept the ravine. Voices clamored in the background: the chief on his radio, Oscar on his, and a woman barking commands from the helicopter's loudspeaker.

Flashlights appeared, their beams racing across the ground as Oscar and the chief hurried to the ledge. Then, the beams disappeared over the edge.

"Can you spot him?" the chief hollered.

"Down there," Oscar said. "To the right."

"Is he alive?"

"Hard to tell from this distance... I think I see him moving."

The chief was back on his radio, updating someone on the situation. Overhead, the helicopter circled, aiming its light into the ravine. In the open side door, a figure stood attaching a harness. They were preparing to drop the rescue worker into the ravine.

"Can you stand?" Ridge asked Elena.

"Yes."

He helped her to her feet. She wobbled, and he tightened his hold around her waist.

Emotion filled his chest to bursting. "I... I don't... I don't know what I'd have done if anything happened to you."

"I'm okay." She clung to him.

"Are you sure?"

"Nothing a little aspirin won't remedy. He knocked me in the head."

"Let me take you to the hospital."

"That's not necessary."

"Elena, you need to be examined by a doctor."

"I'm not going anywhere until Jake's b—" She swallowed. "Until Jake is brought out." She buried her face in Ridge's jacket, a soft sob escaping. "I thought of you. When Jake had me. About what we might have had together. There were so many things I wished I'd told you."

"Shh." He enveloped her in his embrace and rested his chin on her head. "We have our whole lives ahead of us and all the time to say whatever we want."

She lifted her gaze to his. "I'm glad to hear you say that. I…care for you, Ridge. More than I believed possible."

The emotion building inside him burst free. "Good. Because I care for you, too. And if you give me half a chance, I could fall head over heels in love."

"Oh, Ridge. I feel the same—"

His lips on hers prevented her from finishing. Joy and relief and gratitude mingled and lifted their spirits higher still. Elena had survived the ordeal. She was safe in his arms. She'd admitted to returning his feelings.

Whatever challenges lay ahead, and there would be many, they would overcome them together. Ridge believed it with every fiber of his being.

"Come on." He tugged Elena away from the ledge. "You're still shaking."

He made her sit on the ATV while they watched the rescue team workers retrieve Jake. After the medic had been lowered into the ravine, a basket was sent down. The sound of the helicopter blades combined with the chief on his radio and Oscar yelling over the side of the ledge to create a frantic cacophony.

Everything moved at high speed while at the

same time seemed to take forever. At last, the basket appeared, rising from the ravine like an anchor being pulled from the ocean's depths. The basket spun in a slow circle, propelled by the wind generated from the helicopter blades.

As they watched, the basket disappeared inside the helicopter, pulled in by a crew member. The line was dropped again, and the medic retrieved. And then, the helicopter retreated from the area, executed a half-circle turn and flew off.

It was over. Their ordeal had ended.

"Elena?" Chief Dempsey materialized before her and Ridge. "How you doing?"

"I'm all right, Chief." As if to prove her point, she slid off the ATV. "What about Jake? Is he alive?"

"For the moment. What happens next is in the Lord's hands."

The chief's expression displayed only a slight change. Ridge knew the man well enough to recognize his internal struggle. He hadn't wanted to shoot Jake and had only done it to save a life. He'd be grappling with the consequences for the rest of his.

"Part of me still doesn't believe it," Elena said. "Jake was behind everything. The texts. The car tailing us. Probably whatever that thing was that flew past my back patio."

Ridge understood her disbelief. He couldn't imagine his sister and nieces' anguish when they learned what happened. He vowed in that moment to be there for them, whatever they needed.

"Chief," he said. "Will you be the one telling Gracie?"

"Yes. I'm heading there shortly."

"I'd like to come with you."

"I was hoping you'd say that. Tomorrow, whenever you're up to it, we'll need to see you at the station to take your statement. I'm sure the Bisbee police will want to talk to you, too. They're on their way to the hospital. I'll meet them there after I've spoken to Gracie." The chief exhaled a long breath. "I think a lot of people are going to be happy to put this case to rest."

"Jake killed Pete Burnham," Elena said. She took Ridge's hand in hers, her expression filled with sorrow. "He told me everything. He's led a double life all these years."

"I'm looking forward to hearing all about that," the chief answered.

"Me, too," Ridge said.

Elena moved closer. "Would you like me to be there when you tell Gracie? To answer any questions she may have?"

Ridge squeezed her fingers, letting her know how much her sympathy and support meant to him. "Thank you, but I think the fewer people the better. Later, she may have questions for you."

"All right." Elena nodded and turned to her boss. "I'll meet you back at the station, Chief."

"You'll do no such thing." He leveled a finger at her. "You're going to the hospital."

"I'm not hurt."

"Don't play tough, Elena. Ridge told me you took a blow to the head. My guess is you have a concussion." The chief hitched his chin at Oscar, who'd been taking notes and photos with his phone. "Oscar will drive you. That's an order," he said before she could protest.

Oscar. Another person, mused Ridge, who they'd suspected and was innocent.

But was Olivia Gifford? Ridge would tell what he knew about her to the chief and the Bisbee police.

"I'll report first thing tomorrow," Elena said.

The chief shook his head. "You're on leave until admin's cleared you."

"Chief."

"Jake almost killed you. That's no small thing. You'll need counseling, even if you think you don't. You can come to the station tomorrow to give your statement and, like Ridge, talk to the Bisbee police. Not to report for duty."

"Yes, sir."

The older man reached out and clasped her shoulder. "You handled yourself well. Kept your head about you even when the situation got dicey. I'm proud of you. Your father will be, too. You have what it takes to be an excellent deputy sheriff and to go far. I mean it when I say I hope you'll stay in Ironwood Creek."

"Thank you." Elena's words came out choked.

He nodded before leaving them to join Oscar.

Ridge let go of her hand in order to put an arm around her. "I'm proud of you, too."

They didn't have much time alone before Oscar joined them. "Chief says I'm to drive you to the hospital. Can you walk? I'm parked about a half mile down the hill. I couldn't make it any further."

"Take the ATV," Ridge said before Elena

could answer. "Leave it parked at the bottom. The chief and I will walk down."

"Gotcha." Oscar gave a thumbs-up. "Ready, partner?"

"Give us a minute, will you?"

"Sure." The deputy sheriff's smile said he liked the idea of her and Ridge together.

Ridge liked it, too.

When there were just the two of them, he said, "I can meet you at the hospital later. After the chief and I have broken the news to my sister. I'll give you a ride home."

"She and your nieces are going to need you. I'll be all right. You stay with them."

"She may want to go to the hospital. To see Jake. Whatever he's done, they were married for a lot of years, and she loves him."

"I would want to be there if I were her."

"You would?"

"To make peace with myself if nothing else. Emotions are bound to be complicated at a time like this."

"Complicated is an understatement," Ridge said. "I think I'll call my mom on the way to Gracie's house. She'll probably want to stay with Gracie and the girls for a bit."

"That's a good idea. I'm sure Gracie will appreciate it." She hesitated, searching his face. "Your emotions must also be complicated. Jake is your brother-in-law."

Ridge attempted a smile. "Maybe all of us can get a group discount with the therapist."

"You joke, but that's not the worst idea." Elena closed her eyes and sighed. "I'll pray for Gracie and the girls."

"Thank you. They can use all the prayers they can get." Ridge took both of Elena's hands in his and pressed them to his chest, right over his heart. "Speaking of prayers, God answered mine when He saved you."

"Mine, too."

"He brought us together for a reason. I don't want to deny ourselves the opportunity to explore that reason."

She found his hand and squeezed his fingers. "Nor do I."

He drew her close for a kiss, not caring that the chief and Oscar stood twenty-five feet away. He'd almost lost this woman who, he believed with absolute certainty, was the one he'd been searching for his entire life.

"I'll call you as soon as I can," he said, releasing her.

Her answer was to cradle his cheek with her

palm as she looked at him with the care and devotion Ridge was certain mirrored the light shining in his eyes.

The once-noisy night fell quiet around them. Tomorrow would bring a new day and the start of their life together.

Oscar came over. "You ready?"

"Yeah." Elena kissed Ridge briefly on the lips once more before climbing on the ATV.

Seeing her with the other deputy, a memory suddenly returned to Ridge, giving him cause for concern. "Hey, Oscar. Wait a sec," he said.

"What's up?"

"Why were you acting so strange that night you drove up on us behind the bank?"

"You kidding?" The deputy grinned, first at Ridge then Elena. "I was making sure she was all right. We deputies look out for each other. And the fact was, you looked pretty suspicious."

Ridge supposed he had. A moment later, he and the chief watched the two deputies disappear down the hill.

"Quite a night," the chief commented.

"Quite."

"You take care of her, Ridge. If you don't, you're going to have the entire Cochise County Sheriff's Department after you."

"You have nothing to worry about. I haven't told her yet, but I'm going to marry her one day."

The chief squeezed Ridge's shoulder, and the two of them started walking. "Glad to hear that, son. Real glad."

Epilogue

Six Weeks Later

Elena knelt on the ground beside Ridge. The two of them patted the earth at the base of a cluster of gold poppies they'd planted beside the well house. The flowers grew in abundance in Ironwood Creek and around the Burnham ranch. Ridge had dug up this particular cluster and transplanted them to the spot beside the well house where he'd found the gun and the strongbox.

"Before Minnie Pearl eats every wildflower on the property," he'd said earlier while digging up the flowers from behind the barn. Followed by, "Dad always liked these. Called them butterscotch blossoms."

Elena had helped Ridge construct the private memorial to his father, along with several members of Hillside Church. She recruited Mr. Harmon, who, it turned out, was a talented artist, to paint a mural on the side of the well house. He recreated the same hill where Pete Burnham had lost his life. Only rather than depicting a dark scene, the sun's rays stretched down from a vivid blue sky to bathe a soaring dove in golden light. On the ground below, three tiny, indistinguishable figures watched, their gazes raised. Elena liked to believe the figures represented Ridge, Gracie and their mom.

The image evoked feelings of love and wonder and peace. She decided Pete Burnham would have approved, if only because it gave his family comfort. Ridge especially.

He leaned back to inspect their work. "What do you think?"

"They look great." Elena touched a delicate blossom and then placed her hand on his.

Affectionate gestures between them came naturally, as if they'd been together for years instead of weeks. Conversation, too. She was able to open up to Ridge like no one else before. They'd spent hours talking and getting to know each other. And just when she thought she might have learned everything about him, he surprised her with something new. She hoped it would be like that always for them.

Best of all, perhaps, her family adored him. After two visits, they already considered him an honorary Tomes. Elena's mom now had someone new to fuss over and feed, and her dad admired Ridge's impressive rodeo career and cattle ranching ambitions. Her siblings simply thought he was cool.

He pushed to his feet and helped her to hers.

From behind them came Gracie's voice. "Here you go."

Both Elena and Ridge turned to face his sister and mother. They'd come for this unofficial service. Gracie had brought an intricate wooden cross she'd purchased from a craftsman in Bisbee.

"Dad would like this," Ridge said and accepted the cross from her. Then, using a rubber mallet, he drove the cross into the ground, right in the center of the flowers.

Elena watched him from her place on Gracie's right. On Gracie's left stood Ridge's mom, clasping Gracie's hand in hers.

Ridge's sister needed a lot of support these days. She'd taken the news of her husband's double life and criminal history as hard as might be expected and was still struggling. Jake had survived his injuries, though it had been touch and go for days. He was currently residing in jail and awaiting his trial, having been denied bail. The prosecutor had convinced the judge that, because of his connection to the cartel, Jake was considered a flight risk.

So not only did Gracie have to contend with all that, she had to explain to her two young daughters why their daddy wasn't ever coming home again. Eventually, when they were older, she'd have to tell them what he'd done.

Elena felt nothing but sympathy and compassion for Gracie and would do whatever she could to help the woman navigate the drastic changes in her life. While Elena had initially resisted the mandatory therapy, she'd come to appreciate her sessions and seen the value. Hopefully, the support group Gracie had joined, as well as the counselor she was taking the girls to once a week, would help them, too. Ridge seemed to think so.

For now, his mother was driving from Bisbee every weekend to stay with her daughter and grandchildren. Ridge babysat them one day during the week, enabling Gracie to attend appointments with her various attorneys and financial advisor. It turned out that Jake Peterson didn't exist. That had been an identity created for him by the cartel. Which left a lot of legal issues that needed resolving, including a set of paternal grandparents Gracie hadn't realized existed and who lived in Wisconsin.

Her top priority, however, was seeing that she and her daughters had a roof over their heads and a steady source of income. Ridge had dipped into his savings and paid the first installment toward buying out her half of the ranch. More payments would follow quarterly. Additionally, they'd hired a lawyer, and their claim on the forty thousand dollars was expected to be approved in the near future. Gracie had enough to get by on until she found a job.

Gracie hadn't seen Jake since his release from the hospital. She'd yet to decide if she'd attend the trial. As that was months away, she had plenty of time to consider it. And for all anyone knew, there might not be a trial. Jake had been offered a reduced sentence in exchange for information. His lawyer was negotiating with the prosecutor.

Olivia Gifford and her family had left town. The police had questioned her extensively, learning nothing significant. Rumors abounded, however. Elena had her own suspicions.

She thought perhaps Olivia had taken a bribe

from her former boss, the late mayor who was in cahoots with the cartel, in exchange for her silence regarding what she'd witnessed. That would explain her coming into money. And now that Pete Burnham's homicide had been solved, she feared retribution from the cartel and fled the area. Had she kept her mouth shut and not gotten caught up in the thrill of solving a crime like the murder mystery podcasts she liked to listen to, she might not have had to fear for her and her family's safety.

Initially, after Jake kidnapped and attempted to murder Elena, the townspeople had panicked. What if the cartel returned in full force? Clearly, they'd never really retreated. Ironwood Creek could once again become a hub for drug trafficking.

Sheriff Cochrane, whose popularity had risen in the polls since Jake's arrest and the solving of Pete Burnham's homicide, had personally visited Ironwood Creek two weeks ago and assured its citizens in a televised press conference that his crack-down-on-crime program would not only continue, but had received additional funding— a portion of which was designated to securing the area surrounding the town.

Elena had thought his press conference

sounded a little like a vote-for-me-in-the-next-election speech. But, all in all, he was a good sheriff and committed to protecting her new hometown.

"That looks nice," Ridge's mom said when he'd finished with the cross, her smile melancholy. "You'll need to build a little fence to keep that donkey of yours out."

"You're probably right."

He surveyed his handiwork. The cross rose a foot above the blooming flowers, the effect lovely. Elena was certain that Ridge and his family would visit this spot often to reflect and find comfort.

He joined Elena, his sister and his mom. They stood together, holding on to each other and contemplating the memorial.

"I'd like to say a few words about Dad," Ridge said and recounted a favorite story of Pete Burnham taking him prospecting.

His mom and then Gracie followed with their own stories. All positive. Pete had his faults, everyone there knew it, but this wasn't the time to dwell on them. They were here to celebrate the good the man had done in his life, most of which was fathering and raising two fine children. Lastly, Ridge led them in a prayer.

"Dear Lord. Thank You for Your many blessings, among them finally giving us the answers to Dad's final days and what happened. With that knowledge, we can all move on and truly forgive Dad. He was wrong to steal and wrong to believe the end justified the means. But at the core, he was a good man. A kind man. A caring man. True, he didn't always make the best decisions, and it cost him his life. We hope, in Your abundant mercy, You have forgiven him, too, and welcomed him into Your heavenly kingdom. We ask that You stay by our sides as we move ahead in our lives after Jake's betrayal. We rely on Your guidance and Your love. Today and every day. Amen."

A chorus of amens followed.

It was, Elena thought, a fine and fitting memorial.

"We should get going." Ridge's mom glanced at her watch. "When do you have to be there?"

"Four o'clock," Elena said. She was receiving a commendation today in a ceremony at Ironwood Creek town hall. She felt she'd just been doing her job, but the chief insisted she'd gone above and beyond and deserved recognition. "And I need to go home and change first."

They all four started down the rise. At the

house, Elena hugged Gracie and Ridge's mom, confirming they would see one another in a couple hours.

"How's the new deputy doing?" Ridge asked at her car.

"He's all right." She laughed. "The best part is I don't have to patrol the pecan orchard anymore."

"Does that mean you're going to apply for sergeant deputy when Oscar retires in a couple of years?"

The senior deputy had been given the position after Jake's arrest.

"Absolutely." Elena sent Ridge a questioning look. "You won't have a problem with that, will you?"

"Not at all. I rather like the idea of being married to a career law enforcement officer."

"Married!"

"Not for a while." He lowered his lips to her for a warm kiss. "Just letting you know that's on the table for someday."

"I'm glad. I love you, Ridge."

"I love you, too."

Any doubts Elena once had about balancing a career and a husband and children had vanished, chased away by the strength of Ridge's feelings for her. Turned out, she'd just needed to meet the right man.

Thanks to God's many blessings, she had. The past was behind them, and a long life filled with happiness and promise awaited. She need only gaze into Ridge's handsome face to know he was on this journey with her every step of the way.

Texas Revenge Target
Jill Elizabeth Nelson

MILLS & BOON

Jill Elizabeth Nelson writes what she likes to read—faith-based tales of adventure seasoned with romance. Parts of the year find her and her husband on the international mission field. Other parts find them at home in rural Minnesota, surrounded by the woods and prairie and their four grown children and young grandchildren. More about Jill and her books can be found at jillelizabethnelson.com or Facebook.com/jillelizabethnelson.author.

From the end of the earth will I cry unto thee,
when my heart is overwhelmed:
lead me to the rock that is higher than I.
—*Psalm* 61:2

DEDICATION

To those who bravely battle forces attacking their lives (addiction, illness, relationship problems, financial woes, ad infinutum), who daily lean on the Everlasting Rock.

Chapter One

Texas Ranger Brianna Maguire—Bree, if a person wanted to stay on her good side—leaned back in the saddle as she guided her palomino gelding, Teton, down the semisteep grade of a dry wash. Her stomach roiled, but not because she doubted Teton's surefootedness. Images of the too recent shootout between law enforcement and a violent gang of cattle rustlers kept intruding on her concentration and freezing the breath in her lungs.

Had that life-altering event happened a mere thirty-six hours ago? An eternity had passed and yet only a moment since she'd shot a crook, but not in time to prevent her Special Response Team colleague, Will Stout, from taking a fatal bullet. If only she'd been a split second faster, Will might be alive, and his two young children might still have a daddy. But it was the rustler who had survived, though he'd likely spend the rest of his life behind bars and in a wheelchair. If any satisfaction existed in that knowledge, it tasted bitter.

Chipped rock and pebbles disturbed by Teton's big hooves skittered ahead of them into the ravine's mesquite-tufted floor. Saddle leather creaked, the gelding snorted, and Bree began a soft, encouraging patter with her voice. Odors of desert plants and dust teased her nostrils, and she swallowed a sneeze as Teton brought her to the bottom of the gash carved in the terrain by flash floods over time immemorial. Her pulse rate spiked at another splotch of red glistening on a rock. She followed the telltale mark to the right, deeper into this fold in the tableland.

The midmorning sun beat down on Bree's shoulders and she swiped the arm of her long-sleeved shirt across her forehead beneath the brim of her Stetson hat. Late summer's intense heat baked West Texas's arid Llano Estacado prairie, and she couldn't allow sweat to dim her vision. If the sporadic blood droplets she was following came from a human being, she could be on the trail of Leon Waring, the fugitive leader of the cattle rustlers.

In the violent shootout between a joint law enforcement task force and his rustler gang near the town of Levelland, Waring had been wounded. The gun battle had left several dead, including Will, as well as numerous injured, on both sides. Of the criminal gang, Waring and one or two low-level desperados had escaped. A statewide manhunt was underway for Waring, in particular—a manhunt that she was no longer officially a part of due to being placed on leave after shooting someone in the line of duty. Leave was standard procedure, and Bree had no doubt the review of her actions would shortly result in restoration to active service, but she had no intention of sitting out the hunt for Waring.

She was the only one who seemed to think the fugitive, escaping cross-country into the night on an ATV, had headed into the Llano to hide. Everyone else was looking east, where larger towns and cities would afford medical care and a place to hide for a wounded crook. But Waring was born and bred on the Llano, and if his wound wasn't too bad, this was where he'd go. And Bree was just the person to hunt him down. The Llano was her childhood back-yard, too.

So, like any other sensible veteran of law en-forcement, she'd taken advantage of the un-expected leave to go home. But when she'd reached the familiar comfort of the Double-Bar-M, the ranch she co-owned with her brother, she'd saddled up Teton and headed out. Apprehending Waring was a personal mission, even though finding a trace of him in the vast rugged country wasn't likely. She simply needed to feel like she was doing something productive.

Bree had not located the crook's ATV or even ATV tracks, but then the sudden appearance of blood droplets had given her renewed but guarded hope. The blood trail could well come from an animal, and one of God's creatures might need to be mercifully put down. If so, she'd have to deal with the frustration of not locating the violent crook. Too bad the terrain made sneaking up on whatever lay ahead nearly impossible.

Her horse's shod hooves clicked sporadically against scattered stones. As the wash deepened into a canyon strewn with boulders and dark crevices, Bree kept her head on a swivel and her ears perked for any indication of an ambush. Sounds foreign to the natural environment reached her ears and Bree tugged Teton to a halt. The animal stood still, head high, ears aimed forward toward a bend in the canyon. Clearly, the gelding heard the murmur, too.

Human voices?

Bree swung her leg off the saddle and lowered herself to stand beside her horse. She dropped the ends of the reins to the earth. Teton was trained to remain in place when his reins were grounded by his rider. With one hand, Bree pulled her rifle from the saddle holster and unsnapped the sidearm at her belt with the other. She might be happening upon an innocent situation, like cowhands out looking for strays, but she wasn't about to discount potential danger. Not with a desperate criminal at large and the blood trail that had led her here.

Carefully placing her booted feet to avoid loose rocks or brittle vegetation, Bree made her way toward the bend in the canyon. When she reached the curve, she halted and squatted behind a boulder. Slowly, she peered out from behind cover and bottled a gasp.

She'd been right to believe the notorious rustler had fled to the Llano. His burly form leaned up against the cliff wall. A bloody arm hung limply at his side, but the other arm pointed a pistol at a man who stood with his back to her but trained a rifle in the rustler's direction. Apparently, Bree had been mistaken that she was the only one pursuing Waring into the wilderness. Then again, this could be a random encounter between the fugitive and a local hand. The guy was dressed like a rancher in faded and dusty denim pants, a long-sleeved checked shirt, and a sweat-stained cowboy hat. However, with only the broad back of the rifleman to go on, she couldn't claim to recognize the person engaged in the standoff with the wounded rustler.

"I'm more willing to shoot than you are," Waring snarled, a manic glint in his inky eyes. The sheen of sweat coating his scruffy face glistened in the sun. "I'll blast you before you pull the trigger. Now, drop that weapon and get out of here before I put you down."

Bree opened her mouth to warn the guy not to believe Waring would allow him to leave.

"This rifle's got a hair trigger." The man's words emerged, steady as the rock she hid behind. "If you shoot me, it'll go off, and we'll both be buzzard food."

Bree didn't recognize the deep voice. Who *was* this stranger and how had he ended up confidently facing off with a fugitive?

"Now, put your gun down," the man went on, "and I'll do the same. Then I'll treat your wound. You're not looking so well, buddy."

The crook's face crinkled in a snarl and his body tensed, preparing for action.

"Drop it, Waring!" Bree stood tall and stepped forward, rifle at the ready. "If this guy doesn't shoot you, I will."

The fugitive's fevered gaze swiveled toward her, along with the barrel of his gun. As the direction of the rustler's weapon shifted, the rifle in the stranger's grip blasted. Waring's pistol flew from his hand. The crook doubled over and sank to the ground, clutching both arms to his chest. Even if the stranger's bullet had struck only Waring's gun, the impact would have hurt—maybe even broken a bone in the fugitive's gun hand.

The stranger turned his head to Bree and his smoke-gray eyes met her green ones. Nope, this guy was not among her law enforcement colleagues, nor was he a local rancher. She knew all the owners and ranch hands in this area. If she'd ever met this man before, she would have remembered him—not only for his rugged good looks, but from the faint but distinctive scar that arched a one-sided parenthesis from the corner of his left eye almost to his ear and then nearly to the edge of his firm mouth. Whoever he was, the squint lines around his eyes labeled him a long-time outdoorsman, and the traces of silver at the temples of his short sable-brown hair suggested an age only slightly greater than her own forty-three years.

Now, for the big question—was he friend or foe? The guy had shot the weapon out of Leon Waring's hand, swift and accurate as a striking rattler.

Bree kept her rifle at the ready. "Texas Ranger Bree Maguire. And you are?"

Tension drained from the stranger's face and he lowered his weapon. "Cameron Wolfe. You must be Dillon Maguire's sister. He's told me about you." The edges of the man's lips tilted upward in a slight smile.

Bree's gut clenched. Why would this guy know Dillon and what had been said?

The man's smile turned to a grin. "Relax. I'm your new neighbor. I bought the Franklin place."

Bree huffed. She'd known the Franklin heirs were selling out after the death of their father because none of them had any interest in ranching, but Dillon had failed to tell her the place had sold. However, to be fair, she had pretty much blown onto the ranch site and blown right out again on Teton without saying much more than *Hi* and *Be back later* to her brother. Dillon would have tried to talk her out of traipsing the Llano on her own, but the bloody shootout near Levelland had disturbed her on levels she hadn't come to terms with yet, and she'd needed to be alone. Finding Waring's trail was a happy result that she now had to conclude properly.

"Pleased to meet you, neighbor, but I have to secure this prisoner." Reaching for the zip ties she kept in a pouch on her belt, Bree lowered her rifle and stepped past Cameron's tall, sturdy figure. "This man is a wanted cattle rustler and murderer."

A crumpled, bleeding mess, Waring glared up at her as she approached. "I got mean friends with a long reach." His voice came out a breathy snarl. "You won't keep hold of me. They'll kill you."

Ignoring the threats, Bree leaned toward the fugitive. "Leon Waring, I'm arresting you on suspicion of—"

A sharp tug on the ponytail that hung down her back coincided with a rifle blast echoing through the canyon. In her peripheral vision, strands of flame-red hair floated free of her head as time seemed to slow to a crawl. The fugitive's eyes went wide, fixed on her. The rifle in Bree's hand suddenly weighed a ton, dragging against her arms as she forced it up to her shoulder. She began to whirl on the rancher, who must have shot at her, every movement constrained as if by quicksand.

Then a heavy body slammed into her, thrusting her into a crevice in the rock face, and time snapped back into sync. Bree fought, kicking and attempting to head-butt her traitorous neighbor. Her rifle was out of play, crushed between their struggling bodies. Together, they struck the unforgiving stone wall and the shade of the crevice enveloped them.

"Stop fighting," Cameron's voice rasped in her ear. "It wasn't me. Someone's shooting from above."

Bree went still, the sense of his words penetrating her fierce resistance. Every detail of her surroundings etched upon her consciousness—the throbbing of her pulse in her ears, the groaning of the wounded crook on the other side of the crevice, the chill of the rock at her back, and the lingering odor of gun smoke overlaid by the buttery-leather aftershave her neighbor wore.

Pregnant silence fell. Bree's heart hammered in her chest.

Then another sharp report quickly followed

by a third sent shards of rock ricocheting into their meager hide. Most peppered the stone face around them, but one stung Bree's cheek, sending a warm trickle down her face. By her neighbor's sudden grunt, one or more bits of shrapnel must have hit him also.

At best, the sniper above could hold them in the crevice until his ammo ran out. Then they could break cover and go after him. At worst, if this was one of Waring's alleged friends, the fugitive could overcome his wounds and recover his gun. Then she and her new neighbor would be at the ruthless criminal's mercy.

Cam breathed in the earthy scent of horse mixed with a pleasant fresh-rain shampoo the woman used. Her height—approximately five and a half feet if he had to estimate—put the top of her head just under his nose. The crevice in the canyon wall was not nearly big enough for two adults, even if one of them was a slender female. If the gunman above got the right angle for his shot, he could bounce a bullet off the rock right into one of them. Then there was the wounded desperado the redheaded ranger had attempted to arrest. He might recover enough to attack them as well. They couldn't stay where they were in the hope of survival, yet he had no safe exit strategies in mind.

But when had "safe" ever been a part of his life?

"I'm going to duck and roll toward that boulder a few feet from us. Cover me while I do that. From there, I may be able to spot the shooter and put him out of commission."

"Right." Bree jerked a nod. "I'll keep the attacker busy dodging bullets."

Cam grinned, meeting the ranger's steady gaze. She was no-nonsense. No argument. The ranger knew what needed to be done and was ready to do it—an attitude he immensely appreciated. People who ran rather than stood had once cost him everything worthwhile in his life—except faith in God, and sometimes he barely clung to that. Firming his jaw, he batted away the swarming memories and stuffed the pain back down into the black hole where it belonged. Now was not the time to wallow. If ever he permitted that time to come.

With no further thought or discussion, Cam dropped and rolled out of cover. A bullet slapped the rock face above him, but a cacophony of fire from Bree halted the attack. Since she couldn't see the assailant, she might not be sending bullets anywhere near him, but only an idiot would put his head up under that firestorm.

Cam reached the boulder and crouched behind it. He readied his rifle and ventured a peek past the cover of the rock toward the cliff top about fifteen feet up. The ranger's firing ceased and silence rang as loudly as gunfire.

Then the top of a Western hat peeked above the cliff's edge. Cam fired, and the hat flew. A loud yelp carried from above. He'd either hit the sniper or scared him silly. A receding scramble of feet on loose scree met his ears. Had the shooter fled?

Cam turned his head toward Bree, still undercover in the crevice. She met his gaze with wide eyes and a shrug of her shoulders. The shadow of her hideaway softened the clear-cut planes of her face, lending an exotic flavor to her striking features. Bree Maguire was not pretty—that description was entirely too bland. Nor was she beautiful in the standard sense. Yet a guy would look twice when she passed by. For sure and certain. Cam tore his gaze away and concentrated on listening.

No sound came from the wounded man Bree had addressed as Leon Waring. Had the man fled? Or had he retrieved his gun and now awaited someone brave or dumb enough to poke their head out? Must be his day for being brave or dumb because he ventured a peek. Then he drew back, processing what he had seen.

He settled grim eyes on Bree. "I don't think you're going to have to arrest that Waring fellow."

"He escaped?" Her tone held equal parts anger and anguish.

"Eternally."

"Oh." Her eyes rounded.

In the distance, a motor started up. The rumble carried faintly across the tableland. Not a truck-size motor. Probably an ATV.

Cam grimaced. "I think our sniper had enough of people shooting back."

Bree's full lips compressed into a thin line. She took a step out of the crevice, posture alert and rifle at the ready. Her exposure brought no response.

"I think you're right." She nodded at him as Cam stood from his crouch.

He walked toward the still, crumpled figure on the ground near the ravine wall, then knelt and placed two fingers against the man's neck. Cam looked up at the ranger and shook his head.

"He's gone, Ranger Maguire."

"Call me Bree. You've more than earned that

right." Her stiff posture sagged. "I would have liked to bring him in still breathing, so he could answer publicly for his crimes."

"What did the guy do?" Cam rose and faced her.

"He is—*was* the leader of a particularly vicious gang of cattle rustlers. For the past ten months, his crew has been swooping into remote pastures, scooping up whole herds of cattle with semitrucks and leaving no witnesses behind. Lots of murdered ranch hands and hundreds of thousands of dollars of property stolen. People don't realize rustling is alive and well in the West or how lucrative slick operations can be. And then the night before last—"

She clamped her lips shut, and her face washed pale, revealing a scattering of light freckles across her nose and upper cheeks that her tan had concealed. Whatever she had been going to say choked her up considerably.

Cam stopped himself from pressing the issue. He was out of touch with the media reports more often than not, but no doubt, the next time he went to the coffee shop, someone there would let him know what had happened. Rural areas thrived on hearing and telling the latest news to keep life interesting. If he hadn't been camping out hunting strays for the past two days, he'd probably already know whatever had gone on.

He frowned at the rustler's body. "I've got a packhorse at the far end of this box canyon where I've been keeping the strays I've rounded up. We'll probably have to leave my kit behind and use old Myra to haul this guy out of here."

Bree didn't respond. She was staring at Waring's body also. At last, she stirred and looked up at him.

"I wonder who murdered this guy and took shots at us? Was someone trying to shut him up?" She pursed her lips and nodded her head. "Kind of confirms the notion we've been batting around at headquarters. Someone behind the scenes was coordinating the rustling activities—someone intimately familiar with where big ranchers pasture their stock."

"Someone Waring could expose." Cam completed the logical progression of thought.

Bree nodded. "I should go get the satellite phone in the pack on my horse. If you would wait here, I'll just be a minute, Mr. Wolfe."

"Call me Cam. You've more than earned the right."

He deliberately echoed Bree's words and added a grin to cover a sudden, surprising clench in his gut at using the name that went with his new identity. Usually, saying the name, which he actually liked better than his original, didn't bother him. It hadn't mattered the first time he'd identified himself to this woman before the shooting had started. Maybe the discomfort came from repeating the identity to an official of the law. Or maybe his unwelcome attraction to his neighbor added significance to the necessary deception. Except it wasn't really deception. Cameron Wolfe was now his legal name. He squelched the foolish introspection and maintained his grin.

"Cam, it is." She nodded with a smile and turned away. "We need to notify—"

Cam hissed in a sharp breath, cutting off her sentence. She whirled, gaze hunting for danger.

"*You* were the target." The words exploded from his mouth as his gut twisted. "The shooter was aiming to kill you first. If you hadn't moved to bend over Waring at the exact right second, you'd be dead now. The bullet took your ponytail clean off."

What was this woman not telling him about her situation? Could her predicament place him back in the crosshairs of ruthless criminals he'd turned his life upside-down to escape?

Chapter Two

Bree's mouth dropped open as her hand darted up to grip the frizz that stuck out from the scrunchy at her nape. A shudder rippled through her and her heart hammered in her chest. She tore her hand away from the remnants of the thick mane of hair that had been her only vanity. The backs of her eyes stung and she blinked, swallowing against a sudden thickening in her throat. What was the matter with her? Why was she on the verge of tears over a physical attribute that would grow back over time? She should be grateful the bullet had not struck her in the spine.

Gritting her teeth and clamping fists that dug fingernails into her palms, Bree turned away from the concerned gaze of her too good-looking neighbor. Too good-looking? What was she thinking? It wasn't like her to moon over a guy she'd barely met any more than her pragmatic nature would normally mourn a hank of hair. The tragic events of the past two days must be overwhelming her emotions.

Bree's boots crunched over the gravelly canyon floor as she rounded the corner away from the crime scene and marched toward her patient mount. Teton stood, steady and faithful despite the recent gunfire, gazing at her with dark eyes that seemed to hold the same concern as Cam Wolfe's. Was her uncharacteristic emotional state obvious even to an animal?

A pair of tears escaped the corners of Bree's eyes and tracked down her face. The salt stung the cut on her cheek with a welcome pain that brought her spiraling thoughts back in order. No, she wasn't weeping over hair, or an unwelcome attraction to a stranger, or even a close call with a bullet. Those things were distractions from the true grief of losing a dear friend. This type of normal reaction to the death of a colleague was exactly why she'd be required to see an assigned counselor before returning to duty. She had always considered the regulation a needless delay, but maybe there was a valid reason behind it.

"Good boy, Teton."

Bree patted her mount's silky neck then used

the backs of her hands to swipe the moisture from her cheeks. After the gunfight the night before last, she'd been dry-eyed in a numb sort of way. Now, the dam was breaking, but she couldn't let loose yet. Law enforcement business needed to happen first. She pulled the satellite phone from her saddlebag and placed a call to headquarters. Shortly, her captain came on the line and she explained to him what had happened.

For long moments, deafening silence met Bree's terse recounting of events. Then Captain Gaines barked a wry laugh.

"Lieutenant Maguire, if I didn't know what a buttoned-down, by-the-book ranger you are, I'd suspect you went looking for trouble."

The semiamused tone tempered the tongue-in-cheek chiding of this sometimes maverick but highly effective ranger. Bree's spirits lightened.

"Just hunting for peace and quiet, sir. Trouble found *me*." She held back any reminder to her captain of her unheeded insistence to her colleagues that Waring would head for the Llano.

"Humph!" The wordless exclamation said her *told-you-so* had been read between the lines and noted. "And you say there's a civilian involved?"

"A rancher out hunting strays."

"Wrong place, wrong time for him."

"Or right place, right time for me. Cameron Wolfe saved my life, sir."

"Well and good. Well and good." Silence fell on the line again for several heartbeats. "Find a safe place nearby to hunker down and keep the rancher with you so we can get his statement. I'll have a chopper out there ASAP with a couple of crime scene techs and backup for you. Sounds like there are more bad guys on the loose than just the rustling crew we shut down the other night. Hopefully, they're satisfied now that Waring can't talk, but we still need to be cautious."

Bree bit her lip against voicing Cam's conviction that *she* had been the sniper's priority target. What reason could she give for the notion? She wasn't sure she believed it herself, despite the evidence of her missing ponytail.

A crunch of gravel beneath booted feet announced Cam's appearance around the bend of the wash. Bree nodded her acknowledgment of his presence and he sent her a questioning look with a tilt of his head.

"Ten-four, sir," she said into the phone. "We'll be here when the team arrives."

Cam made a wry face as Bree signed off on the call. "Let me guess. No moving the body, and we should make ourselves comfortable until the cavalry arrives."

She chuckled. "No cavalry in the rangers, and we're more likely to ride trucks and SUVs than horses these days, but yes, you have the gist of it. My captain is sending out a helicopter. I expect help to arrive within the hour."

Her neighbor scratched behind his ear and huffed. "My cattle are thirsty and getting restless. You know what can happen if they take a notion to defy the cowboy and seek water. You'll have one trampled crime scene."

"Then we'd best go make sure the herd stays put." She motioned to Cam to head out.

Leading Teton, Bree followed him into the area where Waring's body lay. She didn't even have to tell him to skirt around the edge of the opposite canyon wall to preserve the crime scene. Bree kept her gaze on his moving figure and away from death. She'd had enough of that to last a lifetime. Many rangers went their whole careers without shooting someone or being shot. Bree was no longer among the number of those who hadn't shot someone, though, thankfully, the latter still applied.

Watching Cam stride along was no hardship. The guy moved like a seasoned hunter with the grace of a panther. Definitely an outdoors-man—another factor contributing to her unruly attraction toward him. Bree rolled her eyes at herself. Her psyche must be scrambling for something—anything—to keep her mind off the recent tragedy. Once she'd had a chance to process her grief, no doubt this fascination with her neighbor would fade. Besides, just because he wasn't wearing a wedding ring didn't mean he was unmarried or available.

They rounded another bend in the winding canyon and the lowing of restless cattle met her ears, along with the distinctive odor of a herd. Teton tossed his head and snorted with the cow horse's natural urge to dominate bovine waywardness.

"You'll get your chance, partner," Bree told her mount, who answered with a hot-breathed whiffle against her neck.

Another curve brought them within sight of the end of the dry wash canyon, a wide, rounded area ending in a sheer sandstone cliff striated with rosy Pleistocene-era rock deposits. Against the wall, about forty black Angus cattle mooed and milled, their hooves churning up a low-lying fog of the reddish Llano dust.

Near at hand, a rock-rimmed fire ring sug-

gested Cam had camped there overnight, but
the fire was well out. No smoke drifted from
the ashes inside the ring. A pair of thick packs
rested on their sides near the fire pit. Any tent
or sleeping bag used by their owner was already
stowed inside. Evidently, Cam had been preparing to move out when the confrontation with
Waring occurred.

Beyond the ring stood a pair of horses, heads
up and watching their approach. One was a
short, stocky quarter horse mare, most likely
the packhorse Cam had spoken about. The other
was a magnificent chestnut bay stallion, also a
quarter horse but long-limbed and sleek as a
barrel racer.

Teton and the bay snorted at each other in
unison. Bree held firmly to the reins on her
mount. This was not a good time to start estab-
lishing a pecking order; a kerfuffle that could
happen even between geldings and stallions. The
mare gazed placidly at the newcomers, chomp-
ing a mouthful of dry grass. She plodded forward, coming between Teton and the stallion as
if to say, "Not on my watch, silly boys."

Bree glanced at Cam, who stood, arms planted
on hips, staring at the restless cow herd.

He turned his head and met her gaze. "I think

we can hold them for a while if everything's calm. But if that law enforcement helicopter spooks them, we'd better get out of the way, and the crime scene will be toast."

Bree nodded. "I'll call Cap Gaines and have him notify the chopper not to overfly the area and to land at least a half mile away. The team will have to hike in from there. I know they'll be delighted."

Cam snickered, clearly appreciating her sarcasm.

Bree grinned at him and their gazes held. Heat, not related to the climate, crept up her neck onto her cheeks. Why couldn't she look away? Those gray depths held her and—

A nudge from Teton's nose broke the connection and Bree turned toward her saddlebags, the skin of her face boiling hot. *Get a grip, Lieutenant Maguire.*

Someone needed to tell her heart to stop fluttering in her chest. Hopefully, he had no clue the tough-as-nails ranger was crushing on him like high school was yesterday. The thought doused her in cold water.

Look what havoc had been wrought in her life because of a starry-eyed, youthful romance indulged and then gone sour too late to head off a marital train wreck. Another sort of burn began in her gut. A decade ago, her philandering ex-high-school-jock of a husband had abandoned his wife of fifteen years for another starry-eyed chicklet barely out of her teens. Apparently, Jared hadn't appreciated that Bree had stopped worshiping the ground he'd walked on, expected him to man up and do his share in the union, and was prospering in her career. She had matured and he hadn't. Simple as that.

Or not really.

The scars ran deep, and forty-three-year-old Brianna Maguire didn't do crushes. She barely did romance. Her last date lay far in the rearview and, until this moment, she hadn't minded that fact at all, despite her younger brother's unsubtle hints about getting back in the relationship saddle. Like the career bachelor should talk!

She pulled the sat phone from her bag and firmed her jaw. Gazing across her horse's rump, she noted that Cam had started saddling his bay. Good idea. They should be mounted while they attempt to keep the cattle calm.

As she began to key in the numbers on the phone, a bass *whump-whump* from the air above began to close in on their location. Sucking in a breath, Bree studied the cloudless sky, so blue it practically hurt the eyes. It was way too soon to expect the law enforcement helicopter. A private sightseeing chopper was possible, but to have one flying over this exact location was suspicious. Hopefully, the bird would soon change course.

Still gripping the satellite phone, Bree swung herself into the saddle to find Cam had done the same atop the bay. He headed his horse toward the small herd, crooning at them in a calming tone. The guy had a decent singing voice though Bree couldn't make out the words over the growing noise from the sky. She walked Teton closer to the cattle but refrained from breaking into song. She couldn't carry a tune in a bucket full of holes.

The helicopter noise continued to amplify and the herd milled faster. Bree sent another look skyward. Nothing in sight yet, but the chopper was closing in on the canyon. Had the sniper sent reinforcements? Her heart began to pound in her chest, echoing the cattle's hooves.

Then the bird roared into sight, hovering directly above them. The cattle bawled and bucked as if coming out of their skins. With great bellows, they charged as a single living entity toward the exit from the box canyon. Bree couldn't have stopped them if she'd tried.

Bree gasped as the chopper's side door opened and a dark-clad figure pointed a rifle down at them. She whirled Teton and joined the fleeing melee. Coughing in the red dust cloud, amid the thunder of churning hooves and desperate huff of heaving bodies all around her, an instinctive prayer zipped through her mind, even though praying had ceased to be regular for her.

God, please don't let Teton lose his footing and fall.

The gunman was hardly the only threat. If her horse didn't stay upright with the herd, they'd wind up ground to paste between iron hooves and stony ground.

Swept up in the scrum of the charging herd, Cam leaned low over his horse's mane and pulled his neck bandana over his mouth and nose. His eyes watered and stung in the flying dust, but at least he could breathe without coughing. Next to him, a cow bellowed and went down, redness spurting from its back.

Cam's heart fisted. He hadn't been mistaken about spotting a shooter in the big bird's open door. They were being fired upon from above, and the herd provided no protection for him or for Bree. The helicopter could easily stay with the moving mass and pick them off until nothing remained standing.

Not today.

Saying a silent prayer that Bree was all right, Cam reined Rojo back. In its fear, the animal fought the bit, but Cam prevailed and the chestnut stallion slowed, allowing the herd to press ahead around them. As the last of the bellowing cattle darted past, Cam hauled his mount to a rearing halt and leaped from the saddle with his rifle gripped in his hand. The moment his boots hit the earth, he released the reins and the bay fled, neighing and bucking.

Don't blame you, pal. Flight was the animal's only recourse, but not Cam's. Not in this situation. A piece of him welcomed the fight. Craved it, since flight had been *his* only recourse not so long ago, and the position he'd been put in then had left residual anger he was still working to overcome.

Squinting into the sky against the dust swirling around him, Cam planted his feet and aimed the rifle skyward. As the reddish dust cloud began to settle, the hovering chopper took shape above. Cam pulled the trigger. The chopper moved at the last split second. Cam had missed the cockpit glass he'd been aiming for, but the bullet had struck sparks off the helicopter's undercarriage. The big bird jerked, not from the bullet, but no doubt from the pilot's reaction to the hit that would have reverberated through the cabin.

The shooter in the open doorway of the chopper swung into view. The guy's rifle stopped spitting bullets as he hung on for dear life against the sudden lurch of his aerial ride. Cam pulled the trigger again and embers arced from the bird's metal body near the open doorway. The shooter and his deadly gun disappeared back inside the chopper.

Cam was under no illusion the retreat would hold if the assault from below ceased. He pulled the trigger again and again, aiming for the cockpit glass to take out the pilot or for any part of the chopper that would disable it. The bird began to rise, attempting to get out of range.

Suddenly, a second rifle blasted from somewhere up the canyon, and the chopper's cockpit glass starred. Bree! And with an ace shot. Cam's heart leaped. She may or may not have hit the pilot, but if not, she'd certainly scared years off the person's life.

The chopper's whole body swung around,

presenting its tail to him. The corners of Cam's mouth tilted upward in a grim smile as he took aim once more and pulled the trigger. Metal flew from the tail rotor assembly, and the bird stuttered in the sky. The back end fell, throwing the chopper into a spin. The pilot must still be able-bodied because the big bird sloppily righted itself and began to flee even as it lost altitude.

Moments later, the chopper slid out of sight, and then a loud *whump* carried across the plain. No flames or explosion followed the crash, but a helicopter blowing up on impact almost never actually happened. Cam wouldn't care to guess about the condition of the chopper's occupants, however.

He lowered his rifle and looked around. His camp had been utterly obliterated. The contents of his packs were strewn everywhere, most of the items ripped or flattened. The thunder of fleeing hooves had faded almost to nothing. His effort over the past week of rounding up strays was all wasted now, but at least he was still standing and unhurt. He couldn't say the same for the pair of inert cows lying nearby who had succumbed to rifle fire from above.

Heat flared within him and Cam gritted his teeth. Why were these yahoos trying to kill them, and who were they? He needed to find Bree and ask her some hard questions. Surely, she knew something.

He headed up the canyon, brittle scree crunching underfoot. This mess was the last thing a guy trying to keep his head down needed. Then a thought arrested him midstride. What if the attack had had to do with *him* and not her? If the cartel had located him, they'd have the resources to send in a chopper to take him out.

No. Cam shook his head and continued striding. The sniper who'd killed that Waring fellow surely had to be linked to the assault from the chopper, and he had shot at Bree first. *She* was the target, and Cam was incidental.

Probably.

What if the sniper was connected to Waring, but the helicopter attack was connected to *him*? A sour taste invaded Cam's mouth. He could hardly concoct a deadlier mess if two separate factions were vying to kill them. For now, he was going to go with the more probable deduction that all this led back to the ranger.

The likelihood that his identity had been exposed was slim to none. He'd covered his tracks via his own resources better than the Marshals Service had planned to do. *They* didn't even know where he was, and he wasn't about to inform the Texas Rangers.

"Cam"

Bree's shout jerked him from his dark introspection. Her trim figure rounded a bend in the canyon, and warm relief flooded Cam's system, flushing tension away. They were both caked in red dust and thoroughly disheveled, but alive and well.

Thank you, Jesus!

Cam hurried toward her. "You're a sight for sore eyes."

She swiped at her filthy face with the backs of her hands. "Literally sore. I could do with plunging my face into a rain-filled playa about now."

Cam snorted at the reference to a playa, a natural water catchment dug by the incessant wind on the plain and a unique feature of desert flatlands such as the Llano Estacado. "The cattle and our horses are no doubt headed for one right now—at least, once they calm down from their fright."

"We can look for them after the ranger helicopter arrives to give us a ride out of here."

"We?" Cam lifted his eyebrows.

"For sure. The least I can do is help you round

up those strays again. Besides, I need to retrieve Teton. I'm sure my brother and some of the hands will join us, too."

"I won't turn down the help, but first we should go look to see if some survivor of that chopper crash isn't sneaking up on us to finish the job they started."

Her gaze lifted to scan the canyon rim. "Someone may be injured and need help."

"No doubt about that. As long as they quit using us for target practice, I'm game to try a little first aid. And a little interrogation, too." At her blossoming frown, Cam held up a hand, palm out. "Don't tell me to leave the questions to the professionals. I have a right to know what's going on."

"Fair enough." She jerked a nod, turned, and led the way toward the shallow end of the wash.

No more words were exchanged as they moved through the area where they'd confronted the rustler. Cam allowed himself only a sideways glance at the remains, and he appreciated Bree's wisdom in keeping her head averted also.

Within fifteen minutes, they had climbed out of the wash at its shallowest end and were standing on the level plain. The crumpled body of the attack chopper gleamed under the westering sun about a quarter mile distant. Belly on the ground, the big bird's landing struts had snapped off entirely. Another five minutes found him and Bree approaching the chopper on cautious feet, rifles at the ready.

Cam glanced toward Bree, already angling sideways, putting distance between him and herself so as not to provide targets close together. Good protocol. Also, the woman knew how to move noiselessly over the terrain. Not that they were exactly sneaking up on the location.

There was no cover on the grassy expanse around them. Not a rock. Not a tree. Much of the Llano was exactly like that—flat as the proverbial pancake, except for occasional stone upthrusts or the dry washes that often became dead-end canyons of the sort they'd been in. The rural prairie only naturally supported trees and vegetation other than grass and desert plants near the occasional springs or the seasonal playas that provided much-needed water for livestock, small game and pronghorn antelope.

Nothing moved around the crashed helicopter except for the lazy twirl of the rotors responding to the constant wind. Soon, they drew close enough for the ticking of the cooling engine to reach his ears. Then another sound intruded. Was that a groan?

Cam halted and darted a look at Bree. She returned the glance with a slight nod. He hadn't imagined the sound that could only come from a human throat. The opening of the chopper's side door gaped at them, dark as a cave mouth. The groan came again from the interior.

"Cover me," Cam told Bree as he edged closer.

"Nope," she said. "*You* cover *me*. This is my crime scene."

Cam gusted a sigh but bent his head in acknowledgment. She'd have to answer to higher-ups if she let a civilian usurp her duty as a ranger or get more involved than he needed to be. However, he could argue that he was thoroughly involved.

Dutifully, Cam held his rifle trained at the opening as Bree approached the door obliquely and peered inside. She bent down suddenly, yanked an object out of the chopper, and flung it behind her. A rifle.

"The shooter's alive in here," she said, "but unconscious. I don't know if the pilot made it. From the petite figure and dainty hand limp on the cyclic stick, the pilot appears to be a woman. She's slumped over, not moving."

Cam's legs swished through the yellowed calf-high grass as he approached the downed helicopter. Bree shot him a scowl but didn't order him back. He needed to get a look at the shooter's face. There was a tiny chance he might recognize the guy, and if he could confirm it, he'd know he'd been found and would need to disappear again. If he didn't recognize the guy, he'd stay in limbo on what to do.

Standing on the opposite side of the open door from Bree, Cam peered into the dimness. Gradually, his eyes adjusted and the features of the shooter's pasty, sharp-featured face became clear. No one he recognized, and the ethnicity did not match what would be expected of a cartel *sicario*—one of the ruthless hitmen employed by Raul Ortega, the drug boss who wanted Cam dead at any cost. Of course, Ortega could have gone outside of his own organization to hire the hit to shift suspicion off himself in any investigation, but Cam counted the probability of that move as very low. Ortega was not a subtle guy—he liked to use a hammer for every job—and he hated to outsource anything. Especially something of so personal a nature as his issue with the man Cam used to be.

If only Cam had no reason to know these

details about such an evil man. But he couldn't change the past. He suppressed a shiver from a sudden chill originating deep inside his chest.

Another groan came from the injured shooter, who lay on his back, bleeding from someplace under his thick head of dark hair. Suddenly, the man's eyes popped open. He gazed around wildly then his stare fixed on Bree.

Shakily, he lifted a hand and pointed at her. "You!"

Cam's heart leaped. Was it wrong of him to feel relieved that the bad guy's recognition fell on Bree? At least now that he knew *he* wasn't the target, he could afford to stick around.

It probably wasn't his place, but he needed to help figure out why someone with serious resources like a helicopter wanted Bree dead and help do anything possible to put a stop to the danger. Of course, his unwelcome attraction to the lovely, courageous ranger played no part in his desire to protect. He would keep telling himself that until he believed it. No, he would attribute this compulsion to releasing pent-up frustration over the injustice of his own situation and his determination not to allow darkness to triumph once again.

The shooter's hand had fallen again to his side,

and he had seemed to relapse into unconsciousness as his eyes fluttered closed. But then his hand moved subtly, not like an aimless twitch but in a specific direction. Cam scanned the man's form, straining to make out details in the dimness of the chopper's passenger compartment.

There!

The shooter was going for a knife scabbard at his belt. He planned to try to stab the woman leaning over him.

Pulse-rate suddenly in overdrive, Cam shouted a warning to Bree.

Chapter Three

Cam's outcry reached Bree's ears even as she lunged into the chopper's belly and snatched the tactical knife away from the fumbling sniper. Venom blazed from the man's eyes and then they rolled back in his head as his body went limp. Unconscious for real this time.

Bree's jaw dropped at the frustrated rage that had radiated from the wounded shooter. She didn't recognize him. What had she done to inspire that kind of fury like she'd cheated him of a coveted prize?

Her mind sifted through the myriad arrests she'd made. Sure, any one of those people or their significant others might want revenge, but the timing of the attacks seemed so random if someone from her past was reaching out to hurt her now. It made more sense to connect this animosity to the recent shoot-out with the rustlers. Was there something she didn't know about the incident?

"I'll secure this guy and see what first aid I can administer." Cam motioned toward the unconscious man. "Why don't you go around the outside to the cockpit and check the condition of the pilot."

Scowling, Bree jerked a nod and stomped away. She wasn't angry with the new neighbor who had been such a help, but she was furious with the situation. People were trying to kill her. She needed an explanation for this vendetta pronto.

The faint odor of spilled aviation fuel followed Bree as she marched around the helicopter. At the pilot's door, she peered through an opening left by shattered window glass. The woman wasn't moving. Bree reached through the opening and put two fingers on the artery behind the chinstrap of the pilot's helmet. A pulse throbbed faintly beneath her fingertips. The pilot let out a low moan. Alive. At least for now. A dent in the woman's helmet hinted at possible head trauma, though she'd likely be dead without the helmet's cushion. There was no external hemorrhaging, so Bree was hesitant to move her in case of spinal injury.

Where was the ranger helicopter? Bree lifted her head and searched the sky. A clean blue slate. Not even a cloud in sight. She dropped her gaze to the cockpit, scanning for weapons in case the pilot revived and became hostile like the now-unconscious sniper, but she spotted no guns or anything else that could be used to injure another.

Holding her rifle in the crook of one arm, she rejoined Cam, who was putting pressure on a wound at the side of the shooter's head. The man's feet were bound together by the shoelaces of his army-style boots and his wrists were fastened to each other by what looked like a dirty bandana. Bree huffed in appreciation of the ingenuity and wisdom in securing the suspect. Just because the guy was out of it didn't mean he would stay that way.

Cam lifted his head and nodded toward her. "The guy had a small handgun in his boot. I've relieved him of it, but I didn't find any other weapons. I don't think he has broken bones, but I have no way to tell if there's been any internal injury."

"The pilot's out, too. Possible head trauma and who knows what else. I don't want to move her. There's no cell service here, but if I had access to my sat phone, I could notify headquarters to send medical help. The unit is in my saddle-bag, though, and Teton tore off with the herd as soon as I dismounted to shoot at the chopper."

"Rojo beat feet—er, hooves out of there, too."

"Smart horses. Rojo is a good name for a red stallion."

Cam flickered a smile in her direction. "He's got excellent bloodlines. I wouldn't have used him on hunting strays, but my mare is recovering from a slight hock injury, and the lone ranch hand I've hired so far took the gelding out to ride the fence. My herds—equine and bovine—are sparse until I can get to a stock sale and make some purchases."

Bree lifted an eyebrow. "You're going to raise horses, as well as cattle?"

"That's the plan."

"Then we'd better get after the missing animals as soon as we're done here. No worries about mounts for us. We've got plenty to spare at the Double-Bar-M."

"Thanks." Cam nodded. "I'll take you up on that offer. Now, what's the backstory with our deceased fugitive in the canyon and these two desperadoes here?"

Bree huffed through her nose. This man

probably had a right to know about the law enforcement/rustler shootout that occurred the night before last. She gave him an abbreviated version. He listened with sober attention and only a frown and a nod at the part about losing her partner in the fray.

His demeanor signaled a savvy, steady temperament he'd already displayed in the tense situations they'd experienced. The only part of his response to her story that seemed a bit off was his apparent surprise and an odd hint of relief when she shared that the Espinoza cartel was behind the rustling ring. The impression of his reaction was too nebulous, however, to afford an opportunity for a question, so she pretended not to notice and continued her tale.

"And that's why I was out looking for Waring's trail." She finished with an exaggerated shrug as if she could unload her grief with that simple gesture. "Now, with this mess of the stampede and losing our mounts, the job is not done. If backup would only arrive, we could get on with—"

A faint but steady *whump-whump-whump* began to beat the air. Bree turned her face upward. There! A speck the size of a gnat in the distance.

"And here they come," she said. This desolate stretch of the prairie was about to turn lively.

A touch on her arm drew Bree's attention to Cam, who stood in the shadowed doorway of the downed chopper.

He motioned her to step through the door with him. "Let's be sure it's the good guys before we show ourselves."

Bree snorted. "You think the yahoos attacking us would be sending out a *second* helicopter?"

Cam's shoulder rippled in a shrug. "If they had one, they could have another."

"Point taken." She readied her rifle, stepped into the shadows beside her neighbor, and fixed her gaze on the approaching bird. Less than a minute later, the ranger star on the helicopter became apparent, and Bree let out a breath she hadn't realized she was holding. "It's them." She stepped out of cover and waved an arm at the law enforcement chopper.

Soon the bird lowered itself gracefully to the earth about twenty yards distant, sending rotor wash in their direction. Bree squinted against the grit and headed for the chopper. The side door opened, and a pair of her colleagues hopped out. Horn and Halliday, as mismatched a set of work partners as Bree's office afforded, met her halfway between the two helicopters.

Mitch Horn, a squat fireplug of a fortysomething man, waved toward the wreckage. "HQ didn't say anything about a downed chopper."

"What gives, Maguire?" Tall, lanky Dan Halliday's long greyhound face pulled tight in a scowl. "You okay?"

"I'm fine." She waved a hand in dismissal. "But we have injured aboard the downed chopper. Would one of you radio in for an air ambulance?"

Horn whirled on his heel and trotted back to the ranger bird. But his partner's body stilled as his cop gaze fixed on something beyond Bree's shoulder. She turned to find Cam approaching them with his smooth, big-cat stride.

"Chill, Halliday," she said. "This guy has saved my life at least twice today. He's a local rancher who went out after strays and wound up getting shoved into the deep end of fugitive apprehension and sniper fire."

The other ranger nodded. "Sounds like quite a story to tell."

Behind Halliday, a pair of jump-suited crime scene techs hopped out of the helicopter, bearing their kits in their hands. One of them waved at Bree. She waved back and then returned her attention to her colleague.

"Go ahead and get out your recorder," she told him. "You can take our statements while we wait for the medivac. Cam and I have strays to round up. I'm technically on leave, you know."

Halliday cracked a smile. "When has that ever stopped you from taking care of business? We were told you took Waring into custody out here. Where is he?"

Bree winced.

Cam came to a halt beside her. "Let's just say there's no need to get him to a hospital."

The other ranger frowned and pulled out his cell phone. In the field, witness and suspect statements were commonly taken through an encrypted app on State-of-Texas-issued phones.

"Let's hear it then," Halliday said.

The next couple of hours passed rapidly. The medivac came and went without interrupting the debriefing. Some conversations took place comfortably sitting in the shade of the ranger chopper with bottled water in hand, and some happened while traipsing around the area, in-cluding the dry wash canyon, touring ranger staff and CSIs through the various crime scenes. When they came to the spot on the canyon's rim where the first sniper had tried to kill Bree and had managed to eliminate Waring, the CSIs had a field day collecting bootprints and rifle cartridges.

"Amateur." Cam sniffed.

Bree eyed him sharply. "Why do you say that?"

"He didn't police his brass, and he ran away at the first sign of trouble coming back at him."

"I understand your deduction about the latter, but how would you know the significance of the former?"

Her neighbor shifted his stance from one foot to another and looked away quickly. "Guess it must be because I've read a few true crime books."

Cam's answer came a beat too late to ring genuine. Bree turned away with a soft frown. Her cop senses tingled. Though her new ranching neighbor had made himself a brave and faithful partner under fire, he was now hiding something. His behavior thus far had reflected good character, but the best of folks still had secrets. She'd let the matter slide for now, but whatever he concealed, Bree meant to find out—especially if it had anything to do with the rash of violence going on.

★ ★ ★

Cam brushed aside the pinch of discomfort at Bree's astute question about his knowledge of violent crime scenes. He'd slipped up in making his observation aloud. Maybe it wasn't a good idea for him to spend more time with her, even though he badly wanted to get to know her better. He hadn't felt interested in a woman since... He stopped the thought in its tracks. Best not to go there lest the pain overwhelm him. Bree would read the emotional upheaval in him, and then she'd have more questions he didn't want to answer—couldn't answer if he wanted to keep himself and others safe.

He turned to the stocky Ranger Horn. "Are you finished with Ranger Maguire and me here at the scene?"

Horn looked at Bree, who was studying footprints in the dust.

She rose and nodded toward her colleague. "What are the chances that we could hitch a ride to my ranch? It's a little off your direct route back to headquarters, but it would save us from having to contact my brother and get him to bring more horses. Cam and I would be twiddling our thumbs out here for hours."

"I think we can accommodate." Horn's gaze

lit, and he smiled in a way that hinted at an interest in Bree beyond their working relationship.

Cam swallowed an inappropriate growl as they began moving as a trio for the helicopter. What was the matter with him? Why should he be bothered that someone else found Bree attractive?

The other guy was only a few inches taller than Bree's approximate five-foot-six, but twice as broad. Their ages were similar, and neither wore a wedding band, so the only obstacle to a romance might be any restrictions on dating between coworkers. Cam had no idea what the policy was in the rangers. For all he knew, Horn and Maguire were already an item. The cool dispassion in her gaze toward the other ranger seemed to negate that idea, and Cam's heart lightened. Perhaps Bree wasn't partial to the rough-hewn burly type and might consider a taller, slightly banged-up rancher type.

Then his spirits sank again. Why would she be any more partial to a scarred face with an even more deeply scarred heart? He'd be wise to let any attraction he felt for Bree Maguire die an unsung death—for both their sakes.

Soon the whole crew was strapped into seats in the ranger helicopter. Cam had a window seat with Bree settled in beside him. The thunder of the spooling-up rotors forestalled any conversation. Fitting a headset over her ears, Bree motioned at another headset tucked into a pouch on the back of the seat in front of Cam. He grabbed the headset and settled it over his ears. Not only did the padded earpieces greatly diminish the chopper's roar, but he now could listen in on conversations between the occupants.

When he tuned in, Bree was supplying the pilot with coordinates for her ranch. The big bird lunged into the air and headed in a direction south and east of their location.

Cam gazed down at the receding earth. His gaze stretched far and wide with only the occasional rock escarpment rearing from the flatness or shadowed canyons gouging into the land. It would be helpful if he could spot some trace of his herd and their horses, but nothing jumped out at him. They must be headed in the wrong direction. At least, that deduction would give him a clue about where to look.

In the far distance, cloud-ringed peaks of the Rocky Mountains punctuated the horizon. The Llano Estacado, sometimes translated as the Staked Plains, was one of the largest mesas on the North American continent, covering around

30,000 square miles with an elevation of flat prairie up to 5,000 feet above sea level right here in the northwest panhandle of Texas. The largest cities were Lubbock and Amarillo, thriving on the petroleum and natural gas industries. But most of the prairie supported dryland farmers and ranchers eking out a living in the arid environment through hard work and stubborn grit. The wide-open spaces and the ability to live quietly and mostly unnoticed among a sparse population were factors that had drawn Cam to choose this spot to hunker down and enjoy his privacy and relative safety. Today's events may have blown that aspiration sky-high.

"There!" Cam's heart leaped as he jabbed a finger in the direction of the ground below.

"What is it?" Bree leaned toward him, craning her neck to see out the window glass.

"An abandoned ATV."

Bree instructed the pilot to turn around and lose altitude to hover over the object.

Cam glanced at her taut face. "I'm pretty sure the sniper took off on an ATV. Could he have run out of gas or had a breakdown? If so, he's on foot, and we might spot him."

The ranger shook her head. "I'm inclined to think this is the fugitive Waring's escape vehicle.

Running out of gas after fleeing the shootout was a distinct possibility for him. Probably why he was on foot when you encountered him. I was following a blood trail he left when I came upon the face-off between the two of you."

Cam nodded. "Makes sense."

Bree straightened in her seat and asked the pilot to drop a GPS pin on the location to be investigated later.

Then she offered Cam a smile. "Good eye. I had wondered where his ATV had gone. Now we can wrap up his portion of this saga with a bow."

Cam stifled a snort. Too bad they still didn't have any idea why someone would be so desperate to take Bree out that they'd send not only a sniper but a helicopter to accomplish the goal. By the slight wrinkle in the ranger's brow, she was probably pondering the same issue.

The chopper flew onward and, not long later, descended toward a flat stretch of ground near a sprawling ranch site familiar to Cam from his meet 'n' greet visit with Bree's brother, Dillon, shortly after he'd moved to the area. Cam had deliberately set out to introduce himself to his immediate neighbors to establish normalcy that reduced speculation over the advent of a stranger into the rural area. As far as he could tell, the Double-Bar-M was a crack outfit with a neatly kept ranch house, bunkhouse, and barn, along with a modern machine shed and up-to-date ranch implements. Well-maintained fencing bounded pasturelands populated with horses and cattle. A ranch hand worked a horse in the corral by the barn, but no other human figure appeared to be in sight.

The bird touched down lightly, and Cam and Bree hopped out, crouching low as they scuttled beyond the whirling blades. Cam looked back to see Horn waving through a window at Bree. She jerked a nod at her colleague as the chopper rose. Cam might as well not exist as far as attention paid to him by the man. Yep, the guy had it bad, and Cam determined not to care as he followed Bree's brisk stride in the direction of the low-slung ranch house with its four dormers and front-facing porch. A tall man had emerged from the barn at the commotion of their landing and now ambled toward the house on a trajectory to meet them at the front door.

"Bree, what's going on?" the man Cam recognized as Dillon called as they neared each other.

Bree halted, and Cam with her, at the base of

the two steps leading up to the wooden porch. The man who joined them nearly matched Cam in height but with a lankier build. His features resembled his sister's, but his hair was mahogany rather than auburn, and his eyes were blue.

"Wolfe." Dillon offered him an outstretched hand.

"Maguire." Cam accepted the handshake, their rough-hewn paws clasping firmly.

Then his upper-thirtysomething neighbor turned to Bree, his initial question still hanging in the air.

Bree shrugged her shoulders and shook her head. "A mess, that's what. We tracked down Waring, and he's no longer an issue, but we ended up dodging bullets and shooting down a hostile helicopter."

Dillon's jaw dropped and his gaze darted from her to Cam and back again. "The two of you got involved in a gunfight and fought off an aerial attack? Whoa! That's wild even for you, sis. How did our new neighbor get caught up in this mess?"

Bree's teeth grinned white from a dusty face. "Let us clean up, and feed us, and we'll tell you. But then we need to head out to round up his cattle herd and our horses that got lost in a stampede."

Dillon flung up his hands. "Now you add a stampede to the excitement?"

"Long story." Cam chuckled despite the seriousness of the situation.

"I can't wait to hear." Dillon waved them to the door. "Get on inside. You two look like you've been wallowing in a dry playa."

Half an hour later, Cam joined Dillon and his sister in the spacious kitchen after enjoying a quick shower in the guest bathroom. Dillon had scrounged up a fresh pair of jeans and a shirt that didn't fit too badly. Sunlight streamed in through a wide window, illuminating a sturdy trestle table laden with a platter of thick roast beef sandwiches, a large bowl of potato salad, a plate of freshly sliced tomatoes, and an apple pie.

Cam's mouth watered. He didn't have to be invited twice to sit down and dig in. He ate ravenously as Bree began to fill her brother in about her day on the open range. Cam offered a remark here and there, but she did a clear, concise job with the story, reflecting a long history of writing after-action reports. To give him credit, Dillon seldom interrupted and then only with astute questions. The longer the account continued, however, the more furrowed the man's brow became.

"Someone is out to get you, sis," he declared at the end. "We have to find out who and put a stop to it pronto."

"I couldn't agree more," Cam said. He chewed and swallowed his last bite of a sandwich, wiped his mouth on a napkin, and then set the crumpled paper beside his plate as a tense silence fell on the group. The sudden burr of a ringtone sent a shiver through Cam, and he was pretty sure both Dillon and Bree jumped the slightest bit.

Bree cleared her throat as she swiped her phone from its holder at her waist and looked at the screen. "It's my captain."

She stepped out of the room and began a low-voiced conversation while Cam went to work on a healthy slice of pie. Though he strained his ears, he could make out no words, except Bree's tone grew slightly shrill at one point. As Cam was washing down the last bite of pie with a swig of iced tea, she returned to the kitchen, her freckles standing out on a face washed pale.

"What did you find out?" Dillon beat Cam to the question.

Bree cleared her throat. "The rustler I shot a day and a half ago has regained consciousness, though it's been confirmed that he may never regain the use of his legs."

Dillon grunted, wordlessly expressing how much he cared about the fate of a thief who stole the livelihood from decent, hardworking people and left the dead bodies of innocent ranch hands in their wake.

Cam couldn't say he disagreed.

"But that's not all." Bree's words began to come swiftly and forcefully. "The suspect has been identified as Emilio Espinoza."

A chill gripped Cam's gut. "Related to Alonzo Espinoza?"

Her gaze held steady on his. "Yes, he's the man's nephew."

Dillon planted his hands on the table, palms down, and stood up. "Does this relationship tie in to why someone wants you dead, sis?"

Her gaze shifted toward her brother. "Apparently, a confidential informant told someone in division headquarters that Alonzo has put a bounty on my head."

The lingering savor of cinnamon and apple soured on Cam's tongue. Raul Ortega, the vicious head of the largest and most ruthless gang of drug and people smugglers on the American continent, sought Cam with lethal intent. Now,

Bree was wanted by the head of the second-largest criminal organization. The same guy who was also a deadly rival to the Ortega cartel. The Ortega/Espinoza conflict had already racked up a sizeable body count on both sides of the border, as Cam knew tragically well. Each of these desperadoes was hunting a specific gringo to exact revenge, and the wanted pair—Bree and him—were now together in the same place.

In his wildest imagination, Cam couldn't have devised a more perfect storm. How could they hope to survive?

Chapter Four

Bree locked gazes with Cam. If the guy's skin wasn't so tanned, he'd probably look white as a Texas cloud. Even his lips had paled. Of course, she was shaken, too, but his reaction seemed out of proportion when they were barely acquaintances, and the threat wasn't against him.

What was going on with Mr. Cameron Wolfe? Secrets were in play, and she needed to find out what they were. But not here. Not now. She had enough experience interviewing people to intuit she'd get no plain answers from him. Besides, she'd be fishing in the dark. A little research into his background was in order before she started firing questions. That wasn't snooping; that was the due diligence of a law enforcement official.

Who was she fooling? She was distracting herself from her own situation by speculating about her neighbor. In law enforcement, personnel got used to being the focus of criminals' ire, but a bounty on her head? That was unusual. Then again, cartel leaders possessed resources more significant than most bad actors.

"Sis!"

Her brother's outcry drew her attention to him. Dillon's fingers had formed white-knuckled fists. He'd gone fully as pale as their guest, but with reason. His sister's life was on the line.

"What did your boss suggest?" His voice rasped as if his throat had gone tight. "How are they going to protect you?"

Bree frowned. "They're not."

"I don't believe it." Dillon flung up his hands and then buried his fingers in his thick hair, kneading his temples. "You've been in law enforcement for twenty-five years and a ranger for what now—nearly two decades?"

"Nineteen years." A sense of unreality swept over Bree.

How had the time flown by so fast? She'd been in law enforcement for more than half her life, first in the state highway patrol right out of high school—the very year she'd married her ex—and then in the rangers.

"And they're not going to look after their

own?" Dillon punctuated his question with the side of his fist hammering the counter.

"I didn't say that." Frowning, Bree dropped her gaze. "I can't do what they want me to do."

Cam rose beside her, eyeing her with a thin-lipped stare. "Let me guess. They want you to go into some version of Marshals Service protective custody, and you're not prepared to hide."

Pent-up air gushed from Bree's lungs. This guy got it. "Exactly." She trained a glare on her brother. "If I let some criminal force me out of my life, what message does that send to crooks everywhere and to my ranger colleagues? That a vendetta spooks the law?"

Dillon folded his arms across his chest and returned her glare. "How about that you'd like to go on living while said colleagues figure out how to end the threat? I can't lose you, too."

"I hear you, brother." Her insides warmed. How blessed she was to have family who cared about her. Many people didn't have that precious gift. The sudden loss of their parents a few years back in the crash of their family's small airplane had made the two of them all each other had for immediate family.

"We're going to get through this," she said, "but you know I'd lose my mind stuck in some bolt-hole while others are out there taking care of business."

Dillon's whole body slumped. "Yeah, I get it, but that doesn't mean I have to like it."

"I should go." Cam retrieved his Stetson from where he'd placed it on a vacant chair and plopped it on his head. "You two have more serious things to figure out than rounding up a few stray cattle and quarter horses."

Bree swiveled toward him and planted her hands on her hips. "How were you planning to depart? It's quite a hike between here and your place."

Cam shrugged with a crooked smile that spurred an annoying *ka-bump* in Bree's heart. "Can you spare a cowhand to run me home?"

"And then what? Go after your cattle on foot? Didn't you say that your riding stock was depleted at the moment?"

"My mare should be healed enough to ride tomorrow."

Bree shook her head emphatically, swishing what was left of her hair. "I promised to help round up your animals, and I'd like to get Teton back ASAP. We stick with the plan to go after our livestock. We'll be out on the open range, and the bad guys won't know where to find me."

Her neighbor's smoky eyes bore into her. "They found you pretty handily earlier today."

"Cam's got a point." Dillon's gaze invited concession.

Bree thrust out her jaw. "I believe they were after Waring, like I was. Locating me was a bonus, and then *ka-blooey!* no ponytail."

Her lips trembled as she fingered the frizzy ends of her hair lying against her neck. She needed a haircut to even out her new short do—a truly inconsequential thought compared to living under a death sentence issued by the cartel.

Her brother sighed. "I know the set of your face. There will be no diverting you from your course."

"Then we'd best get to it." Bree smacked her palms together. "We're burning daylight."

A quick study of a satellite map on Dillon's PC revealed the closest wet, nonalkaline playa from the dry wash ravine where the shoot-out had occurred. The herd was almost certainly to be found where hydration and the accompanying plant life for food was available. A rough dirt road led across the Llano to within several miles of the playa, so they could drive a significant portion of the route.

With the help of a ranch hand, they got to work loading three quarter horse mounts and a pack mule into a trailer hitched to a heavy-duty pickup. Then they collected food, water, tents and camping utensils in pannier packs to be carried by the mule. These were thrown into the truck bed. They were fully prepared to spend the night on the range if the herd was not where they anticipated it to be and they had to keep hunting. But if they found the herd quickly, they could all be home by dark to enjoy soft beds for the night.

Bree threw herself into the busywork to keep her thoughts from scampering like a rat in a maze over the horrible development of the bounty on her head. Her life had been upended in an instant. Was she right in resisting the safe course of action? Then again, how long would hiding stave off the forces that sought her? She couldn't think of a more miserable stopgap. No, she had to maintain her freedom and independence until she could figure out a way to end the threat entirely.

But how? The occasional speculative looks her new neighbor sent her as they worked tempted her to ask him what was going on in his head. Maybe he had some ideas. But why should he? The mystery of Cameron Wolfe kept growing deeper.

At last, they piled into the crew-cab pickup. Dillon drove and Cam rode shotgun. He'd offered to take the back seat, but Bree had ended the debate by climbing in behind her brother. Her neighbor had accepted defeat with a chuckle.

"Mr. Wolfe, you seem to have unvoiced thoughts about my situation," Bree said as they passed beneath the wooden sign mounted on twin posts announcing the Double-Bar-M ranch site.

Cam stirred in his seat but did not turn to meet her gaze. "My opinion shouldn't matter."

"I'm not looking for an opinion. I'm looking for insights."

"Please, share." Dillon's glance at the passenger said that he, too, must have noticed their guest seemed to be holding back comments.

Cam huffed. "You're in a tough position, Bree. Going into hiding feels confining and smacks of cowardice to a law enforcement personality."

"How would you know about that?"

He lifted a hand. "I'm just extrapolating here."

Why did Bree feel like Cam was deflecting? How much should she and her brother trust this guy if he was going to be slippery with his language? A chill slithered through Bree's middle. If she hadn't caught Cam in an armed standoff with Leon Waring, she might suspect he was in cahoots with the crook. But the moments she'd witnessed of the confrontation had the flavor of lawman versus criminal. That event, plus a few telltale comments, including the most recent, suggested Cam might have a law enforcement background. If so, why was he reluctant to say so?

Cam's head swiveled toward her, his gaze somber and piercing. "But you do have to weigh in the factor that going on about your life could endanger your loved ones or your coworkers by proximity to you."

Bree hissed in a breath as the words suckerpunched her. "You speak from experience?"

She read the yes in his eyes, but not a word passed his lips. A tic in the muscles of his jaw betrayed a battle going on inside him. Who had he lost? Or had it been his own life endangered by a situation beyond his control?

"Stands to reason, sis." Dillon let out a snort, seemingly oblivious to the byplay between Bree and Cam. "But don't let that thought give you a moment's pause. If you're not going into protective custody with the Marshals Service, then you're stuck with me by your side. Anyone after you will have to go through me. In fact, the more I think about it, the Maguires sticking together is the way it should be."

"No!" The word exploded off Bree's tongue. "I can't risk your life over my own stubbornness."

Silence fell as Dillon guided the truck into a turn from the paved road onto a washboard gravel byway that passed into the deep shade between a pair of stone outcroppings several times as tall as the pickup. Hunching into her seat, Bree stared out the side window as the stone walls slid past. Her stomach roiled with more than the jouncing of the truck. Everything in her rebelled against tucking tail and slinking away, but—

"Look out!" Cam's bellow filled the cab.

Bree whipped her head toward him as a great crash sounded against the windshield. Glass shattered and flew, a few bits stinging her cheek. A larger metallic object whizzed past her face but struck the rear window then fell away somewhere inside the cab. Even as objects zipped around the truck's interior, the men shouted, and a scream tore from Bree's throat.

Dillon must have reflexively mashed his foot on the brake because the rig shuddered and slowed. Scrabbling hooves banged against the floor and sides of the trailer, accompanied by shrill whinnies from the jostled livestock as the tires skidded on the packed earth. Metal groaned in protest as the front left corner of the pickup rammed solid rock, thrusting them to a sudden and complete halt.

Bree's head jerked forward and then slammed back against the headrest. Her senses spun and she fought the blackness edging her sight. She made an uncoordinated grab for the gun holstered at her side. It was her fault that her brother and her newfound friend were in danger. How had she been found already? And would she be able to defend them against the next projectile zipping into the cab?

Cam shook his head against sparkly stars lighting his vision from the jarring halt. Through the shattered windshield, dry heat invaded the cab. Odors of kicked-up dust and crushed mesquite pummeled his senses.

"Get down! We're under fire!"

At Bree's shout, he turned toward the rear seat. The ranger had drawn her sidearm and was swiveling her head this way and that, seeking the threat, but with limited visibility from her position in the back seat.

"We aren't being shot at," Cam said. "A drone crashed into us."

"A drone?" Dillon's voice emerged slightly slurred as he rubbed the side of his head where it must have banged against the side window. "Is that what came at us?"

Bree snorted. "Are you saying someone drove an unmanned, radio-controlled aircraft into our vehicle?"

Cam nodded. "I saw it swoop around the corner of the rock just before it hit us like a kamikaze."

"That's—" Bree blinked at him, mouth agape, like she was at a loss for words. Then her jaw closed and she shook her head. "That's beyond strange. You used an appropriate word, though, Cam. Kamikaze drones are an actual thing. If it had been one, it would have exploded on impact instead of shattering our windshield and itself." She turned her attention to her brother. "Dillon, are you all right? You sound woozy."

"I'm okay, sis." The younger man spurted a chuckle. "Just had my bell rung a bit. My brain is booting up again. I'd go check on the livestock, but I'm not able to get out of the truck. My door is too close to the rock face."

The vehicle jostled as animals in the trailer shifted their weight. Distressed whickers carried into the cab.

"They're alive, anyway, but who knows in what shape." Cam's hand closed around the door latch. "I'll go have a look."

"Wait!" Bree's sharp tone froze Cam in place. "We don't know if someone is out there waiting to take a potshot as soon as we emerge."

"I'll be extra cautious." He nodded. "But we can't sit and wait to be attacked further." Urgency twisted his gut.

"Agreed. I'll cover you as you move." Matte-black pistol gripped in her fist, Bree scooted across her seat to the rear passenger's-side door, lowered the window and peered cautiously out.

"Hold it." Dillon lifted a hand. "Pass me my shotgun from the roof rack back there before any of you venture outside."

Cam mentally kicked himself for leaving his rifle in the truck bed, temporarily inaccessible. At least he had his sidearm, like Bree, but all three of the weapons near to hand in this cab were short-range. Not much good if a sniper lurked outside to back up the drone.

Bree unfastened the shotgun from its secure rack and handed it to her brother. Dillon efficiently checked his load and then nodded at his sister.

Cam studied the pair, and his lips formed a grim smile. These two fit the bill for the Old West expression of "good folks to ride the river with." In other words, solid and dependable in danger and tough times. For someone like himself on the run from trouble, he'd been blessed with excellent neighbors. He could have found peace here in their company if all had stayed normal. But now he was being called upon to fight a battle not his own alongside them—a battle so *like* his own that he couldn't possibly turn away despite the risk of exposing himself to his enemies.

"Ready?" Cam drew his sidearm in his left hand as his right hand tightened on the door release.

"Ready," a pair of determined voices chorused, and a set of green eyes and a set of blue eyes lasered in on him.

Cam shoved the door open and hopped out, his boots sending puffs of reddish dust into the air. Head on a swivel, he searched the surroundings, including the tops of the escarpments bracketing them, but spotted no evidence of hostile presence. Of course, not seeing the enemy didn't mean they weren't there with all sorts of lethal aids like spotting scopes and high-powered rifles. But standing here with the meager defense of the truck door between him and a possible enemy approach would accomplish nothing.

Hauling in a deep breath, Cam transferred his pistol to his right hand and moved toward the trailer. Behind him, the sound of another vehicle door opening told him Bree had emerged to watch his back. Whiffling and snuffling noises from the stock accompanied his cautious progress. With another glance around, Cam stepped to the trailer doors and swung them wide. Equine heads turned to him, and the mule flicked agitated ears back and forth.

"As far as I can tell, they look okay," Cam said, "but we'll have to get them out to be sure."

"I'll give you a hand." Bree appeared around the corner of the trailer.

"And I'll use the sat phone to call for help." Dillon's voice carried from the truck cab.

"Roger that," Bree responded.

Cam met her grim stare. Neither one of them was under any illusion that assistance would arrive quickly at this remote location. The closest aide would come from the Maguire building site, where a grizzled cowpoke with a permanent limp oversaw the care of the ranch headquarters. All the other Maguire hands were out on the range. Dillon had introduced the on-site guy as Angus—Gus for short—the first time Cam had met his neighbor when he'd stopped by to introduce himself. Gus could drive out with the spare pickup and trailer, but how much use he'd be in a potential firefight was unknown. Anyone with legal authority and firearms was a good hour away from their location.

Nope. They were on their own if further attacks happened.

Bree gave him a nod and Cam responded in kind. Then he stepped into the trailer, speaking in soothing tones to the troubled animals. One by one, he led the livestock out and tethered each one to the outside of the trailer. Dillon exited the passenger side of the truck and joined them, toting his shotgun in the crook of his arm and gazing warily around. Cam retrieved his rifle from the truck bed, checked the load, and hovered nearby on alert while the siblings ran their hands over scuffed hides and tested vulnerable legs.

Soon, Dillon stepped back from the mounts, now standing placidly by the trailer, the fright well past. "The mare has a shallow cut on her forelock from a flying hoof, no doubt, but nothing serious, though she's unrideable until it heals. They all seem a little worse for wear."

"Good to hear." Cam continued to scan their surroundings for threat.

Bree stepped closer to Cam. "Then you and I can saddle up, load the mule, and head out. Dillon can wait with the wreck and the lame horse for Gus to arrive."

"Now, hold on, sis." Her brother planted his fists on his hips. "You can't mean to carry on with business as usual. Somebody is out here flying drones, and they clearly knew right where we were headed so they could intercept us. As much as you hate the idea, I think you need to go into hiding. Let the Marshals Service help."

Bree scowled. "I'm safest out on the plain where I can see a threat coming a mile away or hide in endless meandering canyons. If necessary, I can lose myself in the wilderness where it would take an expert tracker to find me."

Her brother's face reddened. "Stop being so blasted independent. Your enemies aren't limited to ground pursuit. And think about me wondering and worrying where you are and if you're all right. These people have resources. They could hunt you down and keep track of you with another drone until shooters arrive. They could—"

"Hold on a minute." Cam interrupted Dillon's strengthening tirade. "I've had a few minutes to evaluate, and I don't believe the drone collision was on purpose. Think about it. Why would the operator destroy the drone when the utility of equipment like that is surveillance, not attack? We don't even know if someone from the cartel operated the drone. Could be anyone out to enjoy a new toy."

Bree snorted. "You don't really believe the innocent drone-flyer idea, do you?"

Cam shook his head. "Not really, but without proof, it's an idea we have to entertain. The drone was extremely high-end, with heavy-duty construction that broke through the windshield, rather than shatter on impact. But I tend to think that the collision was an accident. The stone outcroppings on either side of the road end only a few yards from where we were hit. I saw the drone swoop around the corner of the right-hand rock barely a second before sturdy truck met fragile flying object. The operator couldn't have known we were there. And now, all he or she can gather from any video feed is that their machine hit a ranch pickup with a couple of guys in the front seat. I suspect Bree's presence was hidden behind you, Dillon."

A short laugh spurted from Bree. "And the operator is now stuck explaining to whoever gives the orders how they wrecked their eyes in the sky. I like it."

Dillon crossed his arms over his chest with a scowl. "You do know that's only a theory."

"It's a sound one. Dill, you'll have to stay here and wait for assistance with the mare and the vehicle. Cam and I need to vamoose before anyone sees which direction we're going." Bree's face glowed, a grin stretching her lips.

If he didn't know better, Cam would think she relished the danger. More likely, she was relieved to grab on to a valid reason to take off into the wild rather than surrender to confinement. In that regard, the two of them were simpatico. If only the ploy could guarantee their safety, but fleeing into the Llano was a temporary solution at best.

The day was long gone when Quanah Parker's wily band of Comanche led the US cavalry on a near-hopeless chase across the vast plain sliced by rugged arroyos and winding canyons like the Palo Duro, the second largest canyon in North America. Today, pursuit on horseback had given way to helicopters and drones that were not limited by the terrain or the enormity of the prairie. The deadly criminals *would* find them. Then what?

Chapter Five

Bree gnawed her lower lip as she rode beside Cam across the semiarid tableland. The pack mule ambled behind them. Cam held its lead rope in his sturdy hand, and his head swiveled, gaze constantly searching the terrain. She was doing the same. This trek across the grasslands would have been pleasant and peaceful if they weren't under constant threat.

Saddle leather creaked and the sun-browned native grasses rustled, waving at them as far as the eye could see. The terrain hid depressions— dry washes called arroyos—in folds of the earth, but these were only discerned when one rode up on them. Occasionally, their passage flushed prairie chickens from their hiding places, and the birds scurried away, not taking to the air but warbling in alarm as they disappeared into the tall vegetation. Clumps of cattle grazed here and there, all Double-Bar-M brand since they were still on Maguire property. On the horizon, miles away, lazily whirling blades of wind turbines signaled human encroachment on the vast plain.

"Do you think I'm being stubborn and foolish to refuse protective custody?" Bree practically held her breath, awaiting the answer. Why did she care so much what this man thought? She hardly knew him. Then again, they had already developed the unique bond that only facing down deadly danger together could forge.

Cam frowned beneath the shadow of his hat brim. "Stubborn, yes. Foolish?" His broad shoulders rippled in a shrug. "I can't say I blame you a bit for your choice. Hunkering down in a hidey-hole waiting for who knows what event to set you free from threat in the nebulous future doesn't sound like any way to live. If there was a plan in place to force Alonzo Espinoza to lift the bounty on your head, then I'd say for sure take the temporary arrangement."

"But there is no such plan." Bree scoffed. "How can law enforcement in the US force a cartel leader in Mexico to drop a vendetta?"

"That is a priceless question, and I have no answer. Yet."

"Are you expecting the solution to drop like rain out of the sky?"

Cam awarded her a sidelong look, his expression unreadable. "Let's just say I've submitted the question to the One who has all the answers. When He gets back to me, I'll let you know."

Scowling, Bree guided her horse around a prairie dog hole. The situation she was in seemed like a field pocked with hidden prairie dog holes. One misstep would bring disaster. Maybe she'd already made the biggest misstep of all in going her own way rather than entrusting herself to the legal system she served. If she was making an error, would God protect her from the consequences of a bad decision?

Yet, hiding away indefinitely felt like a worse decision. Like making herself a sitting duck if—no, *when* killers spurred by the bounty on her head located her. Then the guards on duty around her would be endangered, also, as the concerted weight of cartel heavies fell on them. Bree sucked in a deep breath of air laden with the piney-fresh scent of nearby juniper shrubs. No, she was making the right choice. For now.

"Here's the edge of Double-Bar-M land." Bree pointed to a barbed-wire fence line with a gate situated maybe half a football field distant from them.

Soon, they unlatched the gate and moved over onto Cam's Diamond-W property.

"My livestock and your horse should be a few miles west of here." Cam spared Bree a swift grin as they urged their mounts into a slow jog. "Let's go get them. We can drive the herd to the pasture closest to my place in time for supper. I've got spare bedrooms in the house. You can bunk there out of sight and away from home. By now, hostile surveillance might be set up around the Double-Bar-M ranch site, waiting for you to show your face."

"Do you think we got out of there before any of the bounty hunters had eyes on the place?"

"I do. Otherwise, a drone would not have been sent out looking for you. The enemy would have intercepted us in force on the road because they saw you leave the ranch with us."

"Fair deduction. I'm pleased to accept your hospitality. Let me call Dillon to let him know the plan and check how things are going with him."

Bree pulled the satellite phone from the saddlebag. The call went through, but the ringtone went on and on with no answer. Holding a tight rein on the worry that wanted to gallop away with her, she mashed the off button. Was everything okay with her brother?

"No answer?" Cam's gaze rested gently on her.

Bree's gut clenched.

Her neighbor offered her a half smile. "You do know he must have his hands full getting the equipment wrangled out of that narrow roadway. He might not be near his phone."

She let out a long breath. "I know you're right, but I'm tense as a bowstring."

"I don't blame you. Head back there if you want to. I can handle the stock."

Bree shook her head. "It's probably more dangerous for Dillon if I'm nearby."

"So, you're hanging around *me* instead?" Cam grinned. "After all, I'm just the expendable neighbor." The twinkle in this eye let her know he was teasing.

A reluctant laugh spurted between her lips. "You've got me there. Events have sort of gotten away from us, and we're scrambling from one thing to the next. Why are you helping me?" The question burst from Bree's lips. "I mean, you're risking yourself. Why?"

A cavernous silence answered her as his figure stiffened in the saddle. Finally, he angled a grim look in her direction.

"Isn't that what neighbors do? Help each other?"

"This sort of help goes beyond neighborly courtesy."

Cam's complexion darkened and his eyes narrowed. "Let's just say I don't let it stand when people take shots at me, whether I'm the main target or not." His voice had deepened to a low growl. "That experience makes me want to do anything I can to deny these crooks what they want."

Bree opened her mouth and then closed it again. He was right. He'd been in the crosshairs, too, more than once. Her proximity was toxic, but the threat seemed to make Cam dig his heels in deeper. Some folks were like that, but often, they were the sort of people who gravitated to careers like law enforcement or the military. Had Cameron Wolfe always been a rancher? She knew next to nothing about him, but that didn't mean she was comfortable endangering him, and certainly not risking her brother. Simply by being related to her, he could be targeted as a pawn of the cartel to get to her.

Bree's heart did a little jump in her chest.

Maybe Dillon and she should go into protective custody together. She repressed a derisive laugh. Dill wouldn't allow himself to be yanked from his life and hidden away any more than she would. Next time he pressured her to accept the offer of protection, she'd point out that little fact to him.

But where did this thought process leave them? In limbo. A highly uncomfortable place to be stuck, that's for sure. For now, she'd have to follow Cam's advice of coping with this situation one step at a time.

The first step, round up those stray cattle and retrieve her horse.

And there they were, near a halo of lush, green growth surrounding a pale blue stretch of water that covered less than an acre of ground. Last week's unseasonal downpour would have filled the playa's shallow basin. But late summer's unrelenting heat nibbled swiftly away at the wetness, leaving cracked and baking mud around the edges as the water receded. Within a few more days, the wetness would be evaporated. The herds and wildlife would then be dependent for water on the few rivers that cut through the Llano or on occasional springs fed by the underlying Ogallala Aquifer. That's why ranchers and farmers had installed water tanks here and there across the plain.

As if in silent communication, Bree halted her gelding simultaneously with Cam.

The herd and handful of equines milled around the edge of the water, churning the mud. Why were the animals restless? They should be content with their environment. The slow, quiet approach of riders would not have stirred them up.

Bree rose in her stirrups and narrowed her eyes on a distant dust cloud roiling across the plain on a clear trajectory toward the herd. She went quiet and strained her senses to see or hear what approached. The rhythm of hoof beats lacking any engine growls suggested another herd racing for the water. Why were they coming on so fast, almost like the animals had been spooked or were being driven? Either possibility brought up another host of questions, like what had spooked them or who was driving them—unanswerable at this point.

Bree glanced over at Cam, and he met her gaze with raised eyebrows.

"We should intercept the coming herd and slow them down so the whole bunch doesn't stampede."

"We'll have to hustle to swing around to

the far side of the playa before that second herd arrives."

Cam jerked a nod and released his hold on the pack mule's lead rope. "Let's get to it."

By the time she and Cam reached the far side of the playa, the incoming herd had grown much closer. The cloud of reddish dust still obscured most details, but the distinctive grunting of cattle on the move informed Bree's ears. A mass of dirty-brown bovine bodies undulated across the plain toward them. But a different silhouette of horses and riders trailed behind. At least three cowboys.

Cam let out a wordless growl. "Who in the world is driving cattle across my property?"

His shouted question reached Bree's ears above the rumble of the herd and echoed the question in her mind. She'd scarcely formulated the thought when a distinctive crack echoed across the plain, drawing surprised bellows from the herd in front of her and the one behind her.

A whip?

The sound came again, and something like a bee whine zipped past her ear.

Not a whip. A gunshot.

The approaching riders were firing at her and Cam—or maybe just her. Heat roiled through her veins. Being targeted was getting very old, very fast.

Pulse hammering in her throat, Bree leaned over the neck of her horse, reached for her saddle scabbard, and drew her rifle. As she brought the weapon to bear on their assailants, her mount stumbled beneath her, throwing her forward. Then the animal fell headlong. A shriek escaped Bree's throat as her feet left the stirrups and she went airborne.

Shouting Bree's name, Cam swerved his horse toward the fallen rider, who lay flat on her back and unmoving on the ground. His heart filled his throat. Pulling up beside her prone figure, he swung out of the saddle even before his mount came to a full stop.

Bree stirred, blinked, and sat up. A gush of pent-up oxygen left Cam's lungs. She was alive, at least. Assessing any injuries would need to wait. That other herd was bearing straight down on them, and they needed to get out of the way. Not to mention continuing to dodge bullets.

The question of who those other riders might be was settled when the trio opened fire on him and Bree. Nothing legitimate about them. They were rustlers. Or maybe bounty hunters, intent on collecting the price on Bree's head and using the small herd as cover for their approach.

As Cam bent toward Bree, she gripped his arm and struggled to her feet. Despite the jarring fall, she still clutched her rifle in her other hand. Cam steadied her with an arm around her shoulders.

"We've got to get out of here," she mouthed more than spoke aloud. No doubt she was still struggling to breathe after doing a cartwheel and slamming into the hard earth.

Cam darted a glance around. Bree's horse was hobbling away from them, clearly lame. The animal had probably stepped in a prairie dog hole. His jaw firmed. They'd have to ride double on his mount. Then, a whicker behind them drew his attention. Her gelding, Teton, approached, single rein dragging on the ground, the other snapped off short. No doubt stepped on by sharp hooves in this morning's stampede.

As one, Cam moved with Bree and got her on the palomino's back. He had small doubt the animal was sufficiently trained to respond to leg commands, even though Bree would have only one rein in her hand. Of necessity, Cam ignored her pained groans accompanying the effort, but his heart squeezed in on itself. Then he leaped aboard his own borrowed mount, and together they raced out of the oncoming herd's path. A pair of thunderclaps let them know those hostile riders were still shooting at them, but it was extremely difficult to hit a rider on a moving mount while astride racing mounts themselves.

Provoked beyond measure, he lifted his rifle and returned fire, not expecting to hit anyone but hopefully encouraging the attackers to back off. One of the enemy riders flung up his hands and toppled off his mount. Cam's jaw dropped even as Bree opened fire beside him. Neither of the remaining attackers fell, but they whirled their mounts and raced away across the plain.

Not a very gutsy response from ruthless cartel *sicarios*, but standard for crooked cowpokes out to make a fast buck from stolen livestock. It was possible the crooks had no idea Bree Maguire was one of their opponents. But perhaps that was just wishful thinking on his part...

Coughing against the settling red dust, Cam trotted his mount over to Bree, who had brought Teton to a halt. She sat slumped on his back, echoing Cam's coughs.

"Where are you hurt?" he asked.

Bree grimaced at him from a dusty face. Even caked in dirt, this woman was appealing. Cam squelched the unwanted attraction. She wasn't likely to be regarding his grimy, scarred face with similar interest.

"Where *don't* I hurt would be an easier question to answer, but I'm pretty sure nothing is broken, and I'm not concussed. However, I'll probably be one big bruise in the morning. Let's go check on the fallen rider."

"My thought exactly."

They guided their mounts together at a fast walk toward where a riderless horse had stopped to graze and a human figure lay unmoving a few yards away. She kept her rifle at the ready, as did he.

"That was one tremendous shot."

Cam met Bree's sidelong glance. "A major fluke, you mean."

They stopped their mounts near the crumpled figure, who stirred and groaned but didn't open his eyes. Red blood pooled near the guy's shoulder and stained his plaid shirt in the same area, but nothing life-threatening. Something like a fist unfurled from around Cam's heart. He hadn't killed the guy, after all, which was one burden off his conscience. Plus, maybe they could get some information out of the rustler if he came around enough to talk.

"Keep him covered," he said to Bree as he swung off his horse. "I'll get the first-aid kit and check him out."

"Gotcha." She kept her rifle trained on their wounded attacker.

Moving cautiously with one eye on their prisoner, Cam retrieved the medical kit from his saddlebag and then knelt beside the downed range rider. The man was paunchy and scruffy, not an impressive physical specimen. His grizzled hair betrayed upper middle age, past his prime, and his threadbare jeans spoke of a cowpoke in poor financial circumstances. Were money troubles the reason why he'd hooked up with a rustling outfit? Regardless, that was no excuse to be shooting at other people.

Compressing his lips, Cam got to work checking out the man's wound. Turned out to be a through-and-through just below the clavicle. No bloody froth lined the guy's lips, so likely the lung was not nicked. What kept the guy unconscious seemed to be the knock his head had taken against a rock when he'd landed on the ground. Strangely enough, the skin had barely broken, with minor bleeding, yet a growing knot suggested a probable concussion. There wasn't much Cam could do about the head injury, but he disinfected both sides of the shoulder wound and staunched the bleeding with compresses.

"This guy needs professional medical attention, but in my nonprofessional opinion, if his head injury isn't too severe, I think he will recover."

A heavy sigh answered him. "I can't believe I'm calling for helicopter emergency services twice in one day."

"I'm just thankful the callout isn't for either of us."

"I can get on board with that idea."

Cam checked the grizzled cowpoke for any additional weapons to the rifle the guy had been firing at them but found only a buck knife, which he took away and pocketed. Then he finished bandaging the man's wounds while Bree talked on the satellite phone. She called for aid and then reached out to her brother to get and give updates. This time, Dillon answered, which brought a smile to Bree's face.

From her end of that conversation, Cam inferred that salvaging the wreck of the truck and trailer had gone well. When she started telling him about their situation on the range, the tone of the conversation changed drastically.

Her brother's fuming shouts reached Cam's ears, though he couldn't make out what was said. Not that he blamed the guy for getting agitated when his sister kept going from one dangerous situation to the next.

Bree brought the conversation to a firm conclusion, informing her sibling she planned to finish what she and Cam had come out there to do. The woman was the definition of stubborn. If the situation weren't so serious, he'd be tempted to grin in appreciation of a kindred spirit.

Creaking saddle leather let Cam know Bree was dismounting from Teton. He peered over his shoulder to find her approaching her lame mount, who stood nearby, head down. She reached for the horse's bridle, and Cam caught on that she would be switching the intact headgear onto Teton. Cam returned his attention to the downed rustler. A few minutes later, Bree appeared at Cam's side, leading Teton, just as he rose to stand over his patient. The man had begun to groan and flutter his eyelids.

Cam planted his hands on his hips and frowned down at the guy. "I should look through his saddlebags and see if he's carrying some kind of identification. When I looked him over, I didn't find a wallet."

"No need." Bree scowled. "I know this guy. Ben Trout. Born and raised on the Llano. He's bad news with a sad story. Started out young as a decent cowhand, but too much drink and foolish choices in the company he kept led him down a crooked path. Trout's one of the few rustlers that slipped the net during our tragic shootout the other night."

Cam snorted. "I'm surprised he hasn't found a deep hole to hide in, rather than prancing across the range stealing more cows. He must be desperate for money."

"Desperate, for sure. Despite the rustlers' recent losses—or perhaps because of them—the cartel may be holding them to a quota of stolen beef."

"That's cold." Cam snorted. "But typical."

Bree jammed her hands onto her hips, mimicking his posture. "I'm done letting your cryptic comments slide, Mr. Wolfe. If you want me to keep on trusting you, tell me how you seem to know so much about how criminal cartels behave. And don't put me off with any flippant remarks about watching crime documentaries on TV or the internet."

Cam's mouth went dry as he met her glare. What could he tell her? His glance flicked toward the groaning man on the ground. The rustler's eyes remained closed, but he might be hearing every word he and Bree spoke, and despite being headed for the hospital and then to jail, Trout could easily find the opportunity to share his information with someone. Possibly the wrong someone. At the same time, clearly, the tough ranger was through allowing him to skate along unquestioned about his background.

He couldn't mention being a former DEA agent. If he made that claim, she'd check him out and discover no Cameron Wolfe ever on the DEA roster, which immediately would destroy all trust between him and Bree. Worse, alarm bells would sound throughout the law enforcement community. Official attention would come and expose his identity to the Ortega cartel. He'd have to disappear again. His stomach curdled at the thought.

It had ripped him apart to choose the flight route when fight was his natural instinct. But the overwhelming forces arrayed against him at the time, as well as the emotional pain of his losses, had forced him into what he'd regarded as an honorable retreat. He'd gone into hiding in plain sight and on his own terms. But now, even if he possessed the resources to turn himself into someone else again, he didn't think he could bring himself to do it. He'd done all the retreating he could stomach. Stubborn, yes, just like Bree.

He lost himself in her earnest green gaze, and his heart did a little jig. Despite any negative consequences to himself, for the first time in a long time, a part of him ached to share the whole story with someone. No, not just someone—this brave woman staring expectantly at him.

But if he said too much, he would not only risk himself but double the danger to her—and who knew how many innocents—when the Ortega enforcers showed up and inevitably clashed with the Espinoza *sicarios* in their hatred of each other and eagerness to take down their targets. How selfish, not to mention foolish and irresponsible, would such careless transparency be? But he *had* to tell her something, and it would need to be enough of the truth to satisfy her.

God, guard my mouth and give me wisdom.

Chapter Six

Bree all but held her breath for Cam's response to her insistent question. Color ebbed from the man's cheeks, and his gaze tore away from hers as he appeared to study their surroundings. Then he glanced back at her, but the eye contact bounced off and fell to the injured man on the ground. Cam's lips thinned, and he jerked a nod toward no one as if coming to some sort of conclusion.

"I cooperated with law enforcement on a certain project that ended well for some, but not for me." He heaved a deep breath. "I was engaged, but…things happened that changed me. The cartel mess brought tragedy, and—well, the wedding never happened, so I moved away to start over."

The raw pain on Cam's face ripped at Bree's heart. She shouldn't have pried, and yet, for her own assurance, she'd had to understand what was going on with her neighbor. Still, he was telling her the bare bones of what must be a complex and difficult story.

"I'm sorry." Her words came out gently. "Was your fiancée killed?"

Cam grunted as if he'd been struck in the stomach. "No, she survived, but she was an emotional wreck. She fled with important unresolved questions between us. In some ways, that consequence has been more complicated to properly mourn." His mouth twisted in a grimace.

"Very well, Cam. I'll stop badgering you about your personal business. You understand that I need to know anything that impacts my current situation."

"I get it, and I appreciate your discretion."

If the guy looked any more relieved by her backing off, he'd flop onto the dirt like jelly. The reaction sparked her curiosity more than ever, but as she'd promised, she put the matter on a mental shelf. For now.

The cowboy on the ground moaned and started mumbling something. Bree squatted beside him and Trout's eye popped open. He fixed her with an inky stare that started out bleary and then snapped into narrow-eyed focus.

"You!"

"Yep, Texas Ranger Brianna Maguire. And you're under arrest, Ben Trout, for cattle rustling and attempted murder." She briskly informed him of his rights. "Do you understand what I've said to you?"

Trout snorted a phlegmy laugh that ended in a wince. "I got it, all right. But if I'd known it was you I was shootin' at, I'd have made sure to aim my rifle better, instead of just tryin' to scare you off as if you was a hired cowhand. You're worth a pile more money than them scraggly cows."

"I've heard." She infused her tone with enough flatness to hide the cold pang that shot through her at his words.

It was one thing to be told by her boss about the bounty on her head. Quite another to hear it spoken with venom from an enemy.

The rustler squirmed and tried to sit up, but Cam put a boot atop Trout's good shoulder. "Stay down unless you want to be cuffed."

Bree spread her hands. "Sorry, I don't have cuffs on me for this roundup, but I do have a few zip ties." She grinned down at the prisoner, who looked away with a scowl.

"I need a doctor." A whine replaced the harsh tone.

"Air ambulance is on the way," Bree told him. "In the meantime, you can tell me what you're doing trespassing on Diamond-W land, driving a herd of Cameron Wolfe's cattle, and shooting at random people you just basically admitted you had not identified."

The man sucked his lips between his teeth and then smirked. "I don't have to say nothing without a lawyer."

"That's right. You don't. But that doesn't mean your buddies we arrested a couple of nights ago aren't singing up a chorus with your name in the lyrics."

Since she was on leave, Bree was throwing out speculation on what the interviews were yielding with the captured rustlers. But Trout didn't need to know she was temporarily out of the loop.

"Since you've got this guy under watch," Cam said, "is it okay if I go over to the herd, secure Rojo, and check the condition of the cattle?"

Cam's question drew Bree out of her inner mulling, and she gazed up at him. He was frowning and scanning the horizon, clearly still uneasy about their situation. She didn't blame him. Her own senses remained on high alert.

"Absolutely." She offered him a nod. "This

guy's just a distraction from what we came to do. As soon as he's out of here, I'm right with you."

Cam nodded soberly. "If you feel you need to head out on the helicopter with the prisoner, I totally understand."

She shook her head. "I'll zip-tie his wrists to the gurney and make sure someone from the rangers division at the other end to receive him, but I'm staying out here with you."

"And away from the clutches of anyone who might want to corral you into doing something you don't want to do, like going into protective custody." Cam grinned down at her.

Bree grinned back. This guy got her.

He tipped his hat and then climbed onto the mount that Dillon and she had lent him.

Bree returned her attention to the rustler, who appeared to have resigned himself to his enforced repose on the ground. Or maybe it simply hurt too much to move. She settled in, cross-legged, beside him, keeping her rifle in her grasp.

"So, tell me more about this bounty Alonzo Espinoza has allegedly placed on my head."

Trout pursed his lips as if considering the request. Probably figuring out what to say that wouldn't incriminate himself further.

"Don't know much. Just that the young fella you shot and crippled was Alonzo Espinoza's sister's son, and the big cheese's choice to lead the cartel after he retired."

Bree snorted. "I haven't heard of a cartel head yet who made it to retirement alive and unincarcerated. It's a high-risk occupation—as is being a rustler."

"Just sayin' what I heard. Got that? Hearsay only. Nothin' criminal."

"No, but you being aware of the details reflects the sort of people you hang out with."

"Are you judging my friends now?"

"I'll leave the *judging* to the actual judge on the bench. You'll be facing one soon enough."

An uneasy silence fell and a sullen look took up residence on the rustler's expression.

Cattle lowed softly and hoof thuds increased behind her near the playa. A baritone voice, singing a cowboy melody and carrying a tune quite well, met Bree's ears. The familiar odors of livestock and ancient, sunbaked Llano dust filled her nostrils.

Bree's gaze found Cam's tall figure, now mounted on Rojo and guiding the stallion, slow and easy, through the livestock. His head turned this way and that, inspecting the condition of the herd. After being shot at and stampeded, injuries needing treatment were likely and had to be identified and assessed.

Bree's brows drew together. Her new neighbor, encountered so dramatically this morning, exhibited all the earmarks of an experienced and caring rancher. Why did she continue to think his main occupation had been something else until recently? Maybe because of how cool he was under fire. But if it were so, why wouldn't he tell her?

Yet, more troubling to her personally, how come in so short a time, she felt like she'd known Cameron Wolfe forever and would like to go on knowing him for an eternity more? That kind of instant crush didn't happen to Bree Maguire. She knew better. At least, she had until her heart started trying to override her good sense. Bree shook her head as if warding off a pesky horsefly.

Cam must have felt her eyes on him because he turned his head in her direction. He lifted a hand in greeting and she responded the same.

Time passed as Bree kept an eye on the captured rustler and the surrounding terrain for any return of the crook's buddies, perhaps with reinforcements. The westering sun peeked beneath the wide brim of her cowboy hat, though a fresh breeze mitigated some of the heat. Cam continued to work with the cattle, occasionally resuming his crooning. Beneath all the sensory input, her nerves thrummed in anticipation of the sound of an approaching helicopter.

When it came, she physically jerked and rose to her feet, eyes piercing the horizon for a sight of the big bird. Her skin prickled like she was swathed in a blanket of tiny needles, and her grip tightened around her rifle. She whistled Teton over and mounted up.

If she and Cam had to run, they'd do better on horseback. The memory of this morning's chopper attack loomed all too fresh in her mind. The last time they'd expected the good guys to show up from the air, the bad guys had arrived instead, and she and Cam had barely survived.

Rotor rumble began to drown out the thud of milling hooves and lowing of livestock as Cam continued his inspection of the herd. So far, he'd discerned only minor wounds among the cattle that could be treated in the pasture. He might have the vet come out to look at his old pack mare, who sported an angry red bullet graze across her flank. She wouldn't be carrying a load for a while.

Cam lifted his head skyward. The big bird made a speck in the deepening blue sky of impending dusk and the speck grew bigger by the second. The hairs at the base of his neck prickled. He wouldn't relax until he spotted the hospital logo on the chopper's side.

Still crooning to the herd so they would remain calm while the chopper landed, he gradually began urging his mount out of the press of animals and toward Bree, who had remounted Teton. Cam stopped his horse within speaking distance of Bree but far enough distant that the pair of them wouldn't make convenient bunched-up targets. Rojo pranced and snorted, muscles rippling beneath his sleek, red hide. If the need came to run, the stallion was eager to go.

Bree spared them a glance but mostly divided her attention between her prisoner and the sky. The scraggly rustler moaned loudly as he hauled his body into a hunched sitting position. Bree's voice admonishing the man reached Cam's ears as an indistinct murmur—the specific words lost beneath the growing roar of the helicopter. Then Cam made out the markings on the side of the big flying machine and the fist around his heart unclenched.

"It's the emergency chopper."

His cry drew Bree's head toward him and she nodded, a smile breaking out over her face. The bird eased to a gentle landing far enough distant that the rotor wash dwindled to a mere breeze by the time it reached their location, and the herd would not be spooked. Almost immediately, a pair of uniformed emergency medical technicians hopped out, bearing a stretcher between them, one with a medical pack in her opposite hand.

Then, a third figure climbed down—a tall, burly man dressed in a Western-style suit of gray slacks, white shirt, casual sport coat and string tie. The man wore no Stetson on his salt-and-pepper head, but the sun's lingering rays glinted off the star badge pinned to his coat. The ranger's expression was stern. Bree's smile morphed into a scowl.

"What's the problem?" Brow furrowing, Cam shifted in his saddle.

"It's okay." Bree lifted one hand, palm out. "Well, it's not okay, but there's no physical threat. That's my boss, Captain Gaines."

Cam urged Rojo closer to her. "Come to haul you back to headquarters?"

"Try, anyway." She grimaced.

He let out a wry chuckle at her mulish tone. Bree shot him a glare. Swallowing another chuckle, Cam sucked his lips between his teeth and looked away.

The EMTs trotted over to the injured man, Gaines striding purposefully in their wake. Bree's loud sigh carried to Cam's ears despite the fading rumble whine of the helicopter rotors. She climbed down off her horse to meet her boss. Cam drifted Rojo closer to the pair so at least he might catch part of the conversation. Eavesdrop much? No, never. But he was making an exception to the rule today when so much lay at stake that affected him deeply.

"Bree, are you okay?" The man's voice was a smooth tenor wrapped in steel.

"I'm fine, Captain."

"Things can't go on this way." Gaines swept on, scarcely missing a beat for her response.

"I know it's been wild, sir, but—"

"You need to come back with me to Company C headquarters in Lubbock. We can't delay getting you into protection."

"What do you suggest, Captain? That I hole up at headquarters indefinitely? That's not practical."

"Not at headquarters, no, but I'm in discussion with the Marshals Service. Since you'll be testifying at several trials related to the issue that has you under threat with the Espinoza cartel, you would qualify for witness protection through the dates of the trials, followed by relocation."

"No." The single word cracked like a whip.

Gaines lifted a quieting hand. "I know it's not ideal, but it's your life we're considering here."

"Not ideal?" Bree's tone had gone up an octave. "Exactly, it's *my life*. You're asking me to leave my family and my career to become someone else. Not happening."

"But—"

She leaned closer to the captain, invading his personal space. "What are my recourses when the cartel finds me under my new identity?"

Gaines gave no ground as he shook his head. "The Marshals Service is exceptionally good at what they do. They don't lose people unless the subject does something stupid like willfully coming out of hiding or contacting someone from their old existence. And you're not that stupid. At least, I thought you weren't, but you've been testing my opinion of your judgment by refusing to come in."

"I'm on leave, and I have a job to do with those cattle." Bree waved at the herd.

The captain let out a low groan and rubbed his palm across his sharp chin. "You've been attacked twice in one day."

Cam mentally amended the tally to three times, but at least one of those times, the drone collision, might have been by accident. At any rate, he hoped so.

"Only once, sir—" Bree lifted her chin "—when I've had any reason to believe the attackers knew my identity. That was this morning. This afternoon, the three rustlers who accosted us, including Trout over there—" she gestured at the man the EMTs were loading onto a stretcher "—thought we were cowhands trying to stop them from taking the herd. This wasn't a personal attempt on my life. It was standard operating procedure for this gang of rustlers. The cartel does not know where I am right now. They *will* know as soon as I show up at headquarters."

Gaines let out an acquiescent grunt. "I'll grant you that the cartel probably has our office under surveillance, but they won't get to you there." He crossed his arms over his lean chest. "Be sensible. You're endangering yourself and others out here on your own."

Cam bent forward and rested his elbow on his saddle horn. "She's not on her own, sir."

The captain whirled toward him with a deep scowl. "And you are?"

"Cameron Wolfe, the Maguires' neighbor." He sat up tall in the saddle and met the fury with steady eyes. In a way, he didn't blame the ranger captain for his anger and frustration. The man was afraid for his colleague. But that didn't mean Cam needed to back down. "You're on my land at the moment. Bree and I are rounding up the herd that got stampeded during this morning's excitement. I've told her she doesn't need to feel obligated to do that, but apparently, she does."

Gaines narrowed his pale blue eyes. "You're the rancher who accosted Leon Waring and ended up helping fight off a sniper and taking down that attack helicopter."

"One and the same."

"Good work out there." The captain's expression relaxed marginally. "Now, will you please explain to your neighbor here that cooperating with law enforcement, not to mention her boss, is a wise idea?"

Cam chuckled. "I figure she's a sharp woman and can make her own choices."

The man's face reddened and his mouth opened as if to speak.

"No explaining necessary." Bree's brisk tone interrupted the exchange between Cam and her boss. "I am fully aware that I am in danger and that those I love are in danger, and even my work colleagues are in danger if I am in proximity to them. The cartel is not fussy about collateral damage and is not squeamish about using a person's family members to get close to their target. However, my disappearance into protection will not lessen the danger to my loved ones. If anything, that action will increase the risk, as the desperate hitters will be more prone to grab anyone available as leverage to flush me out. The only person who will be safer is me, and I can't put myself first in this situation."

Cam's heart swelled in appreciation of this woman's savvy and unselfish conclusions. If anyone got what she had so ably explained, he did. At one point in his own similar situation, he'd made the same decision she was making—to hold fast and stick it out, trusting for some other solution than uprooting his life. But then things happened and disappearing alone had become the only viable option. Now, Bree was in an uncannily similar position.

Cam jerked a decisive nod. "What she said."
Warmth cascaded through his insides at the
naked gratitude in Bree's gaze upon him.

The captain's sour stare affected him not at all.
If only he could assure Bree this choice would
turn out favorably for her, but her life hung
precariously in the balance, and there was little
anyone could do to affect the outcome but hope
and pray. The cartel was coming for her, and
things were likely to get messy. Cam would do
anything in his power to ensure that any spilled
blood was not hers, but the cartel had numbers
and ruthlessness in its corner. God alone knew
how long they could hold out against the overwhelming tide.

Chapter Seven

Weary and slumped in the saddle, Bree guided Teton to help push the last of the cattle through the gate into the home pasture near Cam's ranch headquarters. Just in time. Full dark spread across the prairie like spilled ink as the last sliver of the sun dipped below the distant mountain heights. Happily, a full moon and myriad twinkling stars studding the blue-black sky shed enough illumination to safely continue moving forward. The cattle picked up their pace, no doubt scenting the good water held in the spring-fed tank that had long been one of this ranch's richest features. Cam had done well to buy the place.

The injured animals trailed along last, but at least they continued onward. Except for the old pack mare and the lame gelding, who would be led to the barn, the other injured animals would have to wait until morning light to be lassoed and have their wounds treated. Tomorrow promised to be as busy as today, but hopefully without interruption by hostile forces.

She was relatively confident she'd spoken the truth to her captain when she'd claimed the cartel didn't currently know her whereabouts. On that premise, Captain Gaines had grumpily left without her in the medivac helicopter with the wounded prisoner. Of course, Dillon would need to be extra cautious going forward in case *sicarios* or cartel spies in the form of people or drones came sniffing around. She'd get in touch with her brother tonight, and they'd have that conversation.

"Let's head on up to the building site." Cam's voice pierced the darkness.

Bree turned her head toward the sound. His horse and rider silhouette stood out as a darker patch in the gloom. Behind him stood an additional pair of silhouettes, the wounded mare and lame gelding, she presumed.

"I'll be right behind you." She kneed Teton forward and took her gelding's reins from Cam, then followed him and his mare at an ambling walk in the direction of the looming barn.

They'd care for the animals they brought into the barn first and then go into the house and look after themselves. As grubby as she felt, a long, hot shower sounded like a major treat. Whether she'd eat something or simply call Dillon and then fall into bed afterward remained to be seen.

"My stomach is eating my backbone," Cam said as if sensing her thoughts about food.

Bree chuckled, the sound tired and faint on the breeze. "My eyelids need propping up. Do you have any toothpicks?"

Cam's laugh warmed her heart. Something about coming in off the range in this man's company felt so right that it was scary. She'd have to watch her wayward emotions and rein them in severely. A life crisis was no sane time to be entertaining romantic notions.

Forty-five minutes later, the horses fed, watered, and injuries tended, Bree and Cam entered through the side door of the Diamond-W's two-story home, a sturdy but plain dwelling that was significantly smaller than the Double-Bar-D's sprawling single-story house. The entrance led into a small mudroom where they hung their hats on pegs and washed up in the scrub sink. Then Cam led the way into a neatly laid out but compact kitchen redolent with the smells of Mexican spices and tortillas. A squat, round woman in a flour-coated apron stood near the stove.

The middle-aged cook grinned at them, brown eyes twinkling. "It is a good thing I heard those cattle bawling from a mile away, so I knew when to put the tamales in the oven. They are almost ready."

"Thanks, Estrella. You're a gem. Did Luis make it back from checking the irrigation lines?"

"Yes, Señor Cam. All was well with the pipelines. He is in the work shed mending a bridle."

Bree appreciated that Cam properly pronounced his hand's Hispanic name as *Lwees*. The knowledge suggested native Southwestern roots, which gave her a hint about Cam's origins. Or maybe it only meant he'd been polite enough to pick up on the pronunciation when he'd first met his ranch help.

Bree responded appropriately as Cam quickly made the introductions between the women, and then he glanced deeper into the house. "Do we have time for quick showers before we eat?"

The older woman waved them away. "The food will be on the table when you return."

Bree followed her host up a set of slightly creaky, original hardwood stairs to a guest bedroom furnished and decorated in a country theme. With a grateful sigh, she lowered her saddlebags onto the padded bench at the foot of the bed. Cam's gray eyes studied her solemnly, and she all but heard his unvoiced pledge: *No one will get to you here.* She met the look straight-on. Her heart fluttered and her stomach did a silly pirouette.

"The bathroom is at the end of the hall." He jerked a thumb in that direction. "I'll be down-stairs in the master. The Franklins upgraded it to include an en suite. We can meet in the kitchen. Estrella's tamales are the best I've ever had."

His slight smirk communicated that he was well acquainted with her fatigue and sympa-thized, but an authentic Mexican dinner was not to be missed.

"I'll be there." She nodded.

He withdrew, and his boots thump-creaked down the stairs. Releasing a long breath, Bree opened one side of her bags and drew out a change of clothing—just a T-shirt and a pair of soft leggings—plus a few toiletries she'd packed in anticipation of a possible night on the range. Sleeping in a house in a bed beat the bare ground in a tent by a mile, but a part of her prickled with unease that perhaps she'd be bringing dan-ger to Cam and his innocent housekeeper and

ranch hand. But that risk would be real anywhere she went. For the moment, her neighbor's
house was as safe as anywhere else.

The shower was as wonderful as she'd anticipated it to be. When she arrived downstairs,
clean and in comfortable attire, Cam was already in the dining room, where Estrella was
arranging the food on the table. From what Bree
caught of the conversation he was having with
his housekeeper, he had been updating her on
their eventful day on the range. The woman was
properly appalled and kept flapping her apron
and making sympathetic sounds. Then, at Bree's
appearance, she smacked plump hands together.

"Sit, sit." The woman waved Bree to a vacant
seat. "You must be starving."

With a nod toward Cam, Bree obeyed the
housekeeper and bowed her head with them
both while her host spoke a simple table prayer.
They dug in, and the meal was beyond scrump-
tious. Bree made sure to express her appreciation
to Estrella, who remained with them, sometimes sitting, and sometimes fetching this and
that, including a plate of flavorful cinnamon
churros for dessert. She did not eat, claiming
she and her husband, Luis, had eaten earlier.
The housekeeper and Cam made pleasant and

relaxed company, but Bree was under no illusion that she, with her drooping eyelids, was any kind of company at all.

As she shoveled the last yummy bite into her mouth, she caught Cam eyeing her speculatively. "What?" She narrowed her gaze at him.

"Sorry." He shook his head. "I was just thinking that maybe Estrella could be persuaded to even out that accidental haircut you received this morning." He ended the sentence with a grimace, clearly recalling the events surrounding that sniper bullet.

Bree caught her breath. "You're right. I need the damage fixed. I've always had long hair. This does feel...strange." She ran her hands through her ragged ends.

"No offense intended. The short style suits you."

"Indeed, it does." Estrella clicked her tongue. "Of course, I will be happy to provide a trim, but in the morning. You look ready to fall asleep on your plate."

The woman let out a hearty laugh that buoyed Bree's spirits. She may have lost a chunk of her hair, but she hadn't lost her life.

"Let me help you with the dishes first." She rose from the table.

"Nonsense, *mi querido*. It is my pleasure to serve such a brave one. Go get some well-deserved rest."

Estrella grabbed a pile of plates and bustled from the room. Cam seconded his housekeeper's urging. Gratefully, Bree trudged up the stairs, flopped into the bed and promptly fell into a deep slumber.

Bree had no idea how long she had slept when a firm hand on her shoulder shook her into startled awareness. Sitting up with a cry, her fist flew at her assailant and smacked a fleshy target. Pain jolted through her fist and up her arm. The shadowed figure at her bedside staggered backward with a deep *whoof*. Bree fought free of her bedcovers and leaped to the floor in full Krav Maga mode.

"Bree!" Cam's powerful rumble halted an instinctive kick before it left the ground.

The last of the sleep thrall fell away from her senses. "Cam? What are you doing rousting me like this? It's still dark out." Her sideways glance at the cracks between the curtains on the window revealed blackness outside.

Cam huffed, a switch clicked, and the overhead light sprang on. Bree blinked at her tall, pajama-clad host, his expression etched in taut planes. The paleness of his thin facial scar stood out against a red splotch where she'd struck him. There would be a bruise.

Bree's hand went to her mouth. "I'm so sorry." Her warm breath feathered against her fingers.

"No matter. Considering the situation you're in, I shouldn't have startled you." His words came out gruff, some deep emotion shading his eyes—not related to being sucker-punched.

Bree's gut seized. "What is it?"

"There's a fire at your ranch. It's visible from here."

"No, no, no!" Heart trip hammering, she raced to the window and threw the curtains aside.

Her mouth went stone dry. It was true. A red-gold stain on the landscape pulsed on the distant horizon. The fire must be substantial to stand out so visibly. Her stomach wrung like a dishrag.

"Dillon." His name emerged in a strangled tone. She could hardly speak for the constriction of her throat. "I have to go."

Bree whirled toward the exit and slammed against a large body adamant to obstruct her way. Sturdy arms wrapped her close, but she fought. If she could get her arms free of Cam's python grip, she'd punch him again.

"Whoa, whoa, whoa!" Cam clutched Bree close despite the sharp kick she landed on his shin, sending pain splintering up his leg. Another bruise for sure. "You didn't let me finish. Dillon's okay. Everyone at your ranch is all right."

She went still as if frozen in place. "What? How do you know?"

"He called me."

Bree went limp, and Cam hazarded releasing her but kept a grip on her shoulders in case she crumpled from the sudden relief. He didn't dare give a second thought to how good and right this woman felt in his arms. Painful kick not withstanding.

She glared up at him. "He called *you*. Why didn't he call me?"

"He knew you'd be furious if you weren't told right away, but he wanted me to stop you from doing exactly what you were trying to do—rush to the scene."

Her eyes flicked from right to left, thoughts clearly churning. "Because the whole purpose of the fire is to draw me out. This was arson."

"Dillon thinks so, though they won't know for sure until the blaze is out. The fire department is there already."

Bree's gaze hardened on him. "What is burning?"

"Your machine shed. The fuel inside the building is causing the blaze to be exceptionally intense."

"Not the house, or the barn, or the bunkhouse?"

Cam's blood chilled. If any of those structures had been set on fire, people and livestock would have been at risk. Not that the cartel would care. This scenario involving only the machine shed showed uncharacteristic restraint.

Bree pulled away from him, hugging herself and pacing. "The arsonist must be a local, not a ruthless *sicario*. Someone after the bounty, but a person with rural roots who would despise injuring animals and prefers not to hurt untargeted people."

"I had about reached that conclusion myself."

She stopped her restless movement and fixed a steady stare on him beneath raised eyebrows. "I would surmise the two rustlers who got away out at the playa as the culprits, except the rustler gang that's been operating around here has the same respect for life as the cartel, which is none. Do I have to start suspecting friends and neighbors now?"

Cam's heart sank. She'd asked a legitimate question—the sort of agonizing idea he'd dismissed to his sorrow at an earlier point in his life. *Please, God, don't let this situation turn out for her the same way it did for me.*

He drew in a deep breath and let it out slowly. "A lot of people are struggling financially, and the bounty is substantial. Desperation makes people vulnerable to temptation. But then, we don't want to jump to conclusions. There could be another explanation."

Bree side-eyed him like she knew he was attempting to soften a bitter blow. "If you think of one, please let me know."

Cam puffed out a dry chuckle. "I'll be sure to do that. But on the bright side, since you didn't come running when the smoke signal went up, anyone on the bounty hunt might decide you're nowhere in the area. The net could widen, taking some of the focus off the immediate area."

"A little breathing room, maybe?" She stopped pacing and faced him, hands on hips. Her green eyes lit with a glimmer of hope.

Cam forced a smile to his lips. Any reprieve would be temporary, but they'd take what they could get. "Lay low here on the Diamond-W like it's your safe house on the open range, and let's see what happens."

Her eyes narrowed. "I hate this."

The vehemence of her tone resonated within him, and he nodded. "I know. I hate it *for* you. In the morning, we can figure out clandestine means to contact your brother and your captain."

"Morning? Isn't it that already? It may still be dark, but it must be after midnight."

Cam snorted. "Technically, 2:00 a.m. counts as a new day, but I'm still all for a few more hours of rack time before the fresh workday starts."

Bree's shoulders drooped. "I don't know if I'll be able to get back to sleep."

"Give it a try. There's always milk that can be warmed down in the kitchen, but Estrella is likely to show up as soon as there's a stir in the kitchen. She'll hover like a mother goose. She and Luis have a small suite attached to the back of the house adjoining her culinary domain, and I know from the experience of trying to sneak out of the house early that she sleeps lightly."

A meager smile brightened the dark expression on Bree's face. "I think I'll crawl back under the covers and try to get my heart rate under control. I'm sorry, by the way."

"For what?"

She tapped her cheek on the location where she had struck him. Cam touched the spot on his face and found a little heat and swelling. He'd have a bruise by the time he woke to start the day.

He grinned at her. "You pack a wallop, ma'am. Remind me not to get in the way of your fist again."

Bree let out an unladylike snort, and Cam turned to go with a small wave. "Sleep tight."

"And fast. I'll be up by sunrise. I don't believe in burning daylight. We've got critters to look after."

He knocked lightly on the doorframe and awarded her a grin. "I'll meet you downstairs for breakfast at six sharp."

"You got it." She answered his grin with her own. "Don't be late."

"As if." He snorted and headed for the stairway, chuckling.

Who would have believed that tense encounter would end on a positive note? Cam's heart hurt for Dillon over the loss of property. What a mess, creating all sorts of headaches. But everyone was still upright and breathing. They'd have to take small mercies where they could get them.

He returned to his Southwestern-themed

bedroom and tucked himself under the covers he had so suddenly vacated. Bree thought she might have trouble getting to sleep again. She wasn't the only one.

Cam closed his eyes, and his last glimpse of Bree, flaming hair disheveled from sleep and green eyes gleaming as if determination alone would prevail against all threats, appeared mirrored against his eyelids. Stubborn. Unconventionally beautiful. Resourceful and undeniably courageous. Those were a few of the descriptors he'd apply to Brianna Maguire. His dainty socialite former fiancée had been this woman's polar opposite, but she'd been the sort of shiny woman the man Cam used to be had thought he wanted. But that was then. His eyes had been rudely opened since.

If he was honest with himself, dealing with Bree's straightforward manner was like a breath of fresh air compared to the demands and expectations Tessa had possessed, envisioning herself as the first lady of a Western ranch empire. Discovering Cam had no desire to play cattle baron—that ranch life meant she would work alongside everyone else—had done as much to end the relationship as her contempt for his resurgence of faith in Jesus Christ. In the end, she'd betrayed him in the worst way possible.

Cam's heart wrung at the memory, but the misery had dulled to the ache of a bruise rather than a deep knife cut.

At the time, he hadn't known if he could survive the pain, especially when her betrayal took a back seat to the other… The cruel knowledge he scarcely dared allow himself to think about. Almost worse than anything the cartel could dish out. Yet here he was—alive but hiding in plain sight. Forevermore not the man he used to be, and perhaps the better for it…if he could ever stop looking over his shoulder for the enemy coming after him.

What a pair he and Bree made. Both of them fugitives, not from the law but from the very criminals who should be locked up. Life could scarcely get more ironic than that. What tomorrow might bring, God alone knew. If the Espinoza cartel had its way, Bree's life would end in bullets and blood. Cam couldn't let them succeed if he hoped to continue living with himself.

But how could he stop the cartel? He had no idea. If only helplessness and despair didn't mock him like dark pits eager to swallow him whole.

Chapter Eight

Bree leaned her folded arms on the top bar of a corral fence, her gaze riveted on the tall figure working with a lovely bay filly. Cam had informed her that he recently purchased the two-year-old for breeding stock, and someone had delivered the animal to the ranch only three days ago. Her neighbor knew his way around horse training, that was for sure. The young animal trotted obediently in a circle around him, where he stood in the center of the corral, holding a rope attached to the horse's halter in one hand and a training stick in the other. The pricked-forward ears and slight angle of the equine head toward Cam indicated the trainer had captured the filly's attention. At a cluck from Cam's tongue and a flick of the stick with a small flag on its end, the horse picked up its pace to a slow lope.

Dust from flying hooves tickled Bree's nostrils and she stifled a sneeze but did not curb the smile that spread across her lips. This was a good life. Fresh air. Honest toil. The sun kissing her skin. Congenial company like the man who captured her attention more than the fine horse he trained. It hardly seemed possible that danger lurked like a predator sniffing at the perimeter of her life. Waiting. Watching. Ready to pounce.

The smile dimmed as she yanked her thoughts away from the dark precipice. Had it really been a whole two weeks since the fire at her place? Bree had kept in touch with her brother, not using her phone, which might be tracked, but Cam's. Dillon was already preparing to rebuild the machine shed, and orders were in to replace the ruined equipment. The destruction was a big-time, resource-stealing annoyance on a working ranch, but no living creature had been hurt. The fire had been officially declared arson, but nobody was yet in custody for the crime. Bree was waiting to hear back from her captain about a lead the rangers were pursuing.

Her heart wrung with an unvoiced plea that the culprit not be someone she knew. It was bad enough to have to suspect every stranger who came through the area without feeling unsafe around friends and neighbors. Not that she'd been out and about so far, but she couldn't pretend the world wasn't waiting for her to rejoin it. Something that probably needed to happen soon.

This idyll here at Cam's ranch had seemed to stretch on forever. Like she'd found safety that would last. Her heart willed the reprieve to go on forever, but her head knew better. Officially, she was using vacation days she had accumulated, and Captain Gaines was continuing to work with the Marshals Service to arrange the dreaded witness protection. Unofficially, she was hiding in plain sight, but realistically, this time on the Diamond-W could only be the proverbial calm before the storm.

With every passing minute, she potentially brought danger to the courageous man and his kind hired help who had taken her in. They— no, *she* needed a plan for when the cartel found her. The thought of leaving everyone and everything to adopt a new identity nauseated her. But what were her alternatives?

Bree had yet to find one, and there had to be a limit to how much longer she involved Cam. Too bad she was reluctant to admit the threshold was upon them and make the break. She was getting too comfortable here.

Bree dropped her arms to her sides and stepped back from the corral. Maybe she should—

"Whoa!" Cam spoke to the colt and brought the animal to a stop.

Bree also froze, gaze fixed on the training scene. The filly turned its nose to Cam and walked docilely, head low and calm, toward his still figure. Cam crooned to the animal and rubbed a hand between its doe eyes. Bree's skin tingled pleasantly as if she were the creature receiving the gentle touch.

Get a grip, Maguire! Bree shook herself and let out a huff that echoed a loud whiffle from the filly now following Cam to the barn.

"Let me brush her down," Bree called, and Cam acknowledged her request with a smile over his shoulder and a wave.

She joined Cam in the dim barn that smelled pleasantly of fresh hay, grabbed a horse brush, and got busy on the filly's sleek but slightly sweaty hide.

Cam patted the horse's rump. "She's coming along nicely, if I do say so myself."

"Agreed. You're a good horse trainer."

"Competent." He shrugged. "Hardly an expert."

The crackle hum of vehicle tires on gravel interrupted their conversation and brought both their heads around toward the ranch yard.

A muscle tightened in Cam's jaw, and Bree's gut twisted. She took a step away from the horse, but Cam raised a forestalling hand. "Stay here out of sight. I'll go see who it is and what they want."

Bree bottled a low growl in her throat. "I hate—" she started, but he was already striding from the barn before she could finish telling him how much she despised being on edge all the time and him being in danger because of her. Not that the observation was new information, but revulsion for the situation had pushed the words out of her mouth.

Laying the brush aside and leaving the filly tied in the alleyway between the stalls, Bree drew the pistol from her appendix carry and crept up to the open door. She didn't have to show herself to listen to whatever conversation Cam conducted with their uninvited guests. Quite probably, the visit was benign, but Bree was hardly going to rely on that possibility, especially when the intruding vehicle seemed to be coming up the driveway entirely too fast.

Remaining in the shadows, Bree put her eye to a crack between the door and the casing. A dark blue SUV with blacked-out windows skidded to a stop with a ping of gravel against the undercarriage mere yards from Cam's stalwart figure. He stood with legs set apart, offering a solid balance base for any necessary action. One hand subtly hovered near his own pistol in the holster on his hip. As he'd consistently proved, the man was no stranger to defending against aggression.

Taut silence fell over the yard. The late-morning heat baked the bare earth with a near-audible sizzle. Or maybe the sizzle was Bree's nerves strung tight as electrified fence wire.

At last, the driver's-side window rolled down and a man's hand reached out, showing a placating palm. A pleasant, round face appeared behind the friendly hand.

"Hola, señor." The man grinned, but the toothy facial expression sent a shiver down Bree's spine.

Maybe the guy was here for an innocent purpose, and she was overreacting, but she didn't think so. Smarmy is as smarmy does, and that too-big grin rang false, which led to expectations of deceptive behavior. Too bad she wasn't close enough to read the guy's eyes, but at least

Cam was, and she trusted him. The visible stiff-
ening of his spine didn't bode well.

"Stranger, whatever you're selling, I'm not
in the market for it." Cam's tone brooked no
nonsense.

"No, no, you misunderstand," the man in the
car protested, starting to open his door. "Let
me show——"

"Stay right there." The barked words and the
big hand on a pistol butt stopped the stranger
midmotion and midsentence. "I don't know you,
and I didn't invite you. If you're some innocent
passer-by who's lost his way out in the boonies,
my apologies. Go on back to the county road
and turn left. Continue in that direction for five
miles and you'll reach a state highway that will
take you to Interstate 27. Road signs will show
how to get to Lubbock or Amarillo or whatever
way you want to go from there."

The stranger's smile disappeared into a sneer.
"I am not lost, and I do not need directions.
You are not a very friendly man, *señor*. I might
become offended at your lack of hospitality."

"Offending you is the least of my concerns.
I've been hearing rumors about cartel hitmen
rampaging around the countryside. In fact, my
neighbor recently lost his machine shed to arson,

so forgive me if I'm a mite protective of my property. Unless you can convince me that you have legitimate business, you'd better turn your vehicle around and vamoose."

The stranger's face turned deep red, and Bree's heart began hammering against her ribs. Violence hung like gunpowder in the air. All it would take is a spark to turn explosive.

Behind Bree, the filly let out a shrill whinny and slammed her hoof against the floor. Even as Bree whirled on whatever threat crept toward her back, she dropped into a low crouch. A shadowed figure rushed at her, and the shotgun in his hands boomed.

At the shotgun's blast Cam involuntarily swiveled toward the sound. But his peripheral vision caught sudden movement from the man in the car. He forced himself to whirl back toward the immediate threat. Bree could take care of herself, couldn't she? *Please, God, make it so.*

Cam yanked his pistol from its holster as the snarling stranger lunged from his vehicle, bringing an automatic weapon to bear on him. Cam's gun spat milliseconds before the stranger's. The man grunted and staggered, throwing his aim off, and the burst of bullets from the automatic missed Cam. But not by much. The hiss of speeding lead nipped his ear. Cam pulled the trigger again, and his assailant collapsed. He rushed forward and kicked the man's weapon away even as another blast echoed from the barn.

Not a shotgun.

A pistol.

Bree.

A weight the size of an elephant left Cam's chest. She was alive and fighting back.

He had to help her. There was no time to address the injuries of the man from the car, who lay still, eyes closed, bleeding from his head and chest but breathing. Cam rushed for the barn but stopped himself from plunging willy-nilly into the dimness where grunts and smacks betrayed an ongoing struggle. At least the shooting had stopped.

Pulse throbbing in his neck, Cam pressed his back against the outside wall and peered around the edge of the door. Bree's pistol lay on the floor. Nearby, she and a wiry man struggled for control of a shotgun. The man was getting a taste of her booted feet and sharp elbows.

Cam stepped through the doorway with a shout. "Drop the gun!"

Wisely, Bree leaped away from her assailant to

give Cam a clear shot at the guy. Not so wisely, the man attempted to bring his weapon to bear on her, and Cam pulled the trigger. The attacker yelped, dropped his gun—finally—and clutched his wounded arm. A high, keening sound came from his throat.

Bree snatched up the pistol and the shotgun then spared Cam a nod. "Thanks. Are you…all right?" Her words came out with a wheeze, like she was struggling to catch her breath.

"Not a scratch. You?" He scanned her figure from top to bottom and spotted no obvious wounds.

"He took a shot at me, and I took a shot at him, but then we were too close to each other. After he knocked the pistol from my hand, I took a shotgun stock to the solar plexus. No bullets, thankfully. But not for lack of trying." She nodded at the door swinging on its hinges behind him.

Cam spared a glance over his shoulder and found the wooden door pock-marked with lethal pellets at about chest and head height. His blood ran cold at the thought of the consequences if the blast had struck her.

"Looks like the guy in the car came in as a distraction so this hombre could sneak up on you." He waggled his gun at the scowling shot-gun–wielder.

"Yep. This was planned." She shook her head. "Apparently, I've been located."

"You should have let me kill you." The wounded prisoner sneered. "You have no idea what's coming for you. There are many of us and only two of you."

"Nonsense." Bree snorted, seemingly breathing easier but rubbing her breastbone. "When you come after one of us, you take on the entire law enforcement apparatus of the great State of Texas."

"Are you certain they will be enough? They are not with you today."

Cam ground his teeth at the sly expression on the criminal's face. "Enough talk out of you. Move." He stepped aside from the door and waved for the man to walk ahead of him out of the barn. "You'll get your taste of Texas law enforcement hospitality all right."

"What he said." Bree stepped up alongside Cam, her face pale but her eyes blazing like sunstruck emeralds.

Side by side, they followed the prisoner out into the sunshine. A sturdy figure in a brightly colored skirt and white blouse rushed at them from the direction of the house. Estrella had a rifle clutched in her hands, but she kept the muzzle pointed skyward as she came toward them.

"What has happened, *señor*?" The housekeeper slowed as she neared, and then she stopped, pressing a fist to her mouth as her gaze swept over the incapacitated bad guys. Estrella huffed, scowled, and then shook her head. "I will call the sheriff and emergency services." Turning on her heel, the woman scurried back to the house in a swirl of skirts.

"Thank you," Cam called after her.

Bree pulled zip ties from her pockets and secured the wrists of her attacker. Droplets of red stained the ground from his arm wound, and he let out a pained grunt as she tightened the binding. Red-faced fury had replaced the pallor of shock on her face, so Cam inferred she wasn't inclined to spare the guy much sympathy. But she did order him to sit down on a nearby hay bale before he fell over.

As he sullenly complied, she grabbed a nearby length of rope and began to bind it around his arm as a temporary tourniquet. Not so devoid of sympathy, after all, or perhaps simply practical about preserving human life, as well as a potential witness to testify that his boss, Alonzo Espinoza, had ordered him to kill Bree. Not that such testimony was likely. Cartel muscle was usually more afraid of their ruthless master than what the US legal system could do to them.

Bree had her would-be killer under control, so Cam allowed himself to take his eyes off her and squat down by the man from the car. The *sicario* had taken a bullet to his upper chest and one had grazed the side of his head, knocking him out. Neither wound bled any longer because the cartel hitman was no longer breathing and the heart had stopped pumping. Cam frowned and heaved out a long breath.

It wasn't the first time Cam had been forced to take a life, but he'd hoped the last time was going to *be* the last time. Now this. But trouble had come looking for *him*, not the other way around, and he'd learned the hard way to respond with appropriate force. Hesitation got you, a colleague, or a bystander, dead. This time, it could have been Bree who might have paid the ultimate price if he hadn't made this guy pay it instead.

"What now?" Bree said from behind him.

Cam grunted and rose to face her. "This one didn't make it."

"I see that." She nodded solemnly. "Thank you. But that's not what I meant. What do I do now? I mean, I know I need to leave here. I've stayed too long." She looked away and pressed her lips together to constrain whatever railing outcry against her situation was striving to leave her throat.

"I know a place we can go."

Bree shook her head emphatically. "Not we. Me."

"I don't think the cartel is going to be happy about my interference. I'll have to lay low, too. We might as well do it together."

A slight glint of humor entered her eyes. "Methinks the Knight of the Range has dubbed himself this ranger's protector. As much as I appreciate the sentiment, I don't think the cartel will bother you if you're not harboring me. How are they even going to find out you killed one of their own? This one can't talk and the other guy—" she gestured to the desperado slumped on the hay bale "—will be in custody."

Cam sent Bree a bleak smile. "Trust me. They'll find out."

The vast intelligence network cartels worked hard to achieve, reaching into law enforcement itself, was another lesson Cam had learned the hard way.

The crunch of feet across gravel drew their attention. Estrella hurried up to them, clutching Cam's phone that he'd left in the house while he'd trained the filly. He reached out for the cell, but his housekeeper bypassed him in favor of Bree.

"It is for you, *señorita*. Your boss."

Bree released an audible sigh and took the phone. Cam eyed her with raised brows. What now?

Their understanding with her division was that anyone needing to contact her would do so through Cam's phone so that she would not have to activate her own and risk being tracked. Estrella had been made aware of this arrangement, and Cam had given her permission to answer his cell if he was not there to do so.

"When I tell him what just happened," Bree said, "the captain will no doubt want to connect with us both and get initial statements." Sidling closer to Cam, she tapped the screen and activated the speaker.

Cam appreciated the inclusion, but his gut tightened in anticipation of what Captain Gaines might say.

"The woman who answered my call said you just survived a cartel assault." The captain's words came out high-pitched and staccato as if pressure were being applied to his vocal cords.

"That's correct," Bree said. "The sheriff and emergency services are on the way. We have one wounded *sicario*, and the other—well, he won't need a doctor."

Her boss hissed in a breath. Glass suddenly shattered in the background, and someone shouted.

The hair on the back of Cam's neck stood on end. "What's going on there?"

"Headquarters has been under attack for the past ten minutes."

Cam's body went rigid. That was the farthest thing from what he'd figured on hearing, but it did explain the extreme tension in Gaines's voice.

"What do you mean?" Bree's tone was shrill.

"Cartel presence has been thick around head-quarters for the past week. We knew they were hanging around to intercept you if you came in, but none of the suspicious characters was doing anything we could arrest them for. But now, all of a sudden, we've got sharpshooters in nearby taller buildings plinking the bullet-resistant glass in our windows with armor-piercing rounds."

All color ebbed from Bree's face and she swayed. Cam caught her arm, steadying her.

"Casualties?" Cam asked.

"Two wounded from shrapnel. We're all taking cover, but—" Somewhere nearby, more glass exploded, and Gaines spat an angry word.

"I'll be there as fast as I can." Bree pulled away from Cam, her expression setting like steel.

"Don't you dare come here," Gaines bellowed. "That's an order. Secure yourself somehow until the Marshals Service contacts you to enter WITSEC. Should only be a day or two. We're done playing wait and hope for the best." Glass shattered again, and the captain cried out. "This can't be happening. We're the law! They're—"

A loud thump sounded, like something falling, and then the call went dead.

The wounded *sicario* sitting on the hay bale began to chuckle. A sinister solo in the stunned silence.

Chapter Nine

The phone slipped from Bree's sweat-slick fist. Cam's hand moved in a blur and caught it even as his fierce gaze seized hers. She straightened her spine.

"You heard the captain." She nodded toward him. "Time to hole up somewhere for a few days. You said you know a place?"

"I do, but I'll tell you about it later." He jerked his head at their prisoner.

Bree glared at the *sicario*, whose gaze met hers. The man's black eyes glittered like wet stones, and his lips seemed set in a permanent sneer. No doubt his ears were perked to overhear anything he could about their plans. All the cartel would have to do was send in a lawyer to talk to the prisoner, and the lawyer would get the information to pass along to Alonzo Espinoza.

Engine noises began to grow from the direction of the county road. Minutes later, a sheriff's vehicle pulled into the yard, followed closely by an ambulance. The next half hour passed in a flurry of activity as the wounded outlaw received first aid. Both desperados were placed into the ambulance; one strapped to a gurney and handcuffed to the railing, the other in a body bag.

The lanky sheriff's deputy frowned at the proceedings even as he took Bree's and Cam's statements. Estrella also served as a witness. She hadn't seen much of what had gone on, but she'd heard things that corroborated the sequence of events.

Bree stood nearby, shifting her weight from foot to foot, as the deputy wrapped up the interview. At last, he put his recorder away and settled his gaze on Bree.

"Too much excitement around these parts." His tone bordered on the accusing.

Standing at Bree's side, Cam let out a wordless snarl. "You can't blame a fellow law enforcement officer for doing her job. It's the cartel who has taken this vendetta to a surreal level. But then, Alonzo Espinoza hasn't been quite rational since his daughter was kidnapped by the Ortega cartel. He got her back by a fluke of happenstance, but now he goes over the edge if anyone messes with his family."

Bree whipped her gaze up at him. How did Cameron Wolfe know unreleased details about Espinoza and the notorious incident in New Mexico? The kidnapping and recovery of Espinoza's daughter, who was being trafficked by the Ortega cartel, had been kept under wraps. All the media had known was that the border patrol and DEA had wrapped up an Ortega trafficking ring with backslaps all the way around.

Then again, Cam had confessed he'd been involved in something with the DEA that had wound up costing him his relationship with his fiancée. Questions for her new neighbor piled up behind her lips, but now was not the time to ask them. Her narrow-eyed gaze on him promised a later discussion, and his slight nod and heightened color indicated he'd received the message.

Bree turned back to face the deputy. "Have you heard anything about what's happening at ranger headquarters in Lubbock?"

The man frowned. "What a mess." He shook his head, not in negation but in what Bree interpreted as amazed disgust. "Heard on the radio that the building got shot to smithereens, but I guess it's over now. Ended as quickly as it started. The cartel soldiers withdrew as suddenly as they attacked. Only minutes before the Lubbock Police Department SWAT team showed up loaded for bear."

"Casualties?" Cam asked the question on the tip of Bree's tongue.

She held her breath for the answer.

The deputy sighed. "Last I heard, there were a bunch of minor injuries from flying glass, but no one in the building took a bullet."

Bree breathed out a long sigh. "I'm so thankful."

"Amen," said Cam and the deputy in chorus.

"I'll get along then." The latter looked from Bree to Cam and back again. "What are your plans?"

Cam's lips flattened into a grim smile. "Let's just say we've got one and leave it at that."

The deputy shrugged and got into his sheriff's department SUV. Bree's eyes followed the dust of the retreating vehicle until the haze dissipated in the heavy air.

Then she turned to Cam with a pointed look. "What next, *caballero*?"

"Let's saddle up." Cam's tone was gruff, and he didn't meet her stare or respond to her designation of him as a mounted warrior. Without another word, he whirled and headed for the barn.

Bree followed on his heels. No conversation passed between them as they prepared their horses for a journey cross-country to where she didn't yet know. That she was content not to ask until they left the ranch spoke volumes about the level of trust she'd developed toward Cam Wolfe. And yet, nagging questions remained. Teeth on edge, Bree gave a last jerk, tightening her saddle cinch.

Estrella hustled into the barn, arms laden with packages. "I have brought you food and supplies for your journey that will last many days."

"You're a gem." Smiling, Cam accepted the packages from her and began fitting them into panniers on the packsaddle. "I'm relying on you and Luis to look after everything while we're gone."

"You may depend upon us."

"I do—too much so, lately. We can talk about a raise for both of you when I return."

"Sí, señor." Estrella's countenance brightened.

Five minutes later, Bree on Teton trailed Cam on Rojo, with the pack mare—not the injured Myra, but an animal that had been delivered to the ranch along with the new filly—ambling behind on a lead rope. They headed in a south-westerly direction.

"Okay, spill," she said. "Where are we headed?"

"The Diamond-W has a line shack on the backside of nowhere." He turned in the saddle as she trotted Teton up beside him. "I found it when I inspected the property prior to purchas-ing it. Used to be a place for cowpokes to stay when they were rounding up strays far from the home place, but the cabin didn't look like it had been used in years. The conditions will be primitive. Plus, we may have to cold camp so no one on land or in the air spots smoke com-ing from the chimney."

Bree jerked a nod. "Do you think a little dis-comfort intimidates me at this point?" She bit her lower lip against blurting out more in the same sarcastic vein.

She hadn't intended her tone to be so snarky—not toward *him* anyway—but she was beyond angry, thoroughly frustrated, and, yes, quite a bit scared. If Alonzo Espinoza was willing to mount an attack against a law enforcement head-quarters on United States' soil, there were no lengths to which he wouldn't go to get her. She'd thought she understood that, but the unprovoked assault in Lubbock brought the truth home to her. Those were her colleagues, her friends, who had been under attack.

At least the siege had been short-lived when other law enforcement agencies had mobilized to aid the rangers. No such rapid response would be coming for Cam and her out on the open range.

He reached over and squeezed her shoulder. The warm, steady touch melted a thin layer of the ice block that had taken up residence in her core. Unless something drastic happened to change her situation, soon she would be saying *adiós* to everything and everyone she'd ever known. Bree's heart tore. How could she go on?

Beneath Cam's palm, the rock that was Bree's shoulder abruptly melted into a slump. How hopeless she must feel. Cam's gut twisted. If anyone understood what was going on inside her, it was him. Telling his own complete story to her couldn't wait much longer, and she might be the only person on the planet to whom he'd feel safe telling it. But first, they needed to get to somewhere relatively safe and out of sight.

Next to him, Bree suddenly hauled back on her horse's reins and stopped. Cam pulled Rojo to a halt and turned the stallion to face her.

Her brows pinched together and faint lines between them formed a *V* on her forehead. "I understand about not lighting the fireplace in the shack, but what will we do with our horses? Their presence will give away our location to anyone scouting the area, especially by air."

"Good question." He offered her a smile that hopefully might relieve some tension. Then again, probably not. Nothing in this situation contributed to relaxation. "The shack stands near a spring-fed stream, and the grass is plentiful. We'll hide our tack in the lean-to attached to the cabin and set the horses free like they're simply loose and grazing a natural pasture. And because it *is* a natural pasture with more arid ground farther away, the animals are almost certain to stick around close by if we need them."

Bree offered a meager nod. "It's not a guarantee they won't wander off, like staking them out on ropes or keeping them in a corral, but I agree with the likelihood of them staying close by. If we're attacked, we may not be able to get to them as quickly as we would like, but in this situation, the emphasis is more on hiding than escaping—at least once we're at the cabin."

"Agreed. To complete the camouflage, we can push any cattle we run across over into that pasture as well. Then it will thoroughly appear to be assorted livestock loose on the range, a natural occurrence on a ranch."

A smirk appeared on Bree's lips and the tension lines on her face smoothed. "You think of everything, Mr. Wolfe. One would think dodging bad guys was a way of life for you."

Cam's jaw dropped, a protest forming on his tongue, but he halted the disclaimer before it emerged in words. Deflection of such remarks had become a reflex with him for self-preservation, but he didn't need that tactic with this woman. What would she think of him when she heard the full truth? He suppressed a shudder and forced a chuckle that came out more like a hiss of steam than an expression of wry humor.

With a narrow-eyed look, Bree bumped her horse's ribs with her boot heels, and Teton moved out obediently. Cam shut his mouth and brought Rojo around beside her. Silence fell, except for the muted thud of hooves against packed earth and the chuff of horses breathing easy. Scents of sage and juniper wafted on a welcome breeze that did its bit to relieve the relentless heat of the sun.

"I need to call Dillon," Bree suddenly exclaimed . "I can't believe my mind has been in such knots that I haven't thought about him. The way the gossip grapevine works around here, he'll soon know about the incident at your place…if he doesn't already."

She swiveled at the waist and pulled the sat phone from her saddle bag. They'd both left their cells at Cam's ranch since they were the devices most susceptible to tracking. It was unlikely even the cartel's considerable resources stretched to the ability to locate a particular satellite phone.

Bree barely had the sat phone in her hand when it rang. She gasped, and the instrument slipped. Cam reached out and caught it. He could hardly blame her for being skittish.

"Let me answer," he said.

She shrugged but didn't speak. Her face had gone so pale the dusting of freckles stood out on her high cheekbones. No doubt, dreading what fresh bad news might be coming this time, recent phone calls having brought nothing good.

Cam pressed the talk button. "This is Cameron Wolfe. Speak."

Heavy breathing answered the brusque greeting. "Bree!" the caller finally blustered. "Is she okay? Is she with you?"

Cam's insides relaxed. He held the phone out

to his companion. "It's your brother. Sounds like he's about to hyperventilate."

Bree wrinkled her nose. "Like I told you, he'd heard already." She took the device from him and put it to her ear. "I'm fine, Dill."

"Where are you?"

Cam winced. Her brother must be shouting for the question to clearly reach him through the handset. Bree's scowl and pulling the instrument away from her face confirmed his deduction about her brother's volume.

"Dial it down, bro," she said, returning the phone to her ear. "Like I said, I'm entirely unhurt… Yes, Cam, too… No, it's better if you don't know where we are or what we're going to do next… Yup, I knew about the attack on ranger headquarters, but I'm not surprised it's on the news already."

Eavesdropping on the conversation between Bree and her brother was a bit like seeing the action of only one side of a volleyball court, but he could deduce the other end of the exchange. It was nice that Dillon had asked after him when his sister's situation had to be demanding every speck of concern in his heart.

"No, I can't come home… Yes, I know you'd do anything and everything to protect me, but it's not going to be enough. We have to face facts." The last part of the sentence emerged with a strangled sob. She took in a stuttering breath and her whole body stiffened as if coming to attention. "The Marshals Service is almost ready to take me into custody. I might never see you again, and that's just the way it has to be. I can't endanger—"

Dillon's outburst on the other end must have been more of a snarl than a shout since Cam couldn't make out the words, only the emphatic tone. Bree brought her mount to a halt and Cam did the same, scarcely daring to breathe as he awaited her response.

"I know you would willingly come with me, Dill." She hung her head, her shoulders suddenly slumping as if the weight of the world had finally crushed her. "I can't let you do that. I don't *want* you to do that. You've got a good life. Live it."

Cam bit down on the inside of his cheek and looked away, blinking against a salty sting in his eyes. Her situation was many times worse than his had been. She had someone who cared enough about her to give up his lifestyle and identity to be with her. No one had volunteered to enter exile with *him*. He envied Bree such a treasure of a relationship, and yet, the willingness of her loved one to sacrifice deepened the tragedy for them both. These siblings would miss each other terribly.

Cam mentally huffed. Doubtful that anyone was missing him from *his* former life. As bitter as that knowledge might taste on his tongue, at least the man he'd been was not the man he was now. He wouldn't go back to his shallow, self-centered old existence even if he could. A life-changing encounter with Jesus Christ had made him a new person even more thoroughly than a change of legal identity. And that was another part of his story he needed to share with Bree before the marshals took her away.

Cam's heart tore. Now, they'd never have the opportunity to explore what might have developed between them if given time and proximity. Their attraction was palpable and growing.

"Cam."

The voice barely impinged on his consciousness.

"Cameron Wolfe."

Bree's exasperated tone pierced Cam's introspection. He shuddered and met her bemused gaze. She'd put the satellite phone away, so he'd missed the end of her conversation with her brother, but he could infer the sorrow.

"I'm so sorry."

"Me, too." She gave a curt nod, set her face like stone and nudged her horse into motion.

Cam followed suit, any further words dying on his tongue. What else was there to say?

Within a half hour of steady, quiet riding, they came upon a small group of cows and calves ambling along in search of good grass and a drink of water. Like cowhands that had worked together for ages rather than a few days, Cam took one side of the grouping while Bree migrated to the other side, and they guided the small herd to a gate that let them into the furthest north pasture of Diamond-W property.

"Only about another hour, and we'll be there," he told Bree as she followed the cattle through the gate that he was holding open.

She nodded without a word, her face slack with weariness. The sun wouldn't go down for a while yet, but he had little doubt she was ready to collapse. The emotional toll of this day had been far greater than the physical. Nor had the blows finished coming. They expected any moment for the sat phone to ring with the Marshals Service on the other end with final arrangements to announce. Who knew? They might show up in a helicopter and whisk her away yet tonight.

Something like cold feathers slid across Cam's skin. His head knew the score, but his heart remained in denial. Wasn't there some other way? There hadn't been for him, but— Cam shook himself physically as he let himself through the gate and latched it. He needed to stop dreaming about what could never be and get his head in the here and now.

All too soon, the one-room cabin, standing squat and shabby like a forlorn sentinel on the bare prairie, came into view. Scenting water nearby, the herd quickened their hooves, though some moved in fits and starts, snatching mouthfuls of good green grass as they progressed toward the spring.

Pulling his horse up near the shack's front door that sagged on its hinges, Cam watched Bree for her reaction.

She snorted a ragged chuckle. "You told me the place wasn't much, and I see you may have exaggerated. There's 'not much,' and then there's 'hardly anything.' Are you sure the structure isn't going to collapse on our heads?"

Cam grinned at her. "The cabin is sturdier

than it looks. I'm torn between thoughts of giving it a little tender loving care and bringing it to useful life again or leveling it. There's even a crude stone-walled root cellar beneath the structure and a cool room hollowed out of stone for preserving meat. Maybe our stay here will help make up my mind."

Bree swung down from her horse and Cam followed her example. In short order, they had the saddles and bridles off their mounts and stored in the lean-to that abutted the square structure. They gave their mounts and the pack-horse some quick brushes to get the worst of the sweat and dirt off for their comfort and so the animals wouldn't look like they'd recently been ridden. Then they turned the horses loose to mingle with the cows at the spring a short way behind the cabin.

"Shall we?" Cam motioned with his hand at the front door as he hefted a pannier of supplies.

"You first." Bree lifted the other pannier. "I'm not sure I'm that brave."

Cam chuckled and stepped up onto the short porch fronting the building. The place wasn't locked. Not much point in it when one of the windows was broken. He simply turned the knob and pushed the door open. An assortment of odors rushed him—dust and must and a bit of musk. Almost certainly, they'd have to chase out a small critter or two before they settled in.

To her credit, Bree didn't flinch or even mention the possibility—er, probability—of rodents. Despite her teasing about not being brave enough to step inside first, she was a ranch girl through and through. An hour later, they had their crude camp established. Matching sleeping bags had been rolled out against opposite walls of the cabin. A small propane camp stove for heating hot beverages or canned stew or beans was set up atop the wood-burning oven they had no plans to use. Canned and dry goods sat sorted on the counter and, finally, the sandwiches and cake Estrella had sent with them for the first meal had been laid out on the table. With matching groans, they settled on the rickety dining chairs to quiet their bellies' complaints.

Cam's muscles ached from the strange and strenuous day they had experienced. Her aches and pains were likely worse, considering she'd gone hand-to-hand with a *sicario*.

"How are you doing?" he asked her as they polished off the cake. "Physically, I mean. I know you're struggling emotionally. Who wouldn't be?"

She shrugged, keeping her eyes averted. "I'll probably be stiff and sore in the morning, but nothing too bad." Then her eyes snapped toward him.

Cam's face heated under the intensity of her stare.

"Don't you have a story to tell me?"

"Would you like to get some rest first? My tale can wait until morning if you're on overload."

"No more delay." The thrust of her chin and the steel of her gaze brooked no deflection.

Cam inhaled a deep breath and then let the oxygen trickle in miserly dribbles from his lungs. Time to come clean.

Chapter Ten

"Everett Davison."

At Cam's emphatic tone and his steady stare, Bree stiffened. The name Davison did ring a familiar bell in the back of her mind, but the details were fuzzy. Some sort of historical figure and something more current as well. She drew her brows together and sifted through her memories from lessons about the American Southwest.

"Start with Elliot…" Cam verbally prompted, and the picture snapped into focus in Bree's mind.

"Elliot Davison, the famous—some would say infamous—cattle baron from the late 1800s in New Mexico Territory. He gobbled up great swathes of land by any means necessary under his Leaning-D brand. Then, sitting on top of the world and poised to become the first governor of the newly formed state in 1912, he died suddenly of a heart attack."

Cam grinned at her, but a certain grimness remained in his eyes. "You recall your South-western history lessons. Elliot's son, Ethan, took the dynasty to a new level with the discovery of oil on the Davison property. However, he never entered politics, though he meant to, but he also died before the dream could be realized."

"Right." Bree nodded. "By the third gen-eration, the Davison name was pretty much synonymous with ranch royalty, and the fourth-generation patriarch, Emeric Davison, became a New Mexico state senator with his eyes on the US senate and maybe beyond. But didn't I hear a few years ago that the dynasty fell apart? Wasn't Emeric Davison found to be complicit in smuggling drugs and people from Mexico? There was a shootout on the property with the Ortega cartel, and people were killed, includ-ing Emeric."

A bright flicker of—what? pain?—lit Cam's eyes, but the emotion was extinguished so quickly Bree couldn't be certain she'd read the response correctly.

"Your recall is spot on." Cam nodded, his expression stoic. "The Leaning-D brand is now defunct, and the property either confiscated by the state or sold off by a scattered gaggle of shirt-tail heirs scrambling to distance themselves from a nasty scandal."

Bree frowned. "So, who is Everett Davison?"

"Me." Cam sat stiffly as if an iron rod had been attached to his spine.

Bree gaped at him.

"At least, I used to be." His lips pressed together into a thin line and his gaze fell away.

"Your real name is Everett Davison?" Bree blinked at him. "And you are a member of *that* Davison family?"

"Yes, to the latter. Emeric's only child and direct heir, in fact, but no, to the former. Everett Davison *used* to be my name. I am now legally Cameron Wolfe. According to a private bit of family lore, my several times great-grandmother's maiden name was Wolfe. Camille was a kind and Godly woman, by all accounts, and not a fan of her husband Elliot's tactics in chasing after riches. When I was forced into hiding, I wanted to connect back to an ancestral line with positive associations and yet have a name that was unlikely to be linked with my prior identity."

"Wow!" Bree lifted her camp mug to her lips and sucked in a deep draught of cool spring water to counteract a mouth suddenly gone dry. Then she clanked the metal cup onto the rough-hewn table. "You must have a long story to tell. So, give." She narrowed her eyes on Cameron—no, Everett—no, Cameron. At least, that was who he claimed to be now.

Cam's face reddened under her glare. He heaved a great sigh and shook his head. "It *is* a long story and not a pretty one. I'm here now, living the simple, rural life that suits me, and I hope, with an integrity too many of my ruthless ancestors lacked."

Bree's heart panged at the anguish in his tone. He'd seen some ugliness, that was for sure, but how much of the mess he'd been exposed to, he had yet to disclose. "Were you there at the end for the gunfight?"

"I was." Raw anguish masked his face. No mistaking the pain this time. "I got this from a close-quarters knife fight in the melee." He brushed his fingertips across the scar on his face.

Silence fell, and Cam slurped a drink from his cup. Bree held her gaze on him, waiting quietly for him to gather himself and proceed.

Cam set his mug on the table and nudged it reflexively one way and then the other with the fingertips of opposite hands. "I was the inadvertent catalyst for the implosion of my family and the fallout that hurt some and helped others, but the chain of events started years before that senseless gun battle. How to begin…where to begin?"

His face went slack, as if he were meditating deeply, and then his jaw firmed and he met Bree's eyes. "Young Everett's mother divorced his father when he was six years old. She took her financial settlement and left him with his dad. He hardly ever saw her after that. You would think the situation would cause father and son to grow close, but that's not what happened." He let out a thin chuckle.

Bree opened her mouth to speak, but he lifted a forestalling hand, so she closed it again.

"Everett was a bit of a throwback child," he continued, "at least as far as his father was concerned. He took to ranch life like an eagle to the air. Not the ordering-things-done-from-the-office, cattle-baron lifestyle, emulating the dad he never clicked with, but the hands-on, nitty-gritty work of wrangling cattle and horses, imitating the ranch foreman he followed around like a gangly puppy.

"Daddy Emeric didn't approve, but he was too wrapped up in his own busy schedule to interfere much when the boy was little. He had visions of his son realizing the family dream of going big into politics, and he maneuvered like a Formula One racing driver to make the kind of social connections that would set his son up for success. Emeric did so well at it that he ended up a state senator himself. The only rain on his parade was young Everett refusing to engage in politics in his footsteps. The contentiousness got so heated that as soon as Everett was old enough, he left his beloved ranch."

"Ouch!" Bree leaned forward and touched Cam's knee. "That must have hurt."

"Like an infected wisdom tooth." He nodded. "But then, Everett found his second great career love, law enforcement. He ended up a DEA agent."

"Wait a second." Bree sat back in her chair. "I thought you told me you 'cooperated' with the DEA in taking down a human-smuggling ring, not that you were an agent yourself."

He grimaced with a shake of the head. "At the time of the events at the Leaning-D, I was no longer a DEA agent—but we're getting ahead of the story."

"So, you were a civilian when the bullets were flying at the ranch? Just like now with all we've been dealing with?" Bree's gut went hollow. "Living through this situation with me now has got to be like a nightmare déjà vu."

"You have no idea how accurate your assessment is. There's more. A lot more." The words emerged in a taut, inflectionless string. All color drained from Cam's face and his hands resting on the tabletop formed white-knuckled fists.

"I'm listening. Go on." She resisted the urge to reach out to him again.

A comforting touch wasn't welcome at this moment. She'd been there herself when the pain was too raw and the slightest well-meaning sympathy would trigger protective walls snapping into place to contain the hurt. If Cam was going to get through this tale, she needed to let him tell the story at his pace.

For him, speaking it out loud could also be a form of processing trauma. Bree knew that well enough from the aftermath of her failed relationship with her ex-husband. At least she had enjoyed a childhood of close family life with loving parents. Apparently, Cam was unacquainted with that priceless benefit. How he'd turned into the fine man she'd come to know and appreciate, Bree could scarcely comprehend.

"Unbeknownst to our stalwart hero—" Cam

let out a self-mocking chuckle "——Daddy had a secret weapon in his arsenal by the name of Tessa Harding. And, boy, was she the nuclear option. She blew poor Everett's life compass off the map. For her, he'd give up what she called 'the risky law enforcement life.' He'd even return to the ranch where Senator Papa waited with his agenda. Everything was going to plan for Tessa and Emeric, and then the ranch got ahold of Everett once more.

"He realized he'd come home, and he wasn't going to leave again for any sort of campaign trail or the halls of government. In fact, the socialite life that was oxygen for Tessa polluted Everett's nostrils like toxic fumes. Tessa and Papa pitched all kinds of fits, so Everett started spending days at a time out on the range, wrestling with his fascinated devotion to Tessa, his loathing for the political machinations that invigorated his father, and his need to make some sort of peace with all of it that didn't involve him selling his soul. That's when he restarted his childhood habit of reading his generations-removed-grandmother's Bible by campfire light."

Something long dormant in Bree's heart stirred and she shifted uncomfortably in her seat. "Camille Wolfe's Bible?"

"Yep."

"Did the reading help?"

"Beyond my wildest dreams. Reading through the Gospels and my dear ancestor's notes in the margins overhauled my thinking and set me free from my problems without changing my circumstances one iota."

Bree's facial muscles tensed. "What do you mean by that?"

"Jesus made Himself real to me in those pages and confronted me with my selfishness."

"Selfishness?" Bree snorted. "Sounds like you were in the fight for your life as you needed it to be."

"Exactly. *My* life as *I* wanted it to be. Absolutely self-centered, fighting tooth and nail for *my* way. But this newfound awareness of my own failures didn't mean I needed to surrender to other people's selfish agendas. No, I needed to listen to the One who has always had my best interests at heart. I had never given two minutes thought to what God might want from me and for me. To say I was humbled and stunned was putting it mildly."

Suddenly consumed with a need to know what had come from this personal epiphany, Bree leaned toward Cam. "What did you do?"

He laughed, a free and light sound that contrasted starkly with his dark mood moments before. "I stayed in camp with no other humans around for three more terrible, wonderful days."

"Terrible?"

"Yes, the most horrifically excellent days of my life. God shone a spotlight on my life, confronting me with all the specific instances where I trampled others or disregarded them to advance myself. I had a stellar record with the DEA, not just because I was a good agent—which I was—but because I didn't care who I hurt or slighted to make a success of my career. I *had* to show Daddy I would make something of myself without his influence or his money. Under Divine scrutiny, I was horrified by the callous person I'd become. By the time I was done humbling myself and repenting in that remote campsite on the backside of nowhere, I felt clean and whole for the first time in my life."

Bree's insides roiled. What should she make of this raw testimony? Surely, all this humbling and repenting didn't apply to *her* life, did it? Just because she'd stopped being a church-goer after the divorce— She ruthlessly shut down that avenue of introspection. Her wounds were her own to lick. God understood that, didn't He?

Cam's eyes glowed and he let out another laugh. "Just the memory of that special time basking in the Lord's presence reminds me again to stop focusing on myself or negative situations."

"Sounds terrific." Bree snorted. "I wish that were an option for me."

Cam's unguarded yet unflinching stare riveted Bree to her seat. "Isn't it?"

Her insides curled away from the soul-baring look as if Someone else were gazing into her depths through his eyes. What did He see?

She knew. Yes, in the secret place of her heart, she knew He'd found the fears and insecurities that kept her presenting a tough face to the world and guarding every scrap of independence like her own personal Fort Knox. What would happen between herself and God, between herself and this man, if she let her guard down? Did she have the courage to find out?

From the expression on her face, something he'd said had disturbed Bree deeply. Not his intention in his soul-baring. He'd only been seeking to communicate clearly. But her eyes darting here and there, settling on nothing, and the flatness of her expression betrayed discomfort and probably a significant inner battle. What that meant related to what he'd told her, Cam had no way of knowing. Had she suddenly started to mistrust him because of the faults he'd confessed?

"It's okay." He lifted a hand in a placating gesture. "I'm not expecting anything from you, and I'm not about to skip out. I'm here for the duration."

Bree's leaf-green eyes landed on him. "I know you're not leaving, but I still don't understand why not."

"Maybe it would help if I finished my story. I haven't spoken of this to anyone since the debrief with law enforcement after the shootout."

"How long ago was that?"

"Two years of hiding and wandering. It's taken me this long to work through all the legalities in a way that didn't leave a public record for the Ortega cartel find and to locate a new place to call home."

Bree frowned down into her empty mug. "I appreciate you being willing to tell me about a horribly painful incident, and I want to hear it." She rose from her rickety seat, her gaze doing that darting thing again. "But I need some time to process what you've told me so far. Besides, I'm bushed. Can it wait until to-morrow morning?"

In the growing dimness of the unlit room at dusk, Cam studied her weary posture and took note of the dark circles under her eyes. "Sure. Get some rest. We can go at this fresh tomorrow. Who knows? Maybe inspiration will strike and we'll come up with some ingenious way of thwarting the Ortega cartel permanently without uprooting you from your life."

Bree let out a sound like a cross between a snicker and a snort. "I won't be holding my breath while I'm dreaming of rainbows and lollipops."

Cam laughed. "Fair enough. I'm all for being realistic, but I'm not giving up either."

He busied himself cleaning their food mess and putting away the few eating utensils they'd used while Bree sat down on her sleeping bag and removed her boots. Then she curled up on top of the sleeping bag with her back toward Cam. The cabin was too warm and stuffy to allow for slumber inside covers.

His eyes swept the small, musty room. The sun was down, but the moon was bright, and objects indoors had become hazy shadows. To avoid exposing the cabin's occupancy, they could not light a lamp. Turning in for the night made sense. But first he moved carefully to the gaping hole left by the broken window and peered out into the night.

Slowly moving lumps of darkness betrayed livestock ambling across the grass. In the near distance, a cow mooed, probably summoning a wayward calf. Insects hummed, a few flitting by him into their meager shelter, along with a breeze barely cooler than the still-warm, sage-laden air on the cusp between summer and fall on the Llano Estacado.

Not long now, and the temperature would fall significantly. Winter wasn't a time to be caught roughing it on the Llano prairie. A resolution for Bree's situation needed to be found and acted upon swiftly. If only it didn't appear her single viable option was disappearing into witness protection. He would miss her more than made any sense to him, considering the short time they'd been acquainted.

Was there anything he could do to change what seemed the inevitable course of events? After all, he was acquainted with Alonzo Espinoza. Some might even think the drug lord owed him a favor. Cam let out a muted snort. Doubtful Espinoza did the math that way after all that had happened. Besides, reaching out to the head of the Espinoza cartel risked exposing himself to the Ortega faction. It was widely known that the rival cartels had spies embedded in each other's organizations. But did the risk outweigh the potential benefit if Alonzo was inclined to listen to Cam's—er, Everett's plea for clemency toward Bree? He would have to reach out under his old identity. A shudder ran through Cam's body.

With a sigh, he turned away from the window. He should get some shuteye, too. If a person or a machine came within the vicinity of the line shack, the animals would be disturbed and their sounds of alarm would wake him up.

Cam removed his boots and then lay down atop his bag, which did little to soften the hard floor. Sleeping outside on the ground might have been marginally more comfortable. Maybe they could do that tomorrow night, weather permitting.

Sleep proved elusive. Like chasing happiness, it darted away just beyond his reach the more he strained for it. Finally, he sat up and scrubbed his eyes with the heels of his hands.

"Cam?" Bree's soft voice reached him across the dark space that separated them.

"Yup."

"You can't sleep either?"

He chuckled. "Nope."

A rustling came from the opposite side of the shack and her shadowy form sat up and turned toward him, her face half lit by the moonlight seeping in through the window opening. "I think I need to hear the rest of your story. What happened to Everett Davison on the Leaning-D in New Mexico that has Cameron Wolfe ranching in Texas on the Diamond-W?"

He swallowed against a dry throat. Might as well throw the punch line out there. "Everett Davison saved Alonzo Espinoza's daughter's life."

"What?" The question came out a strangled screech. "No way! Why did you save that piece of information until now? How? You have some explaining to do."

Her incredulous outrage brought a grin to Cam's face that quickly fell away as he considered the rest of the tale he was about to share. He rested his back against the wall of the shack and let his mind roam into the past. How could he encapsulate a wild jumble of actions and reactions into a few intelligible sentences?

"The day I broke camp from my life-changing retreat on the range and began my return to ranch headquarters," he began in low, slow tones, "I ran smack into a hidden compound of human traffickers in a remote area of the Leaning-D. They had a shack not much nicer than this one located in a snug little canyon. A trio of armed thugs were in the process of herding a group of teenagers and children out of the building and into a small haulage truck fitted for off-road travel. I was on a ridge overlooking the activity, and they didn't spot me. Naturally, I wasn't about to let them get away with their human contraband."

"Of course not, but what could you do? You were all alone."

Cam shrugged, though she probably couldn't see the gesture. "There were only three bad guys, but the situation was tricky because I didn't want to give them an opportunity to harm the kids, which they might do if they felt cornered. Let's condense the story and say I got out ahead of them and arranged for some sharp objects to give their truck a flat tire. While a pair of them were replacing the tire, I crept in and knocked the one guarding the children unconscious. Then it was easy to get the drop on the other two because they'd had to lay aside their weapons to change the flat."

"Just another day at the office? Not hardly!" Bree laughed. "Don't tell me. One of the children was Alonzo Espinoza's daughter. *You're* the guy who thwarted Raul Ortega's plot to revenge himself on his arch rival by taking his enemy's youngest child. Law enforcement kept your name out of the news."

"Got it in one guess."

Something like a growl came from Bree's throat. "I hate it when innocents get caught up in evil grown-ups' vicious games."

"Me, too. If I didn't *know* that somehow no suffering goes to waste and that Divine justice will ultimately and eternally be served, I would be in despair over humanity and this messed-up world. Not that I have any easy answers about bad things happening to innocents, but at least I can now say I trust the One who does. That wasn't always the case."

"Hmm." A floorboard creaked as Bree shifted to a new position. "I don't think I'm where you're at yet on the subject, but let's move on. What happened next?"

"Fair enough." Cam lifted a silent prayer for Bree to make her peace with God. At least, he was wise enough to know praying was the best thing he could do. How the struggle between bitterness and faith came out was an intensely personal thing. "Oddly, after the authorities came and hauled the creeps away and took custody of the trafficked children, my father joined me in lobbying for my name to be kept out of the news releases. I thought he'd leap on the incident as an opportunity to thrust me forward into the limelight or at least to toot his own political agenda as a law enforcement advocate. The reaction to avoid publicity was highly suspicious to anyone who knew Emeric Davison. That's when I first began to dread that my father knew something about the trafficking that was happening on his property. To say I was torn up about the idea would be an understatement."

A soft, whining sigh came from Bree's side of the cabin, her sympathy unspoken but clear. "Completely understandable."

"I wish I could say that was the end of the story and my suspicions subsided." A sour taste formed on his tongue. "But things escalated and got more complicated from there. The one bright ray in the murky mess was that all the children were returned to their families, including Espinoza's daughter. Cartel chief or not, the

US wasn't about to withhold his daughter from him. What a political nightmare that would be. The other side of the coin is that my name got back to Espinoza as his daughter's savior and to Raul Ortega as the one who thwarted his act of vengeance on his arch rival."

"Yikes!" Bree let out a low whistle. "All of a sudden, you got plopped into the middle of a blood feud between ruthless men."

"Brianna Maguire, you are perspicacious as always." Cam laced his tone with irony. "The end of the nightmare for those kids was just the beginning for me. I—"

"Shh!"

Bree's sudden shush froze the words in Cam's throat.

"Do you hear that?" Her words were an urgent whisper.

Cam held his breath and strained his ears. Outside, the cattle's lowing grew more frequent, and hooves thudded on the hard ground. Not stampeding, but uneasily milling. Then above the animal sounds, a faint, unnatural buzz sent chills cascading through his body and stood his hair on end.

A drone had found them. Or maybe not found them...yet. But the eyes in the sky were searching, and if the mechanical creature was roaming in the dark, the equipment must include night vision and possibly infrared capabilities. Their heat signatures inside the cabin would glow brightly, a place where the livestock would not be.

Cam rose and snatched up his rifle, boots and saddlebags. "Down into the stone cool room beneath the cabin. Now!"

Wordlessly, Bree grabbed the same items and followed him to the trap door against the far wall. Something like frozen barbed wire twisted Cam's insides. They had seconds to disappear into the manmade stone cavern—if that long. Their response to the incursion might already be too late.

Chapter Eleven

As Cam flung the cellar door wide open, Bree's pulse thundered so loudly in her ears that the smack of the door against the floorboards barely registered with her. A black hole gaped inches beyond her sock-clad feet. Ice congealed in her middle.

How could she make herself jump down in there? How deep was the pit? Did any creepy crawlies, or worse, a venomous snake, await her?

A snap near at hand drew her attention and a muted, blue glow flowed around them, not likely visible outside the cabin. Cam had activated a glow stick, no doubt from his pack. He tossed the stick below, and an expanse, void of any threatening creatures, took shape. The dirt floor of the cellar lay about six feet beneath the shack, and there was a rickety-looking ladder, which they didn't have time to test or use.

Inhaling a deep breath, Bree jumped into the

hole then swiftly moved out of Cam's way as he did the same while pulling the trap door shut. Dust puffed up around them, and a musty, damp odor pervaded the space. Bree bottled a sneeze.

Cam scooped up the glow stick and jabbed it in the direction of the cellar's far wall. The area continued longer than where the cabin's outer wall must extend, and the rough-hewn, mortared rock walls gave way to the solid, human-chiseled stone of what might have been a tiny natural cavern before people had fashioned it for use as a cool room. The nearby spring may have originally carved the hollow in the rock, though the water no longer flowed there.

Crouching, Bree scuttled toward the cover of the stone alcove where no heat signature could betray them to those who hunted their lives. Cam did the same, his height forcing him to bend nearly double to avoid hitting his head on the ceiling. Breathing raggedly and huddled together, they pressed themselves against the farthest wall of the small cavern.

Their escape into the earth had consumed mere seconds. But had they been fast enough to avoid detection? They would have to wait to find out. But for how long did they dare crouch here, cornered with no way out, if they had been detected and armed enemies even now converged on their location?

Cam stirred and began tugging his boots onto his stockinged feet.

"Good idea," Bree murmured and copied him.

Now they were ready to move at a moment's notice, but they had nowhere to go. A bitter taste invaded Bree's mouth. Is this what their lives had come to? Crouching in a hole, waiting to be discovered and snuffed out?

No, she didn't dare think such hopeless thoughts.

But what hope did she truly have left? If they escaped this cabin with their lives, she had days or maybe only hours before she would be torn from everything and everyone she had ever known in order to be relocated where no one and nothing was familiar. Cam's assistance to her must surely be common knowledge now. Did that mean he would need to uproot himself and run again, also?

Bree's heart did a little hop. Could they go away together? No, wait, that was silly. They barely knew each other. Why would he want to tie himself to her for the foreseeable future? How ironic that doing what was right in bringing evildoers to justice during that shootout with the rustlers would end up wrecking her life and damaging her brother, her work colleagues, and her new neighbor in a cascade of consequences.

There must be a solution. What am I not seeing?

Her only answer came in outer silence, marked by the solemn thudding of her heart.

Next to her, Cam stirred and drew himself up into a cross-legged, seated posture with his back resting against the stone wall. "We may be wise to spend the rest of the night here."

Bree let out a groan. "I hate this fleeing-and-hiding routine. I so badly want to bring the fight to the crooks, but going on the offensive against a monster criminal machine like a cartel is sure suicide."

"Isn't going on the offensive what law enforcement is all about?"

"Sure, but the legal apparatus is a behemoth in itself, designed to take on the worst of the worst." She assumed a similar posture to his and hugged herself against the chill of this microcavern that felt more and more like a tomb. "When an individual is singled out for attention from the criminal element, the whole balance of the struggle is taken out of the equation. You, of all people, know this. What's your point?"

"My point is since we're cooling our heels down here—literally—I should probably finish my story. I have the glimmerings of an idea, but I want to see if you discern it also."

"An idea? Really?" Bree squinted at her companion. The glow from the stick was fading, leaving more shadow than light in their alcove.

"It's extremely dangerous, and you're going to hate it—though probably marginally less than your current alternative of witness protection."

"Stop with the teasing already and tell me."

"The end of the story first."

"No rush. I've got all night."

At her dry tone, Cam chuckled, and Bree managed a slight smile, her heart lightening marginally. This man was truly extraordinary. Everything in her wanted to get to know him better. The usual flashing red light of stop-and-go wariness when she considered a potential new relationship had flipped to solid yellow with flickers of green sometime during the past weeks' idyll spent living and working alongside him on his ranch.

During one of their long conversations, she'd even opened up enough to share the bare facts with him surrounding her prior marriage and its ending. His compassionate response, minus any hint of pity, had left her with the sense he had reason to understand her pain. She'd like to know more details about his past relationships that would have given rise to that impression, but she hadn't pried. As they continued to get to know one another, she trusted the subject would be explored in due course—provided they were given enough time.

Going into WITSEC would end the possibilities instantly. If Cam's nascent idea had any merit at all, she would have to leap into the project with both feet.

Maybe. Her old habit of caution nudged her.

"Where did I leave off?" Cam asked.

"Your name got outed to both the Espinoza and Ortega cartels. I can guess the consequences. Espinoza wanted to reward you and Ortega wanted to kill you."

"Right on both counts. Alonzo's version of rewarding me was summoning me to a face-to-face meeting with him."

"And you went?"

"One tends to comply when you're grabbed off the street and thrown into the back of an SUV at gunpoint."

"Friendly!"

"Exactly what cartels are famous for."

They snickered almost in unison.

"The guy really did think he was being magnanimous when he offered to bring me in on his move to take over the Ortega smuggling route that went straight across Leaning-D range, especially when he pledged not to traffic humans, only drugs."

"Why would Espinoza think you'd be interested in replacing one cartel with another in exploiting your property?"

Silence fell for a heartbeat as Cam visibly cringed in the fading illumination of the glow stick. "Apparently, my adversarial relationship with my father was common knowledge. Alonzo thought I would enjoy betraying him while enveloping myself and my ranch under Espinoza protection."

Bree gasped as the implications cascaded over her. "In effect, you would become a puppet of the Espinoza cartel, dependent upon it as a shield. Plus, the offer revealed that—"

"My father was actively cooperating with the Ortega cartel." The words snarled from Cam's mouth. "Up until that moment, standing before Alonzo Espinoza, I had only suspected the worst. Clung to a shred of hope that it wasn't so. Now I knew, and I could no longer pretend my family name possessed a shred of honor."

"Oh, Cam, how devastating." She released a deep groan. "Intending to do you a favor, Espinoza wounded you deeper than a bullet from an Ortega gun."

"Thank you." Cam hung his head. "It means a lot to me that you understand."

"Of course."

Cam seemed to shake himself, and he lifted his chin and met her gaze. "Naturally, I turned down the so-generous offer. I half expected a shallow grave to follow my defiance, but Alonzo declared he was releasing me with my life for saving his daughter, but to expect no further favors."

"Right! You saved his daughter from untold horrors, but the best he could offer in response was to *not* kill you when you turned down a so-called business opportunity. How messed up is that?"

"Twisted thoughts are a symptom of a dark heart."

"Deep. Almost sounds like a Scripture verse, but I don't recall the quote."

"It's not directly from the Bible, though the principle is there. The incident with Alonzo Es-

pinoza did remind me of the verse from Prov-
erbs that says, 'The tender mercies of the wicked
are cruel.' The context is the care of animals,
but to cartel leaders, people are cattle to be ex-
ploited."

"I can't disagree there. Where's this idea of
yours? I thought, for a minute, you were going
to offer to contact Alonzo Espinoza and trade
my safety for the favor he owes you for saving his
daughter. But now it sounds like that obligation
is off the table, at least in Espinoza's reckoning.
Not that I'd want you to risk yourself making
a deal with the sort of human snake that would
turn around and bite you as soon as false promises escaped his mouth." As the last of the light
from the glow stick winked out, Bree's gaze
linked with Cam's. Was that tenderness in his
expression? Her heart fluttered. "What?"

"You are a remarkable woman. A genuine
protector and person of integrity. I'm blessed to
have met you."

Thankfully, the inky atmosphere hid the hot
flush that washed Bree's face. Involuntarily, she
leaned closer to him. He must be doing the
same because his warm breath touched her lips.
Anticipation of the earth-moving kiss tingled
through her. And then—

The world exploded in heat, light and thunder. Pain splintered her psyche and the relief of nothingness swallowed her whole.

The explosion's brilliance seared Cam's eyeballs and he squeezed his lids closed even as he threw himself at Bree. Too late to spare her much except to absorb the brunt of the falling rubble. Dislodged stones pelted him and bits of hot rubble stung his back. A muted roar, snap and crackle let him know that fire was actively consuming the main portion of the cabin. At least, in the stone alcove, they were sheltered from the worst of the flames, though the heat washed in waves across him. Smoke bit his lungs and he coughed.

Pulling the bandana around his neck up across his mouth and nose, he pulled away from Bree onto his elbows. She lay limp on the ground. Cam's heart stuttered. He opened his watering eyes and scanned her pale face in the flickering gloom.

"Bree!"

He quickly touched her throat and found a pulse. Then he put a finger close to her nose and her exhales puffed around it. *Thank You, God.*

She was alive, at least, but how injured he had yet to determine.

Somehow fresh air mingled with the smoke, alternately providing good breaths and tainted breaths, depending on the fluctuations of the breeze that swirled around them. Still coughing, Cam sat up and looked around. The cabin had collapsed entirely into the cellar, and the God-created night sky glimpsed between burning wreckage replaced the shattered, human-made roof.

A deep groan, followed by a wracking cough, came from the woman beside him. She stirred and attempted to sit up.

Cam pressed her down with a hand on her shoulder. "Take it easy until we see where you're hurt."

Bree's eyelids fluttered. "Where I'm hurt? Try everywhere. And nowhere, too. I think it was just the concussion of…whatever that was."

"You have a concussion?"

"That's not what I meant." She rubbed her forehead, smearing dirt and soot. "It was the pressure, like being crushed by a wall of super-heated air."

"That's what explosions are like." Cam slumped beside her. His own wounds smarted, but so far he didn't think anything major had been injured. He'd know more when the adrenaline wore off and they tried to move. "I think we can safely deduce our presence in the cabin was detected, but unless someone was standing out there with an RPG to shoot at us, I'm fairly sure we were hit remotely by an actual kamikaze drone."

"Not like the regular drone that hit Dillon's pickup truck."

"Correct."

Bree sat up with a high whine and gritted teeth. "Then our attackers think they got us."

"I'm sure they're hoping so, but I'm equally sure they'll send someone to check and confirm. Probably in the morning."

"Then we need to get out of here as quickly as possible."

Cam frowned at the dying fires dotting the main cellar area. "As soon as it's safe to move out of this microcavern and climb the stone wall."

"Our horses." Her eyes went wide. "They will have run away from the explosion."

"No doubt, but I hope they didn't go far. I think the spring of water will draw them back in this direction, at least by morning. How are you at riding bareback? I assume our saddles are toast."

"We'll manage." Bree suddenly hiccupped on a catch of breath. "Oh, Cam!" She threw her arms around him and sobbed. "Again…we made it through an attack…but we can't…survive much longer."

"We'll either have to get you into witness protection, or we'll need to stage a showdown."

"Stage a what?" She pulled away from him, moonlit tears glistening on a pair of scowling cheeks.

"It's either full retreat with the hope that you're never found wherever the Marshals Service places you, or we take control of the situation and draw the enemy to us where he—or rather, *they*—can be neutralized."

She scrunched her eyebrows together and glared at him. "You want to lure Alonzo Esperanza *here*?"

"Not here, necessarily, but to the United States at a place of our choosing. And not just Alonzo, but Raul Ortega as well. We won't get one without the other."

"How do you propose to pull off that feat?"

"You are the bait for Alonzo, and I am the bait for Raul, and they are the irresistible lure for each other. If they each think they are going to be able to get their targets of revenge and take out their rival forever in one fell swoop, neither one will be able to resist showing up in person on this side of the US/Mexico border. Then, if we're prepared and waiting for them, they can be arrested and locked up where they belong."

She gaped at him like a beached fish and then suddenly snapped her jaw closed and scowled. "I hate the idea."

"I knew you would."

"It's going to be so dangerous."

"Yup."

"Let's do it."

Cam grinned. He couldn't help himself. "I knew you were going to say that, too."

Bree swatted him on the arm and he winced at a stab of pain.

"You *are* hurt." She moved closer to him, scanning him up and down.

"Scorched by sparks here and there and bruised from flying debris. But since I don't seem to be bleeding out, we need to get as far away from here as we can before more enemies arrive. We can assess injuries and perform first aid later."

"Gotcha." She scooted toward the opening of

the stone hollow with her rifle in one hand and her saddlebags in the other.

Cam opened his mouth to call her back and insist on venturing into the still-smoldering wreckage first. Then he shut his jaw. Bree was a trained Texas Ranger. She knew how to handle herself in risky situations.

He scuttled out in her wake, acrid smoke biting the back of his throat, but not in health-threatening amounts. Gradually, they weaved around shattered pieces of furniture and shredded wall and floorboards. A shard of metal gleamed up at him from the devastation. Possibly a piece of the drone that had wrought this havoc.

They came to a cellar wall and Cam assessed the stones and masonry for hand-and footholds. They didn't need to climb up far. The cabin had been thoroughly leveled by the blast, so the top of his head came nearly even with the ground above.

Bree turned to him. "Just make a stirrup with your hands. I can step into it, and you can hoist me up. Then I'll turn and grab the supplies from you."

"Sounds like a plan."

Cam did as she asked, and soon she crawled

onto terra firma with a groan that hinted she had a few bumps and bruises herself. Lying on her stomach, she reached down, and he handed her his rifle and bags. Using the holds he'd spotted, he hauled himself out of the hole that used to be a cellar. A moment later, he flopped down beside Bree. The cool grass soothed his slightly fried back.

She got to her feet and did a slow 360-degree turn. "I don't see hide nor hair of livestock. Which way would you guess the horses went?"

"Whichever direction got them away the fastest from the danger." Gritting his teeth against a pained hiss, Cam stood beside her. "But I doubt if they ran too far from water. If we want to catch them, I think we'll have to wait near the spring and hope they show up before the cartel scouting party arrives to confirm their kill."

Bree huffed. "I don't think we have a lot of choice. We need mounts to travel fast. Hoofing it cross-country in cowboy boots won't get us far enough away from here to avoid detection by the bad guys come morning. In fact, on foot and without cover on this prairie landscape, we'd be completely vulnerable."

"To the spring it is."

Cam led the way to the patch of wet ground

that marked the tiny spring bubbling to the surface, tracing a short path across the terrain and then, just as quickly, diving underground again. Maybe he should dig a well here and tap into the aquifer that was clearly down there. He shook himself as he located a dense huddle of shrubbery where they could shelter and await the horses' return. Now was not the time for planning and dreams. Then again, why not think positively?

If their desperate ploy went awry, as it so easily might, this could be one of the last times he entertained practical dreams for his ranch. Failure to stop both Alonzo Espinoza and Raul Ortega meant no more future for Bree or for him. And certainly not for them together. For a reason he didn't care to examine at the moment, that thought hurt most of all.

Chapter Twelve

Something cool and bristly brushed Bree's cheek and she swiped at it without opening her eyes. Whatever had disturbed her slumber went away and she drifted toward oblivion once more. Then the bristles feathered her skin again, accompanied by a loud, snuffling warm breath washing across her face. She jerked awake and sat up. Her sudden movement prompted a startled whicker and the thud of trotting hooves retreating. She turned her head to find a familiar equine rump moving away from her. What? Where was she?

"Teton!" Her involuntary cry drew Bree fully into the waking world.

The sky had begun to pale, revealing a sepia landscape dotted with grass clumps waving in a steady breeze. Heaviness tinged the air as if the environment were waiting for something momentous. A storm may be brewing, though as yet the clouds were scarce overhead.

Bree shook herself physically. How could she have fallen asleep after the events of last night? Curled up on the lumpy ground in the sparse cover of a juniper bush, no less? She shook herself. Why she'd fallen asleep didn't matter, though exhaustion and trauma probably explained it. What mattered was that the horses had returned, exactly as dawn was breaking, and they needed to vacate the area.

Battling the aches and pains of stiff muscles and bruised bones, Bree struggled to her feet, keeping a firm grip on the rifle she'd slept with clutched to her chest. Where was Cam? Her gaze scanned the area. Teton hadn't gone far— just to the edge of the spring, where he had stuck his nose in the water. Cattle also had gathered around, but no Cam and no Rojo, or the pack mare either.

Her throat tightened and her heart rate sped up. He wouldn't leave her. Had something happened? No, surely she wouldn't have slept through anything dramatic going on nearby. But maybe he'd left to look for the horses and run into the bad guys. No, that dire scenario didn't work either. At least, not very well. She'd heard no gunshots. However, if Cam had been threatened at gunpoint and captured, no one would necessarily have fired. Bree's head spun and she matched the movement with her body, searching in every direction as far as her eye could see in the growing light.

"Bree!"

Cam's distant call fell sweetly on her ears. Bree turned east and flung up a hand to shade her eyes from the sun's first piercing rays. She smiled. The man certainly did make a striking figure on horseback, even riding bareback without a saddle or bridle. He'd found Rojo, and the stallion was evidently well enough trained to allow him to mount and would accept guidance from knee pressure. The pack mare ambled along in the wake of the magnificent pair.

Bree waved and then scooped up her saddlebags and headed for the spring. At her approach, Teton lifted a dripping muzzle from the water and turned his head toward her, ears pricked in her direction. As she neared, he stepped out and met her.

"Hey, boy, did you have a scare last night?" She rubbed his muzzle then moved along his side, rubbing his shiny coat with her palm. The smoothness of his skin and the familiar horsey scent calmed her riled nerves. "You look like you're all right. No injuries from flying debris or anything."

Continuing to croon kind words, she stopped near his withers and hopped upward so she practically lay sideways over his back. Teton turned his head, ears waggling back and forth. Bree grinned at him and swung her leg over the top so that she ended up sitting in the spot where a saddle would have been. The bags sat awkwardly across her legs, but it was the only place for them where they wouldn't slip off, and the rifle rested in the crook of an elbow.

Winding the fingers of one hand through Teton's thick mane, she clucked at him and nudged him with a knee in the direction she wanted him to go. The gelding snorted, possibly a mild grumble at the odd arrangement, and headed for the approaching party of Cam, Rojo and pack mare. As soon as she and Teton converged with them, Bree brought the gelding to a halt, and Cam did the same with his stallion.

Her gaze narrowed on Cam. Now that she was close to him, his bedraggled condition became apparent. Dark ash smeared spots and stripes across his face. His jeans showed dirt and tears. And scorched holes on the arms and shoulders of his shirt exposed the red marks of first-degree burns.

Bree clucked her tongue. "You need treatment."

His teeth gleamed extra-white in his filthy face as he offered a grin. "Not to mention a bath, but first aid for minor injuries and other such luxuries are far down on my priority list. Let's grab a drink at the spring, fill up our canteens, and get far away from here." He tapped Rojo's ribs with his heels and moved toward the spring.

Bree followed without another word. Soon, humans and animals were hydrated and heading onto the prairie.

"This direction seems random." Bree shot her companion a sharp glance. "Where are we going?"

"For the moment, it *is* random. We need to get out of sight of the cabin. Where do you suggest for an ultimate destination?"

"Home. I just want to go home." She heaved in a deep breath and let it out slowly. "Do I sound pitiful?"

Cam shook his head. "You sound correct." His tender gaze soothed her raw nerves. "We'll have to sneak onto your ranch to avoid potentially hostile watching eyes, though, hopefully, they may already think we're dead and be gone. We need to talk to Dillon privately in person to recruit him into our plot to trap the cartel bosses."

"About that." Bree bit her lower lip. In the morning light, the idea appeared ludicrous, suicidal even.

"We'll talk further later. Let's move!" Cam kicked Rojo into a ground-eating lope.

Bree had no choice but to follow suit, though her gut churned in sync with writhing thoughts. Or maybe her problem was hunger. They had jerky in their packs but no time to eat it until they were out of range of an aerial spotter heading for the destroyed cabin. Then again, the cartel might be in no hurry and opt for a low-key overland approach.

Hopefully, the latter. She'd had her fill of aerial threats. Besides, she and Cam would have more time to get away if the enemy were approaching overland. A growl formed in Bree's throat. She'd had her fill of running from danger, too. Maybe taking their lives in their hands and running toward the threat really was the only sensible option in this appalling scenario.

Gradually, the familiar thud of hooves against the ground and the rhythmic bunch and stretch of Teton's muscles beneath her lulled her tension. If the situation wasn't so dire, she could enjoy this ride. Her gelding loped, ears perked, and neck stretched out, his nose parallel to the stallion's haunches. Both animals seemed to feel the urgency, yet they were finding pleasure in the exercise, at least between gusts of wind that seemed to be growing more frequent and pelted them with dust. Teton snorted against the unpleasantness, and Bree fitted her bandana over her nose and mouth.

Then Cam's torso swiveled toward her and he pointed to their right. Bree turned her head, and her breath caught in her throat. In the distance, a streaky wall of blackness had formed, led by a hedge of wind-churned dust. Judging from a faint but growing rumble, the dense veil of water appeared to be rushing straight for them. The storm hinted at by the heavy air at dawn was here—a last hurrah of rain before long dry months arrived. Heavy rainstorms on the Llano were no joke. The force of the periodic deluges had dug the ravines, wadis and canyons that scarred the prairie and sometimes sent the rivers into devastating flood stage.

Instinctively, Bree nudged Teton away from the approaching storm. Even as she did so, a crack of thunder rolled across the plain with an accompanying flash of lightning. They couldn't hope to outrun the weather, but they needed time to locate some sort of shelter, however meager.

Rojo inserted himself in Teton's path. The gelding protested with a jerk of the head and a whinny, but he slowed to a walk. Bree clung precariously to her position atop a horse with no saddle.

"What was that for?" She scowled at Rojo's rider.

Cam's dark gaze flew skyward but not in the direction of the wild weather. Bree looked up. Ice stabbed her chest. A speck in the distance barely stood out from the gathering gloom, but she had no trouble recognizing a helicopter heading their way. The beat of its rotors had been masked by the rumble from the maw of the storm.

Bree fixed a grim gaze on her companion. "Our shelter is the storm itself. It's the only alternative. The chopper will have great difficulty flying in that weather, and whoever is inside the bird certainly won't be able to spot us."

Cam's lips quirked into a wry half smile. "So, we choose the lesser of two evils." His glance turned to the snarling, flashing turbulence fast approaching. "Though I'm not certain if there's much difference."

Silently, Bree's heart agreed as they kicked their mounts into a run toward the dubious protection of thunder, lightning and torrents of rain. The dust storm enveloped them first, and then great droplets of water began to pelt them. All at once, as if they'd passed through a veil, the world turned to water, roars of thunder and flashes of blinding light. The scent of ozone hung in the air.

The lesser of two evils? Perhaps facing bullets would have been wiser.

Bree's head whirled under an assault of sensations. Lances of wind-driven water stung her skin, and her drenched clothing hung heavy on her body. She could no longer make out her companions through the sheets of water that clouded her vision in the gloom. Teton's heaving body beneath her became as slippery as a greased pole. She clung desperately to his sides with her legs and a convulsive, two-handed grip on his mane.

Then he stumbled and all contact was lost. She flew through the air and landed awkwardly in slimy muck. Pain speared through her left shoulder that had taken the brunt of the impact. For long moments, Bree lay on her side, fighting for breath. At last, she forced herself to sit up and then to stand, trembling in the deluge that had cooled the temperature by at least twenty degrees. If she didn't drown, hypothermia was a possibility.

Blinking against veils of water and choking in attempts to breathe, she hunted for a glimpse of her companions, either man or animal. Nothing and no one. She stood alone in the storm. A powerful gust of wind staggered her, and she slipped and fell to her knees in rising muck. Agony sliced through her injured shoulder.

She might not make it out of this storm. Thunder cracked and lightning ripped the air all around. One such strike could easily hit her, and that would be it.

However, even if she did survive to see the sun again, only one question would remain. What if the bad guys found her first?

Leaning low over Rojo's neck, Cam clung to his horse while his head turned this way and that.

"Bree!" The cry barely left his throat, swallowed in a gargle of airborne water.

The torrent and tumult isolated him as if he and his mount remained solely existent on the planet. The eerie sensation chilled him more than the abrupt drop in temperature. Shivers cascaded through his body, which Rojo's quivering hide seemed to echo.

He would have to trust God to bring him and Bree together again after the storm passed. And it *would* pass. Cam forced his overwhelmed senses to focus on that truth. He urged Rojo to slog ahead through the deepening muck on the ground. Their pace necessarily slowed to a near crawl. His stallion's breathing came in grunts as the animal fought to draw air out of the saturated atmosphere. This aboveground situation came as scarily close to swimming under water as the real thing.

Time inched forward, conditions worsened, and Rojo stopped still, head hanging, chest heaving. Cam clung to the stallion's back as if his life depended upon remaining mounted, which was not far from the truth with the level of water swirling around them up to Rojo's knees. They must be standing in a dip in the terrain for the runoff to be this deep.

Where was Bree? Was she all right? *Please, God, help her.*

He took a breath, and no water invaded his nostrils. Was the rain's intensity receding? Cam lifted his head slightly. Needles of wetness pelted his face, but the dense darkness of the storm appeared paler. He could make out bushes and trees around him. His heart lightened.

Then, as if to mock his resurgence of hope, a deep boom shook the earth, simultaneous with a brilliant flash. Cam's eyes slammed shut against the searing light. An electrical charge stood his hair on end, and Rojo surged forward, nearly unseating him. Had his grip on the horse's mane not been all but frozen in place, he would have been thrown. As it was, he slipped from side to side on the animal's slick back.

All thoughts of maintaining possession of his rifle in the crook of his arm or his saddlebags across his lap were forgotten. What happened to those items, he had no idea. They were lost to him as horse and rider plunged across the landscape in frantic leaps and splashes.

Then, as Rojo's heaving lessened, the light strengthened and the storm's tumult noticeably abated. The stallion plodded forward, movements now slow and weary. Cam sat up fully on the animal's back and looked around him.

The plain now flowed with a film of water,

in places cutting into the earth, perhaps marking future ravines and washes. The sky still dripped moisture, but in plinks and plops here and there, not breath-stealing torrents. Twilight yet gripped the air through dense cloud cover, but the sun's rays were attempting to peak through. Tempest had given way to a steady breeze that promised to dry the ground…eventually.

Cam didn't recognize his location. Nor did he spy another person, or animal, or any of his lost property. He could remain there and hope that Bree caught up to him. She'd been behind him. Or he could go looking for her. But where? In the storm, she could easily have become disoriented as to direction and ended up anywhere. She could even be trapped, wandering in circles, somewhere in the maelstrom proceeding across the plain in his wake.

Taking no action when action was possible went against his nature, so Cam seized the only alternative that offered the slightest possibility of success. He turned Rojo around and moved toward the receding storm, not fast enough to catch up to it, but with a steady pace that might bring him into contact with someone emerging from its grip.

Thankfully, there was no sign of the helicopter overhead. The bird had no doubt been forced to flee before the violent storm. However, the cartel *sicarios'* urgent orders to eliminate Bree might have forced a foolish decision to carry on. In that case, Cam didn't give the chopper much chance of having remained aloft. He might possibly come across the wreckage, but hopefully, he wouldn't. Not so much because he cared if the cartel minions were hurt but because he didn't want to take time out of his search for Bree to deal with survivors. Cold-hearted? Maybe. But he knew his priorities.

Movement caught his eye, and he squinted to make out a living figure emerging from the storm about a football field's distance from him. Teton. The gelding was limping and riderless. Cam's heart filled his throat. Bree had been thrown and could be hurt...or worse.

No. He couldn't allow himself to think that way. Bree was strong and resourceful. She had to be alive...somewhere. But she was alone and on foot, possibly injured, and almost certainly needed his help.

Cam called to the gelding, and the animal turned toward him and Rojo, increasing its pace with a welcoming whicker. Not severely lame after all.

"Where's your rider, boy?" he asked the gelding as they approached each other. Not that he expected an answer or even, as might happen with a dog, for the horse to turn and lead them in search of its mistress.

A whinny came from another direction and Cam looked around to find the mud-stained mare trotting to them, seemingly the least worse for wear out of them all.

"Good girl," Cam told the mare as she drew near. "Now, the gang's all here except for an all-important one. Let's find her."

The storm had drawn significantly away from their little grouping and appeared to be dissipating in strength and size. Cam urged Rojo to lead out in the tempest's wake. Calm now covered the land, the clouds had broken up, and the sun's rays were beginning to warm Cam's shoulders. His shivers lessened.

Gaze straining this way and that, Cam prayed under his breath. The longer they went without finding Bree, the greater the turmoil grew inside him—almost mimicking the intensity of the thunderstorm. Where was she? What could have happened? Visions of her trudging through the storm's darkness and tumbling into a wash filled with roiling water attacked his imagination. He worked hard at shoving the unproductive fears away, but the longer they went without locating her, the more likely such a scenario became.

There!

Cam rushed Rojo in the direction of an unnatural lump huddled among flattened grasses. His shoulders slumped as he made out the remains of a modest-size tent sitting near a swamped fire ring. Then a crawling sensation went through him. People had been camping out here recently. The tent's canvas wasn't nearly so weathered and tattered that the small shelter had been abandoned in this spot for any length of time.

Sicarios on the hunt for Bree? Quite possibly. And where were the campers, whoever they might be? They clearly weren't anywhere in the vicinity of this site. Had they fled from the storm on horseback or perhaps on an ATV? There was no way to tell. Any telltale tracks had been thoroughly washed away.

Cam left the site and continued with his quest, but more cautiously than ever. If the campers had been cartel hitters, they could still be out there, and they were likely to be armed, while the storm had stripped him of his rifle and the pack that contained his handgun. If the wrong people discovered him, he was absolutely vulnerable.

Rojo stepped carefully down a hillock into a small dip in the landscape where a temporary river ran with a swift but shallow current. On the far side of the water's flow, a set of smallish bootprints led to the edge of the rivulet, which must have been considerably higher only minutes ago, and then the tracks turned and led away from running water.

Cam's heart leaped. Those had to be Bree's tracks. She'd turned aside from crossing on foot and gone in search of easier passage. His eyes swept the area but spotted no movement. Disappointing, but at least he was traveling on the right trajectory. Cam urged Rojo across the water and began following the traces the wanderer's passage had left.

He wanted to call out for her but held himself back. If bad guys were out there, he couldn't afford to draw their attention.

Cam turned and checked what might be behind him. The other two horses had fallen back as they stopped now and then to graze. They'd be all right. He could return for them, but he couldn't wait. He urged Rojo onward.

Many fruitless minutes later, the stallion

topped a rise and a flat vista spread before him. Across it, a small figure staggered along. *Bree*. Her name whispered gratefully through him.

Then movement drew Cam's attention below and to the left of him along the slight ridge he'd climbed. Barbed wire wrung his guts. A man stood behind a juniper bush, lifting a rifle to his shoulder with a bead on Bree.

Cam could shout and warn her, but how would that help when she had no cover? He could race toward the gunman, but he'd surely arrive too late to stop the man from taking his shot. There was only one thing he could do. And that was both.

Bellowing Bree's name, Cam clapped boots to Rojo's sides and charged the cartel hitman— knowledge of the futility of his actions nipping at his heels.

Chapter Thirteen

At the urgent shout of her name from a familiar voice, Bree whipped around. A bullet sizzled past her ear, accompanied by the sharp report of a rifle. Automatically, she crouched and raced away from the danger in a random zigzag designed to make herself a more difficult target. But if the gunman was as nearby as the sound of the shot would suggest, her evasive maneuvers may be worthless.

Masculine shouts from the hillside behind her drew her head around. Distracted, she stumbled over some small obstacle on the ground and fell to her knees in the muck. Pain lashed through her and she ground her teeth together. Even such a soft landing jarred her injured shoulder. The joint was probably dislocated. Not a fatal injury but debilitating when she needed to be swift and agile.

Come on! Get up, woman!

Bree struggled to her feet even as another bullet zipped past, preceding a rifle report by a split second. Groaning, she slogged onward. Her bootfalls splashed water in all directions, further drenching her sopped clothing. The thunder of her pulse in her ears muted other sounds. Any moment now, a bullet would end her senses and sever all connection to this world.

Then Cam's voice again, shouting her name, cut through the fog of fatalism. Bree slowed and turned. Atop the hillock, he stood tall, holding a rifle on a man who crouched on his knees with his hands raised. Cam had disarmed the *sicario* and stopped the attack.

Bree inhaled a sharp breath. Her legs went wobbly and she almost fell again. *Thank you, Cam. No, thank You, God. You sent Cam here in time.* Her thoughts drew up short at the unaccustomed release of prayer. Cam's testimony had deeply impacted her.

By an act of will, battling exhaustion all the way, she trod up the hill to them.

"I am so thankful to see you." She stopped several yards short of the prisoner with his captor.

The disheveled, dark-haired Hispanic male kneeling in the mud was short and wiry. His black eyes gleamed at her like cold pebbles. "You cannot escape us forever, *chica*." His tone dripped venom.

"You have not done well so far." Cam snorted. "I'm sure Señor Espinoza is pleased."

The *sicario*'s face reddened and his mouth opened.

"Oh, hush!" Bree snapped. "I'm tired of threats from your ilk. When we want you to speak, we'll ask you something. And, believe me, the rangers will have lots of questions for you."

The man's lips pulled back in a toothy sneer, but he remained quiet.

Cam nodded toward her. "We need to get to the nearest civilization so we can call your headquarters for an aerial pickup. The time for running and hiding has passed."

"You lost your saddlebags and sat phone, too?"

"Yup. But I ran across Teton and the pack mare a little way back. They stopped to graze, so we should be able to pick them up relatively quickly."

Warmth flooded through Bree on the realization that her horse had survived. "How was Teton?"

"Probably sprained a front hock, so he's not

rideable, but we can put you up on the mare. Our guest here—" he gestured toward the captured hitman "—can take shank's mare."

Bree chuckled at Cam's usage of the old vernacular for walking. "We'd best get going then. Lead on."

"You're injured." Cam's narrow-eyed gaze assessed her. "I can tell by the way you carry yourself. Your shoulder?"

She resisted the impulse to shrug—an agonizing prospect. "I'm going to need a doctor to put it back in the socket."

Cam growled wordlessly, then motioned with the end of the rifle for the *sicario* to get up and walk ahead of them. The man complied with exaggerated swagger and a scowling face. Bree took up the rear position, clutching her injured arm to herself with the opposite arm to minimize the painful motion of her shoulder. Check that. Rojo took up the rear position, responding to a cluck of the tongue from his master.

Bree's estimation of Cam as a horse trainer continued to elevate. When word got out of his skills, he'd be doing a brisk business. That was, if they could ever bring this horrible threat from the cartel to a close…and if they survived the process.

Several miles of plodding as the ground grew ever dryer beneath their feet brought their bedraggled party in sight of a pair of horses contentedly foraging in the grass. At their approach, Teton's head came up with a snort. The animal started to trot toward them but soon slowed to a limping walk. Bree groaned. Hopefully, Cam's assessment of a strained hock was the worst of the damage. She wasn't the only one who needed medical attention.

Teton reached her side and Bree wrapped her good arm around his neck and buried her nose in his mane. The gelding let out a soft whicker as the familiar horsey odor settled her frazzled nerves. The situation could be a lot worse. She or Cam or both of them could be dead. And yet, somehow—and she could only thank God's grace—all of them, human and animal, had survived everything that had been thrown at them.

"Let's get you up on the pack animal."

Cam's gentle voice near at hand drew Bree's head around. He stood nearby, his gaze and his rifle trained on their prisoner, though his words had been for her.

She let out a brief chuckle. "How are we going to go about that gymnastic feat? You can't take your attention off the cartel hitman, and I can't get aboard a horse on my own."

"I guess we'll improvise." He shrugged with a rueful grin. "I can spare an arm to lift you up if you can be in charge of swinging your leg over the mare's back."

Bree grimaced. "We'll make it work."

She'd continue walking under her own steam if she thought she could handle the distance, but weakness saturated her limbs. Getting astride a horse would take every ounce of energy that remained to her. If only they didn't also have a prisoner to guard, the maneuver wouldn't be so tricky. But they did, and she had to do her utmost not to distract Cam too much from guard duty. She didn't trust the gleam in the *sicario*'s eyes or his crafty expression.

Together, the little troupe of people and animals walked up to the pack mare, who gazed at them placidly, her jaws working a mouthful of sweet grass. Bree took up a position next to the animal, and Cam encircled her waist with one arm.

"Ready?" he asked.

Bree gripped the horse's thick, coarse mane in one fist and flexed her knees to assist Cam's efforts with a hop of her own. "Let's mount up."

Her feet left the ground and her stomach reached the level of the animal's broad back. She heaved herself forward, letting out an involuntary cry as her shoulder screamed in protest. Cam's head turned to her. The *sicario* let out a feral snarl. Bree's peripheral vision caught brisk movement as he charged them.

Cam whirled on the threat, his support leaving Bree. She landed hard with her stomach against the mare's spine. The breath left her in a *whoof* even as the rifle roared and a masculine voice howled in pain.

The horse hopped once then broke into a trot across the prairie while Bree clung on like a sack of grain lying across the mare's back. Her own plight barely held Bree's attention as her mind clamored with a vital question.

Who had been shot, Cam or the hitman?

Standing over the wounded *sicario*, Cam shook with the effects of adrenaline. The tussle had been close, but when the rifle had gone off as they'd struggled for control of the weapon, the bullet had struck the cartel hitman in the meaty part of the thigh. The *sicario* lay groaning on the ground and clutching his leg. But by the moderate though steady blood flow, he had not been hit in the artery and was not rapidly bleeding out.

"Now, what are we going to do with you?" Cam's tone emerged as a husky growl. "You can't walk."

"Help me." The man gasped. "I'm going to die." His eyes were wild with panic.

"Not so tough now that it's you that's taken a bullet. Relax. You'll live if you follow my instructions."

The man stared up at him, blinking rapidly.

"Take off your belt," Cam instructed. "Then bind it tightly around your leg above the wound. That'll stop the bleeding. I don't have anything for first aid or to help the pain. Sorry."

Well, sort of sorry. Not very noble of him, but he didn't have much sympathy for a guy who made a business of going around killing and torturing other people in service of trafficking drugs. The bullet the man had taken was a direct consequence of exactly that sort of activity.

Grunting and moaning, the *sicario* went about following Cam's instructions while Cam searched the area with his eyes for what had become of Bree. The mare had been startled when the cartel killer had attacked, but Cam had had no time or attention to see which direction the mare had headed with her precious cargo. Pent-up air gusted from his lungs as he spotted the pack animal ambling in his direction with Bree sitting astride her back.

Soon the pair drew close enough for Cam to discern the deep pain lines bracketing Bree's mouth and the pallor of her face. It must have cost her a lot of agony to get fully upright on the mare and bring her under control, but Bree had been up to the task. Cam's chest filled with a tender emotion. Admiration, yes, but also something more that he wasn't yet ready to identify.

"You're not hurt, are you?" Bree's query came out in a thready voice, another indicator of deep pain.

"Not me, but this guy isn't doing so well." He nodded at the *sicario* huddled on the ground.

She let out a disgusted sound. "What are we going to do with him now?"

Cam sent her a wolfish grin. "Leave him for the buzzards and coyotes."

The hitman released a string of Spanish curses while Bree simply raised her eyebrows.

Cam shrugged. "He can't walk, and we don't have a mount for him. Therefore, here he stays until we can send someone back for him."

"Your logic is impeccable." Bree nodded. "Let's be on our way."

The hitman continued to curse them. Bree shot an icy look in his direction and commanded him to shut up in fluent and emphatic Spanish. The cartel tough guy complied.

Cam swallowed a grin as he got down on his haunches in front of the *sicario*. "You had better hope it is your people who find you." At the suggestion of this very real possibility, the anger faded from the man's face and his look grew warily hopeful. "If you are rescued by your compadres, be sure to tell Señor Espinoza that Everett Davison asks the favor of him that he forget this vendetta against Ranger Maguire in honor of his daughter's rescue from the Ortega cartel. The debt will then be fully paid."

The hitman's eyes grew big enough to show the whites all the way around. "*You* are Everett Davison?"

Cam gave a solemn nod and then rose to his feet. "*Adiós*. We will send law enforcement to collect you. If you are still here, they will take you in, and you will go to prison."

The *sicario* began spitting curses again as Cam mounted Rojo. He paid no attention, and neither did Bree as she fell in beside him, riding away from the wounded man. Silence reigned between them until they were well out of the cartel hitter's earshot.

Then Bree sidled closer to him. "You must think the *sicario*'s people will get to the wounded man first before US law enforcement. Why is that?"

Cam sent Bree a wolfish grin. "I didn't search him and relieve him of any communication device. He must have one. I'm sure he's using it as we speak."

"I should have learned by now that you always have a reason for whatever you do or don't do." Bree pursed her lips and her gaze turned introspective. "Do you think Alonzo Espinoza will entertain the idea of calling off the hit on me in gratitude toward you?"

Cam shook his head. "If I thought that, I would have approached Espinoza with the deal sooner. But, no, cartel heads have a skewed idea of honor, if they have any at all. As I told you, Alonzo figured I'd been repaid when he let me walk away alive from my refusal to let him traffic drugs across Davison land."

"Then your message left with the wounded *sicario* was the initial gambit to get the attention of both Alonzo Espinoza and Raul Ortega.

You think word will get back to Ortega that you're alive?"

"I'm nearly certain of it. The two cartels spy on each other relentlessly."

"And that knowledge will spark your ploy to draw both drug kingpins into the US after us as vendetta targets and in hopes of personally eliminating each other."

"To be hoped, but it's an uncertain prospect. We'll need to sweeten the bait, so to speak."

"What did you have in mind?"

"I'll fill you in fully when we talk to your boss at ranger headquarters. You'll all need to hear the last episode of my family tragedy—the part where my father was killed in the cartel raid—for my plan to make full sense to you."

A rush of emotion threatened to overwhelm him at the mention of the horrible day of the shoot-out on the Davison family ranch. Iron willpower barely managed to contain the fury and grief he'd been processing since the event. Judging by the gentle look Bree laid upon him, his pain had probably bled through his voice and expression despite his best efforts.

Silence fell, save for the thud of hooves against rain-softened ground and the swish of wind in the grass. The fresh odors of nature after a cleansing rainstorm always lightened Cam's spirits, though it had been terrifying at the time to pass through the violent weather.

Next to him, Bree let out a soft moan and shifted on her horse's back. Cam's heart wrung. If he could take her pain on himself, he would. They needed to find help soon. He strained his eyes, scanning the horizon. There. A distant line of electrical power poles indicated the strong possibility of a road running parallel, and a road would inevitably lead to human habitation. By his estimate of their location, his ranch site and the Maguire ranch site were far away. A road offered a better opportunity to make human contact that would get them to a hospital or clinic.

He urged Rojo to move faster. Not a trot. That would hurt Bree too much as she matched his pace. A fast walk, though, would get them to the roadside soon.

Within a few minutes, they were climbing a gently ascending berm toward the pavement. They came to a stop inside the fence line near a gate fronting the road. In the distance, a vehicle began to take shape, rapidly approaching their location. Cam tensed, poised to wave down what appeared to be the ubiquitous pickup that nearly everyone had around here. Few rural residents drove anything so mundane as a car.

The truck—a white Ford—slowed as it neared their location. Cam narrowed his eyes to make out whether more than one person occupied the cab. Yes, at least two heads showed over the dash. And what was that object the passenger was waving around like a thing he meant to use?

A gun!

Cam's heart leaped into his throat as he raised his rifle.

Chapter Fourteen

Heart hopping around in her chest, Bree reached over with her good arm and pressed the muzzle of Cam's rifle downward. That was close. They were wound too tight. There had been enough gunfire. They didn't want to invite a needless battle.

"No threat. That's the Trent brothers. Local gun enthusiasts. Wave them down."

Cam shot her a wide-eyed look and obeyed, whipping his arm up in an exaggerated stop gesture. Bree held her breath. The vehicle was almost level with them. The occupants might not see them, or if they did, may not understand the need to pull over. After all, people around here waved at each other all the time.

The truck swept past them and Bree slumped, air gushing from her lungs. Ah, well, maybe the next vehicle would stop. No, wait. The pickup slowed, halted, and then began to back toward them, angling onto the gravel shoulder.

Cam shot a grin at her. "One ride to the hospital coming up."

He dismounted, and Bree allowed him to help her do the same. Her knees nearly buckled when her feet met the earth. Weakness washed over her with a fresh burst of pain.

Cam turned away and slapped the rumps of their mounts, sending them back onto the prairie. They should be safe enough until they could be found and retrieved. Then he opened the fence gate, and Bree allowed him to support her through it.

The truck stopped and a door clicked open. A hairy face peered out at them, only the brown eyes and broad nose visible between a prolific beard and thick mane that looked like it hadn't met a comb recently. Except for their insistence on owning a late-model pickup and their avid acquisition of all the latest firearms, Able and Arnie Trent lived a rustic life, mostly off the grid. But they were decent sorts, as showed by their readiness to stop on the highway for bedraggled strays along the roadside.

Arnie squinted at them. "You-all look like you've been dragged through a knothole backward."

Bree let out a weak chuckle as Cam drew her through the gate and onto the roadside.

"She's hurt," he said. "We need to get to a hospital as quickly as possible."

Able poked his head forward, staring at them past his brother's beefy body. The only difference between his facial appearance and Arnie's was a lighter shade of brown hair.

Able let out a low whistle and clucked his tongue. "We just came from Lubbock. Got this piece." He waved the large, black pistol that had sent Cam into defense mode. "But we can turn around and go back. No problem. Hop in."

"Thanks!" Cam opened the rear door of the club cab.

Bree attempted to raise her leg high enough to ascend into the cab but couldn't succeed. Cam's arms came around her and lifted her onto the seat. She managed to scoot over and let him inside, too. Cam ensured her seat belt was securely fastened while Arnie wasted no time in turning the truck around and whizzing toward the city. Bree slumped against the seat and faded in and out of awareness as the brothers' voices prattled on and on about their gun collection and the new hunting dog they were training.

In typical Texas mind-your-own-business fashion, their hosts didn't ask what had happened, probably assuming Bree had taken a tumble from her horse, which was the truth, but not all of it. Their mounts lacking saddles or bridles must have sparked curiosity in the brothers' minds, but they refrained from poking their noses into the matter. Bree silently thanked God for the small mercy. If Able and Arnie were not aware of the cartel's price on her head, she didn't want to be the one to inform them.

At long last and yet in a surprisingly short time, the Trent brothers pulled up outside the emergency entrance of the University Medical Center in Lubbock, Texas. As Cam helped Bree out of the truck, she made a mental note that Texas Rangers' Company C headquarters was also here in the city. A very good thing— if they could get to it without running afoul of cartel presence in the area.

She opened her mouth to discuss the issue with Cam, but he bellowed out a cry for medical staff to bring a wheelchair as he guided her sagging body toward the entrance. A flurry of activity followed.

An hour later, Bree rested on an emergency room bed, her shoulder thankfully whole and in place once more. The pain persisted but at a much lower level. Her arm was cradled in a sling, and she'd been instructed to keep the limb quiet for a few weeks to let the injury heal.

Then she would need physical therapy to restore strength and mobility. The muscle relaxant she'd been given prior to the doctor manipulating the joint back into place had Bree's entire body lazing against the mattress in a semiliquid state.

Should she be concerned about her current vulnerable condition? Somehow, she couldn't bring herself to care. Where was Cam? He'd been taken away to another cubicle to have his burns treated.

The curtain around her cubicle twitched aside and the man she'd been wondering about stepped in, allowing the folds of cloth to join once more and give them an illusion of privacy. Even though people couldn't see them, voices carried quite clearly throughout the area. Cam still wore his ragged clothing, but white bandages showed through the holes in his shirt, and his color looked healthier.

He scanned her up and down. "How are you doing?"

"Better. I'm amazed at how much a dislocated shoulder hurt."

"I'm not. Been there, done that." He shrugged. "How about we take off out of here? We may have only a narrow window of time to reach the shelter of your headquarters before our presence in the city becomes known by enemy forces. I'd be surprised if they aren't watching area hospitals, since I'm sure they've discovered we survived their kamikaze drone. Especially if the *sicario* we left on the prairie has managed to make contact and update them about us."

Bree grimaced. "Movement requires energy, a commodity I'm a bit low on at the moment."

"Good thing this place has wheelchairs." He offered a slight grin. "I called for a rental car to be delivered out front. Should be here any minute."

Gritting her teeth, Bree forced herself to sit up and then turn with her lower legs and feet dangling off the side of the bed. "Get me to a phone first so I can let my captain know to have a welcoming committee ready to let us in and guard our backs while we make our grand entrance."

Cam shook his head. "Already done. I got one of these from the hospital gift shop." He waggled a burner cell phone. "We can keep in touch en route and let them know our ETA in real time."

"Excellent. While we're loading up, I can

make a quick call to Dillon and let him know to round up our horses and treat Teton's injury."

"Again, done. He's extremely worried about you."

Bree stared up at him, eyes wide. "You think of everything."

He snorted. "I wish, but I have to leave that omniscience stuff to God."

Bree had no ready answer to that observation. Her head still balked at yielding her trust to God, but her heart was more than halfway there. She wasn't prepared to talk about such eternal matters with anyone. Yet.

Soon, they were whizzing down a city highway toward Company C HQ. The activity of getting from the treatment room to the vehicle had roused Bree from lethargy. Seated on the passenger side of the midsize sedan, she kept her head on a swivel in search of hostiles following them. Cam's eyes flicked continually from the rearview mirror to the side mirror, watching for the same.

Less than a mile from their destination, Cam's body jerked. Pulse rate ramping up, Bree turned her attention toward him.

"What is it?"

"We've grown a tail. Big, black SUV three

vehicles back. I've seen it one too many times." He let out a derisive snicker. "The bad guys never seem to get creative with their style and color of pursuit cars. Boring!"

Bree hugged her injured arm close as Cam increased their speed, not recklessly fast, but flirting with the edge of safety. He would probably have taken their velocity into the stratosphere if they didn't have to exercise a modicum of care for the traffic around them.

"Take this next right turn," Bree told him, violating the GPS directions. "It's an obscure shortcut that should bring us around the back of the ranger building. We'll take the lesser-used entrance to the underground parking garage."

She activated the phone in her hand that Cam had handed her when they'd gotten into the car at the hospital. Her captain answered on the first ring, and she informed him of their proximity, their route, and the presence of a tail.

"Keep coming." Captain Gaines's tone was grim. "I'll have ranger vehicles close in around you and cut them off."

Bree smiled. Gaines was a good leader. He must have deployed ranger units to be ready and waiting on the streets as soon as he'd found out they were on their way. Now, she and Cam just had to traverse the final half mile without being shot.

She looked over her shoulder, and her stomach clenched. The way that SUV was bullying heedlessly through traffic and creeping up on their backside, they might have only seconds before their pursuers came close enough to open fire.

The rear window of the rental car shattered just as Cam whipped the vehicle around the final corner toward ranger headquarters. The report of the gun echoed between surrounding office buildings. A three-story, square, brick-and-stone edifice loomed ahead of them. Ranger Company C HQ. Straight ahead, a set of steel-reinforced garage doors grew ever closer. Thus far, the sturdy portal remained closed, and another barrage of gunfire hammered behind them. Pings on the body of the car informed Cam the trunk had taken hits. He started to holler at Bree to get down, but she'd already done so while speaking urgently but quietly on the phone.

Suddenly, multiple siren whoops bombarded the air, originating from different directions. Ranger vehicles converged from side streets. The attack vehicle behind them began to slow down and fall back even as the garage doors in front of them started to rise. For the remaining nail-biting yards between them and safety, Cam held their vehicle's speed steady. Finally, the car plunged through the opening into the relative dimness of the secure parking garage.

He brought the rental to a stop at the bottom of an incline, and ranger personnel filled in behind them with impressive efficiency, guns drawn and aimed at the ever-narrowing opening onto the street as the doors rumbled shut with maddening slowness. At least, slow was the impression on Cam in the moment. He had no doubt that, in reality, the doors closed more quickly than average, given their use in a law enforcement building.

Cam opened his door and emerged from the driver's seat. Mingled odors of vehicle exhaust, oil and cool concrete met his nostrils. Bree had already piled out of her side and was peppering ranger buddies with questions regarding the attack on the headquarters building yesterday. From what he overheard, their second-hand information that injuries had been minor was correct. Another item for which to give thanks.

The tall, lanky ranger who'd been introduced as Dan Halliday out at the helicopter crash site a little over two weeks ago strode up to Cam and stuck out his hand, just like he'd done at their first meeting. Cam shook with the man. Then the ranger turned away and began to move toward metal doors with a sign saying Elevator above them.

"Follow me. I'll take you to Captain Gaines. He's waiting upstairs."

Cam gazed around warily as Bree joined him, along with two other rangers, the stocky Mitch Horn among them. The man's gaze on Bree continued to betray more than collegial interest. As much as the yearning look raised Cam's hackles for a personal reason he wasn't yet ready to confront, his wariness possessed another source.

He was beyond certain that someone in this unit, perhaps someone who walked with them this very moment, was in the cartel's pocket. Actually, he hoped that was the case to bolster the likelihood of success for his plan to lure out the cartel kingpins, though he hated the idea for Bree's sake and the morale of her ranger company. Everybody got smattered with mud when a dirty law enforcement member was exposed. He'd experienced the ripple effect during his tenure with the DEA.

At last, the elevator delivered their little

troupe to the third floor. They strode, almost in lockstep, into a busy bullpen full of desks and moving bodies, and faces staring into screens. Carpeting throughout the area kept the noise muted, though the racket was distinctly familiar to Cam from his earlier career.

At their appearance, silence washed in like a wave as attention was drawn and conversations and typing ceased. The hush continued as Dan led them into a spacious glassed-in corner office facing the bullpen. It had apparently taken some rifle fire through a window in the outer wall, which was now covered by a solid sheet of metal. The repairers had made do with slabs of Sheetrock to temporarily mend the missing interior panes.

They stepped into the office where Gaines stood behind a bullet-scarred wooden desk. Only Mitch, Dan, Bree and Cam entered the room. The other rangers peeled off to continue regular duties.

"We made it, Captain Gaines." Bree stopped in front of the desk. "Thank you for the assist."

"Good to see you're whole. Well, almost." The captain motioned to Bree's sling.

Then he turned his attention toward Cam, who met the man's assessing pale blue gaze with an evaluating look of his own. Bree thought a lot of her boss. Cam wanted to do the same, but caution held him back. Even the big cheese of an outfit could be compromised. At the same time, he respected Bree's character evaluations. She was the epitome of a skeptic and didn't give trust lightly. For the moment, Cam would give Gaines the benefit of the doubt.

The man nodded solemnly and held out his hand. Cam took it and found the grip firm but not aggressive. Signs of a confident person. Another tick in the positive column for the captain.

"Good to see you again, Cameron Wolfe. I keep hearing good reports of you from my people, including Bree, and she's hard to impress."

Despite any lingering misgivings, the words brought a grin to Cam's face. "I've noticed, sir."

"Thank you for staying by her side through this. Can we get you anything? Food, beverages, a change of clothes?" His grizzled eyebrows went up as those pale eyes glinted with understated humor at their disheveled appearance.

A chuckle escaped Cam. Yes, he was going to have to like this guy.

"All of the above, thank you," Bree answered for them.

Gaines jerked his square chin at Dan and Mitch. "Round up some food and clothing while Bree shows Cam to the locker rooms. Let them freshen up, hydrate and eat. Then we'll have a strategy summit right here." He nodded at Bree and Cam.

"Thank you, sir," Cam said. "Any word on the attackers in the SUV who chased us here? Were they apprehended?"

"Affirmative. We've got a pair of cartel members in custody, but they're low-level thugs, not seasoned *sicarios*. I doubt we'll get much useful intelligence out of them."

"Too bad, but congratulations on the arrest."

"Follow me." Bree motioned, and Cam exited the room behind her.

A reprieve was welcome from the revelations he must make to lay the case for his strategy to capture the cartel heads. And a hot shower, clean clothes, and a meal sounded beyond great. A long sleep was also on the list of necessities, but that would have to wait until after the difficult conversation with the captain.

As if Bree and Cam shared an unspoken agreement to take a break from heavy topics while they refreshed themselves, only conversation on mundane matters passed between them while they went down to the first level above the parking garage. She showed him the men's locker room and then went off toward the women's.

By the time Cam had enjoyed that hot shower he'd craved, a set of clothes had found their perch on a bench by the lockers. The pants and shirt fit him reasonably well, and the socks were one-size-fits-most. He tugged his boots onto his feet, feeling clean and as alert as he was going to get short of eight hours of uninterrupted sleep.

As he reaffixed his watch around his wrist, Dan showed up, and they joined Bree and Mitch in the hallway. Another ride on the elevator brought them to the second floor, where they were showed into a small conference room where paper sacks emitting savory scents awaited them.

"Want us to wait around here in case you need anything else?" Mitch's tone dripped hope.

Bree shook her head with a perfunctory smile. "I know my way back to the captain's office. Dealing with us must have set you guys back on your workday, so don't give us another thought."

Mitch's face fell, and Dan flickered a brief smirk behind his partner's back as he followed the man out the door. The shorter ranger wasn't fooling anybody about his interest in Bree. Except maybe Bree, who seemed oblivious. Cam suspected she was feigning ignorance to avoid the awkwardness of acknowledgment, but the time was fast approaching when the matter would need to be addressed head-on. Now was not that time.

Bree took a seat at the table. "I'm so hungry, I could inhale this meal, bag and all."

Consuming the thick deli sandwiches, chips and gourmet dill pickle between healthy swigs of water took little time. Again, Bree seemed disinclined to talk about the situation they were in.

Soon, they headed back upstairs and reentered Captain Grimes's office.

The man greeted them, remarked how much better they appeared, and motioned toward a pair of guest chairs. Cam settled into a seat, and Bree did the same with a wince and a tiny groan. The captain came around his desk and shut the door, then returned to perch in his desk chair, leaning forward.

"What can we do to end this?" His gaze rested on Bree. "If there's any other option, I don't want to lose a fine ranger to WITSEC. On the other hand, we can't have your life constantly in danger."

"The life of a ranger is inherently dangerous."

Gaines shook his head and wagged an admonishing finger. "Not like this."

Bree hung her head. "I know." She heaved a long breath. "Cam has an idea, but it's risky and doesn't come with guarantees."

"By all means, let's hear it." The captain laid his hands flat on the desktop and shifted his focus onto Cam.

The pale stare sliced into him like a laser beam and heat jolted through him. Moment of truth. The whole truth and nothing but the truth. He was about to break a vow he'd made to himself to never speak of those final intense moments of gun smoke, blood and fear when his father died and the woman he'd thought loved him had betrayed them both in a scramble for wealth and self-preservation. Cam's throat tightened as memories attacked. If only his ex-fiancée's betrayal and his father's death had been the worst events that day.

Chapter Fifteen

"My legal name is Cameron Wolfe, but my birth name is Everett Davison."

Bree resisted the urge to take Cam's hand as he began recounting his pain-filled history. She sensed her touch might be an unwelcome distraction. He seemed to have drawn in upon himself, and his voice was thin but as strong as a sheet of tungsten metal.

Gaines had the good sense to remain silent while Cam went through the parts of his story Bree had heard already. Her captain's only reaction was an occasional flinch or a repeat of the muted intake of breath that had greeted Cam's opening revelation about his identity. But then the saga moved into new territory and Bree sat gripping her chair with white-knuckled fingers.

"We thought we were safe. That the worst was over after the Ortega human-and-drug-trafficking ring had been shut down on our property and Alonzo Espinoza allowed me to walk away from his proposition to take over the smuggling route through our land. My father was now under a public cloud of suspicion regarding his possible involvement in the Ortega ring, but nothing could be proved. He did resign from his position as state senator and then came home from the capitol. He also brought my ex-fiancée with him, scheming anew to realize his political aspirations through me reconciling with his dream wife for me and assuming my 'rightful place—'" he bracketed the two words with air quotes "—in high society. The atmosphere in the house was naturally strained, because I *knew* my father was involved with the cartel, and I had no interest in renewing a relationship with my ex. Despite my rekindled love for ranching, I was seriously considering leaving the Leaning-D permanently when the enraged Ortega cartel struck our home site."

A sharp gasp left Bree's throat and her face heated as she clapped a hand over her mouth. It was one thing to have read the lurid accounts of the tragedy in the newspaper and listened to the sensational reports on television. But hearing the brutal fact stated from someone who'd been there, and in the overly flat tone and bald brevity that signified great emotion held in check, was quite another experience. Bree's heart wrung like it would spring from her chest, and her hand flew to his. His return grip around her fingers quickly became almost painful before his chest heaved and he gradually calmed. Cam released her and visibly shook himself, his eyes fixed resolutely on her captain.

Gaines cleared his throat. "You don't need to share details of the battle. We already know several ranch hands and your father were killed before sheriff's deputies and border patrol agents arrived to help. Go ahead and move on to how this event ties in with getting the price lifted from Brianna's head."

"Thank you. I don't believe I will offer graphic descriptions. No one needs those visuals in their head."

Bree bit her bottom lip. She heard what he wasn't saying—that *he* could not escape those visuals. He carried them with him on the inside. The level of horror that Cam had experienced and the faith-filled grace with which he managed the scars impressed her beyond words. If only she could claim she possessed a similar level of faith.

Cam shifted in his seat. "I do need to color

in a few details of another sort far worse for me but that were never released to the public."

"Go on." The captain nodded, face pale as if dreading what might be revealed.

"I didn't find out until afterward, and I was somehow still alive, that my ex-fiancée had initiated the attack on her signal right before she took shelter in the safe room of our house. When I released her from the safe room afterward, and she saw what had happened, she was hysterical and blurted everything out to me. But no one else heard her confession. Raul Ortega had made a deal with her. If she would pick the optimal time for them to overwhelm the ranch, they would spare her life and cut her in on the money made through a reestablished smuggling route across the property."

"What?" Bree shoved back in her chair. "How is it possible she would have any ownership or say over Leaning-D property? She wasn't married to you."

"Yes, she was…at least on paper."

Bree joined her captain in gaping at Cam.

He let out a harsh snicker. "She'd lied to my father and claimed to be carrying my child, which wasn't even possible. Gleefully expecting an heir who might prove more malleable than

I was, my father forged a marriage certificate meant to prove she was my wife at the time of my death. Unbeknownst to him, she also fully expected my father to be killed during the attack, leaving only her in charge of the ranch as my grieving widow."

Bree's thoughts tumbled over themselves, struggling to comprehend the implications of what he'd said.

"Your father was in on the scheme?" she finally blurted.

Cam nodded. "Only he didn't think he was supposed to die in the attack. I was."

Silence fell as if all oxygen had been sucked from the room and every inhabitant had been robbed of the ability to breathe.

Hot tears sprang from Bree's eyes and bathed her cheeks. After such a devastating betrayal, how had Cam found the will to go on, much less to establish a completely new life and continually show himself to be a genuinely decent and selfless human being? Most people would be mentally and emotionally wrecked and bitter to the nth degree.

Her own experience of betrayal from her ex-husband, minor in comparison to Cam's, had soured her outlook on people. She knew that it had. Why else had she never attempted another serious romantic relationship? She couldn't blame her inability to commit to another man on cynicism from negative experiences with the worst sort of people endemic to her job. No, she'd allowed the wounds of a failed relationship to fester and draw her away from God and from deep personal connections with people.

God, I repent of my bitterness. Help me to let it all go, to forgive my ex, and to heal. I want to be the sort of woman with whom Cam might consider exploring a relationship.

There, she'd admitted it to herself and to God.

Cam's witness had fully broken through her defenses. Now, they simply needed to solve the little problem of the vendetta against her life.

Simple? Ha! Try mortally dangerous on every level. But she was not going to run. Stand and fight remained the only option to achieve a life worth living.

Cam studied the expression on Captain Gaines's face—a scrunch-browed cross between horror and puzzlement. Apparently, the man was as appalled as Bree over the things he'd shared, but no doubt still wondering how his tragic mess contributed to solving Bree's.

"Now, I'm getting to it." Cam leaned toward the captain seated on the opposite side of the desk. "I've always needed to hear corroboration of Tessa's awful tale about my father's betrayal from another source. I don't trust her to have been truthful about my father's involvement, though I don't fully disbelieve her either. I know the man's obsessions too well. However, I've never been able to get the satisfaction of confirmation from an independent source. Raul Ortega is the *only* other source, and I need to be looking him in the eye, reading his expression, when I have the conversation. He will believe my reason for contacting him for a face-to-face meeting."

Bree reached over and gripped his arm in a python squeeze. "You can't risk yourself like that. He'll come to kill you."

"Not if I offer him something he wants more than me." Cam met her stricken gaze.

She gasped. "Alonzo Espinoza."

"Bingo."

Bree sat up stiff. "That's right. We talked about it. I'm the bait for *him*."

"Wait, wait, wait." Gaines lifted his hands, palms outward. "You can't mean to lure both cartel heads to some place on US soil."

"Exactly."

Bree's voice melded with Cam's as they stared in unison at the shocked ranger captain.

The man scowled like thunder. "And just where, pray tell, will this fateful meeting happen?"

"I'm thinking back where it all began," Cam answered.

Bree canted her head at him. "Where we rangers had the shoot-out with the rustlers?"

"Farther back—a place Ortega and Espinoza will know about."

"The shack in the middle of nowhere on the Leaning-D where you first rescued those trafficked girls." Bree nodded, her eyes lighting up with something like hope.

"Not happening." Gaines let out a snort. "New Mexico is outside ranger jurisdiction."

"Precisely the point." Cam met the man's ice-blue gaze. "Ortega will be supremely comfortable with the location because his cartel is familiar with every nook and cranny of the area. And Espinoza is less likely to think it's a trap because the location isn't on Texas soil, where Bree is headquartered. After I talk to Ortega, I'll speak with Espinoza and trade him the location of Ortega's meeting with me for canceling the contract on Bree's life. He'll jump at the chance to personally end his rival."

Bree frowned. "Sounds like a potential blood-bath. They'll both come with massive troops."

"I don't think so. They'll be traveling across a hostile border and will need to move as surreptitiously as possible. I estimate maybe a handful of bodyguards for each of them, and we—" he swept his finger around at the three of them "—will arrange for a specially selected, but highly trained group of law enforcement to be waiting for them."

"Hmm." The captain sat back in his chair, twiddling his fingers against his desktop as his gaze turned introspective.

Cam fell silent and Bree was wise enough to do the same.

At last, the man sat forward and stopped the rhythmic drumming of his fingertips. "I assume this skilled task force will need to be formed on the down-low with as few people as possible having any awareness of what's about to happen."

Cam nodded. "Correct. But I'm risking stepping on your toes with what I need to say next. I'm happy to be seen around ranger HQ associated with Bree. And I want it to get out that

Bree and I are going into hiding at a certain location in New Mexico. The information will get back to Espinoza and confirm the message I'll give him on the phone, as well as the one I've already sent through to the cartel boss via one of his *sicarios* today. However, I don't want anyone but you, Captain Gaines, to know about the deeper plan to lure in both cartel leaders."

The captain's expression flattened. "Because one of my people is compromised?"

"Isn't it obvious?" Bree let out a hiss. "How else were those rustlers prepared when we attempted to take them into custody three weeks ago? They ambushed us, and people are dead, including my partner."

Unresolved grief leaked through her tone and Cam's heart tore. She'd have some healing to do once this mess was settled.

The captain sighed. "I don't disagree with you, and I plan to flush out the mole as soon as possible."

"Maybe during the process of this sting operation," Cam said, "the culprit will betray himself."

"Or herself," Bree inserted.

Cam shot her a sidelong glance.

"What?" She blinked back at him. "Dirty

rotten cartel moles can be female, just like righteous rangers. I'm equal opportunity that way."

He chuckled and shook his head, then turned his attention to Gaines. "Who do you know that could capably and quietly make up this task force?"

The man grinned. "I've got a good friend who's an excellent sniper in the Marshals Service, and he may have a trusted buddy or two itching to take down mega-bad guys. Also, the New Mexico State Police director owes me a favor, and I know he's not in the cartel's pocket. He'll have some good people who will leap at this opportunity with both feet." Gaines chuckled and rubbed his hands together. "Actually, the NMSP director will probably figure I'm *doing* him a favor for letting him in on this gig. He'll likely invite me to ride along on the mission." If smug had a face, it was the ranger captain's in that moment.

Cam chuckled and Bree let out a little huff. They both knew how law enforcement folks thought. Getting in on the action was a bonus, probably one the captain hadn't experienced in a while.

Gaines shoved his desk phone toward Cam. "Make your calls."

Cam shoved the instrument back at him and pulled out his burner phone. "The calls need to originate from a regular but unregistered number, not the blank number designation of law enforcement. And I'm going to have to reach out first to clandestine contacts developed while I was in the DEA before I'll be granted a direct conversation with the cartels' head honchos."

"Got it." Gaines nodded. "Bree?"

She grinned. "I'll take him to my office for his calls, while you make yours, Cap."

"I've always liked how you think, Lieutenant Maguire." The man winked and grabbed his handset.

Bree rose and Cam followed her on a straight shot through the busy bullpen toward the closed door of an interior office at the other end of the room. It didn't appear to have taken any damage from the recent assault on ranger HQ. On the way, she greeted coworkers, both men and women, who seemed extra interested in their movements. Cam saw what she meant about the possibility of a female mole, but he couldn't help but suspect at least one of the pair of male of rangers they'd come into operational contact with during this messy affair.

Was Mitch's seeming romantic interest in

Bree a cover for his dark intentions? Or maybe the scoundrel was lanky Dan with the laid-back personality? Which one?

Cam shook off the questions as Bree ushered him through a door marked with a plaque that read Lieutenant Brianna Maguire. He sat down, cupped his burner phone in his hand, and released a long breath. Everything rode on the success of the conversations he was about to have. So wound tight was he, that he jerked when Bree's hand gripped his shoulder from behind.

"Wha—"

"Shh. I'm going to pray."

Cam's jaw flopped open. Miss Independent was going to ask the Almighty for help? A smile formed on the inside of him, but he didn't let it out. Instead, he bowed his head.

"Dear God," she began, "I'm rusty at this talking-to-You business, and I'm sorry for that. My fault. I'd like to work on the issue, but I'll need time and opportunity to do so. If You'll just see fit to guide Cam to the right contacts and give him the right words to say to everyone, up to and including the cartel heads, I'd be grateful. That's all I'll ask for right now, but I'm sure there'll be more requests to come. In Your Son's name. Amen."

Bree came around to the front of Cam, went to her desk, and flopped into her desk chair like she'd worn herself out. Then she grinned at him.

"Go for it, cowboy."

Cam grinned back, his heart suddenly a thousand pounds lighter. Whatever happened—and the outcome was far from certain—something great had happened today. Was this the start of a trend? He had to hope so, but he needed to remember the old warriors' maxim that plans were necessary things but rarely survived beyond first contact with the enemy. After that, anything could go wrong.

Fortifying himself with a deep breath, Cam's fingers began to tap the keypad of his cell.

Chapter Sixteen

The southwestern New Mexico Bootheel was like a different planet from the northwestern Texas Panhandle. Standing outside the smugglers' adobe shack on former Leaning-D property, now in the custody of the state, Bree scanned her surroundings. While the Llano Estacado was an unending vista of grassy plains sliced with hidden draws and arroyos, the terrain here was rugged, with many milestone upheavals of land and even mountains in the near distance. The climate was drier here, especially after the Llano's recent rainstorm, and a bit warmer, though with a hint of higher elevation chill in the breeze that cooled her skin under the merciless, nearly noon sun.

Bree looked up, and her gaze fastened on a hawk lazily whirling on the thermals, eyeing the ground for prey. She shivered, giving thanks she was too large for the raptor to hunt. But others were coming who considered her the mouse in their sights.

A crickety chirp from a nearby cuckoo cut off her morbid thoughts. Then the odor of broken sage preceded the crunch of footsteps on brittle weeds and drew her attention to a tall figure approaching from his scouting expedition around the property. If only she could enjoy exploring the unfamiliar landscape in the company of the man striding her way, but she was all too aware of the minutes ticking toward the time for the fateful rendezvous.

This was really going to happen. Tingles swept across her flesh. Both cartel leaders had taken the bait. They seemed to have believed Cam when he'd assured them that only he and Bree would be present at the rendezvous site. Of course, Cam hadn't been lying. It was only the two of them here in the cup of the small valley where the shack hunched, crumbling and brown. Her gaze scanned the ridged heights several football fields' distance away where Marshals Service snipers and Dillon, an unsung sharpshooter himself, held overwatch.

Cam stopped beside her, and Bree sent him a nod, not quite managing to smile. The pins and needles attacking her insides didn't allow a light gesture. Nor did Cam smile. In fact, his face seemed to be battling a frown, resulting in an eerily blank expression.

"What happened to her?" To break the heavy silence, Bree blurted out the question that had been plaguing her for a while.

Cam's brows lifted. "Who?"

"Tessa. She admitted to those horrible things. Is she in jail?"

"Not hardly." He let out a sound like a cross between a snarl and a grunt. "Like I said, I'm the only one she confessed to, and then just at the spur of the moment in a sudden fit of hysteria after the fact. With the issue being her word against mine, there was insufficient evidence to charge her with anything. I knew I needed to disappear—and fast—so I pretty much left her in my dust while I went off the grid until I could arrange a new identity. Happily, I knew a judge who facilitated my name change and then sealed the records. I assume Tessa slunk off to Los Angeles, where she always said she wanted to live. The place is a rich hunting ground for someone looking to cash in, literally, on her good looks and sophistication."

Bree's hands balled into fists. "That just makes me mad. The woman got off scot-free."

Cam chuckled softly, and his features relaxed. "No worries on that score. I'm fully convinced no one gets away with anything in this life. They either repent and get it forgiven because of Christ, or if they don't repent and a natural, human consequence like prison never happens, they still have to answer for it before God. His justice is forever trustworthy and absolutely inevitable."

"Huh! I guess you're right."

Cam's body stiffened. "I think I'm right, also, that Ortega is almost here."

He pointed and Bree followed the direction of his finger toward a dust cloud wafting upward on the horizon. Yesterday, at the ranger headquarters, Cam had told the cartel leader a rendezvous time twenty minutes before the time he'd given Espinoza, so Ortega was certainly prompt, if not a bit early. Cam had also predicted to her and the law enforcement team that the man would travel overland because his people had long experience with the terrain. Espinoza, he judged, would arrive by air, and Bree wasn't going to doubt him.

"Time to take our places," Cam prompted.

Involuntarily, Bree ground her teeth together.

Was she ready? No choice. This was happening. She whirled on her boot heels toward the shack.

"Wait!" Cam called.

Bree turned to him and he wrapped his solid arms around her. She leaned into his embrace and stared into his smoky eyes. A yearning in their depths snagged her breath away. But he only leaned down and kissed her cheek then released her and stepped away. A little wobbly on her feet from the warmth of his lips, even in so innocuous a touch, she sent him a nod and then marched to her post.

The adobe shack's interior clung to last night's desert chill and goose bumps formed on her arms beneath her long-sleeved shirt. Holding her eyes wide to force them to acclimate to the sudden dimness, she moved over to a glassless window aperture. She took the sling off her left arm and then picked up with her right hand the rifle she'd left propped against the wall beneath it. She was Cam's first line of defense if Ortega decided to renege on his word about renouncing his vendetta against Everett Daniels if Alonzo Espinoza were delivered into his hands.

What had Cam told her once? Cartel leaders weren't very skilled with honor? Well, they'd soon find out. Meanwhile, Cam stood out there unarmed and prepared to have a tough conversation with his arch nemesis.

Bree lowered herself to one knee and propped her left elbow on the chair she'd positioned for the purpose of supporting her weak arm as it helped her aim the rifle out the window. She was careful to let only the tip of the muzzle show out the window opening. That way, Ortega would have the hint that Cam had cover in place and yet not tip the balance toward aggression that might kick off a gunfight. If everything went perfectly, not a bullet would be fired. If things went radically south, then hot lead could pepper the air like a kicked hornet's nest. No one wanted that—probably not even the cartel members—because some of them were likely to get shot. Cam was at the most risk of all.

Bree's stomach clenched as a dirty-white, off-road vehicle that looked like a Jeep and a panel van had had a baby began to trundle down the dirt track into the valley. Cam stood solid as an oak. What must he be feeling? Was sweat breaking out on his skin like on hers? His face, in profile to her, showed no emotion.

The thick-wheeled van with roll bars came to a halt in a cloud of dust about twenty feet from the shack. The van's windows were too dark to see how many people were inside. No one moved, not Cam or anyone in the vehicle. Bree's heart pounded against her rib cage.

At last, the van's front passenger door creaked open on grit-clogged hinges. Half a moment later, the rear side door behind the driver slid back. Simultaneously, a pair of armed *sicarios* stepped out on either side of the vehicle. The men's hardened glares swept the area and they held their automatic rifles ready to deploy at split-second notice.

Bree's finger cupped the trigger of her weapon. Any further aggression on their part would invite a warm greeting from her.

Then the *sicario* by the rear door nodded to someone inside, and a man of average height and build stepped down onto the ground. Ortega, she presumed. The cartel boss wore shoes so shiny they glinted in the sunlight and a suit cut like it cost more than Bree's annual salary. Designer sunglasses perched on his nose, hiding his eyes, but something in the intensity of his look reached Bree and a chill coursed through her. Otherwise, his features appeared regular, unremarkable even, though his thick, graying hair betrayed a stylist's touch. Take away the display of wealth, however, and this man looked like nothing special. She'd walk by him on the street and not give him a second glance.

Flanked by his bodyguards, Ortega strode toward Cam. "Well, well, the disappearing Everett Davison has reappeared. I half thought I would be meeting a puff of smoke." The trio halted several yards from Cam.

"I'm real enough, Ortega, and so is my promise to deliver Espinoza. He should be here soon, but you will have plenty of time to prepare a suitable welcome for him. I hope to be long gone."

The cartel head let out a hearty chuckle. "You are your father's son, devious and ruthless."

Bree was close enough to note the jerk of a muscle across Cam's cheek. No doubt he hated being compared to his father.

"As I mentioned on the phone—" Cam shifted his stance, leaning slightly forward "—I have one question to ask you about the attack on our ranch, and I will need to you take off your glasses when I ask it."

"Very well." Ortega swept the sunglasses from his nose and into his left hand. "What do you want to know?"

Cam's Adam's apple bobbed as if his throat constricted. "Was my father in on the plot to ensure the demise of his son and snag a tragic and sympathy-grabbing headline? Certainly, facing down a cartel raid on his ranch headquarters would be proof enough to debunk the rumors and assure the public that the Davisons were not in collusion with the cartel, would it not? Voilà! Political career resurrected." His tone was paper-thin.

"That was two questions, but I will answer simply." The cartel boss sneered a nasty smile. "If losing you meant regaining his aspirations of political power, the price was not too high. You know Emeric—or rather, *knew* his deepest fears and his highest hopes. You embodied both of them. When you refused to fulfill his hopes, he couldn't allow you to continue existing as his deepest fear—a better man than him."

Cam visibly jerked with every crushing phrase, but Ortega only shrugged. "You should take his desire to snuff you out as a compliment."

"Excuse me if I don't." Cam's words emerged in a gruff snarl.

Bree's heart wrung like a sodden dishrag. His pain must be beyond imagination. Then she shoved emotion away as Ortega and his men stiffened, their attention drifting skyward. Was

Espinoza approaching from the air, like Cam had predicted? He was early, too. If so, everyone standing there was a sitting duck.

Far from appearing alarmed, however, Ortega's face bloomed into a broad grin. "You never asked me why I attacked your ranch. *My* purpose was to kill every insolent one of you, but you survived...until now. Today, my purpose is the same, and will include my only rival. It is good that I have taken precautions." He turned slowly about, motioning toward the hills and ridges.

Bree's blood ran cold. Had Ortega's *sicarios* silently overwhelmed her brother and law enforcement personnel on overwatch? Did the enemy now surround them, lying in wait for the Espinoza contingent to join the slaughter? Were they all about to die?

As a shout and then a gunshot echoed from a ridge, chaos began to reign. Cam dropped to the ground and rolled away into the cover of a pile of dry but thick logs intended once upon a time for the shack's fireplace. He'd stored his rifle there. Theoretically, Bree and Cam could communicate through a side window adjacent to the log pile, but the gun thunder was too loud for a voice to carry. She was comforted as to Cam's well-being as a rifle spoke from that location. Bree went back to her own job.

Gun blasts filled the air and bullets flew, not just from the ridge but from the air above them. Bree couldn't see the helicopter, but she could hear it. More hitmen piled from the off-road van and poured lead skyward while the first two bundled their chief into the vehicle. Even as she joined the fight, winging one of the *sicarios* and knocking him off his feet, Bree deduced from the starred but not shattered windshield, and the impotent ping of bullet rounds against the van's body, that the vehicle must be armored.

Bullets began pouring her way, and she had to pull to the side of the window so the adobe brick would offer some shelter while she continued defending herself and, hopefully, Cam, too, since they were roughly in the same location. The new position didn't offer her the best view of the enemy positions and strained her injured arm, but she made do with what she could get, methodically driving the crooks back from her position.

Then she paused in firing, the odor of cordite from repeated rifle fire swirling around her. Had she heard right? Yes, the helicopter noise had grown exponentially greater. A grim smile creased her face. The New Mexico State Police choppers had ridden to the rescue. The battle wasn't over yet, but it soon would be.

About a hundred feet beyond the van, a helicopter whirled to a crash landing against the side of the valley. Had to be Espinoza's ride. The bird lacked law enforcement insignia. Several people tumbled out and fell to the ground.

A bullhorn from above commanded the remaining *sicarios* to drop their weapons and lie face-first on the ground. They obeyed without being told a second time.

Elation left Bree's mouth in a whoop that came out embarrassingly loud in the sudden silence. "We did it, Cam. It's over."

She paused to hear his answer. There was none.

On leaden feet, Bree staggered over to the window that looked out on the woodpile. Her heart stopped beating, and her body froze. No sound reached her ears but the shattering of her heart.

Cam slumped, facedown, over the wood stack, rifle clutched in his fists and his blood painting the logs a deep crimson.

Epilogue

Cam struggled awake to the rhythm of an annoying high-pitched beep. At least the sound was faint, but then again, teasing him from barely audible range was part of its annoying quality. Then came a rustle and the pleasant odor of fresh rain touched his nostrils. He knew that scent. A warm presence loomed over him and his eyes popped open.

Bree gasped, recoiled, and then fairly pounced on him, gripping his hands and leaning close over his bedside. Bedside? Yup, he was in bed, but not his own. Hospital? Check. Now he knew where he was.

Cam gazed up at Bree beaming down on him. When did she grow so beautiful? Dumb question. She had always been beautiful; he was just appreciating it more every time he saw her.

"What—"

"Shh. Save your questions." She placed a finger over his dry lips. "I've got to tell the others. They'll want to be here."

"But—"

She flitted out the door. "Hey, everyone. He's awake." Her excited voice carried to him as the door swished closed behind her.

Cam had barely started to feel bereft when Bree came back, followed in procession by her brother Dillon and her boss, Captain Gaines, both beaming like she was. He couldn't help but smile back.

"We got 'em, my boy!" Gaines's voice held a crow.

"Raul Ortega and Alonzo Espinoza are in custody?"

Bree must have noticed the hoarseness in his voice because she put a straw to his lips and he gratefully sucked in cool water.

"You're half right." The captain's expression sobered, but only slightly.

"Apparently, Ortega was mortally wounded by the time they got him back into that van." Bree gave him another drink. "He didn't make it."

Dillon stepped up beside his sister. "Espinoza didn't fare too well in the helicopter crash. He's likely to join his nephew in a permanent wheel-chair. They can share an accessible prison cell."

Bree gripped Cam's hand again. It fit there, and he wasn't about to let it go any time soon.

"We almost lost you." She started blinking rapidly and he tried to sit up so he could pull her close, but pain lanced his side and he fell back. "Oh, no, you don't, buster." She pressed firmly on his shoulder. "It's bed rest for you for as long as the doctor says. You lost a lot of blood, plus your spleen."

Cam grunted. "How about the law enforcement personnel? Everyone okay?"

Gaines matched his grunt. "Bumps and bruises and a few minor bullet creases. Everyone will live to fight another day. And one of our captives, Espinoza's right-hand guy, has been talking our ears off since his boss is in custody, too, and he doesn't have to fear reprisals. I'm extremely disappointed to tell you that Mitch Horn was on the cartel's payroll." The man's face reddened in a stern expression, like he was equal parts offended and furious. "He and a rancher neighbor of the Double-Bar-M kept the cartel informed of law enforcement plans and cattle locations, respectively."

Cam frowned. "*I'm* the Double-Bar-M neighbor, and I assure you it wasn't me working with the rustlers."

"Our neighbor on the *other* side of us." Dillon chuckled. "It was him who burned our machine shed down."

"Sorry to hear about all that betrayal." Cam scrunched his brow, looking from Dillon to Gaines and back to Dillon again. "I was worried about you. That initial rifle blast and shout came from where you were holed up on overwatch."

The man shrugged. "That was me dealing with the two-legged rattlesnake from the Ortega cartel who tried to ambush me."

Bree scowled, clearly not a fan of the danger to her brother. "The would-be bushwhacker will be taking a vacation to Club Fed as soon as they discharge him from the hospital."

Cam chuckled at the reference to a federal penitentiary but cut the mirth short at a sharp protest from his side. Bree's hand was still in his and he gave it a squeeze. She started beaming down at him again. He could get lost in her eyes. How sappy was that? He barely noticed a pair of soft footfalls retreating from his bedside, overlaid by muffled masculine chuckles. The door wheezed open then shut and Cam was alone with Bree.

She cleared her throat. "You have a lot of healing to do."

"You, too."

"But—"

"You're carrying grief you need to work through."

She huffed a breath and nodded. "You're right. And you—I can't believe—I mean—"

"I'll heal, too. More than physically." She'd been referring to the confirmation from Ortega about his father's bad intentions. "You'll help me."

"We'll help each other."

"That's what people who love each other do." He studied her brightly blushing face. "I know I love you. You do love me, too, don't you?"

"Whatever gave you that idea?" The words were skeptical, but the tone was tender, and she smiled as she said them.

He smiled back. "You don't have to tell me with words. Kiss me if you do."

And she did.

★ ★ ★ ★ ★

A NOTE TO ALL READERS

From October releases Mills & Boon will be making some changes to the series formats and pricing.

What will be different about the series books?

In response to recent reader feedback, we are increasing the size of our paperbacks to bigger books with better quality paper, making for a better reading experience.

What will be the new price of Mills & Boon?

Over the past four years we have seen significant increases in the cost of producing our books. As a result, in order to continue to provide customers with a quality reading experience, the price of our books will increase to RRP $10.99 for Modern singles and RRP $19.99 for 2-in-1s from Medical, Intrigue, Romantic Suspense, Historical and Western.

For futher information regarding format changes and pricing, please visit our website millsandboon.com.au.

Romantic Suspense

Danger. Passion. Drama.

Available Next Month

Colton Undercover Jennifer D. Bokal
Second-Chance Bodyguard Patricia Sargeant

LOVE INSPIRED

Cold Case Kidnapping Kimberly Van Meter
Escape To The Bayou Amber Leigh Williams

LOVE INSPIRED

Search And Detect Terri Reed
Sniffing Out Justice Carol J. Post

Larger Print

LOVE INSPIRED

Undercover Escape Valerie Hansen
Hunted For The Holidays Deena Alexander

Larger Print

LOVE INSPIRED

Witness Protection Ambush Jenna Night
A Lethal Truth Alexis Morgan

Larger Print

BRAND NEW RELEASE!

A hot-shot pilot's homecoming takes an unexpected detour into an off-limits romance.

When an Air Force pilot returns to his Texas hometown with the task of passing along a Dear Jane message to his best friends ex, the tables are turned and she asks him for a favour…to be her fake fiancé in order to secure her future. But neither expects the red-hot attraction between them!

Don't miss this next installment in the Cowboy Brothers in Arms series.

In stores and online October 2024.

MILLS & BOON

millsandboon.com.au

Keep reading for an excerpt of a new title
from the Inrigue series,
HOMETOWN HOMICIDE by Denise N. Wheatley

Prologue

"9-1-1. What is your emergency?"

"Someone's trying to break into my house!" a woman screeched into the phone.

Operator Nia Brooks shot straight up in her chair. The buzz within Juniper, Colorado's communications center was louder than normal as the phone lines had been dead for hours. Increasing the volume on her headset, she scanned the computer screen for the caller's location.

"What is your address, ma'am?"

"Three eighty-two Barksdale Road."

"And you said that someone is trying to break into your house?"

"*Yes*. A man has been banging on the back door and fighting with the knob for several minutes now. I'm here alone, and…"

The woman fell silent. A loud thud penetrated Nia's eardrums, followed by a deep, muffled howl.

"Do you *hear* him?" the woman hissed.

"I do," Nia replied, forcing a calm tone as her fingers flew across the keyboard. "I'm already in contact with the police dispatcher alerting them to the situation. Law enforcement should be heading your way. Just stay on the line with me—"

"Listen," the woman interrupted, her voice breaking into a jagged whisper. "I told you I'm here by myself. I don't have any weapons. If this maniac makes his way inside my house, I have no way of protecting myself. So *please* tell the authorities to hurry up!"

She paused at what sounded like a bat pounding the door.

"Leave me alone!" the woman screamed. "I'm on the phone with 9-1-1 and police are on their way!"

"Yes, they are," Nia assured her. "I can see that law enforcement is en route to your house. And they're aware that this is a high-priority emergency situation."

Quivering sobs rattled Nia's headset as the woman whimpered, "They need to hurry up and get here. This man is about to break down the door. When he does, he might try to kill me!"

"Are all of your windows and doors locked?"

"I think so—yes. I turned off all the lights, too, hoping that would somehow run him off. Obviously it didn't work."

"Well, the secured windows and doors should keep him at bay until police arrive. In the meantime, I'll be right here on the line with you. What is your name, ma'am?"

"Linda. Linda Echols."

"Okay, Linda. When the knocking first began, did you happen to take a look outside and get a glimpse of the man?"

The woman paused, only the sound of her unsteady breaths swooshing through Nia's headset. "I—I did. Just once. When the banging started. I looked out to see what all the commotion was about and tried to tell him that he had the wrong house, not realizing he was trying to break in. He insisted that he was exactly where he was supposed to be. But he's dressed in all black and looks to be wearing a mask and—*wait!* I think he might be…"

She went silent again.

"Linda, talk to me. Tell me what's going on. I don't hear anything."

"Yeah, neither do I. Maybe he finally decided to stop—"

Boom, boom, boom!

Nia cringed at the rapid succession of thumping. "Linda?"

Silence.

"Linda! Are you okay? What is he doing now?"

"He just picked up one of my patio chairs and is slamming it against the window! He's gonna break it and get inside. I need for the police to get here. *Now!*"

Just as Nia enlarged the map on her screen and

checked the responding officer's location, a message from dispatch flashed below it.

Inform the caller that police are on the way, but due to construction they've been rerouted, causing a delay.

Clenching her teeth, a frustrated grunt gurgled in Nia's throat. This was the hard part of the job— the part that she couldn't control. It pained her, being on the front line with the victims from behind a desk as opposed to in person.

"Where are the cops?" Linda rasped. "Are they almost here?"

"They're still on the way. But there's roadwork near your home that's blocking the direct route. So as soon as they get around that they'll arrive at your house. And like I said, I'll be right here with you until they—"

Crack!

Nia jerked in her chair as the sound of shattering glass pierced her ears, followed by Linda's guttural scream.

"He's getting in!"

Inhaling sharply, Nia asked, "He's getting inside the house?"

"Yes! He just smashed the sliding glass door!"

Nia pounded the keyboard with an update to dispatch while clambering footsteps stuttered through her headset.

"I'm still here with you, Linda. What's happening now?"

"I'm running upstairs to hide inside my bedroom closet. *Please* tell the cops to hurry up and get here!"

A faint shuffling echoed in the background.

"He's inside the house!" Linda whisper-screamed as the sound of shoe soles squeaked across the floor.

"Hey!" a gravelly voice roared. "Get your ass back down here!"

"Linda," Nia began, struggling to maintain her composure, "are you inside the bedroom yet?"

"I am now."

"Good. Make sure you lock the door. Can you push a dresser or a chair or some sort of heavy object in front of it?"

"I can try, but I don't think I can move this chest of drawers across the carpet!"

Eyeing the map on her screen, Nia checked the responding officer's location. Her chest tightened at the sight of the vehicle's marker. It was at a standstill.

The intruder's demands boomed in the distance, followed by Linda's hysterical cries.

Bam!

"He's forcing his way inside the bedroom!"

A throbbing pain pulsated over Nia's left eye. She pounded her fist against the desk, watching helplessly as the responding officer's vehicle finally began to move.

"Linda, the police are making their way to your

house. Is there anywhere inside the bedroom you can hide? The closet? Or bathroom?"

The other end of the call went silent.

"Hello?" Nia called out. "Hello! Are you still there?"

"I'm gonna kill you," she heard a man grunt. *"Linda!"*

A jarring thump preceded heaving gasps.

"I'm gonna kill you," the man muttered again over the sound of gut-wrenching gurgling.

Nia's body weakened at the thought of Linda being killed.

Come on! she wanted to scream after seeing that police were still several blocks away from the victim's house.

Just as she typed another message to dispatch alerting them to the severity of the situation, the call dropped.

ubscribe and all in love with Mills & Boon eries today!

ou'll be among the first o read stories delivered o your door monthly nd enjoy great savings.

WE
SIMPLY
LOVE
ROMANCE